THE
FATED BORN SERIES
BOOK THREE

FATED SWORN

Kristin L Hamblin

FATED SWORN

Kristin L Hamblin – kristinlhamblin.com

© Cover design: Franziska Stern - www.coverdungeon.com - Instagram: @coverdungeonrabbit

Editing by Kelley Lynn of Cookie Lynn Publishing Services

Map by Angel Perez

Library of Congress Control Number: 2023915841

ISBN: 978-1-959230-02-1

For Mom and Dad. I wouldn't be who I am today without your love and support.

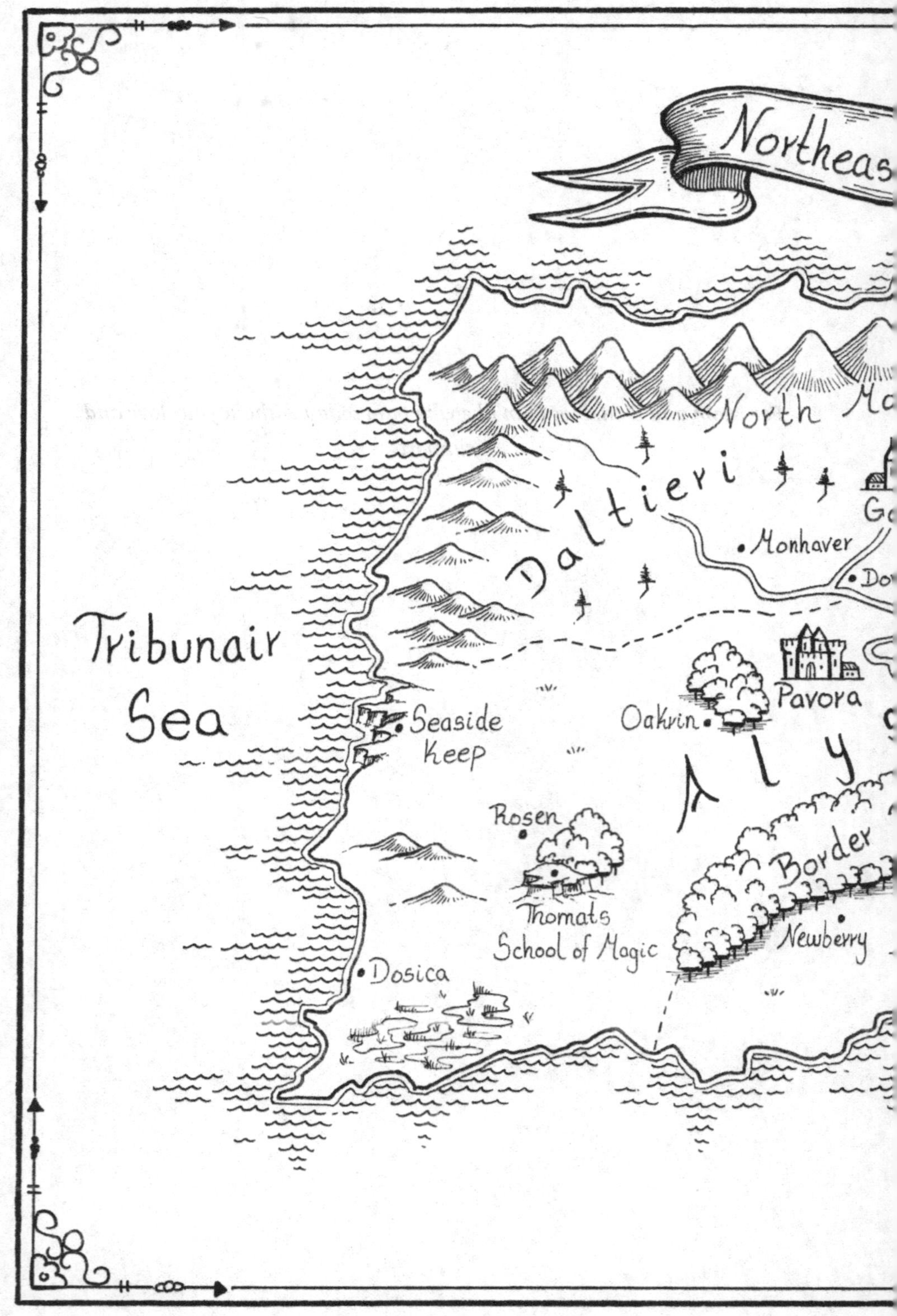

Northeas
North Mo
Daltieri
Monhaver
Go
Do
Tribunair
Sea
Pavora
Oakvin
Aly
Seaside
Keep
Rosen
Border
Thomas
School of Magic
Newberry
Dosica

st Thera
ountain
Docimer
Kestrea
Gull Island
Emerald
Ocean
adren
Crosston
Maze
over
Berrington
Cristanfani
Caprina
s i e s
Creadel
Wood
N
Terca
Sengi Desert
Salaya
Ardenis

CHAPTER

ONE

Bastien braced himself as a meaty fist slammed into his face. Locked in place by the two boys holding him, he grunted with the full impact of the blow. The dark room spun with the faces of the gang, cheering and pumping their fists, eager for more action.

Kolb's knuckles struck Bastien's body for the third time, followed by white pain and the trickle from a fresh cut high on his scalp. He could conceal the wound later. Bastien spat blood on the floor at the old guy's feet. His captors tightened their grip to a bone-grinding hold, but it wasn't necessary. Bastien wouldn't attempt escape. He knew better.

Every punch was one Olin wouldn't have to take.

Bastien tensed, readying for more. Kolb's jowls were red, and sweat beaded the stubble on his upper lip. He reared back, and his fist flew with the weight of his thick body. The boys cheered as Bastien's head snapped back from the force. Like all the times before, he imagined the pain as something making him stronger—imagined it laying another shield over his heart, cushioning him from his dismal past and even more dismal future. He imagined if he took enough hits, eventually he'd be untouchable.

"I don't like to do this, Bast." Kolb shook out his hand and wiped blood on his dirty trousers. "Every time the guard sees one of us running around looking like you do right now, it brings trouble down on us." He towered over Bastien—as if he needed more power over a fifteen-year-old. "If you weren't the best thief we've got, you know where you'd be. You and Olin." Kolb knew where to place a hit to do the most damage. Decades of running this street gang had taught him all sorts of nasty tricks.

Bastien held Kolb's eyes, refusing to glance toward the dungeon, but the boys' murmurs said that everyone recognized the implied threat. Kolb hadn't locked him up in a long time, not since he became the top earner in the gang, but the threat made his heart leap. A week or even a day in the cells meant no money, and no money meant no food, and winter came early in the city of Docimer.

Kolb looked away first, scanning the crowd of boys until they landed right on Olin, easily a head shorter than the rest. The kid's wide eyes vanished too late. Kolb took a casual step away, but Bastien clenched his muscles, having learned that ploy long ago. Sure enough, Kolb's fist hammered him in the gut, the hardest hit yet. The air whooshed out of him, and Bastien's captors let him go as he bent over coughing, clutching his middle.

"Let this be a lesson to all you new kids. Don't think some long-timer is gonna help you. You want to live here? You want to learn how to fight and fend for yourself, protected from the eyes of Captain Cerick? It comes with a price. No leaving 'til you pay the price." Kolb turned to Bastien, who'd regained his breath, crouched on the balls of his feet. "And if you leave, you do it alone. Take one of my boys, and you're both dead."

Speech over, feet pounded up rickety stairs, leaping over the missing step as the room cleared out, leaving Bastien behind. Only Olin stayed. They were right to make themselves scarce. Kolb was always cranky, but he usually didn't stop at one when he was out for blood. All he needed was a reason, and not even a good one.

Kolb followed last, deliberately slow. He turned off the last oil lamp on his way up, leaving them in darkness.

Bastien sighed at the pettiness, and with relief that Kolb hadn't pursued Olin.

Olin stumbled his way over, tunic too big and trousers too long. "Why do you do it, Bastien? He'll never let me go, not while it keeps you here, making him his riches." Olin pushed his unkempt hair behind his ears as Bastien rose, taller than him.

Even in the dark, Bastien saw the hero worship in the young boy's dark eyes, heard the weak wheeze as he breathed, and knew exactly why he stayed when he'd paid his debt long ago.

Bastien wiped the blood from his face. His headache dulled to a minor annoyance. "Don't worry about me. You just take care of yourself. We'll find a way to get you out of here."

Olin's stick-thin frame shook with a cough as his glance betrayed his thoughts. The dungeon, as the boys liked to call it, was empty but for a few chairs, a rotting wood floor, and the open cells Kolb had built, with shackles and everything.

Bastien patted his back. "Let's head up. We'll get an early start tomorrow, and I'll show you how to spot a good target."

Olin nodded, and they trudged in the dark toward the stairs. It'd be the hundredth time Bastien had taught Olin his tricks, but the kid wasn't cut out for a life of thieving. He'd caught the wet-cough at the orphanage as a baby and barely survived. It slowed him down, made it impossible for him to get away. But if Kolb wouldn't let Bastien pay off Olin's debt, what choice did they have?

Two flights up in the forgotten, rotting building, Bastien and Olin stepped carefully and climbed onto their pallets among the already sleeping boys. The room was stifling with all the bodies so closely packed, but Bastien considered it a blessing. All too soon the cold would return, making every bit of their nearness a necessity.

They called it the House, because as Kolb liked to remind them, it would never be a home, and best they knew the distinction.

Bastien sighed and pulled his thin blanket to his chest, exposing bare feet. Narrow shafts of moonlight filtered through a boarded-up window—the only source of light. Snores and quiet sobs, the usual nightly chorus, floated over the room, and Bastien was thankful to survive another day. Though, it was no life.

Orphaned. Abandoned. No family or money. Kolb had sucked all the boys right into this life with promises of protection and riches. Now it was the only thing they knew. Bastien was sick of lining Kolb's pockets. When Olin earned enough to pay his way out, they'd leave and start their own gang, one that benefits all, and not just its leader.

A slow-building sensation began in the pit of his stomach. He stifled a gasp. Anticipatory tingles ran up and down his body. Eager, he cleared his mind and let the powers that be take over. It had been several months since he'd had a vision.

He forced a slow blink, and when he opened his eyes, his view had shifted to another scene. Instead of the dark, dingy room of the House, he viewed himself, overlooking a crowded street from above. There was no mistaking his town, and from the angle, he stood on the balcony of this very building. Stone houses and shops rose up the mountain in switchbacks to his right. Snow capped the highest peaks. People dressed in their finest lined the street below, an odd sight for this part of town, even for a main road.

The green valley rolled in the far distance. Down the hill, a silver glow caught his eye. The light held him in its grip as it built, traveling closer as it rose with the incline of the road until it revealed the most beautiful woman Bastien had ever seen. The glow surrounded where she sat perched on her horse as she smiled, waving to the crowd. Her dress shimmered with the steady movement, and pale golden hair cascaded down her back beneath a silver crown that rested on her long ears. She drew nearer, surrounded by a small guard with eyes that darted everywhere. The crowd below oohed and awed with delight, but Bastien didn't dare tear his attention away from the mysterious woman.

Then her gaze shot up, and she locked depthless turquoise eyes onto him. Into him.

Bastien's vision vanished. His heart, which had been so full, deflated with a force that knocked the breath from him. He gasped, dashing tears from his eyes. A loud snore brought him back to reality, and he immediately stifled his emotions. The contrast between the beautiful scene he'd just witnessed, and the dilapidated prison he willingly remained in set his chest to aching.

He looked at Olin—dirt-smudged face, torn clothes, snoring softly on his side—and the twenty other kids surrounding them. The few treasures Bastien hadn't hidden around the city—his knife, coin pouch, makeshift lockpicking kit—lay tucked inside the pockets of his vest, the only place he trusted. His most prized possession. It had taken him many months to save up enough for a quality fabric that wouldn't tear with the weight of his stolen treasures, then many more months to sew the pockets just the way he wanted them. More than one gang member had threatened to steal his vest should he ever remove it. He never had.

All of it, even the vest, seemed so insignificant in this moment. Never before had he been so dissatisfied with his life.

He didn't know who she was, but the promise in those eyes made him want for better. A better existence than just surviving another day living off the streets. In the brief glimpse, he pictured a different life, one that was free of the worries he carried now. The hope would fade, he knew, after his vision came true and he saw her. His visions always came true.

That's what happened with the vision of Olin. He'd seen himself helping the boy when Kolb tricked him into joining and had helped ever since. The vision of Olin had felt just like this, hopeful and bigger than himself, like he was meant for more than just this wasteful life.

Whoever she was, and whenever she'd arrive, he had to be there. He had to.

CHAPTER
TWO

Bastien flitted between wagons and market stalls, dodging people amid the unusually condensed street crowd. No one noticed they'd helped line his pockets as he made his way to his destination. An apple here, a coin pouch there; as much as he'd been looking forward to this day, there was no way he'd pass up the opportunity this crowd presented. Pointless to deny the survival instincts honed since before he could remember.

Besides, he'd be in big trouble if he reported back to Kolb empty-handed. Even with his debt paid off, he owed the inflated rent to stay by Olin's side. Plus, though Kolb had caught him last month, the boss had no idea how often Bastien slipped extra coin to Olin.

Every day.

While he walked, Bastien bit into a sweet chocolate chip scone, its fresh warmth heightening the flavors. It had always been one of his particular favorites. The baker had been too preoccupied exchanging coin with several hungry customers to notice its absence. As Bastien wound his way through Cart Street, the women's poufy skirts were as abundant as the disdainful looks from the men—as if he were some common thief off the streets. *The nerve!*

Truthfully, he should have gone a different way to get back to his part of town, but this was faster, and more profitable—nothing but rich folk here, where people had coin to spend on pointless things like flowers. The thick stench of a dozen meshing perfumes coated his tongue and overtook the lingering flavors of chocolate. It was clear everyone had come for the same reason he had. They crowded in for the best spot along Mountain Way, the widest road to the palace. The roar reverberated off the stone and mortar buildings only to be quickly sucked into the extensive wardrobe of the rich. They'd braved the crowds, like him, all to catch a glimpse. Just one look at their visitor.

Queen Faelyn Rylandor of Alysies.

Rumor had circulated the streets for weeks, and Bastien had gathered every morsel he could, hoping this was connected to his vision. It had to be, right?

After so many years of no contact, King Bautamin had invited the queen to Kestrea's capital to enter into some kind of trade agreement with Alysies. Most people agreed it would help their economy. No matter what brought her here, she was due to travel down this very street sometime this morning, and Bastien planned to have front-row viewing.

A rare beauty, she was said to be. Most spoke with scorn, claiming she wasn't even human. 'Fae,' they called her, with pointed ears, limitless magic, and a kingdom regaining its power in the world. They said she didn't age, that she'd been alive for over a century and still looked fresh and young. Except for the promise in his vision, Bastien wouldn't buy into what everyone was saying. He still half expected a fancy carriage with closed curtains, and a slim chance peek at an ancient lady's wrinkled hand.

But he could hope.

"Hey!" A lanky gentleman grabbed Bastien's wrist as his hand slid out of the man's pocket.

Bastien's heart pounded. Several nearby heads turned toward them. Keeping hold of the coins, he twisted out of the man's grip where his thumb and fingers came together—an old, sloppy trick. Then he was off, weaving between the mass of bodies, away from the shouts. The man had no chance of catching up. The other boys in the gang weren't as tall, but Bastien made up for it with his speed and balance. He lost the man in the crowd and kept going. Skirting around the corner of a cobble store, he slipped into a shadowed alley and stopped, back against the cool brick. The grainy edges pulled at his hair while his breathing slowed.

That was closer than anyone had come to catching him in years. He'd let his boyish fantasies distract him. But, where was that kid? Olin should have already been here.

Bastien stepped away from the brick just as Olin emerged from the crowd.

"I'm here! Like you told me." Olin, four years younger than Bastien's fifteen, trundled forward. His dark hair was made light from road dust kicked up by the crowd. Like Bastien, he wore a dirty brown tunic two sizes too big. Bastien's old shoes—an absolute necessity in the winter this far north—kept Olin from being barefoot.

Bastien pulled a smushed peach tart from his pocket. Olin's eyes opened big as saucers, and his grin lit his dirt-smudged face.

He grabbed the treat, shoving half in at once. "Is this why you're late?" he asked around a mouthful.

"I'm not late, but we're about to be. Let's go." Bastien led the way through the crowd, and Olin followed, finishing off his breakfast.

They were half a block from Mountain Way, and it was slow going, even without pickpocketing along the way. He'd already met Kolb's quota for both him and Olin.

Since Olin had shown up two years ago, his life had become much more difficult. Olin hadn't grown up on the streets. He'd stayed at an orphanage on the west side until he'd been too old to earn a spot amongst the established street kids. It had taken Bastien a year of watching his back to recoup his reputation for helping a kiddie.

Finally, they reached the spot Bastien had found ahead of time from his vision. The House. The building abutted the street and had been bought by Kolb when deemed uninhabitable. Spectators lined up in front, but no one went inside. Bastien and Olin cut into the back alley and through a side door well-known by the gang.

Bastien followed Olin through the dusty bottom floor and up the rickety stairs to the top with the missing floorboards. The small balcony was sturdy enough to hold two boys. When they got there, three other boys were already in their spots.

Olin stopped in his tracks and shot a gaze at Bastien. The boys, all Bastien's age, turned. Bastien threw his shoulders back and narrowed his eyes. He looked each one in the face, only silence between them. The three boys exchanged glances, then left without a word.

Bastien took their place on the balcony without looking at Olin. "Best view in the city. How lucky are we?"

"Real lucky, Bast." Olin stared after the boys, likely worried about getting beat up later for this.

Bastien would never be Kolb's second because it was common knowledge he wanted out, and Kolb didn't like him. Though, he commanded just as much respect as a second. The boys' bellies were fuller with Bastien around, and food talked in the House. They knew better than to touch Olin.

They had a good view of the wide street from the balcony. The crowds formed distinct lines on either side, smiling, talking, laughing, but always with one eye toward the south. Good, he hadn't missed her arrival. His heart kicked up for a few beats. This had to be his vision coming true—the balcony, the people below with heads turned in anticipation. He was really going to see her.

He kept his mouth shut, even as Olin studied him. His excitement was more emotion than he usually let show, and the kid recognized it. She was almost here. It was almost as if he could feel her coming closer, like a faint tug to his middle.

Now all they had to do was wait.

CHAPTER

THREE

The long, dirt road reached out before Faelyn and her party. The last endless stretch before they'd finally reach their destination. She hadn't left Alysies once in the fifteen years she'd been queen, but this was necessary. Sunlight warmed her through her riding leathers. Guards on horseback wearing blue armor surrounded her and Amerae, her friend and lady-in-waiting. Conversations filtered in and out over the chirps of birds and the crunch of dirt beneath their horses' plodding hooves.

"I still don't see why Kian got to remain behind," Amerae grumbled from her saddle. Her braided chestnut hair fell past her shoulders, and she wore loose skirts beneath her belted sheath.

Faelyn gave her a sideways look as the trees and country road blurred by.

"Okay, fine, it was my idea for him to stay and me to go." Amerae squirmed. "But I'm regretting it."

Faelyn chuckled. "You said that days ago. I still insist you will be used to riding again by the time we return to Pavora. Kian must oversee things in my absence. Your place is here, with me." She turned to the guards flanking them. "We'll rest here." It had taken a

11

long time for her to get used to giving orders and being a leader. Now, it was a normal part of life, and necessary to ensure her people remained safe.

The trees thinned to a meadow, and it was time to prepare before reaching Docimer, the capital city of the sleepy kingdom of Kestrea. Faelyn dismounted, patting her black mare on the neck. A servant, Meribeth, took the reins. Majestic would get a good rubdown and a carrot or two.

The guards surrounded them, positioning the carriage on the road ahead. Faelyn studied her dusty clothes and smoothed back her limp, oily hair. She had picked this spot because of the trickling creek nearby.

One must look one's best when meeting one's future husband.

She sighed, loud and long. Amerae met her eyes but didn't comment. As Faelyn's friend, lady in waiting, bodyguard, and closest confident, she knew Faelyn hated everything about what they were here to do.

Faelyn slipped off her shoes and walked ahead, shaking her head at the guards not to follow. The cool grass tickled her hot feet as the sounds of the wind in the trees and the chirps of insects slowly came alive the further she went toward the creek. Hoofbeats, jangling reins, and the smell of horses had plagued her for too long.

She looked back once to see Amerae exchange a long smile with Nolan. He locked eyes with her while still directing orders to the guards. Amerae usually hid her feelings for Nolan, out of respect for her duties to the kingdom, but it didn't take Faelyn's ability to notice the budding romance between them.

Faelyn kept going, pretending not to notice. She wouldn't do anything to stop their affections. Amerae hadn't shown interest in anyone since Michael died in the battle of Pavora.

At the creek, Faelyn stripped, washing in the cool water while the maids arranged her clothes. A towel awaited on a rock when she finally emerged, but she only used it for privacy. She commanded the wind to dry her skin and hair, then slipped into a proffered dress—

blue satin with silver fletching, the colors of her kingdom of Alysies. It sparkled in the morning sun with dozens of dazzling gems. The maids braided half her pale golden hair up into a crown, and the rest flowed down her back.

Amerae kept watch, one eye on the sword she was polishing, and one on the horizon for potential danger. Unnecessary, really—Faelyn would hear any bandits or wild animals coming before anyone else did—but she took her job seriously.

Amerae swiped the sword through the air with a whistling sound. "Prince Rory won't be so bad, my queen." Words she had spoken many times. "I hear he has a lovely disposition."

Faelyn forced a smile as they walked back to their entourage, missing her own sword at her hip. "Unity between our two kingdoms is vital. I know that more than anyone. With this alliance, Daltieri will stand alone in any quest for vengeance. We will be able to attack them from all sides if they try to retaliate from their loss at the battle of Pavora." Words she had spoken to herself many times. "And we need that bridewealth to fund our recovery efforts." In addition to their support, Kestrea had promised money for her hand. Money they sorely needed.

She would not become her father, leaving her kingdom undefended and unprepared. A marriage alliance was an unbreakable surety. Never mind that Kestrea failed to aid Alysies when Daltieri invaded. Tucked away in the northeast, without much land to fight over, they'd known peace for too long while Alysies took the brunt of the opposition. Now Daltieri, Kestrea's neighbor to the west, threatened to encroach. The reports confirmed as much. The threat forced the otherwise secluded King Bautamin to welcome Alysies in with open arms, and Faelyn had come running. Her life belonged to her kingdom, and there was no room for old grudges, or for love. She'd accepted that when she'd accepted the throne.

No other kingdom would aid Alysies outside of simple trade agreements, not with their current struggle to rebuild from Daltieri's reign of terror. They'd tried, Acantha above how they'd tried, but it would take many more years before they were strong enough to be a formidable ally. The promise of Faelyn's hand was all they had left to barter.

Then there was the matter of producing an heir so her succession went undisputed should she pass away—unlike what happened when her father died. As vital as that critical detail was, having children was the furthest thing from her mind.

After a quick meal, she remounted Majestic, and they trotted down the road. The guards unfurled banners bearing her Rylandor family crest in the royal colors. They billowed from the carriage at each corner and from half the guards on horseback. The size of their force, twenty guards and a dozen servants, was as much for show as for protection. Upon Kian's insistence, they even had a trumpeter to announce their arrival.

They'd stopped at several Alysian towns along the way, and Faelyn had yet to successfully stifle her giggles when they arrived and were heralded in. Amerae rolled her eyes each time, but Faelyn knew she felt the same. The presentation and its show of strength and unity was one of the most important parts of ruling her kingdom.

So, Faelyn donned her crown—white gold instead of yellow like her father's which was locked away at the castle. Her new crown sat lighter upon her head, more suited for extended periods of wear. Head held high, her keen eyesight took in the capital city as it blossomed before them.

Docimer was set at the base of a looming mountain. At this distance, the contrast between the green of the valley and the rising black rock was mesmerizing. Tiny bunches of brown homes and shops speckled the side of the mountain. Alysies didn't offer such sights, and the view always took her breath away. White clouds caressed the tallest peaks, and the sun shone on the sprawling city, which grew larger as they approached.

A cloud of dust morphed into distant riders—likely their welcoming party—racing toward them down the road. Faelyn's guards tensed, always expecting the worst after their years of war, and she sensed their unease in the air.

"Easy boys," Nolan said.

Faelyn nodded appreciatively. Nolan had proved invaluable since helping them defeat Lord Jamison and reclaim Alysies. She valued him all the more due to his heritage. Nolan was a descendant of Mary, the woman who'd raised Faelyn from a baby since her mother had died at birth, and her father had refused to speak to her until her eighteenth birthday when he'd been murdered in front of her. She was glad Kian had insisted Nolan captain this expedition.

The party slowed as they approached. They wore helms and oiled armor with simple leg coverings, bearing their own banners of green, and a crest with a golden sun. Nolan spurred ahead to meet them, along with two more of her guard. Faelyn put a smile on her face, and her assembly came to a stop.

Ten pairs of eyes from the citizens of Docimer fell on her, studying every facet, from her simple silver crown revealing pointed ears, to her black horse—but mostly her ears. She bore their scrutiny with practiced ease. This kingdom would have heard only rumors, and the undercurrent of hostility was something it had taken her own people time to overcome. Whether they knew it or not, people feared that which was different from them.

When their leader came forward, the party bowed low in their saddles. "I am General Mins. We are here to escort Her Majesty, Queen Faelyn, to the palace." The general was decorated with stars and medals, though he couldn't have much battle experience.

"I am Captain Nolan. Your assistance is appreciated." Nolan nodded.

Mins looked away from Nolan and eyed Faelyn. His long, brown hair shifted as he quickly looked down. Though his face was tense, his fear abated and she sensed he was pleased. He must know why she was here then, though they hadn't spread the news of the engagement outside of their inner circles.

"Captain Nolan, I advise Queen Faelyn to ride within the safety of her carriage. Quite a crowd has gathered for the arrival. The royal guard and local militia may not be enough to guarantee her safety."

Nolan let out a small sigh, audible to Faelyn, making her fake smile turn earnest. "My queen wishes to be visible to the people."

Not everyone could accept the rule of a fae queen and a woman, and reports said there would likely be resistance because of her ears, but she'd convinced Nolan she would be safe without being hidden away in a carriage.

Mins hesitated, then gestured to his men. They split, half in front and half behind, and were on their way. The city of Docimer grew bigger and bigger as they neared, until only the outskirts and the large stone palace at the top of the hill were visible, built into the mountain itself. The splendor of the palace outshone hers in Pavora, its white marble hewed from the very mountain from which it stood. Historically, Kestrea was the less prosperous of their two kingdoms, but not since Faelyn was little.

The murmur of the crowd reached her before she saw them. They passed through a stone gateway on the edge of town, then slowed to a walk. Even on the outskirts, with nothing more than the most humble of homes, people lined the street. Farmers, bakers, soot-smudged miners, mothers with young children clinging to their dresses—all had come to see the spectacle. And they didn't even know why she was here. Nothing had been announced yet.

They didn't know they looked upon their future queen.

Conjuring up a small amount of magic, Faelyn made herself glow with radiance. It shimmered off her satin dress and her mother's turquoise stone that never left her neck. She smiled at the people, like the many times she'd done this in Alysies while they struggled to rebuild what Daltieri had wrought for so many years. All part of the show.

Parents held their children high in the air, townspeople pointed and gossiped, and onward their horses carried them, over the one long road leading up to the palace.

As much as she dreaded this day, she couldn't deny a pull she felt, leading her on. It grew stronger the further into town they went. It was indescribable, like something had tenderly cocooned her soul with the most delicate and pleasant of touches and drew it forward with whisper-light tugs. Perhaps this was where she was supposed to be. Maybe the Fates had decided something should go right in her life.

Oh, she shouldn't think that way. Her dark past had been overcome, and they'd won back her kingdom. She was surrounded by friends and people who loved her and would lay down their lives for her. Why couldn't she be happy and not want for more? Faelyn shook her head. *I* am *happy and don't want for more, save for better protection for my people.*

Still, her smile became more genuine the further they drew to the palace. The delicate tugs grew ever stronger. Overall, the excitement of the crowd drowned out their hostility and curiosity. It was easy to ignore any glib remarks.

"Finally excited about meeting the prince?" Amerae's raised eyebrow cut into Faelyn's thoughts. She realized her heart rate had steadily increased. "You're grinning."

"Am I?" She eased her grin to a more subdued smile. Her cheeks burned. "Is it not right to be excited?" She waved to the crowd, ignoring Amerae's pointed stare.

"No, it's perfectly all right. I'm just beginning to worry about Majestic under all that bouncing you're doing." Amerae gave Faelyn her most innocent clear-eyed look, even adding a few bats of her eyelashes.

Faelyn scowled and stopped bouncing. Amerae flashed a wide smile, but Faelyn only returned it for a moment before her attention was drawn elsewhere. The pull—there was no other way to describe it now—reached a new intensity. They'd entered a busy area full of shops and buildings several stories high. Where most of the buildings in Alysies were made of wood cut from the thick forests, Kestrea buildings were made mostly from blocks of stone.

With the crowd so thick, each person clamored for a view. Faelyn looked ahead, toward the palace, now towering in the distance, but that's not where her gaze wanted to be.

She blinked and tilted her head up and right. When she opened her eyes, they locked on a boy standing at the rail of a balcony. His long sandy-colored hair was disheveled, hastily tied back in a low tail. His clothes were bedraggled and torn. There was nothing remarkable about him underneath the dirt. Nothing except his eyes. They were wide open, taking her in, and the lightest shade of blue she'd ever seen. Lighter than her mother's turquoise necklace. Brighter than any sea she'd had the privilege to witness during her long life. As blue as a wispy sky.

"My queen?" Amerae's voice drifted to her from afar.

The boy studied her with an intensity beyond his years. He didn't point or whisper like the other townspeople. There was a resolve in him. She tried to read him, but there were too many others.

Too soon she passed the building. Only Amerae's hand on her shoulder kept her from swiveling around to find him again.

"Is everything all right, Queen Faelyn?" Concern laced Amerae's voice, and she leaned forward, brows drawn in worry. "Did you sense danger? Ill intent?

Faelyn blinked rapidly. Nolan had a hand on the hilt of his sword, shoulders tense and eyes darting to the crowds.

"Everything is wonderful," she said, loud enough for her guards to hear.

Nolan studied her, then eased his grip.

Faelyn turned to Amerae; she couldn't turn around or her guard might worry again. "Did you see that boy?"

Amerae looked behind them. "I saw many boys." Her eyes flitted upward. "One, in particular, watched you most intently. He seemed familiar, but I've never been to this kingdom. And I'd remember those eyes. Do you know him?"

"No. Of course not." They continued down the road, but the pull was no longer in front of her. It lay behind, lessening the longer they traveled. She wanted to turn around, but her purpose for coming here lay ahead.

Their party passed through a thick guarded gate, then up several stone switchbacks before reaching the palace courtyard. An entourage of soldiers and servants lined up to greet them, and her thoughts turned away from the peculiar pull behind her. It was time to meet the king.

Faelyn dismounted, letting her reins drop for a servant to handle. King Bautamin himself strode down the marble façade steps to meet her, with his overly large crown, red silk tunic stretched tight over a large belly, and a red-cheeked smile. He inclined his head, then took the liberty of seizing Faelyn's hand and kissing it with wet lips. He avoided looking at her ears as if they'd burn his retinas.

The courtiers scattered among the outskirts had no qualms loudly voicing their strong opinions about her unusual appearance.

"Queen Faelyn. The rumors of your beauty precede you, though they do not do you credit." He dropped her hand, and she resisted the urge to wipe it clean.

If she hinted at the rumors circulating about his appearance, she doubted he'd like it much. "King Bautamin, I'm delighted to meet you. Where's Prince Rory?"

Bautamin's eyes crinkled. "Your voice is like a bell, my dear." He held out his arm, so Faelyn took it, and together they walked toward the palace doors. The shuffle of dozens of servants and guards resounded behind them. "After such a long journey, I assumed you'd like a moment to rest and refresh before meeting my son. I assumed correctly, yes?"

"A brief respite would be most welcome, Your Majesty." Faelyn delivered her lines with a warm smile, but inside she itched to get on with things. All the formalities and rules of court were enough to make her want to leap out of her own skin. So much time wasted on pleasantries and everyone trying not to offend everyone else. In some ways, her childhood as a shunned lady of the court was easier. No one expected anything of her then.

After Nolan secured the rooms, Faelyn was escorted into an exquisite suite. Exquisite, if one liked dead animal décor. The skin rug and fur blankets covering everything, she could ignore, but the mounted bear head above the four-poster bed was too much. Decorations aside, the suite was large and plentiful, with enough rooms for her servants to each have their own, should they wish.

Refreshments of sweetmeats and a bubbly drink were delivered, but not until the door closed and it was just she and Amerae did Faelyn let loose a long breath and slump in the fur-covered settee.

"I'm sorry, my queen, but it does get quite cold here in the winter. Animal hide is good for warmth I hear..." Amerae trailed off at Faelyn's tight frown.

"Life is funny sometimes, Amerae." Faelyn laughed to herself. "Did you know forty years ago I was shoveling horse manure in exchange for a barn loft to sleep in? And I had more freedom then."

"Marriage is a big commitment, Your Majesty. It's only normal you'd feel you're losing your freedom." Amerae picked at the fur of a blanket draped over the arm of the settee. "But at least King Bautamin promised that Prince Rory would rule with you from Alysies, so you won't have to look at the hideous décor for long." Amerae smiled in encouragement.

"It's not much of a commitment. Prince Rory will grow old and die, then I'll find a new kingdom to align with." She shouldn't shove Amerae's efforts away so thoroughly. This whole mess wasn't her fault. Besides, it wasn't a mess. The plan to safeguard Alysies with a marriage alliance was going perfectly.

Amerae frowned. "Why don't you take a nap while we wait?"

"I have a better idea. Let's slide the furniture aside and have a duel." Faelyn hopped up and pushed the settee against the wall.

Amerae groaned, but helped.

Faelyn grabbed her sword from the pile of things deposited by the palace servants. The familiar weight sang in her hand. She would duel out her frustrations while waiting to be summoned to meet her future husband.

FOUR

Bastien walked the crowded streets in a daze, only just managing not to trip over his ill-fitting boots. The sights around him passed in a blur. His vision had come true. A queen. She'd been real, and looked right at him like he wasn't the nothing he'd spent his life believing.

Olin punched him in the arm, and he looked up. They'd been walking toward the palace.

"Where are you going? You're gonna get us caught." Olin glanced at the guards down the road, now eyeing the two dirty street kids.

They shouldn't have come so far from their turf, but all he could think of was Queen Faelyn. No one even seemed to mind her ears—he certainly didn't. They didn't lash out or call her names like he'd expected. She was like an angel sent from Acantha above. She radiated with beauty, and she'd looked at him—*him!*—as if she felt the same pull he did.

No, impossible. It was his cursed eyes she'd noticed. He shook his head, coming to his senses. He pulled Olin off the streets just as an armed guard stepped from the wall in their direction. They turned a corner and hurried back to their part of town.

He ignored Olin's worried look and rubbed his eyes. They'd caused him trouble more than once. The lightness of them made him too identifiable. He kept his head down as a rule while in the crowds. Kolb had almost decided not to take him in because of their bright color, but most seven-year-olds weren't as quick-handed.

Picking up speed, Bastien rounded a corner and slammed into someone. The impact threw him back into Olin's legs. Pain bloomed in his rear end. He winced and sat up.

His eyes went wide as he beheld the captain of the city guard picking up a boy off the cobbled street. The boy dusted off his fine clothes, not a hair out of place on his blonde head, then glared at Bastien. He looked familiar, but how would a misfit ever cross paths with a rich kid unless he was robbing him?

Maybe he had robbed him before.

Donned in a crisp green uniform, shiny sword strapped to this side, the captain stepped in front of the boy, his frown deepening as his gaze flickered between Bastien and Olin. Bastien's legs tensed to run—run for his life—but he stayed firmly in place. He swallowed the lump lodged in his throat.

Captain Cerick. The man all street kids were warned to avoid. Your life was in his hands if he suspected you of breaking a law. He was dressed in full honor guard regalia with a dark silver finish and two green medallions set on each shoulder to show rank.

"Where you going in such a hurry, boy?" Captain Cerick came closer.

Bastien shot to his feet, cursing his bad luck. He'd just roughed up someone important to the captain of the guard. Olin's rapid breathing behind him reminded Bastien he couldn't flee.

"My apologies, sir. My brother and I were just heading home." Bastien lowered his eyes in a show of respect, though he'd rather spit on the captain's boots. He and his men had beat up more than a few of his gang. He backed a step, forcing Olin to move with him.

"Yeah? Looks to me like you're common street thieves. Torn

clothes, greasy heads, baggy pants with extra pockets. Employed by a gang lord? You boys were warned to stay away from the palace."

"No sir, we aren't thieving. Just trying to get a view of the fae queen." He prayed the captain would believe the half-truth and stay away from his pockets.

"Captain, I would teach this boy a lesson." The boy, who looked to be Bastien's age, stepped from behind the captain, shoulders squared.

The boy's commanding voice set Bastien on edge.

The captain's eyes went wide. For a moment he looked almost panicked. He opened his mouth, but then the boy nodded his insistence. Cerick turned a steely gaze to Bastien.

Why was the captain taking orders from some rich kid?

The boy, in all his rich, clean finery, clenched his fists, stepping forward eagerly.

Bastien blinked. They may have been the same age, but the boy was half a foot shorter and scrawny as a fish. His stance was all wrong, unbalanced as if he might topple himself over with a strong enough punch. Despite his riches, he wasn't a trained fighter. He hadn't had to hone his fists as weapons for as long as Bastien. It'd be no contest.

Except Bastien couldn't win. Beating up the rich boy was a much worse crime than accidentally knocking him down. He'd be locked away for sure. And maybe that was the boy's intent. The captain's expression promised retribution, and Bastien's heart kicked up with real fear.

"Put your hands up and fight, thief." Cerick beckoned to Bastien and motioned the nameless boy forward.

Bastien raised his arms, curling his fingers into tight fists and wrapping his thumb around his second and third knuckles like the older boys had taught him. The boy charged. It took everything Bastien had not to punch back but to pivot and avoid the hit. He'd been in numerous fistfights, but he'd never thrown a match before.

The boy stumbled behind the power of his swing when he didn't connect. Bastien bounced, swerving to face him. And waited for him to recover. *Horseshit. Absolute horseshit.*

"You can do it! You're faster than this street vermin." The captain shoved Bastien from behind.

The boy reared back and punched. Bastien let the blow connect. His cheek exploded with pain, but he didn't drop. In a well-practiced maneuver, he ducked the follow-up hit, then uppercut the boy in the chin.

"Shit!" *Oh, shit.* Bastien watched as the boy sailed backward, landing hard. What had he done? Bastien's limbs locked in place, his gaze on Olin's terrified expression from the side of the alley as the captain strode forward. A gauntleted hand struck him on the back of the head, dropping him to hands and knees.

The boy stood, rubbing his jaw. Hate and embarrassment burned in his glaring eyes and reddened face. He strode over to Bastien and kicked him hard in the side, sending him sprawling.

The boy leaned over close, his breath hot. "What's your name, thief?"

Bastien stayed silent, breathing through the pain and watching Olin back up into a wall behind the captain. The city guard didn't need another way to identify him. Captain Cerick approached Olin with cruel intent in his long stride.

Olin's knees shook and his eyes went wide.

Don't do it, kid.

"It's Bastien," Olin squeaked. "I'm Olin. We work for Kolb."

Bastien closed his eyes.

The rich kid didn't even glance in Olin's direction. "Bas-tea-in?" He gave a mirthless laugh. "You could hang for this, thief. You have no idea who I am. You're lucky we have somewhere to be. Captain Cerick, let's go."

The captain nodded to the barely-out-of-the-nursery rich kid and followed without question. With a pleased smirk, and without a backward glance, the pair left him bleeding in the alley.

Clearly one of those hits had addled Bastien's brain. The Nightmare of the Streets cowered to no one and left no thief unpunished.

Olin knelt next to him. "Why'd you hit him? They could have done so much worse to you."

"I'm fine, thanks for asking." With a groan, Bastien pushed himself to a sitting position. The world spun and pain washed over him in waves. Blood trickled down the back of his head. "What do we say, Olin? When you've got nothing—"

"You've got nothing to lose," Olin finished. Under his breath, he added, "Except your life."

"Nah, they don't kill kids for thievin' in this city." Beating up rich kids, sure, but Olin didn't need the reminder. Bastien rubbed his tender ribs. Not broken.

"Fifteen is hardly a kid, Bastien."

"What of it, eleven-year-old?" Bastien flashed him a good-natured smile and punched him in the shoulder. Olin scowled, but didn't rub the spot. "Come on, we've got to get back to the House."

Bastien led the way between back alleys, away from the palace and down the hill toward their section of Docimer. It was one of the toughest places to get a good hit because all the residents were either as poor as he, or twice as suspicious. They rarely hunted in their district.

Olin still lectured behind him. "You've paid your debt, Bast. Go back to the orphanage. Maybe they could get you an apprenticeship somewhere. You're smart, you know."

Bastien frowned with familiar sadness. "I'm too old for an apprenticeship."

The lady who ran the orphanage, Miss Bannings, had been like a mother to the orphan kids. She taught him to read and write. At night, she'd let him curl up in a chair with her and she'd brush his long hair, telling him how handsome it made him. He'd abandoned her the first time Kolb had laid eyes on him, promising a better life that never came. Bastien used his first stolen coins to buy food for the orphans and a new shawl for Miss Bannings, but she told him she couldn't accept things bought with his thievery. He was so ashamed, he'd never gone back. He'd never told her how much her care and love had meant to him.

The time had long passed to cut ties with the gang, but he couldn't think about that. He couldn't even think about his brush with death in the form of Captain Cerick. His thoughts turned to Queen Faelyn and the hope for a better life he'd felt in her gaze.

Maybe he could rise up and be more than his mistakes, be someone worthy of her attention.

Olin spoke over his musings. "I'm sorry I told them our real names. I panicked. He was going to arrest you."

Bastien glanced over at his friend. Olin's eyes were downcast, trailing the cobblestones beneath his flopping boots, hands shoved deep into his empty pockets.

Bastien clapped him on the back. "You did good. He would have arrested me for sure. We need to find out who that kid was though. Did he seem familiar?" He cut over, following a shortcut that ran through the ruins of an old building.

Some of the tension left Olin as he shook his head.

They'd escaped what could have been a disaster. One thing was for sure, Captain Cerick wouldn't forget his face, or his name. Things were going to get much harder.

CHAPTER

FIVE

Faelyn held up a hand, breathing hard. Amerae grinned and pulled her practice sword out of a high strike.

"You've been practicing those techniques I taught you." Faelyn wiped sweat off her brow, then tossed her sword on the fur-covered chair.

Amerae leaned her hands on her knees. "Coming from you, that's quite the compliment."

A knock on the door made them jump. A guard answered it, and someone from the hall said, "His Highness will see Queen Faelyn now."

Faelyn shoved sweaty hair off her face. The guard looked to Faelyn, and she gave him a quick nod. He eyed her training attire before turning back to the page at the door. "Her Majesty will be out shortly."

Faelyn locked wide eyes with Amerae for half a beat before flying into action. She ran into her room to her trunk, stripping off her tunic and pants.

Amerae's feet pounded to the maid's wing. "Double time, ladies.

This is an emergency." Their gasps and rushing steps carried to Faelyn's room.

By the time the maids surrounded Faelyn, she had her dress halfway over her head. They helped navigate it the rest of the way. Amerae pushed Faelyn down into a chair that wasn't there a moment ago, and one maid went after her hair in a whirlwind frenzy of combs and picks, while another redid her makeup.

Faelyn squeezed her eyes shut and hoped for the best. Part of her wouldn't mind showing up a sweaty mess to such an important first meeting, but that was the part of her that continued to resist this life. She tramped her down.

Someone nudged her foot with a pair of silken shoes. She lifted her feet, and they slipped them on. A spritz of perfume nearly made her gag. When the maids had packed her trunks, they assured her perfume was all the fashion, and that it only smelled strong to her.

"It'll cover the stench of sweat, my queen." Amerae couldn't disguise the amusement in her voice.

Someone tugged on her arm, so she stood and opened her eyes. The mirror in front of her proved that her team had transformed her within just a few minutes. The pearly-green dress widened at a flattering spot on her hips, flowing down to golden slippers. They braided her hair up off her neck, which was still graced by her mother's blue stone. Her turquoise eyes looked more alive than she felt.

Another knock sounded on the door, more urgent than before.

Faelyn lifted her skirt in one hand and, holding her chin high, walked out of the bedroom and toward the door.

"Wait!" Amerae darted to the vanity and snatched up Faelyn's circlet. She cast a hard look toward the maids.

They gasped, realizing their error, and rushed forward to secure it in Faelyn's hair

A page waited for them in the hall. He dipped his head, his feather cap bobbing. "If you'll follow me, Your Majesty."

Faelyn trailed him, along with Amerae, a few servants, and the rest of her guard behind her. Conversations flitted to her sensitive ears as they traveled the many corridors and wings that made up the palace. Nothing interesting. Maids cleaning empty rooms, discussing their latest love interests, or their charges' disgusting habits.

It seemed they'd never arrive at the throne room. Amerae's frequent sighs provided a measure of entertainment along the way. The clacking of her guards' boots echoed endlessly in the marble halls. She was glad for the strong perfume to cover the smell of the mounted animals gracing every alcove. Eventually the corridor widened, the paintings on the walls grew larger with more ornate frames, and the space opened into a receiving room with marble columns and high ceilings. An elaborately carved set of double doors with gold detailing and flanked by guards meant they had arrived.

Faelyn dropped her skirt, took a slow breath, and stilled her hands to her sides. Through those doors was her future husband. Her heart steadied. It wasn't her forever, and it wasn't today.

The palace guards opened the doors, but she was too far back to see into the room.

The page rushed forward. "Your Majesty, King Bautamin of Kestrea, and Your Highness, Prince Rory of Kestrea, may I present Her Highness, Queen Faelyn Rylandor of Alysies." He bowed deep at the waist, flourishing his hand and feather cap, then backed away with his eyes down.

Faelyn pasted a small smile on her face and walked forward, entering the throne room. Similar to her own, the room boasted high ceilings with plenty of open space. But where hers had tapestries portraying Alysian history, this one featured marble busts of men on pedestals and a wraparound balcony.

Avoiding the dais, she glanced briefly toward the members of the court who stood on either side of the room. She'd expected this to be a more private affair, though maybe for Kestrea her presence was a cause for celebration. Alysies was a powerful ally for any kingdom.

The people, dressed in their wool and long sleeves for the cool northern summer, watched her closely as she ascended toward the dais. Eyes alight with curiosity, their whispered conversations accompanied smiles and feelings of relief and appreciation—also not what she was expecting. There was hardly a word about her ears. Most of the comments centered around her beauty, and their protection from the Daltieri threat.

Faelyn's smile turned genuine. If she could really help these people in tandem with helping her own, then her sacrifice would be worth it. The only person she'd ever considered marrying, she couldn't have. Kian was approaching middle age, and though that made no difference to her, they both knew it was for the best.

Faelyn purposefully avoided looking at the prince as he fidgeted in his seat. Instead, she stared at King Bautamin sitting erect on his throne. She curtseyed at the appropriate time, lowering her head as a show of respect. Lifting her face, she finally met the boy prince's brown eyes. Prince Rory looked younger than she expected a fifteen-year-old to look. He was dressed in crisp, green silk with gold buttons and red accents. The collar fastened up to his neck, and he pulled at it in regular intervals. His back was straight and his blonde hair perfectly trimmed. By the time they would wed in five years when the prince was old enough, he'd probably pass as handsome.

King Bautamin dipped his head. "Thank you, Queen Faelyn, for joining us. If you feel rested enough, let's start with a tour of the palace. You can get to know Prince Rory, and it would give you a feel for the people you'll one day be ruling by my son's side." He watched her closely.

No need to remind him they'd be ruling from Alysies. The practice wasn't standard, but her advisors assured her it was all in the document.

"Do you not wish for me and Prince Rory to sign the agreement first?" That must be the purpose of the witnesses, after all.

The boy prince's eyes lit up at the sound of her voice. He leaned over his father. "Let her wait," he whispered. His voice was quiet enough, but Faelyn heard, and it made her frown.

The king patted his son's hand. "We'll sign them in a few days, at a celebration feast I'm holding in your honor."

Faelyn expected the feast. Obviously, they simply couldn't sign the engagement agreement and journey back to Alysies that very day —too many ridiculous formalities—but the delay still chaffed.

She reformed her plastered smile. "I'd love to see the palace."

CHAPTER

SIX

"Kolb wants you."

Bastien looked up from where he and Olin played chess on the floor. Half the pieces were missing or broken, but they made it work with their own version of the game.

Shawn, the boy who'd spoken, kicked at the board, scattering the pieces. Bastien shot to his feet, but he wasn't willing to do much to Kolb's second in command. Shawn only had the position because Bastien had turned it down. He'd seen what Kolb was about and wanted no greater part in his underhanded dealings than absolutely necessary. Kolb was as slippery as a snake, and so was his temper. Best to stay out from under him and his second if he wanted to make it out all right in the end.

They'd only take it out on Olin.

Shawn glared as Bastien moved passed. Bastien smiled reassuringly at Olin's worried face, unintimidated by a jealous second-rate whose power only existed because Bastien had allowed it. The stairs creaked as he wound his way to the second level.

Two boys guarded Kolb's door, but they moved aside to let him in, giving him the eye. The office was a different world than the rest

32

of the House. Bastien stepped out of a life of poverty and neglect, and into a richly furnished room that he'd once feared ruining with his soiled clothes.

Kolb stood at the window, looking down into the street. Probably trolling for his next kid to snatch.

The door closed behind him, and Bastien waited in silence. He'd looked up to Kolb once, would have done anything for him. But when Kolb invented the piss-poor rule about not helping the other boys pay their debts, admiration turned to resentment.

Kolb faced him. He lifted a glass off his desk and sipped the golden liquid. Liquor bought with the boys' slave labor. "Still upset about my punishment, I see."

"No, Kolb." The injuries from the beating had healed long ago. Even his fresh wounds from the run-in with the captain the day before were better.

A drop splashed on Kolb's silk shirt, turning it dark as he took another swig. "Good. I have a job for you."

Kolb's jobs were never fun, never optional, and usually ended with someone in pain. "I'm not your lackey second, Kolb. I've paid my debt."

Kolb's amused smile disappeared. "The boys need to see you're still under my command. You live in my House, after all. And I heard you almost got caught by the captain of the guard."

Of course he had. "Nothing happened."

Kolb leaned forward, his tell before he delivered the line he knew would trap you. "I have Olin. I'll use him if I have to, Bastien. You know I will."

Bastien clenched his fists. "What's the job?" Kolb must need him very badly.

Glass in hand, Kolb pointed at a wrapped package on the desk. "I need you to deliver this to someone. They are waiting."

"Who, and what is it?" The small rectangular box could hold anything. Kolb didn't need Bastien to make a simple delivery—there'd be a catch at the end.

Kolb shrugged. "A friend of mine. Roman. He's waiting for you behind that pastry store I sometimes buy you kids treats from."

Bastien crossed his arms and leaned against the doorjamb. "You'll have to be more specific. You never buy us anything. And what's in the box?"

"Rue's Bakery is what it's called. Roman will be in the alley behind. He's a big investor, so don't mess this up." Kolb flipped a gold coin toward him. "Buy the boys something after you're done."

Bastien snatched it from the air without breaking eye contact with Kolb. *A gold coin!* This was ten times the biggest payment Kolb had ever given, and Kolb didn't often pay. Bastien removed any facial expression and pocketed the precious coin. There was always a catch. The bigger the payment, the bigger the danger.

"It's illegal, but that's all you need to know. Don't get caught with it or I'll invent a new punishment for you. Maybe I'll finally shave your head." Kolb turned his back on him to refill his glass from a decanter on the table.

Bastien prided his long hair. It helped him blend into a crowd and made it easier to hide. Kolb must have noticed his attachment to it.

He ignored the threats and scooped up the lightweight package, tucking it into his vest pocket with the coin. Everything about this screamed foul, but if he refused the task, Olin would be the one to suffer the consequences. He'd have to be careful.

He left without a word and pounded down the stairs. Olin jumped up from the reassembled chessboard on the floor.

"I'm making a delivery. Best if you wait here." Bastien patted Olin on the back.

"Why can't I come? Maybe we can nab a few pockets on the way."

Several heads, including Shawn's, turned their way.

"That's good thinking, but this is for Kolb." Bastien stared into Olin's innocent eyes, trying to impress upon him the importance he stay behind. Whatever mystery surrounded the package was bound to be trouble.

Olin nodded and flopped back down on the splintery floor, frowning. "All right."

Bastien smiled and flipped the gold coin, catching it in his palm. "I'll bring you back something sweet."

Olin's brown eyes lit up. Whispers broke out around them. Olin's grin followed him out the door.

Bastien whistled as he walked the familiar alleys, avoiding the main streets. The bakery, famous for its frosted treats and the best fresh bread this side of the city, was not far. But he'd have to skirt around Makers Market to avoid any guards.

He took the package out of his precious vest. It didn't weigh anything. He shook it, hearing only a slight rattle. It didn't smell like anything ominous—no herb or poison he knew of—so he put it back.

Enticing scents of cinnamon and roasted meat accompanied the noise of the always-open market on the other side of the building. Once clear, Bastien slowed, listening for guards. His street instincts had him scanning each intersection. Out of habit, he took the least direct route to the bakery.

Before he turned the final corner, he peered around. Roman, one of Kolb's oldest acquaintances, leaned against the wall behind the bakery. He wore his silk finery, lest anyone mistake him for the criminal Bastien knew him to be. No one else was in sight.

Head swiveling to inspect each side street, Bastien turned the corner and walked toward him.

Roman watched him approach, holding out his hand when Bastien got close enough.

Bastien pulled the package from his vest and passed it over.

"Thanks, kid." Roman dipped his head and walked away.

Bastien watched him leave, then shrugged. It was one of the easiest tasks he'd ever done for Kolb. So where was the catch?

The coin simmered through his vest. Now time for the reward—Olin would love something sweet.

Free of the illegal package, Bastien circled around the building to the front of Rue's Bakery. The window boasted an assortment of sugared candy and cookies, cakes and tarts, and baskets of baguettes like bouquets of flowers. A gold coin would be enough to stuff all the boys at the House with sweets, and some change leftover for Olin. It'd be nice to earn his treats the honest way for a change.

Townspeople stared at him warily as they passed in and out of the store. Bastien looked down at himself. He dusted his permanently dirty trousers and smoothed back his long hair. He wiped at his face with his dirty sleeve, then entered the shop.

The smell of baking bread and sweet frosting swirled over him. He breathed in through his mouth, almost tasting the treats. Winding through the many tables covered with mouth-watering goodies, he caught the wary eye of the few patrons.

The baker looked up from the counter, flour dusting his front. "Young man, you can't be in here. Please leave before I call the guard."

Bastien took the coin from his pocket. He bit it and then held it up for the baker to see. The baker frowned and went back to kneading his dough. Bastien smiled and grabbed a basket, filling it with savory cookies.

The door banged open, causing Bastien to spin around. Roman stormed in, eyes alight in fury. Five guards pushed in behind him. The townspeople screamed and darted back—away from Bastien. Had Kolb double-crossed Roman? He set down the heavy basket and widened his stance.

Arm outstretched, Roman pointed. "That's him! That's the thief who stole my money. Look, look there! He's got the coin in his hand right now!"

Bastien's mouth dropped open.

The guards drew their swords and approached. The baker ducked under his counter.

Bastien clenched the coin in his fist until it dug into his flesh. He shook with anger. This store butted up to another. No back door. The front door loomed behind Roman's superior smirk, but guards blocked the way. As fast as he was, they could still kill him if he tried.

He threw the coin over the counter to the baker. "For your trouble."

He launched a table full of beautiful pastries toward the guards. Sugared delicacies flew through the air. Bastien dashed toward the front, aiming for the barest of openings between the guards as they raised their arms against the assault.

Bastien skidded on his knees toward the space between the guards' legs. They surrounded him, two grabbing his arms while three pointed their swords. Roman must have made quite the scene to attract five guards for one teenage coin thief. Or they'd been waiting for him.

The guards hauled him out of the bakery.

Women with hands over their mouths stared in astonishment, whispering to each other. Men stepped forward, ready to assist the guards in bringing a criminal to justice. Bastien let their gasps and murmurs blur as they hauled him down the street. His eyes widened, and he fought back uselessly as he realized where they headed. The one place he feared going. Robbers' Round.

He had only himself to blame. He'd walked right into Kolb's trap.

It was so close, they didn't bother with a barred wagon. They walked him straight to Robbers' Round, a raised patch of land in the middle of the busy Maker's Market square filled with an assortment of torture devices. They could cut off his hands, hang him by his neck, lock his ankles in an elevated stock and let him starve for days, or to death. Everything he'd ever done, the skills he'd learned, the routes he took, the lessons he taught Olin, all revolved around how to not get caught and be brought to Robbers' Round. The punishment depended on the mood of the Round's captain that day. There was no way of knowing what fate he marched to, but odds were, he wouldn't come back from it.

Why would Kolb do this to him? What about Olin? He would be sitting at the House, alone, watching the door, mouth salivating for the treat Bastien promised.

His feet hit the grassy knoll, and a crowd of market-goers surrounded him. Gawking. Pointing. Gossiping.

"Would it help if I told you I didn't steal that coin?" His mind grabbed at clouds, trying to find a way out of this. His breath sounded loud in his ears.

"Shut up." The guard behind him shoved him up the hill.

They stopped in the middle of the small plateau, and the captain approached. Captain Cerick. Cocky with a deep scowl and something to prove, wearing the medallions that marked his rank.

The captain stopped a single stride away, satisfied recognition in his eyes. "Crime?"

The guard who pushed him spoke first. "Stealing, sir."

"Search him."

Rough hands patted Bastien down, searched the pockets of his trousers, and removed his boots and vest.

Bastien eyed his precious vest, ignoring his rapid heartbeat. "I expect that back when you're done."

The guard shook it upside down, but all that fell out were his lockpicking kit, a knife, and a few crumbs.

Captain Cerick snapped his fingers, and the guard delivered him the vest. He took it in two hands at the top and pulled in opposite directions, trying to rip the fabric. It didn't tear. Bastien smirked.

So did the captain. He snapped, and a guard withdrew his sword. Bastien clenched his jaw. Cerick held the vest up, and the guard ran his sword through the priceless vest, tearing the fabric in two.

It fluttered to the ground as he looked Bastien right in the eye. "The cage."

No! Bastien jerked his arms out of his captor's grip. He dashed for the cover of the market. A guard caught him by his long hair, yanking him off his feet. Bastien landed on his back, the air driven from his lungs. Swords went to his neck, and he was hauled up. He coughed, catching his breath, then they threw him backward. He crashed into cold metal, and the door slammed closed.

"Raise him up." Cerick watched with a bored frown as a crank was turned, winding the rope attached to the cage.

Slowly, Bastien's small metal prison—barely big enough to stand in—left the ground. His breathing slowed as he scanned the faces of the large crowd already readying their rotting fruit and vegetables.

Of all the things in Robbers' Round, Bastien feared the cage the most. Suspended in the air, there was no protection from the cold nights. He'd seen people freeze to death when the guards forgot to get them down. How long would they keep him here?

He'd crossed the captain of the city guard. They could keep could him forever.

Why now? What had he done to make Kolb betray him like this? He'd been a fool for not seeing it coming. How would Olin survive without him?

He gripped the bars as the cage lurched to a stop. The boos of the crowd crescendoed as the guards cleared away. Bastien stared out over the market, face expressionless—nothing to show the fury within but the white of his knuckles.

The first few projectiles fell short, but then a tomato hit the bars and exploded over the side of his face. The putrid juices ran into his eyes and down his back. He didn't flinch. Every hit thereafter was kindling to the fires of revenge that turned molten inside him.

Kolb be damned to the dark depths of the Hereafter.

CHAPTER

SEVEN

From high above the busy market, Bastien hung in his cage, heart heavy as he watched the people at market around him. For two days, the iron bars dug into his legs where they dangled through the holes. For two days, people bombarded him with rotten vegetables and animal dung. For two days, not a drop of rain fell to quench his growing thirst. The stench flooded his nose and mouth with each breath, and the flies swarmed, undeterred by his feeble swatting.

And now, of all times and places, Kolb strode up to him, no doubt to make things worse while Bastien slowly wasted away in this cage of sure death. The thick man strode passed the bored guard with barely a nod, a smirk on his whiskered lips when he spotted the chosen method of Bastien's imprisonment.

"I'm surprised to see you here, Kolb." Bastien's voice came out convincingly strong despite his weakened state.

Kolb stopped just shy of the ring of filth surrounding the cage. Raising his voice to be heard, he said, "I tried to keep away, but I couldn't pass up the chance to make the last days of your life more miserable."

"Why'd you do it?" Bastien's forehead rested against the bars as he looked down. He hated that he hadn't been strong enough to resist asking. Kolb was nothing better than a dirty thief praying on innocent children, but Bastien had been a sure deal, a steady source of coin with the leverage to keep him in check. Things shouldn't have turned out this way.

"You haven't figured it out? You used to be smart."

Bastien thought back, as he had many times over the last couple of days with nothing else to do but keep the flying refuse from his eyes. This whole thing started when Kolb sent him on the damned assignment. He'd threatened to use Olin to force him to go. He'd also mentioned Bastien's run-in with Captain Cerick. The captain had many connections in this town and was known for his ruthlessness, but he'd let Bastien and Olin go without a word after that boy had ordered him to.

He blinked down at Kolb, a slow thought dawning on him. "The captain got to you?"

"Pah, water under the bridge, or cage, in your case." Kolb saluted him with a waterskin and tipped it back in his mouth to reveal the luscious, sweet water.

Bastien almost fainted from the sight. His sandpaper tongue scraped through his dry mouth. Whoever that boy was that Bastien and Olin had encountered in the streets must have been very important. So important Bastien had forfeited his life with a single misplaced punch. The captain had either paid off or threatened Kolb to get rid of him. Likely the latter. Heat flushed through his body.

If he was to die, this was his last chance to help Olin, even if a slim chance.

He shifted his aching arms. "I'll forgive you, and I won't hunt you down when I get out, if you'll free Olin of his debt."

Kolb let loose the most dramatic belly-shaking laugh Bastien had ever heard. "You know, I believe death will do you good." He turned to walk away.

"Last chance, Kolb. I will not die, and you don't have to either.

Let Olin go." Bastien was only half bluffing. There had to be a way to escape and go back for Olin.

"Your Olin is hurt, Bast." He shook his head like he was truly sorry. "He shouldn't have left to find you when the gang learned you'd turned traitor."

Cold fear ran down Bastien's spine. He gripped his cage tighter, the slants cutting into his palms. "You're lying." But Kolb wasn't lying at all.

"I'll see you in the Hereafter, Bastien."

Bastien shot to his feet. Kolb walked away and didn't look back.

"No!" Rage leaked through his normally tight control, fueling his starving body. It'd always been easy for him to keep his head in the face of all his hardship. Only Kolb's constant threat to Olin's safety had ensured complacency. Olin wasn't safe anymore.

Bastien's muscles tensed, and he threw his weight into the side of the narrow cage, then again, back and forth. The cage swung back and forth more wildly with each toss of his body. It didn't fall.

"Hey!" The guard stumbled from his post. "Stop!" He hesitated, looking toward the palace, then ran off through the market.

Bastien bent down and jumped, hitting his head on the top, but slamming his feet down on the bottom. The beam holding his cage groaned and shook. Bastien drew a breath and looked up. He did it again, slamming his weight as hard as he could. Then again, and again. Little by little, the wood rattled more, and soon he detected a barely audible splintering noise. But his strength was fleeting. If he could hold out long enough, it just might work.

A fresh crowd gathered, attracted by the spectacle. A short while later, head aching and bleeding, several footsteps approached. He kept going. He was close. The metal wiggled more and more.

A twang was followed by a sharp stabbing pain in his calf. He cried out, trying to grab his leg in the small space. The arrow had grazed him. Several city guards in dull, silver armor surrounded him below, crossbows and swords at the ready. Blood dripped from his leg where they'd shot him.

"Is your cage not to your liking, boy?" the lead guard asked, his deep scowl and long scar evident beneath his helmet with the ridiculous green plume. At least he wasn't Captain Cerick. "Let's fix that. Get him down." He didn't take his eyes off Bastien, but a pair of guards broke away and rushed toward the post.

They hit a release lever, then unwound a crank. Bastien cursed his bad luck as the thick rope wheeled through the pulley, and his cage lowered to the ground. There was no telling what they were going to do, but he had an idea, and it wasn't good. He clenched his teeth tight to keep from pleading for his life. His slow sure death had just become a quick one, and he'd never make it to help Olin.

He watched the sprawling view of the market vanish, along with his hope of escape. On the ground, the lead guard unlocked his cage and others hauled him up. The rest bared their blades in warning.

Bastien smiled through the nervous fluttering in his chest. "Can I get a drink of water?"

The lead guard's lips thinned, then he turned on his heel. The guards dragged him across the small clearing, past a tempting watering trough, but did not stop to allow him a drink. The lead guard bypassed the gallows and headed to the stocks. Bastien's eyes widened. They didn't mean to end him quick. This was worse. Much worse.

He jerked his arms, freeing one from a surprised guard who cried out. The rest tackled him before he got any further. Their heavy armor crushed him to the ground.

"Since you're afraid of heights, this may be more to your liking." The lead guard's voice was faint against the scrape of gravel beneath him and the punches and kicks to his sides.

Swords drawn, two guards grabbed his wrists, and two more grabbed his upper arms. He pulled uselessly against them as they yanked him forward, dragging him on his knees. The wooden flap of the stocks hinged open. They pressed his arms into the cutouts, then pulled him forward and shoved his head down. With a resounding whack, the flap closed over his arms and neck. The click of the lock made it official. He was going nowhere.

"How about that drink?" he asked.

Some of the guards chuckled as they scuffled away. He craned his neck, but couldn't see past their waists until they disappeared out of sight. A minute later, a bucket came into view. Its contents sloshed back and forth, sending beautiful droplets of water flying through the air as the guard walked toward him. The drops landed on the parched ground, which soaked them up greedily. Bastien licked his lips. The guard lowered the bucket to eye level.

The anticipation was almost too much to bear. Bastien opened his mouth. The guard reared back and splashed the contents of the entire bucket in his face. Bastien swallowed the mouthful he'd caught and saved his satisfied smirk for after he'd lapped up the drops spilling down his face.

"Captain Cerick sends his regards." The guard's feet trudged away.

Bastien clenched his teeth against a biting remark sure to get him kicked in the ribs. His hands went numb within minutes. His arms and neck ached fiercely, and his head weighed a hundred pounds. He must have dozed at one point because the splat of something hitting his back jolted him awake. The sun had moved further through the sky. That much he could tell by the shadows on the dirt below. He flexed his fingers against the pins and needles running up his arms. Someone behind him he couldn't see kicked him in his rear. A child, by the laughing and quickly retreating footsteps.

At least before, the bars and height of the cage had shielded some of the attacks. He hoped Olin was okay, that he was with a healer. Bastien strained against the board, using his bare feet to kick against the gravel. It didn't budge.

The bottom half of a strolling couple came into view. The woman held her skirts in one hand, and her lover's arm in the other. When Bastien twisted to look at their faces, she raised her chin and looked away. The man spit on him as they passed.

Bastien sighed. No one was going to help him. He was about to enter his third day with no food, and hardly any water, and already the air felt colder tonight. Hopefully, Olin had taken his blanket before someone else got to it. His stomach rumbled, but he shook it off. He'd endured worse hunger and worse cold before; he could endure this. So he settled in for the long, lonely night, thankful to survive another day, and worried for his friend who might not.

After days of palace tours, garden strolls, and endless dining, Faelyn eagerly agreed to King Bautamin's suggestion of a city tour. He hoped a relationship would blossom with the frequently absent Prince Rory, while she hoped to discover something to take back to her engineers in Pavora. Already, she'd seen amazing techniques the city used to support the houses and shops built into the steep hills and switchback roads.

After lunch, the king, the prince, and Faelyn entered a covered carriage accented with gold. Guards from both kingdoms rode and walked ahead and behind, making it more than obvious who sat within. Faelyn watched as building after building slipped by, longing for the oak trees of Pavora Woods. When King Bautamin cleared his throat, she realized she'd been neglecting the point of this tour: to spend time with the prince.

Faelyn pulled her gaze from the window. "Prince Rory, what do you like to do for fun?" This exercise was futile; he'd be an entirely different person by the time they wed, with different values and leisurely preferences.

He squinted at her. "I enjoy riding. I would normally be in the country now." His tone was accusatory.

Faelyn's smile slipped. "Well, I won't linger, so you can get on with your riding in the country."

Prince Rory caught his father's disapproving stare. He frowned and turned away.

"And what's your favorite activity here in the city?" The conversation was very one-sided, but she hadn't expected any different. It was hard to think of him as her future husband, so she didn't. She thought of him as what he was, a child. He behaved younger than his fifteen years.

"I like spending time with my uncle." He looked toward his father who watched him closely. "He's captain of the city guard."

Faelyn nodded as he went on about the street criminals his uncle had caught, but she couldn't pay attention. Her gaze was drawn toward the window as a unique feeling stirred her from a three-day slumber. Their carriage had slowed, and smells accosted them through the open window; animal waste mixed with the pungent smells of a spice stall.

"Can we turn here?" she asked, pointing out the window. Something pulled her toward the mass of people and shops that made a lively market square.

King Bautamin smiled and gave orders to the guards. "Commerce thrives here in Docimer." Their party turned and headed into the market.

They became engulfed by the shouts of salesmen proclaiming their wares and people haggling for better prices. Paths twisted off the main road, leading to more shops, and peopled milled everywhere, carrying their baskets and bundles. They stopped to gawk as the guards urged them off the road. It was a curious route, but a good place to get the feel for the city, she supposed.

The king was watching her again, so she poked her head out the window to get a better view. The scene reminded Faelyn of a celebratory market day in Pavora, but maybe it was bigger than usual due to people being drawn to the king's carriage.

Her eyes took in, then quickly dismissed the people and their wares, searching for something beyond, in the center of the market. Between a pair of stalls, she spotted a patch of green, a grassy hill in the middle of the market. As they drew closer, the pillory and empty hanging cage made it clear what this was: the location for public imprisonment and execution. Punishment for thieves and the like. Though Faelyn considered it savage, all big cities in Alysies had them. There were more brutal ways of punishing thieves, which she'd quickly outlawed when she became queen. Daltieri liked to remove hands or digits, even for first-time offenders.

King Bautamin cleared his throat, trying to draw her attention away from the dark spot of their tour.

She gave him a quick glance. "Don't worry. Pavora has two such squares. They are unfortunately necessary at times to keep the peace."

"That they are indeed, Your Majesty." His friendly smile returned.

Faelyn felt a sharp tug, which brought her attention back to the yard. Magic? One of the stocks was occupied—some poor thief who'd done something terrible enough to get his head and wrists locked tight. Caked-on filth covered him, but she couldn't look away. When they passed to the front of him, he glanced up, locking pale blue eyes right on her. She gasped in recognition.

"Queen Faelyn?"

The concern in King Bautamin's voice made her look at him. His brow was drawn. The prince glanced from her to him, and she lowered the hand covering her beating heart.

"That boy... Your guards have locked up a child, Your Majesty."

He peered out the window, then slowly drew his gaze back. Curiosity coated the air. They both knew that children weren't above stealing, or being punished for it, and the boy appeared older than the word "child" described, but surely, he didn't deserve it.

She risked another glance at the boy as a woman hurled a head of cabbage. "Please don't tell me that children are put into stocks in your kingdom, King Bautamin. I'm not sure if I can condone that kind of leadership." *Stupid*. What was she saying? Let him go or the engagement was off? What was wrong with her?

But, already the day had a chill to it, and she'd seen grown men die of the elements. She couldn't let this boy be another victim. "He can't be much older than your son."

Prince Rory tried to peer out the window, but his father held him back. Rory crossed his arms and huffed.

King Bautamin's mouth parted. He blinked a few times, gathering his wits. "That doesn't appear to me to be a child, Queen Faelyn. Would you call my son a child? I certainly don't allow children to be put into the stocks in my kingdom." He put a finger to his chin. "I know what we'll do." He snapped his fingers outside the window, and a guard appeared. "Find out the prisoner's age in the stocks and his crime."

The carriage continued to move slowly through the market. Faelyn kept her hands folded in her lap, smiling every so often at Prince Rory, and fighting the pull to look back out the window. They passed the hill before the soldier returned.

"Your Majesty, the boy is fifteen and is being held for stealing from a noble and trying to escape custody." The soldier bowed from his horse to the king.

The same age as Prince Rory.

King Bautamin glanced at Faelyn. Her heart beat against her ribcage, threatening to reveal her strong desire for this boy's safety. The tug pulled her gaze behind them, but she resisted.

Refusal coated King Bautamin's essence. He was going to say no. The boy would die, and the world would no longer be graced by his presence, and the pull to him would be no more. It was fate. Fate wanted her to intervene, and there was only one thing she could do. She let loose magic on the king. Slow and subtle, so as to avoid detection by the mage disguised as a soldier outside the carriage.

What she did was illegal, punishable by death, even for an allied queen. But that didn't matter. She continued her fake smile, conjuring feelings of youthful innocence inside the king, capitalizing on his love for his son as he pondered how best to handle the situation. No words passed between them, but slowly, his resistance crumbled.

He looked up at the guard still riding beside them. "Fifteen, you say?"

"Yes, Your Majesty."

Faelyn sent one more subtle wave of guilt and love into the king. The mage-soldier looked sharply in their direction, and Faelyn cut off the magic.

"That does seem young for the stocks. And how long has he been there?" Bautamin glanced at his son, still pouting beside him.

"Two days, Sire."

Two days! He couldn't hope to survive much longer in those conditions.

The king nodded. "That sounds long enough. Have him released at once."

"Yes, Sire." The guard bowed low again, then raced back to relay instructions.

Faelyn smiled openly at the king. The pull to the market lessened the further they traveled, but peace settled over her. The tour had been a success after all. "We have trouble with child gangs too, but I started a fund for these children to receive help, to have a place to turn to for education and food instead of being locked into a gang."

King Bautamin returned the smile, but it was entirely forced. "Let's get back, shall we? Or we won't have time to prepare for the feast."

Faelyn enjoyed herself at the feast, despite her distraction; she'd had Nolan send someone to find out more about the nameless boy, but so far had heard nothing. Spurred by the victory in freeing him, she ate fine foods and reveled in the high spirits of the northern kingdom. After the sixth or seventh course, the betrothal contract was brought forth and set upon a special table flanked by golden candelabras and a bejeweled inkwell. She swallowed back any misgivings—her people needed this alliance—and signed her future away with a flourish. Urged by his father, Prince Rory did the same. The crowd cheered, and eventually the feast ended, as did her visit to the cold city. It was time to go home.

CHAPTER
NINE

A guard strode up to Bastien, eyes narrowed in clear anger. His boots stomped against the dirt, and he was followed by two companions. Nothing good could come from the anger roiling off them, but even Bastien's thirst and the ache in his limbs had fallen into the back recesses of his mind.

It was her again.

Bastien felt that unmistakable tug toward the carriage. It drew his eyes like a flower to the sun. The glow of her pale golden hair and her striking turquoise eyes had been worth the pain of craning his neck. He'd held his heavy head up until his muscles quivered and splinters lodged in his skin. The carriage was out of sight by the time the guards stopped in front of him. His head dropped from the strain. Let them beat him. What more could they do?

"I think there's some cabbage left if you're hungry," Bastien said into the boards of his prison. "That last one was only half-rotted." And he'd have eaten it if he could've reached it.

The jangle of keys caught his attention. A guard unlocked the stocks with a click. The bar lifted from his neck and wrists, and firm hands tossed Bastien on his back. The freedom of movement sent glorious pain shooting down his every bone. Blood rushed into his head and hands, and joy overrode the fear of what they planned for him next. His raw wrists begged to have feeling rubbed into them, but he lay unmoving on the hard ground, too stiff to get up.

The lead guard stood over him, a scar on his cheek, and his teeth gritted behind lips parted in a snarl. Bastien mentally prepared for a hard kick to his side.

"You're free to go, vermin, by king's command." The lead guard spat at Bastien's feet, then strode off, followed by his companions.

Bastien glanced toward where Queen Faelyn's carriage had disappeared, then back to the guards. Was it some kind of trick? "So you don't want to dine with me?" They ignored him, and Bastien ignored the rotten food. His street-sense detected no ill intentions from them.

Free, just like that. But, why?

Well, he wasn't about to lay there and wait for them to change their minds. He rolled over and pushed to his knees, then his feet. His legs gave out after two steps, and he went sprawling to the ground.

Come on. Olin needs me. He pushed up again and stumbled to the watering trough.

A layer of sludge covered the top. He shoved it aside and stuck his whole mouth into the dirt-flavored water. Drinking deep mouthfuls, he savored every gulp. Water had never tasted so good. His belly sloshed by the time he was done, making him queasy. The rest of the water turned foul as he scrubbed the caked-on food and animal waste off his body the best he could, getting soaked. He shivered. The day grew colder.

Good enough. Bastien stumble-ran out of the quieting market and down the familiar back alleys of south side.

He rounded the corner of the general store and stopped when he spotted Shawn leaning against the wall, eyes alert for a potential mark. Kolb's second. Before Bastien could backtrack, Shawn turned, spotting him. Shawn's arms went slack, and he glanced in the direction of the House. Bastien sensed his fear.

Bastien's heart sped, and he pushed himself toward the House. Was Olin worse off than he feared? He'd only been gone mere days. How bad could he be already?

His weakened legs tripped him up as they tried to keep up with his mental pace, passing people making their way home with baskets and children in tow. He twisted around carriages and hopped over familiar ruts in the road. What would cause Shawn to fear him? Something was wrong.

Movement to his left caught his attention. *Shawn!* He traveled almost parallel to Bastien, one street over. *He's trying to beat me back to the House!* If Bastien hadn't spent the last days being starved to death, there was no way Shawn could win. But even with as much force as Bastien could muster, Shawn pulled ahead, and Bastien lost sight of him.

Minutes later, Bastien burst into the side door of the House. Conversation halted immediately. Most of the boys had returned—there wasn't much in the way of activity once evening fell. The older ones wouldn't meet his eyes. The younger ones who didn't know better looked at him with fear.

"Where is he?" Bastien's voice carried through the room, cold and deadly, as much a warning of his wrath as they would get if someone didn't speak up.

Shawn was nowhere in sight.

Ben, one of the oldest and one Bastien trusted, shifted his gaze toward the stairs leading down to the dungeon. Bastien strode across the room, the boys clearing a path, his footsteps the only sound. He descended the steps two at a time, whipping around the turn at the first landing.

He got to the bottom just in time to see Kolb unshackling Olin from the wall, Shawn at his elbow. Olin slid down the wall to the ground, head lolled to the side, and didn't move. The air smelled of blood. Bastien trembled with worry at the empty look in Olin's eyes —the vacant stare of one who'd lost all hope. A look he'd seen many times. A look he'd thought he could protect Olin from.

Kolb dropped the keys and drew a knife. "How in the Hereafter did you escape?" He took a casual step closer to Olin, angling himself behind Shawn. The stress roiling off Kolb's second said Shawn did not want to be where he was, but he didn't move.

Bastien shifted his stance and curled his fists. "Freed, by king's command. Imagine that, eh?"

Kolb pointed his knife at Olin. "And you've come crawling back to your friend."

"I promised I would, didn't I?" Bastien shifted his gaze to Olin, concern overtaking anger. "He's hurt. Let me help him."

Kolb smiled, slow and controlled. "Sure, Bastien. Sure." He stepped aside, taking Shawn with him.

Bastien walked slowly across the room. "You okay, buddy? I'm here. I told you I'd take care of you." Olin turned his face up to Bastien. His wide-eyed fear was as plain as the bloody gash on the side of his face.

Bastien reached down, placing a hand on Olin's cool cheek. Debt and the threat of pursuit no longer mattered. Both Captain Cerick and Kolb wanted Bastien dead. Nowhere in Docimer was safe. It was time for them to leave the House for good.

"Get him!" Kolb shouted. He pushed an unsuspecting Shawn who went tumbling into Bastien.

Bastien shoved Shawn out of the way. Teeth bared, Kolb swiped his knife at Bastien in a move that should have gutted him. Bastien caught him by the wrist and threw his weight forward, taking them both to the ground. The knife clattered across the floor.

Dizziness made the room spin, but adrenaline surged through his body.

Using one hand to pin Kolb's arm to the floorboards and a knee on the other, Bastien unleashed his remaining strength. Kolb struggled under Bastien's fists, threatening and cursing, calling for the other boys, but he couldn't throw him off. Bastien was too strong, and Kolb too weak and heavy.

Rich off the struggles of those looking for help. Fat off the sweat of younger boys' brows. Powerful off the years of holding invisible shackles to their legs.

One last punch and Kolb fell unconscious. Bastien looked up, panting, hands aching. Shawn was gone. Olin, face blank, laid a hand on his shoulder.

Bastien wrapped his arms around the boy he considered a brother and wept for them all. Olin didn't hug back at first, but then wrapped weak arms around him.

"I'm sorry, Olin. I promised to protect you, and I failed."

Olin patted his back. "No. You saved me. I'm okay because of you."

Bastien released him and peeked at Kolb, wincing at the sight. Kolb was a bloody mess, the weak rise and fall of his chest the only indication he wasn't dead, though that didn't mean he'd stay that way.

The slam of a door and the pounding of boots on the floor above sent Bastien's heart racing. Very few people had boots in the House.

Bastien stood and pulled Olin to the hall that held the cells.

"No, Bastien. What are you doing?" Olin tugged, but was too weak to resist.

"Shh! You have to hide. Shawn got the guards." Bastien helped Olin into the first empty cell. "If this goes south, you know where I keep my stashes. Take them. Say you found a honey spot. Don't give it to Kolb all at once. You'll be free." Olin could never flee by himself without first paying his debt—they'd hunt him down.

Bastien ignored Olin's reaching hands and the fierce shake of his head. He gave him a reassuring smile and a nod, though it was entirely empty, and raced back into the dungeon.

The guards, Shawn in tow, arrived at almost the same time. When Shawn saw Kolb's prone and bloody form, he vomited all over two of the four guards' boots. Bastien ran over to them, waving his arms and looking wildly around the room.

"Guards! Thank Acantha. This man tried to kill me! With that knife, see?"

The strong hands of a guard gripped his shoulders and shook him still. "Just look at this." There was such recognition in the guard's voice that Bastien studied his face. He had a long scar on his cheek. "We let the vermin go, and he returns to the nest to eat his kin." The very guard who'd released him stared him down with eager eyes. "You best not hope to survive this misadventure, boy."

Someone yanked Bastien's arms behind him. He reacted instinctually, throwing his weight into the guard in front of him. The guard stumbled, snarling and pushing back. Cold shackles locked in place around his wrists.

"The stocks are too good for this one," the scarred guard spit, hate in his eyes. "Take him to Kingsguard."

Kingsguard Prison?

They hauled him backward. The days without food caught up to him, and the fight left him. Olin was safe, and with any luck, Kolb would die from his injuries. At the very least, he'd not be able to function as a tyrant anymore.

As they dragged him up the steps, Bastien prayed Olin would remain put.

"Acantha above, look at this mess." The guard's voice trailed up the stairs. "We're looking at murder if he doesn't survive."

"It was self-defense!" His pleas fell on deaf ears. It was worthless. They already knew him as a criminal, newly sprung from the stocks. Now they'd take him to Kingsguard.

The prison wasn't a place from which many returned, but those that did had stories to tell. Maybe they'd feed him.

The cold dark of night hit him as they hauled him from the House. A barred wagon was already waiting. They shoved him in alongside an unshaven man who reeked of booze. Better than what Bastien smelled like.

He gritted his teeth at his growing anger. Kolb deserved what he got, but Bastien should have been smarter. He'd been given a second chance to help Olin, and he'd failed again.

A guard slammed his hand against the bars where Bastien

leaned. Bastien jumped, narrowing his eyes, and the guard laughed as the wagon rolled away. Bastien stared up at the stars, barely visible between rooftops and torchlight, ignoring the older man and his stench.

The prison was located near the guard barracks to the west of the palace. Was Queen Faelyn still there? Did she sense him drawing nearer? Though, he couldn't sense her now. That pull had left with her. But, what had it meant?

Bastien let loose a long, slow breath of air. It turned to fog in the chilly air. When they reached the prison, their wagon passed through a guarded gate, then another. As each one closed behind him, his future became bleaker. Not that it was ever very bright. A thief whose only true friend had been used as a tool to control him, then set up to die when his usefulness had worn out. He'd never hoped to be someone worthy of a queen's hand, or even a fine lady's, but now all he hoped for was another chance at freedom and to know Olin was okay.

The bored guards didn't glance up as his wagon rolled by. They didn't care that Bastien was being locked away, that this was possibly the last time he'd breathe the free night air. He sat up, opening his lungs and filling them until he thought they might burst. The drunken man snored beside him. The flickering torches lit up the prison complex, and the wagon pulled up to a wooden door with a barred window.

All too soon, they stopped. A new guard opened the wagon, and Bastien climbed down before they hauled him out. Thank the Fates for his foresight, because his travel companion received a rude awakening when he was hauled sleeping to the hard ground.

"Welcome to Kingsguard Prison." The guard stood with feet apart and hands on his hips. His trimmed beard moved as he spoke, delivering a speech he probably said a dozen times a day. "You will await here until the judge decides your fate. Dinner has already been served, so it's off to your cozy quarters."

A different guard shoved Bastien forward, so he allowed himself to be led into the prison. The door shut behind him—one more door between him and all he'd ever known. The air smelled of rot and human stink. The stone floor seemed to squish beneath his bare feet. Cells, mostly empty, lined each corridor they took. Metal bars revealed threadbare cots and rotting chamberpots. The press of gazes from the few watching prisoners made him shiver. A bearded man flashed him a haunting grin as the guard stopped and opened a cell with a set of keys. The guard jerked his head, gesturing Bastien to get in.

With a gulp, Bastien stepped inside. His manacles were roughly removed, then the door closed with a reverberating bang behind him. One more door to add to the countless others. The guard didn't utter a word as he walked away, then Bastien was alone. He stood staring at the wall, lines cut into the stones by some poor soul who'd probably stayed in here until he died a sorrowful death.

Would that be his fate? Couldn't be. He hadn't done anything wrong.

His grumbling stomach, a steady drip nearby, and the cough of a nearby prisoner were the only sounds. Prisoners. Because that's what he was now. A prisoner. Not an orphan, not a street thief, not a brother or a friend or a man with a future. He was the fastest, the strongest, the smartest. How did things end up like this?

"Hey. Hey, kid," someone whispered.

Bastien turned to see the man in the cell diagonal from him, face pressed to the bars. He wore a grizzled beard that spoke of many months of being locked up. Like Bastien, he was barefoot with bedraggled clothing.

"Come here," he whispered.

Bastien raised an eyebrow. He was already as close to the bars as he could get.

The man laughed at his own joke. "It's okay. It's scary when you're new here and don't know what's what." He glanced both ways down the hall and lowered his voice. "We could be friends, help each other out."

The man was crazy. Bastien turned around, took two small steps to his ragged bed, and lay down. His weary body welcomed the relief, the feel of the pallet not much worse than the floor he slept on at the House.

The pallet's smell confirmed Bastien's theory about the previous tenant. It stunk of someone who'd slowly rotted away right on this very spot. He squeezed his eyes closed, ignoring the whispers of his new neighbor. Then he shut the last door, the one on his heart. There was no future for him anymore.

He was never leaving Kingsguard Prison.

CHAPTER

TEN

Bastien licked up the last smears of slop, barely resisting the temptation to gnaw on the bowl. It was the first meal he'd eaten in days, and as unidentifiable as the substance was, it eased the ache. He downed the cup of water in two gulps, then set it aside and rose to pace his cell. The guard had refused to answer any questions when he'd dropped off breakfast, so Bastien had no idea how long he'd be locked away.

The pacing did little to relieve his tension. Two and a half steps and he was already on the other side.

"You okay over there, kid?" The grizzled man sat on the floor, one leg outstretched, the other bent at the knee and resting against the bars.

Bastien stopped. "I'm fine."

"Ah, so you can talk. Are you ready to hear my proposal?"

"What proposal?"

"The one where we help each other out." He lowered his voice to almost barely audible. "I can get us out of here."

Bastien rolled his eyes. "Save your breath, stranger. There's no escaping this place. Besides, I may be judged innocent." He sat, leaning his back against the cell door.

The man let out a wheezy laugh. "They don't put innocent people here, kid. The best you can hope for is a fine." He shuffled in his cell. "But by the looks of you, you don't have the means to pay any fine. So if I were you, I'd get real comfortable in that cell, just like my buddy whose bed you now sleep in. He'd been there ten years before the Fates took pity on him."

The marks on the wall were lined up in neat rows and numbered too high for Bastien to bother counting. The stark white contrasted with the dreariness of the stone wall, threatening to blind him. What would become of Olin after ten years? Twenty?

"Or." The man let the word hang in the air, an offering Bastien had only to reach and pluck for the taking. He dropped his voice to a whisper. "We can escape."

Bastien shook his head.

"I know a way out of here. You help me, and me and my boys will help you on the outside. We'll get you out of the town, keep you from getting caught again."

"Why don't you get your boys to help you?" Bastien asked, without turning around.

"Simple. They—"

A door banged and footsteps sounded down the hall. Bastien backed away from his bars. The grizzled man resumed his casual pose, and soon a guard appeared. Featureless beneath his helmet, he paced down the hall and stopped in front of the grizzled man's cell.

The guard kicked the man's leg. "Away from the door."

He acted as if he had something to prove, the worst kind of guard to have around. Bastien stayed clear of them in the streets. He'd have to do the same here.

Jaw clenched tight, the man scooted back to the wall. Bastien arranged his face as the guard turned toward him. A flicker of recognition alighted in the guard's eyes. Bastien studied him closer.

Acantha above, of all the rotten luck. It was the guard with the scarred cheek from Robber' Round who'd arrested him.

Scarface's mouth formed a slow smile.

Bastien's fingers clenched into fists.

"Bastien, no last name. Awaiting judgment for attempted murder." He stated the charge as if intentionally trying to rile Bastien.

Bastien gave only a nod. With arrogance like this, ignoring him would ignite his rage.

"You attacked me," Scarface said with a sniff.

Bastien's palms grew slick beneath his clenched fingers, but he didn't respond.

"Well, so long as we are in agreement. And now I know which cell is yours." The guard turned on his heels and marched back down the hall.

Bastien remained frozen, trying to discern what he meant. Did he leave in a hurry so he could report the incident from earlier? The guard could say just about anything, and it'd be his word against a thief and attempted murderer.

"Did you attack a guard, kid?" Surprise colored the stranger's tone as he stood, peering at Bastien between the bars.

Bastien uncurled his fists, avoiding the question. He hadn't attacked him, but the guards wouldn't see it that way.

"Then you need out worse than I thought. How about our bargain? You help me escape; I'll help you on the outside. My boys are waiting, but they can't get in."

"No deal." Bastien remained on the hard ground against the back wall of his cell, the stranger hidden from view.

He had the best chance of returning to a normal life if he stayed put. If he tried to escape, they'd catch him and hang him for sure. Even this conversation could get him killed.

Not much later, the scarred guard came back. His footsteps preceded him, so Bastien didn't look up this time. He passed without pause or comment, then passed back again. There weren't many prisoners on this row that Bastien could tell. Maybe one or two at the very end. He crept to the bars and looked out, but the guard was gone. A little while later, the guard did it again. This was repeated off and on until a different guard replaced him, taking up the same schedule.

When a ladleful of slop landed in his neighbor's bowl, saliva filled Bastien's mouth. He hadn't expected a noon meal, and his stomach grumbled in anticipation. The slop hit his bowl, some splashing out, followed by a hunk of bread that bounced over the soiled floor. Bastien scooped up the bread, ripping it apart in his teeth. He worked over the tough bite until it was soft enough to swallow. He pulled off another hunk, then grabbed his slop and stuck it in, soaking up the juices.

He raised the piece to his mouth, and stopped. Memories swarmed him.

When Bastien was a boy of seven, excited by the prospect of joining such a powerful man who'd promised him riches in return, he'd left the orphanage. Young, impressionable, and oh, so trusting, Kolb used him for errands. There was a plant, he'd said, that grew especially well here in the north. If Bastien was a good boy and found this plant, Kolb promised a reward.

"Where can I find it?" he'd asked. "What does it look like?"

Kolb hadn't looked up from his desk, merely pointed. "In the woods east of the city, at the edge of the trees, there is a meadow. The plant grows low to the ground and sports delicate, dark purple flowers with five petals, even in the depths of winter. Dig it up, roots and all, but don't touch them."

Kolb had given him the first pair of gloves he'd ever owned. Following Kolb's careful instructions, it had taken him two days to travel to the woods and return with the flowers. His reward was admission into the gang, which he came to realize was the worst punishment a kid could hope for.

He'd never forget that pungent smell. The intensity of a startled skunk mixed with a sickly sweet rose.

He'd also never forget what happened to the leader of a rival gang Kolb fed the plant to.

Purple Borahella.

Though diluted, the scent clung to his slop. *Captain Cerick.* Bastien threw his bowl down. He stared at the thick slime, slowly chewing his bread. He raised his head.

"Hey, stranger. Don't eat the food. It's poisoned."

The sounds of chewing from across the hall stopped.

Bastien stepped to the bars to hear groaning.

"You're right, kid. Oh, my belly." The stranger had his back to the bars, and he rocked his body back and forth.

"How much did you eat?" Bastien's tone bordered on panic. Even if the stranger's plan was a complete lie, the hope of escape would die with him if he'd eaten too much Borahella.

"Couple bites," he groaned.

Bastien paced his cell, tension easing a bit. "I don't think it was enough to kill you."

A grunt and the splash of vomit hitting stone was the only reply. The stranger collapsed to his side, hurling his lunch, then hurling up nothing in dry heaves. Bastien hoped the stranger would survive. If the food was to be poisoned, Bastien would never make it to freedom. He'd die of starvation first. And if the vindictive captain was set so on killing him, his only chance may lay in whatever the stranger offered.

Sometime later, the whack of a stick banging on the bars sent Bastien skittering to his feet. His fuzzy head took a moment to clear itself. How long had he been asleep?

A new guard stood next to his cell.

"You have a visitor." The guard turned to someone Bastien couldn't see. "You have five minutes."

Bastien clutched the bars. Why would Olin risk coming to see him?

A woman stepped into view, her skirts outdated, but clean. Her graying hair pinned up and immaculate beneath a bland headscarf. Tears slipped down her face.

"I warned you not to join that gang, Bastien. I begged you." Miss Bannings, from the children's orphanage, dabbed at her eyes with a handkerchief. "I'm going to plead with the judge, try to get you released back to my care."

Bastien unhinged his jaw and pressed closer against the bars. It'd been eight years since he'd left her, and he never thought he'd see her again. Memories of the care and love she'd freely given threatened to overwhelm him. There were so many things he longed to tell her, but instead, he asked, "Is Kolb still alive?"

She dabbed at her eyes and nodded. "He's alive. Maybe they'll only make you pay a fine. We'll find a way to pay it, so you can come back to the orphanage where you'll be safe."

Warmth touched his heart, pushing aside some of the bleakness of his surroundings. Miss Bannings had always seen the bright side of things. She'd always told him he was special, and when the fire had burned down half the orphanage, and he'd survived unscathed, she never believed it was his fault. She was as wrong then as she was now. Even if he was released, he'd be no safer on the outside. The captain would never stop hunting him. She'd always be at risk.

He changed the subject, not wanting to give her false hope. "I never got a chance to thank you for all you've done for me. Take care of Olin, will ya? Watch out for him should he need a place to stay."

Miss Bannings lifted her hand, as she would to stroke his cheek or long hair, and instead put her palm against the bars. "You can find a way to help Olin once you're out and with me."

He gave what he hoped was a convincing nod. "Just in case. Protect him just in case."

"Bastien, my child." She swallowed, eyes shifting. As if steeling herself, she took a deep breath. "Protecting Olin won't change the past."

Bastien flinched. Pain lanced through his chest, bursting open packed-away memories and sending anger bubbling to the surface.

Something stirred within him, but he pushed it down, down, down. He would not unleash emotion on a woman who'd been so kind to him. "You need to go."

A sob escaped her, and she reached through the bars. He took her hand, savoring its familiar warmth. "I'm sorry, Basti. But it's true. Come back to the orphanage. I'll take care of you. This isn't you. You're better than all this."

He let go of her hand, eyes stinging, and smiled. There was nothing more to say.

The guard stepped out of the shadows where he'd been breathing loudly, waiting. "Time to leave, ma'am."

Miss Bannings covered her mouth, eyes creasing in a last look. "I'll do what I can, Basti. You do what you can, too. It's never too late to choose the right path."

The guard stepped forward. Miss Bannings flinched and walked away.

Bastien stared at the empty spot, absorbing the last of her love.

"So, you ready to hear the plan, kid?" The stranger's voice came out raspy.

"No." Bastien sighed. "So you're still alive, stranger?"

He coughed. "Heh, I think so. And the name's Tave."

Bastien stepped to the bars and peered down the hall both ways as far as he could. Miss Bannings was gone. He poked his ear through, listening for anyone nearby, but only the constant dripping and distant muffled voices accompanied his thoughts.

Bastien awoke, thrown from a restless sleep by a sharp sensation from inside his chest. It didn't hurt, but left him gasping for breath. He rolled to his side and clutched at his heart. Queen Faelyn. The tug to her, it hadn't been truly gone, but now it was ripped away.

She'd left the city. He didn't know how he knew this, but he did.

The absence stole away the last of his joy, joy he didn't even know he had. He sat up, panting in the dark.

He had to find her. He had to escape.

"Tave," he whispered, listening for guards. "I'm ready for your plan."

Tave stepped into view, looking pale behind his long beard, but otherwise all right. His mouth formed an anticipatory smirk. "You get me out, and I help you on the outside, right?"

Bastien narrowed his eyes. "Right." There was no other choice. He had to get out to find Faelyn and figure out this connection between them.

"My friend, the one who died in your cell, he'd been working on a plan for a long time. Got in good with a guard-in-training, who just so happened to graduate and hasn't been back. But this guard left him a parting gift, which I will bestow upon you. My friend died before we devised a plan to use it. I've spent the last year perfecting that plan, waiting for someone like you to come along."

Bastien leaned forward, intrigued. "What do you mean, like me?"

"You see, you possess something rare, something extraordinary, that I require to execute this plan. If it wasn't for you, it wouldn't be possible."

Bastien shuffled his feet. "What do I possess?" He held his breath.

"Two working legs and the fact that you've been placed in that cell, where my friend hid the key to unlock our doors." He smirked.

Bastien's shoulders drooped. "Really? That's the grand plan? You have a key in my cell, and you need me to get you out?" He scanned the small space with new eyes. No cracks or crevices, nor chips in the stone big enough to hide a key. A glance up revealed only dried moss-covered stone.

"Oh, kid. Did you hear nothing I told you? Without me, you don't know the guard rotations, the route to take out of here, what to do with the double gates, and you certainly won't get out of town before they catch you."

He was right, not without wasting more time to learn what Tave already knew. "I get you out of the cell, you get me out of the prison and out of town?"

"That's the deal."

"Why didn't your friend just give you the key before he died?" Something about Tave's plan didn't add up.

"He didn't trust me not to leave him. He was waiting to get better, only he never did." Tave shrugged. "He was right, of course. He was too weak to escape, and I would have left him."

The clank of the slop cart echoed down the hall. Bastien and Tave dropped back. He sat on his pallet, studying the cell. Somewhere in here was a key to freedom. As Tave's bowl was filled, Bastien patted on the nearby wall, jiggling the immovable stone and tapping to listen for hollow spots.

When his bowl was filled, he rushed to it, inhaling deeply. No trace of Purple Borahella, but any number of other poisons were odor and color-free, and Bastien had no way of identifying them. The food smelled as dead and disgusting as ever.

"Is it safe, Bastien?"

"It's free of Borahella. That's the only one I'm familiar with." Bastien chewed his bread, waiting for Tave to eat his slop first.

"Ugh," Tave said. "Tastes awful. Same as always."

A little while later, Tave was still alive. Bastien shrugged and gave in, hunger overriding logic.

A bit after that, Bastien felt fine. He fidgeted with impatience. "Where's the key, Tave?"

Tave looked up from where he lounged beside the cell bars. "Under your pallet, there's a stone that pries up. Might take some effort. That's good thinking, though. Best make sure it's still there and not found by a chambermaid or something." Tave chuckled to himself.

Bastien pulled his mat aside. It was stiff with countless years of grime and several layers of threadbare blankets stuck together. The stones beneath were less dusty, but none stood out immediately as being loose.

Keeping his ears open, Bastien knocked on the stones one at a time with the side of his fist, testing the feel and sound. Closer to the wall, a rectangular stone made a sound just slightly higher in pitch than the others. He noted it and continued. When he'd tapped every stone, none had moved, and only the one had made a sound different than the others. He stuck his fingers in the edges, pushing down into the seam. With a good enough grip, he pushed in deeper. The stone popped loose, clanging against its neighbors.

Tave cursed, and Bastien held his breath. No one came. He removed the stone, revealing an unimpressive iron key with a metal marble hanging from it by a thread. The key was cool in his palm when he lifted it, and the marble surprisingly heavy. He stepped to his door, comparing the key to the hole in the door across from him.

"Well, spit it out, kid. Did you find it?"

"I found it, and it looks like it will fit." He didn't dare try it in his own door. He placed it back in its hiding spot, covering it with his mat.

Fate, it seemed, was interfering on his behalf once again. He couldn't help but wonder who in Acantha was watching over him.

"Yeah!" Tave slapped the bars and pumped his fist. He stuck his hand through, pointing. "We leave tomorrow. After dinner."

CHAPTER
ELEVEN

Faelyn gazed out the carriage window, ignoring Amerae's frequent glances from atop the horse beside her. The city passed by in a blue blur of morning fog and sleepy residents. The path was clear this early, so their company made good time down the mountain.

But part of Faelyn wished they'd go slower.

A sad ache blossomed in her chest that threatened to part her lips and bring tears to her eyes, which was ridiculous. The prince was awful, and her people needed her to return. She'd done what she came to do. Her kingdom was allied, and in five years she'd be wed. The thought of home brought peace, but her eyes kept drifting back toward the heart of the city.

No one had questioned her when she'd chosen to ride in the carriage instead of horseback—the inexplicable sadness left her with no desire to force another smile—but it wasn't in character, and Amerae worried. Faelyn sensed it with every breath. She smiled up at her friend, catching her gaze once again. Amerae sent a small smile back, then scanned the city streets for potential danger.

The ache grew, much to Faelyn's irritation. For distraction, she opened her magic, pulling fog from the air and creating a small sphere of water. She shaped it into abstract forms, the tightness in her chest lessening. What was the matter with her? She certainly had no romantic feelings toward Prince Rory. If anything, she had to work hard on not resenting him and her future entrapment. But the ache felt familiar, much as it did the day Kian left Thomats School of Magic. She had told him who she really was and rejected his marriage proposal. Rejected him.

Faelyn poked her head out of the carriage and looked down the path, the sphere of water hovering above her hand. The city gate was near. She breathed a sigh of relief, forcing the air through the tightness of her chest.

The carriage passed beneath the gate. Faelyn cried out, bending over. The water lost form and splashed to the carriage floor, soaking the hem of her dress. Her hands gripped her knees as the painless ripping sensation eased.

The carriage came to an abrupt halt, and Amerae flung open the door.

"Faelyn! My queen, what's happening?" Amerae jumped inside and gripped her shoulders.

Outside, swords unsheathed, and her guards shouted as they surrounded the carriage.

Faelyn took a shaky breath. The feeling—like having a piece of her torn away—had passed, but left her empty. "I don't know what happened. What did you see?"

"You cried out as if someone had shot you with an arrow. You doubled over. Are you hurt?" Amerae's hands fluttered over her.

Faelyn looked up into her eyes. "You didn't see anyone nearby?" The sensation, however brief, had been magic of a new kind. An attack by an enemy mage? A quick scan with her magic revealed no nearby mage crystals.

Amerae looked back out the door, catching Nolan's glance from where he watched the scene unfold. He gripped his sword and barked commands to search the perimeter.

Amerae closed the door. "No one. What happened?"

"It could have been a mage. Or a magical trap." Faelyn shook her head and forced her back straight as a board. She struggled for words. "It felt like I lost something important, a pain that wasn't pain. More emotional than anything." Like, just for a moment, she'd never be happy again.

Amerae raised an eyebrow.

"Okay, I suppose that doesn't explain anything." In fact, it sounded crazy even to her ears. She had to maintain control. She adjusted her tone, disguising any hint of her distress. "Order the party to continue. You can remain in the carriage if you wish."

There was a fine balance between their friendship and their necessary roles as leaders, and Amerae juggled it well.

"Yes, my queen." She left Faelyn alone and relayed the commands.

The ache and tightness in her chest were gone. She'd passed through the gate, and after a moment of weakness, was back to normal. The water rose from the floor and her dress, following her command. She sent it out the opposite window in a blob as Amerae reentered the carriage.

Maybe the city had protective wards around it... but they'd been lowered upon her arrival? Maybe the others couldn't sense it because they couldn't access magic.

"When we return to Pavora, I want Kian to gather the mages and devise a set of wards around the city."

"Wards?" Amerae adjusted her sword as she settled against the soft, cushioned bench.

"Yes, like a shield around the city. An approaching enemy would trigger an alarm. If it's strong enough, maybe it could keep an enemy out."

"We have scouts and sentries to warn of enemies. Plus spies in every kingdom."

Faelyn frowned. "And now we'll have wards."

The entire party breathed a sigh of relief when they crossed the border back into Alysies. The pine trees on one side looked the same as the other, but home was home. Even the horses pranced easier. When they were a day's ride away from Pavora, Nolan sent a scout ahead to announce their arrival. They camped that night, though they could have continued on and reached the castle by nightfall. She'd learned it was better politically to make an entrance.

In the morning, Faelyn mounted her horse, and they departed, eager to be home. Majestic kept speeding up, and Faelyn reluctantly pulled her back, though she was just as anxious. Finally, they crossed out of the thick Pavora Woods and into the city.

The outskirts painted a different scene than the one Faelyn had returned to when she'd come to reclaim her throne over fifteen years ago. The paved streets were free of trash, and the homes and buildings were all in good repair. It would take many more years before the city and the wealth of the kingdom equaled that of Kestrea thanks to her inept father, followed by the rule of a kingdom of tyrants.

Thankfully Daltieri had suffered a blow with the complete cutoff of trade and the loss of precious funds and resources from Alysies. They were recouping too, and it bought Faelyn precious time to prepare.

The cheers of the townspeople reached her before she saw them. Faelyn had ordered the news to be heralded around town before their arrival. When they neared the closest market square, smiling faces lined the street. Women threw flowers, children jumped up and down, and the men clapped with enthusiasm as her company paraded down the road.

Faelyn didn't have to force this smile. These were her people, and she'd worked hard to earn their love, suffered much to have come this far. She opened her heart, soaking up every grin and peel of laughter, every pleased thought of joy and admiration, of loyalty and devotion.

Their queen had returned, securing their future, and they welcomed her home. Music burst alive at random from assembled revelers as they continued their march to the castle. Drinks and fresh bread traded hands in between spontaneous dancing. Young men and women linked arms and twirled in the alleyways. Faelyn longed to join in the celebration.

She laughed right along with them, accepting flowers from the children, and waving to the crowd. It was good to be home. Too soon, they reached the castle's outer wall and passed through the gate. The celebration continued on without her in the streets. Here, in her castle, was a new kind of celebration.

The castle turrets, though not as splendid as a towering mountain, cast long shadows over the white stone courtyard. Flowering vines and mature trees complimented the sweet scene that greeted her.

Servants and royal guards lined the courtyard from the outer gate to the rising driveway up to the castle steps. Faelyn dismounted, and her people bowed low in unison. The depth of the respect that laced the air was equal to the love and relief they radiated at her return. Since taking the throne, she'd never been away this long, never had a chance to experience what her people truly felt for her.

She didn't realize she was crying until the first tear slipped down her cheek.

"I've missed you all, too. Please, rise." She flicked the tear away, returning eager smiles as she ascended the stairs to the castle doors.

Two guards held the doors open, and she entered her home. Her eyes softened at the familiar tapestries and décor. Not a dead animal in sight.

"Lord Kian is waiting for you in the council room, Your Majesty." A servant, Marissa, curtsied, keeping her eyes down.

"Thank you, Marissa. I will see him now."

Amerae stepped beside her, two ladies-in-waiting in the background. "You don't want to freshen up first?"

"No, I've waited long enough." Holding her dress up, Faelyn hiked through many corridors and up two sets of stairs. She couldn't wipe the grin from her face.

Guards opened the doors of the council room, and her longtime friend stood from his charts and notes.

Kian Foster grinned behind his low bow. "Welcome home, Your Majesty."

Faelyn crossed the room filled with maps and scrolls, bookshelves and the general untidiness Kian preferred. She rounded the long table and wrapped Kian in a tight hug. His gray whiskers tickled the top of her head, but his hold around her waist was as tight as ever. Age may have been catching up with him, but his strong spirit remained.

Faelyn pulled away first. "What news, Kian? Did you solve the world's problems in my absence?"

Kian chuckled, grabbing his mage staff as they sat in the tall, straight-backed chairs. "Not hardly, my queen." He proceeded with the usual run-through. "The annual taxes came in, and it's more than what we expected. King Wesli wants to further trade routes and proposes we allow him to cut a wider path through the south border woods."

Faelyn frowned. King Wesli had inherited the throne of Creadel after his father, King Jeffe, passed away a few years ago. She hadn't returned to the kingdom—or the farm—that had once been her refuge. They'd been too busy rebuilding Alysies. Though she thought of Ellowen and the family who'd taken her in often.

"Ha, I knew you wouldn't like that idea. Still, the border woods stretch a good ways and really hampers trade."

Faelyn narrowed her eyes.

Kian smiled. "Okay, we'll put that one up for discussion amongst the reigning lords." He grabbed a piece of paper from in front of him. "Daltieri continues to ignore our peace emissary. In fact, Astin believes they may eject him from the kingdom soon. Our spies confirm their continued effort to recoup their economy, though no word on an invasion, either in Alysies or Kestrea. The hope, of course, is that your alliance with Prince Rory will curb their efforts."

He put his paper down and looked up. "There is one new development, though. They've begun a road. Through North Mountain. Our spies believe they are trying to regain the sea access we've denied them. They'll build a seaport, becoming more self-sufficient. While that poses no immediate threat, you may yet see something of it in your long life. I doubt it will happen in my lifetime."

Faelyn tsked to cover a wince, glancing at the deepening lines on his face. "Mages live forever." She sat straighter, smiling slyly. "So Prince Rory was charming."

"Infatuated already, Faelyn?" He placed a finger against his cheek and leaned forward in his chair, eyes alight with interest.

A slow smile spread on her face. "Why yes, Kian. How did you know?"

"I've never seen you so happy. All those years I tried to convince you to accept my hand, and the man who finally catches your eye is a fifteen-year-old." The smile stayed plastered on his face, but Faelyn felt his old pain.

For a moment, images flashed in her mind of a young Kian with his strong, youthful arms wrapped around her waist. A warm cape given to hold the cold at bay when she thought she'd never know love again. They'd known each other for over twenty years now, and would never be what they once might have been.

"When I accepted my place as queen, I gave up my right to choose, or at least to choose for selfish reasons. Now I must do what is best for my kingdom. Right now, that's Prince Rory." Her gaze drifted to the map on the table. "When he grows old and dies, and I'm still young and all my friends are gone, it will be a new prince." Her eyes flashed to his. "Whatever it takes. I won't be the ruler my father was, and I won't see Alysies fall to the hands of a foreign kingdom ever again." Her hard words covered her old wounds.

"I know, Faelyn. I know." He patted her hand, resting his fingertips longer than necessary. "It's my fault anyway."

"Oh, please don't, Kian." Faelyn pushed out of her chair. "Don't you know the guilt is already more than I can bear? You could still marry, you know. I wish you would."

"And miss the chance to simmer your guilt? Never." He gave a half-smile. "And you keep me way too busy for any wife to want me."

Faelyn groaned, covering her face with her hands. Kian spoke the truth. He was vital to the success of her kingdom. Without him, it wouldn't even be hers in the first place. As much as she tried to convince herself he wasn't still here because of his love for her, she knew it wasn't true. She'd have done him a favor if she'd forced him away, but Alysies needed him too greatly, as did she. He was a constant reminder of her selfishness, and when she thought of him that way, it only made her feel even more selfish.

He rolled his mage staff back and forth along the edge of the table. "I'm sorry to ruin your good mood, Faelyn. Where's the smile from a moment ago, and what's brought it about?"

She pursed her lips. "It doesn't seem right to say anymore, but I will. I was thinking, aside from your stubbornness, everything is right in the world. The kingdom is growing and prosperous, our enemies are at bay, and the people have finally accepted me, fae features and all. Plus, Niri says I'm close to completing my lessons to become a master mage." Niri, her long-time red-headed friend from Thomats, had come to Pavora to be Faelyn's head mage and assist with training.

"And you're engaged to be married, of course."

She looked at him down her nose. "Of course. That too." Never mind that she didn't love Prince Rory, not like the way her parents had loved each other. The love of her people would always outrank her own happiness.

She smiled. "Everything's perfect."

CHAPTER
TWELVE

Breakfast and lunch slop were poison-free. That is, Tave, Bastien's unofficial and unwitting poison checker, hadn't succumbed yet. Bastien tried to get details of the plan from Tave all day, but his pleas went ignored. The suddenly-mute stranger wouldn't say a word. Bastien hunched over his bowl, scraping the last of the slop up with his stale, crusty bread. Lunch slop was the only time they got bread, and he wouldn't waste a crumb.

"Hey, Tave. What'd you do to get in here?" Bastien bit the words out, not bothering to disguise his irritation. He knew nothing about the man who, in a few short hours, he'd be trusting with his life and future.

"You're with Kolb's gang, aren't you?" Tave's reply was the first all day.

Bastien started. "What of it?"

"I've heard of you. Made Kolb a lot of money." A hint of excitement colored Tave's tone.

Bastien stayed silent. Anyone who'd done business in the streets would know Kolb, so it wasn't strange he'd heard of Bastien. But he wasn't about to offer up his life story. Let Tave have to pry information from him for a change.

Tave grumbled. "I'm in here for stealing. Food. Couldn't pay the fine."

Bastien nudged his bowl with his toe. "What about your boys?"

"My boys? Yeah, they're my brothers, and they're as poor as me."

Bastien was certainly no stranger to stealing food to survive. "Why won't you tell me the plan?"

"Just be patient, kid. We'll get out when I say, but first—"

"Quiet," Bastien hissed.

Tave stopped talking, and footsteps sounded down the hall in an arrogant stride Bastien already recognized. Scarface was back. Bastien was fairly certain Kolb had coerced him to finish the job he'd started.

Bastien backed to his mat, lay down, and closed his eyes. He hadn't spent his life on the streets studying guards and people to learn nothing. Some guards you were to stay away from, and some people had a darkness in them that, unless you were in a position to fight it, was better left alone. Darkness cannot be fought by darkness.

The footsteps reached his cell. "Still here?" A shuffle. "And by the whisperings, it sounds like you've made a friend."

Was that why Tave had been poisoned too? There was maybe one other prisoner on their row, too far down to see, and Bastien hadn't heard him retch. Bastien opened his eyes to stare at the wall. The hidden key throbbed beneath him, threatening to scream its location.

"I know what you're thinking. Powerful guard thinks he can do anything he wants." His voice rose. "But I worked hard to get here, and someday I'll be captain. Maybe even someday soon if certain people make good on their promises." He clicked his tongue. "Now, you best eat up, or you won't make it to your trial."

Bastien kept his mouth shut. The guard seemed awfully interested in Bastien's eating habits.

Scarface slammed something against the bars, sending echoes crashing. "Look at me when I'm speaking to you, or I'll haul you from that cell and introduce you to the hole."

Bastien tensed and opened his eyes. Even without knowing Tave's plan, he was fairly certain that spending time in whatever 'the hole' was would ruin it.

Scarface snatched a ring of keys from his belt. "Know what? I never thanked you for attacking me. Think it's time we remedy that."

Bastien shot to his feet, directly above the key. Scarface had the door unlocked in a matter of moments. Tave cursed from his cell.

Scarface grabbed him by his filthy tunic and yanked, slamming him against the stone wall. Bastien's teeth bashed together, and his gaze involuntarily trailed to where the key pulsated in rapid-fire beneath him. Had he secured the pallet well enough?

Scarface's hot breath rolled over him, eyes ready for a fight. No matter. Bastien could take a hit, so long as he didn't search the cell.

"Everything all right, Dain?" A new voice cut through the tension, steps coming closer.

Scarface Dain's grip slackened, but he didn't break eye contact. "Captain Brunber. This prisoner mouthed off to me." His hard voice held a flinty edge.

"Typical." Captain Brunber stopped outside the cell, older, with a broader chest and shoulders. "Well, they did say he was a troublesome one. Give him the standard treatment." His tone was casual, like beating up prisoners was a regular thing. "You're in eastern block when you're done here."

"Yes, Captain." The smile in Dain's voice was unmistakable.

The captain walked away. Bastien flexed his abs as Dain reared back and punched. The blow hit Bastien's stomach, sending him to his knees. He sucked in a breath, positioning himself over the key.

"Ah, no," Dain said. "You don't get to keep your precious blanket." He kicked Bastien in the side, knocking him off the pallet.

Pain blossomed in his ribs. His eyes went wide as Dain ripped the stiff blankets off the floor and tossed them out the cell door. The stone above the key sat in place, but dirt had been visibly rubbed off where he'd pried it up. His heart pounded in his ears.

Dain's gaze trailed over the small space. He seemed to stare right where the key pulsed from the ground. "What's this? You think you're too good for this place?" He lunged and kicked Bastien in the side again. "Enjoy the rest of your pitiful life."

Bastien coughed, eyes burning with unbidden tears.

"Be thankful Captain didn't order me to withhold your meals." He grunted and stepped out of the cell, slamming the door and locking it.

The guard left, and Bastien caught his breath, smiling as the pain slowly ebbed away along with his racing heart. He crawled to the door and met Tave's wide eyes. "I hope you ate enough lunch because dinner is not an option."

Tave hesitated as if he wanted to say something else. Instead, he said, "That's what I was thinking, kid."

Hours after dinner arrived, Bastien sat staring at it, waiting for Tave to say something. Anything. The foul smell of the Borahella wafted over him every so often. For as ruthless as the scarred guard Dain was, he wasn't very smart. The pain in Bastien's ribs had blessedly abated.

Time ticked by, marked only by the walkthrough of random guards, and the dripping that had increased to a stream, hopefully meaning rain. While it would prove for a miserable night if they were soaked, the cover would help them escape.

He shot glances at Tave, who lay stretched out along the bars, back against the wall with his eyes closed, perfectly at ease. More than once Bastien thought about throwing something—poisoned slop—to scare Tave and break the unrelenting tension.

He'd been given absolutely no instruction, but the key and the attached marble rested beneath the stone, digging deeper into his thigh with each passing moment. Warmth stirred within him as he focused on the marble, but he dare not examine it. Too risky. His mind drifted to Queen Faelyn and her long golden hair. That irresistible pull toward her. The way it felt like he'd never taken air before that moment, and now his body was left lacking.

A faceless guard walked past, then turned the corner out of sight. Tave raised his head, and Bastien pried up the stone, snatching up the key. Then Tave closed his eyes again, leaning back.

Bastien groaned in exasperation.

"Jesting." Tave grinned. "Let's go."

Bastien hopped up and reached through the bars around to the lock on the door. The key fit perfectly. With a slow turn, the lock clicked. Bastien's heart leaped. Withdrawing the key, he pushed the door, and it opened on silent hinges. He stared with wide eyes. *It really worked!*

"All right, now do mine." Tave glanced down the hall.

Bastien stepped out of his cell, reveling in the freedom of movement in that simple action.

"Come on, hurry."

Bastien frowned and unlocked Tave's cell. Tave pushed on the door. The grating screech of the hinges stumbled them both to a gasping halt. They locked eyes.

"Nothing to be done for it." Tave pushed another half-inch. The screeching echoed down the hall.

"Wait. Use this." Bastien darted to his cell and grabbed his bowl. He dipped two fingers into his moldering slop and then coated the hinges in a thick layer.

Tave raised an eyebrow. When Bastien finished, Tave gave an experimental push. The hinges didn't squeak. "Good job, kid. You're handy to have around."

Bastien grinned. Compliments were a rare thing in his life.

"Let me have the key." Bastien held it up, and Tave snatched it. "We'll need this again."

Bastien ignored the warning in his gut as the metal marble dangled from Tave's hand. "What's that thing hanging from it?" Again, a sense of warmth stirred within, and—white light flashed within the marble. Bastien gasped.

Tave pocketed it. "None of your concern, kid."

Bastien closed his open mouth and shook his head clear. The torchlight had reflected on the marble, that was all.

"Follow me and keep your mouth shut if you want to keep your head." Tave stalked down the hall, the opposite direction of the only way Bastien knew out of there.

He hurried to catch up to him. *When you have nothing, you have nothing to lose.*

Their footsteps shuffled quietly over the slick stone as they passed snoozing prisoners and empty cells. After several more turns, Tave unlocked an unoccupied cell and shoved Bastien in.

Bastien's heart leaped. He threw up his hands in an effort to grab the door and keep it from closing.

"Move, kid. Hurry." Tave stepped into the cell and shut the door. He pulled Bastien against the wall.

Bastien stared at Tave, breathing heavily, dumbfounded. After countless minutes, his heart still raced. Any moment their cells would be discovered empty and they'd be caught.

Through no signal Bastien heard, Tave said, "All right, go."

And they were off again. They saw no guards along the way, but moved faster and faster, at the risk of drawing more attention. They passed a cell, and on instinct, Bastien glanced in and jerked to stop. A bony man sat cross-legged on the floor staring right at him. Drowning in his clothes, the man didn't react other than to blink a slow blink.

Tave doubled back. "Keep moving. We're on a schedule." He grabbed Bastien's arm, then stopped.

Bastien's heart beat in his ears. The bony man cocked his head and raised his hand. He held a finger to his lips, then his mouth split into a decaying smile. "You won't make it." His eyes rolled around in his skull. "They'll catch you."

Bastien looked down the hall. A guard would appear any moment.

"Come on." Tave tugged on his arm, and they surged ahead.

Unease nearly gave way to panic, and he stepped more cautiously until at last, they came to a door that wasn't a cell. Tave stuck the key into the lock, waited what felt like an eternity, then turned it. He waited another eternity, then finally cracked open the door. The pounding of heavy rain in the dark of night was the most beautiful sight Bastien had ever seen. The smell, so crisp and full of promise, chased away the reek of the prison as quickly as the chill in the air chased the heat.

Tave leaned his head into the rain, looking left and right, then pulled Bastien after him and against the wall. He shut the door and locked it from the outside.

They'd made it to the back of the prison. Torch-lined walls loomed past the yard thick with pouring rain. Bastien was already soaked through, and it was the best feeling in the world.

"Don't smile yet, kid. That was the easy part."

The smile fell from his lips. The rain was too thick to see the guard towers along the walls, but they were there. And many more guards would be on the prison roof, trained and ready to shoot them full of arrows if they revealed themselves. How were they going to get past the wall? Or the wall after that.

Tave looked left and right again, then to Bastien's jaw-dropping disbelief, stepped away from the wall, right into the open courtyard. And kept going.

"Tave, you'll be shot!" Bastien kept one hand on the prison wall, as if that sparse contact kept him shielded from the danger ahead.

Tave didn't stop or turn around. "Come on, kid. Almost there." His voice was faint from the blanket of rain.

Bastien groaned. Tave was going to get them killed. His fingertips broke contact with the wall as he darted forward, quickly reaching Tave's side.

"No sudden movements, Bastien. Don't do that again." Tave looked ahead and all around, eyes intense.

Bastien nodded and followed Tave's example of keeping a lookout. He'd always had a keen eye, but he didn't see any movement from the guards. Was the prison not guarded as well at night?

When they'd made it halfway across the clearing, a bell tolled. The frantic clanging shot straight to his limbs, turning them into pudding.

"Run." Tave smacked Bastien's arm, urging him forward.

Bastien ran with all his might, quickly leaving Tave behind. He reached the wall unharmed, but there was nowhere to go. There was no gate on this side of the prison, no door or ladder, just a towering, never-ending barrier between him and freedom.

Tave slammed into the wall beside him. "Damn it. Come on."

Tave ran ten yards down the wall and stopped. He jumped up, grabbing at something.

A rope! He caught it and climbed. Bastien ran and jumped, catching it on the first try, and climbed close on Tave's heels.

Shouting sounded behind him. Bastien climbed faster, hand over hand on the rough rope—easy, like scaling a building. Tave made it to the top of the wall and disappeared. Rain pelted Bastien's face. A twang, then something bounced off the wall near Bastien's head. He let go of the rope with his legs, using only his arms to carry him as fast as he could the last few feet up the rope.

He hoisted himself over the lip of the wall and threw himself behind a battlement. Three guards, dead and bleeding, lay around him. Tave crouched with a bloody sword, peering over the other side of the wall.

Horror pooled into Bastien's stomach. "You killed these guards, Tave. You killed them." He hunched over and grabbed his knees. So much blood. He'd seen kids hurt before. It was part of life on the streets. He'd even come across a couple dead people before, frozen during the cold Kestrea winters. But this was different. He flinched as arrows pinged off the wall and ground around him. "And I'm with you. They'll think I did it."

Tave looked over, a new rope in his hand. "Kill or be killed, kid. Keep going, or stay here and die." He shrugged and disappeared over the side of the wall.

Survive another day. That was his and Olin's daily motto. He forced his gaze away from the bodies and pushed up to a crouch.

Staying low, he reached the other side of the wall. He grabbed the rope and flung himself down, using his feet to slow his momentum. His hands burned against the coarseness. When he landed, feet splashing, he turned to the sound of swords clanging.

Scarface Dain and none other than Captain Cerick had engaged Tave in a fight to the death. Beyond them, another rope hung from the second wall, swaying in the wind and rain like a call to freedom.

Tave moved like the wind, dodging and weaving around the two guards. Captain Cerick swung, but Tave blocked and thrust toward Dain. The blow glanced off his thick armor. Tave spun and slashed, blocked and hit. It was a mesmerizing dance, but his hits slowed the longer Bastien stood there. Slop wouldn't sustain anyone for long.

Bastien scanned the outer wall for guards. Seeing no one, he bolted around the melee for the rope. He almost reached it, then the whoosh of sound made him jump sideways. Captain Cerick's sword clanged against the wall beside the rope.

Cerick's crazed eyes locked on Bastien's for a heartbeat before he charged. Bastien braced, calling up every bit of street fighting skills that had been beaten into him. Cerick held his sword like a battering ram and charged. At the last moment, Bastien twisted out of the way. Captain Cerick's momentum carried him past. Bastien raised his foot, planting it on his back and shoved. The captain stumbled forward, but caught his balance, keeping firm hold of his sword.

Bastien tensed, then a gurgling cry sounded behind him. He spun. Tave, breathing heavily, stood over Dain, who lay face down on the watery ground, blood running from his neck.

"No!" Cerick's wide eyes narrowed in a look of murderous fury. He raised his sword and sprinted toward Tave.

Tave held his sword ready in both hands. Cerick swung, but Tave batted his sword out of the way. Off-balance, Cerick slipped in the mud and went sprawling. Tave readied what surely would be a killing blow. Bastien couldn't look away.

Shouts rang out from the wall, halting Tave mid-swing. He looked up, then ran to the rope without acknowledging Bastien. He threw his sword to the ground and climbed faster than someone should be able to after starving for so long and enduring so much.

Bastien gulped, backing up to the rope. Captain Cerick fumbled through the mud. He'd lost his sword, but Bastien only saw Dain's lifeless body. The blood that flowed from him formed a river of red, intent on staining everything in its path.

Captain Cerick found his sword just as the rope smacked Bastien in the back of the head.

Bastien jumped, grabbing the rope as high up as he could, and climbed. His arms burned with effort as Cerick's footsteps sloshed quickly through the mud. *Almost there.*

Screams sounded from above. The rope jerked as Cerick climbed up behind Bastien. Adrenalin shot through him, and Bastien pushed himself faster. He was almost to the lip of the wall when Cerick's hot hand wrapped around his ankle and yanked.

CHAPTER

THIRTEEN

Holding tight to the rope dangling from the prison wall, Bastien kicked against Captain Cerick's iron grip. Panic seized his lungs.

"You harmed my nephew and you killed my guards. You're not getting out of here alive." Cerick tugged harder.

Bastien's grip slid on the rope. He kicked again, trying to dislodge the captain's firm hold.

Cerick grunted with effort under the weight of his heavy armor and yanked again. "Shoot him!"

Arrows pinged off the wall around him, not getting too close to the captain. Bastien tightened the grip with his hands and released his leg from the rope. He looked down, caught a dark glimpse of twisted hate in Cerick's eyes, then kicked with all he had. Heel met forehead again and again until his ankle pulled from Cerick's grasp. The captain slipped backward off the rope, landing with a crash at the bottom.

Bastien hauled himself the rest of the way. At the top, more dead guards littered the path. Tave finished off one, shoving him over the edge, just as two more guards approached at a run. Arrows from

89

outside the wall took them both. Another rope led down to freedom. Tave hurtled himself over the side without a backward glance.

The bell still clanged, accompanied by the sound of guards shouting and running. Cerick had righted himself below. His lips pulled back in a snarl. He raised his sword, pointing it at Bastien like a promise to hunt him to the ends of Thera.

Bastien skidded across the slippery stone, grabbed the rope, and scaled down. They had to stay ahead of the soldiers. Tave had surprisingly waited for him at the bottom.

"Thought you lost your courage." He clapped Bastien on the back. "We have to get over the ridge." He pointed and then ran.

Bastien chased after him, following where he stepped. Now that they'd made it out of the glow of the prison torchlight, the rainy night made the world dark as pitch. His body felt weaker than it ever had. The adrenalin that had fueled his flight was wearing off, and intermittent slop preceded by days of starvation wouldn't keep him going much longer.

They both stumbled up the hill. Even through the rain, the pounding of hoofbeats and the howl of dogs sounded behind them.

Bastien nearly cried out in relief when they crested the ridge and saw light. Two men stood with four horses. Their forms were dark outlines behind a white glow emitted from some kind of staff. They had swords at their sides, and one held a bow upraised. Tave reached them first, and the two stared hard at Bastien.

"He's with us." Tave threw the reigns of the fourth horse at Bastien.

"Where's Buno?" the bigger man of the two asked.

"Buno's dead. The entire guard is on our heels." Tave mounted. "Let's ride."

Bastien had never ridden a horse before, though he'd seen them plenty. He climbed on the saddle and gripped the reins hard in his hands.

"Yah!" Tave and his friends spurred ahead, flicking their reins and digging their heels in their horses.

Bastien kicked his horse's sides, and it shot forward. The world became a bouncing blur of night and rain. The only thing keeping him from falling to his certain death was his iron grip on the reins. But, he was free.

At the back of the pack, he shouted to the horse. "Turn! We have to find Olin!" He jiggled the reins, but the horse only barreled ahead, following Tave's lead. Soon they'd pass the outskirts of town.

Bastien looked left, to the trees and rocks whipping by. He couldn't jump. He'd be killed. The guards shouted behind him, ready to recover his mangled corpse should he try to leave Tave.

Redoubling his grip, he murmured an apology to Olin on the wind, and a prayer for his safety, then held on for his life as the group rode on. He'd find a way to come back. When it was safe.

The wind and rain whipped his face and long hair as they descended the mountain, eventually passing through the grassy plains and into the safety of the trees. Bastien filled his lungs with cold, free night air.

The guards did not catch up to them. Bastien lost track of how much time and how far they'd come. His butt was numb and sore. Every muscle was clenched tight in an effort not to fall. He'd already decided just how he'd tuck his body to avoid a tumbling death should he go over.

The view didn't offer much. Aside from the wet trees, he had only the three men in front of him to study. Tave rode in front, in his threadbare tunic and torn trousers, followed by a bigger man in a leather vest. His quiver hung on his back beneath dark hair and a bald spot. The shortest of the three rode directly in front of Bastien, a man in dark robes with a curious wooden staff always in his hand.

The rain finally stopped, and the sky lightened, but still, they continued on, though not so fast as before. Bastien had never been away from the city before. He and Olin had talked about all the places they'd see one day. They wanted to take a boat to Gull Island and eat lobster. They wanted to go to Alysies and see the famous mages of Thomats. Maybe even travel south to the Sengi Desert where it was said it never snowed. Maybe none of those things would ever happen, but they'd dreamed. Now, who knew?

He'd explain it to Tave when they stopped. If they ever stopped. He had to go back for Olin.

Following single-file down a narrow trail, they made it into a thicker part of the woods far south of the city. Bastien's horse slowed along with the other horses. Drips of water from the trees rained as they passed, ensuring Bastien remained wet and cold. Just when Bastien could go no further, Tave called a halt.

The three men got down from their horses. Bastien peeled his hands off the reins. Angry blisters tore his skin, sending sharp pain over his palms. He held his shaking hands in from of him, examining his wounds. The other riders moved around their horses, readjusting reins and saddles with no apparent injuries.

Tave approached. "Time for a rest, kid. Dismount and follow us. There's a clearing here." He noticed Bastien's upraised hands. "Not a rider, eh? We'll patch those up in a bit. Next time, hold the reins loose in your hands."

"But I'll fall off the horse."

"Nah, you won't. I'll show you what to do. Now, come on." Tave stepped back and stroked his beard.

Bastien swore Tave was covering a smile. He threw his leg over the horse. His aching joints protested, seemingly stuck. He slid down the saddle and kept going, landing hard on his butt. Acantha above, it hurt. And he hadn't the strength to care.

Tave's laughter broke through his hand. His brothers, as Tave referred to them, chortled from beside their mounts.

"What's wrong with my legs?" Bastien pointed his bare toes, stretching out his locked limbs.

"You'll get used to that, too." Tave pulled him up.

Bastien held in a cry of pain. They each walked their horses down a narrower trail that wound downhill over roots and leaves. The others had no problem, but Bastien couldn't seem to get his knees to go together. He was sure they'd touched when he walked before. The three brothers laughed at his expense the whole way to the clearing.

By the trampled grass and underbrush, it was obvious even in the scant light that the small clearing was used often. The trees pressed in on them from all sides providing a sense of protection and safety. Surely the guard couldn't track them here. How far would they pursue them? Probably not this far, except that Tave had killed some of them.

The brothers took unsaddled their horses and rubbed them down. They unpacked supplies, then the bigger man lit a small fire while the robed man laid out pallets. Bastien held his reins, watching them while the horses huffed and shifted behind him. He debated taking a nap where he stood. But Olin waited.

Tave looked up from where he was speaking to the bigger man. He gave a small smile, patted his brother on the back, and walked over to Bastien. "The most important rule is to take care of your horse."

"I can't stay here," Bastien said. "There's someone waiting for me. He's in trouble."

Tave exchanged glances with his brothers. "You can't go back."

"Watch me." Bastien readied to jump in the saddle.

"You're a criminal. You go back, and they'll hang you. They know where you live. They know who you love."

The breath knocked out of him. He froze where he stood. It was true. Tave murdered guards to help them escape. Bastien was a criminal without ever having done anything wrong. But he knew how to go unseen. He'd moved around Docimer like a ghost many times.

Tave went on. "If you don't think your existence puts him in danger, you're a bigger fool than I thought." There was more pity and understanding in Tave's voice than anything, and that only made his words all the more convincing. He knew what Bastien was being asked to give up. Forced to give up.

"It'll die down," Bastien said. "They're after us now, but that won't last forever." Would it? Would Olin really be better off without the kind of trouble Bastien could bring upon him? The clear answer made his stomach churn. Without Bastien, Olin was just another street urchin who had access to all the hidden gold he'd need to slowly buy his way out of captivity. With Bastien, he would be a wanted criminal, always on the run, and always in danger.

"Let's take care of your horse." Tave didn't speak on it further as he showed Bastien how to unsaddle his horse and brush the sweat off. "Since you're one of us now, you have to learn our ways if you want to survive."

"Who says he's one of us?" the bigger brother asked from beside the fire. His irritated tone contrasted with his jolly nature up to now.

The pan he held wafted the most delicious scent Bastien had ever smelled. Meat sizzling in its own juices and dried herbs. Bastien's mouth watered.

Tave narrowed his eyes. "Sit down, all of you."

The brothers listened, taking a spot around the fire—even the quiet one in black. Bastien sat beside Tave, while his eyes stayed locked onto the pan of food.

"Bastien, this is my older brother Brock." The bigger man with plump cheeks, wearing a thick leather vest over a tunic and trousers, nodded. "And this is my younger brother, Micah."

Micah didn't nod, but pulled his staff closer. The wood bulged out at the top with four holes too dark to see into. Bastien stared hard at it, feeling the same warmth in the pit of his stomach as the marble he'd found with the key. It was like a savory stew just after taking a big bite when his body was at its peak need. He wanted more, even as his mind sought to run far away from it.

Micah leaned forward, blocking Bastien's view.

Bastien blinked. "You all don't look alike."

"We're brothers in arms, as you can one day hope to be. And you're well on your way, with what you did back in the prison." Tave took out the key with the silver marble from his pocket, rolling it between his fingers.

Micah's gaze went straight to it.

So did Bastien's. "What is that?" Similar to Micah's staff, the ball emitted the same warmth into Bastien's gut.

"Who are your parents?" Micah's deep voice cut through Bastien's focus.

He looked at Tave, whose eyes turned intense, watching him closely. Brock moved meat onto four small tin plates.

"I never met my parents. I was left at an orphanage as a baby." He brushed his hands against his filthy trousers. "What does it matter?"

Micah stared at him hard, silently taking a plate from Brock.

Tave answered for him. "Hey, we all have sob stories." He tossed the marble to his other hand. "And we all have hidden talents." Tave took a plate. "My new friend Bastien was the best thief in the best gang in the city, if by best you mean the most profitable. So, one could say Bastien was the best thief in Docimer. We could use a guy like you, if you want to continue on with us." Tave held out the fourth plate toward Bastien.

Bastien's mouth watered anew, and he reached for the plate. A warning buzzed in his head, and he hesitated fingertips away from the best meal he'd eaten in weeks. Tave said he'd been locked up for stealing food for his family. Bastien had sensed the lie, but now it was clear. This was a band of thieves, not a family, and they didn't steal only food. Taking the plate from Tave meant signing himself over to another gang when he'd just escaped the last one with his life. *Survive another day.*

Bastien withdrew his hand. He'd find some other way to survive. Maybe he could find honest work in the next town. Or the next kingdom. He'd come back for Olin when it was safe.

An appreciative gleam entered Tave's brown eyes, and the pride it gave Bastien almost broke his stern composure.

Tave set the plate on the ground. "You're no fool, kid. But neither am I. You wouldn't be here if it wasn't for me, so you owe me, whether you realize it or not."

Bastien resisted the urge to cross his arms. "I got you out. We're even."

Tave raised an eyebrow. "How about a deal? You come with us, take Buno's place, help us with a few jobs, and if you don't like it, you'll be free to go with your share of the money. We split everything equal. I won't force you to stay." Tave picked up the intoxicating plate off the ground.

Bastien leaned forward. "And what about these two? Will they force me? Why is he dressed so different?"

Micah huffed into his plate.

Tave smiled. "Micah is a mage."

Bastien's eyes opened wide. "Like a real mage, from Thomats?" He'd encountered very few who could do magic, and it only led to tragedy.

"There are many schools better than that decrepit place," Micah said.

Bastien had always heard Thomats was the best on Thera.

Tave held the plate out. "Yes, like a real mage. Now, come on, eat. I won't take your soul to pay for supper."

Bastien snatched it from his hand. He shoveled in bite after bite of thick, juicy sausages and fried potatoes. He couldn't chew fast enough. The flavors burst over his tongue, demanding more. When his plate was empty, he licked the last of the juicy potato crumbs, then drank down the water Tave passed to him.

His body demanded more, but Bastien was no stranger to hunger. If he ate anymore, he wouldn't keep it down. In a moment he'd feel full enough, and Tave knew it too. No more food or drink was offered to him.

"So, what's your last name, Bastien?" Tave asked, setting his plate aside.

The familiar sting of having nowhere and no one to belong flared along his insides, but he didn't let it show. "Don't have one."

Tave smiled. "Good, none of us do either. Safer that way. In fact, Tave's just a nickname." He pointed in mock warning. "And don't even think of asking my real name." He winked. "Now get some sleep."

They stayed in the clearing that night. Neither Brock nor Micah would talk to him, but he suspected why. Lying down on his pallet, he knew all these things—the horse, the plate, the pallet—belonged to their friend. The man who'd died in the cell before Bastien came along. Micah and Brock had been expecting to be reunited with their brother in arms, and instead found Bastien, a kid. A common street thief was all they saw, and he didn't even care. He had nothing to prove.

I survived another day, Olin. You will, too.

The stars had never looked so clear, away from the burning lights of Docimer. When he focused, it almost felt as if someone was looking back at him.

He closed his eyes and dreamed of golden hair and warm stew.

CHAPTER

FOURTEEN

Bastien's eyes snapped open, and he sat up. Dread wafted on the cool breeze. His new companions lay on their pallets around the smoking remains of their fire, sound asleep. The ground was thick of blue, predawn mist. Morning birds chirped a slow, sleepy song.

He pushed his thin blanket aside and stood. His breath fogged the air as he stared at the dark trees. His heart raced. Warning bells went off in his head, like the time just before he'd almost pickpocketed an undercover city guard.

Then he heard it. The sound of distant hoofbeats.

"Tave, wake up! They're coming!" It wasn't a simple passerby, this was several riders. It had to be the guard, here to avenge their fallen comrades.

Tave and his gang blew out of their beds. They snatched the blankets as they ran to the horses.

"Move, kid!" Tave yelled.

Bastien grabbed up his pallet, hauling his gear toward the horses. Tave, Micah, and Brock already had their horses saddled and were cinching the straps.

The pounding hoofbeats drew nearer.

Bastien snatched his saddle off a fallen log and threw it on the horse. One stirrup and strap caught underneath. He tugged until they popped loose. Heart pounding, he fed the straps through the holes, tightening them as best he could.

"Shit." Tave strode over in a panic and shoved Bastien back, unfastening the straps as fast as he could.

Cheeks burning, Bastien pounded his blanket into a ball and shoved it into a saddlebag.

Tave untwisted a few places and refastened. "The horse holds air to keep the strap loose. The saddle would slip right off." He put his back into tightening until the horse let go of its held breath.

Smart creature.

Horses crashed into their clearing. They blocked the path. Bastien grabbed his reins as Tave rushed to his own horse, drawing his sword. The surrounding trees and shrubs were too thick to escape with the horses, and they wouldn't make it far on foot.

Bastien's hands shook as he threw his leg over the saddle and prepared to run. Brock nocked an arrow and fired again and again as the guards swarmed—around ten of them.

Men screamed, and blood spurted into the morning sky. The guards fired crossbows back, forcing Tave's gang into the brush for cover. The horses reared and fought against the stabbing limbs and thick briars.

Micah pulled ahead and raised his staff.

"They've got a mage," a guard shouted. His cry cut off with a gurgling sound from his throat before he fell from seemingly no cause.

Micah's staff glowed like a white lantern spotlighting the enemy. The guards hesitated, shielding their eyes.

Brock's arrows kept the guards back, but it was only a matter of time. Bastien scanned their ranks. One of the guards was more decorated than the others, and he stared right at Bastien.

Captain Cerick. He raised his sword and pointed in the same

accusatory way he had at the prison. Like a promise. With a yell, he charged forward.

Bastien reached for his knife and gasped with remembrance. It was gone. Confiscated by the guards. Sweat broke out along his forehead. Weaponless and with no idea how to control his horse, his muscles bunched against the attack.

Tave bolted in between them, meeting Cerick blade to blade. They traded blows, circling each other on their horses. The other guards rushed to attack, but Brock and Micah held them at a distance. Cerick's training couldn't match Tave's skill. With the sharp screech of grinding metal, Tave swirled his sword around the captain's until it dropped out of his hands.

Tave smirked, but another guard swung at him from behind.

"Watch out," Bastien yelled.

The blow glanced off Tave's saddle, smacking the horse's rump. It shied, then reared, throwing Tave to the ground. His horse bolted.

Bastien jumped down and ran to defend Tave. He grabbed Cerick's sword from amongst the leaves and held it up like he knew what he was doing.

The guards still outnumbered them, fighting their way toward the three brothers, and Bastien had thrown himself in the thick of it. Tave groaned on the ground. A short distance away, Cerick drew a dagger.

"Get up, Tave." Bastien stood over him, sword raised and ready for an attack. The twang of bows and screams of fallen guards surrounded them.

"Thanks for the heroics, kid." Tave pushed to his hands and knees.

A little silver ball rolled out of his pocket, right to Bastien's feet.

"Your marble." Bastien grabbed it. Warmth and dread spread through his body. His mouth dropped open, and his thoughts went to Micah.

Pain exploded in his back. Bastien cried out, turning as the sword withdrew from his flesh. Blood coated inches of the tip. The guard reared back to strike again. Fear from his heart and pain from his back struck him like a second blow. The combination dropped into his stomach. Joined with the alarming warmth, it drew strength without his consent. Magic bubbled to the surface.

How was this possible?

The marble in his hand lit up, glowing as bright as the coming day would be. Power, like a second wind, streamed into him. Endless power that overshadowed the burning wound and his hot, seeping blood.

The guard's sword struck out for Bastien's neck—and was shoved back by a blast of air. Bastien gave in to the magic and punched with his fist clenched over the glowing marble. The guard flew to the ground.

Bastien spun, crying out in pain. Tave had charged after Cerick.

"Men, to me!" Cerick shouted, but there were so few left.

Two guards broke from their fights with Brock and Micah and raced back to Cerick. The captain looked over his shoulder, a murderous promise in his eyes, then retreated from the clearing, out of sight.

Bastien stood panting and bleeding, shoulders heaving as he gazed into the light from his fist.

Who are you, boy? Micah's voice streamed soundlessly into his head.

Bastien gasped and shot his gaze to Micah. The mage's unflinching face promised he would get the answers he sought.

The trees tilted, and the sky spun in circles. Bastien dropped to his knees, the blood turning cold on the back of his tunic.

"Damn it all, he's hurt." Tave sounded faint, as if speaking through a thick blanket.

Bastien shook his head and lay down on his stomach. The cool, moist leaves felt good on his cheek.

"Micah, heal him." Tave's voice was impatient, but the words came across as a command.

"He can heal himself." Micah loomed over Bastien, gripping his staff.

Bastien looked at his hand with the marble, still glowing. The warmth in his belly had intensified, but it made him so tired. The marble was stealing his strength. It was ridiculous. Why did the marble need to glow, anyway? The sun was up, bright enough to see by.

"Stop it, marble," Bastien mumbled into the leaves. They were so cold.

The marble listened, and the glowing ceased, so Bastien didn't chuck it into the woods.

"He can't heal himself, Micah. He can't even keep his head up."

Instead, he closed his eyes and went to sleep.

"One of his parents was a mage. Kid from the streets, this was his first time around a mage crystal. No one would have suspected."

An irritating nudge on his shoulder brought Bastien to full consciousness. He squeezed his eyes tight, but the nudge came back. Then it came again and again until it shook his whole body and he finally opened his eyes. The sun beat down, blinding him. Tave's face interrupted his view.

"Welcome back, kid." He smiled.

Bastien rubbed his eyes. "Are they gone?"

Tave glanced sideways at Brock. "Who?"

"The guards. Will they come back?"

"Oh. Yeah, they're gone. Probably the thought of two mages and a swordmaster scared them off." Tave laughed. "But they know where we are. We have to leave." He nudged Bastien on the shoulder with his boot again. "So get up."

Bastien pushed to his elbows, head throbbing, mouth dry with thirst. "Two mages and a swordmaster?"

"Never mind, kid. Let's go. But Micah will have questions for you."

Bastien climbed to a crouch, then stood. His tunic stuck to his back. He pulled it off, twisting to look. Dark, dried blood covered him to his knees.

"They stabbed me." He touched his back with gentle fingers, and then, feeling no pain, pressed harder. "My wound is gone." He met Tave's eyes.

"Micah healed you. Mages can do that kind of thing." Tave handed Bastien his reins.

Stupefied, Bastien accepted them, and Tave moved on to mount a horse that must have once belonged to a city guard. Keeping his head down, Bastien peeked at Micah. The mage looked weary, slumped on his saddle, making his short stature even smaller. He caught Bastien's stare, lines around his eyes like a permanent scowl.

Bastien looked away and mounted his horse. While he positioned himself, he felt around his pockets. It was no surprise the marble was gone, and he was relieved. He didn't want to ever touch that thing again.

Tave and Brock spurred ahead, horses dodging the corpses of the guards. Bastien couldn't look away. More innocent lives to add to his list of misdeeds. He couldn't go back to Olin now. He'd find a way to make sure he was okay.

Bastien gave his horse a nudge, following the directions Tave gave him the day before. His horse obeyed, following after them. Micah bolted in front of him, blocking his path as the others disappeared up the trail.

Micah held up the despicable silver marble. "I'm sure you were expecting this back, but this is not a trifle. It's a sacred thing one must earn. You are not worthy." He pocketed it into his robe and adjusted the grip on his staff.

Bastien's gaze flicked to the rounded top. The warmth blossomed anew. "Keep that away from me." He tightened his fist around the reins.

Micah snorted. "Why?"

"It nearly killed me." He'd never felt so weak before, even after days of starvation, and it wasn't the blood loss, though that probably hadn't helped. The marble had used his own strength to fuel the magic.

Micah closed his mouth and cocked his head. His eyebrows scrunched together, and his eyes moved back and forth like he was searching for something. Then, at once, a slow smile spread on his face.

"I don't know how you figured it out," he said, "but keep it to yourself, or I'll turn my power on you again." He tilted his staff forward. "You remember how that felt, don't you? That inexplicable weariness?"

"You stole my strength?" Did Tave know? Bastien flicked the reins, and the horse moved with him, likely just as eager to be away from Micah.

"Yours and everyone else's. Tell the others and die." Micah laughed and sped after Tave.

Bastien gritted his teeth. What had he gotten himself into?

CHAPTER

FIFTEEN

Leaves and twigs slapped at Bastien's face and legs. Micah's robe mocked him as they traveled through the woods. Brothers, Tave had called them. But they weren't as close as Tave thought. Micah probably stole their energy too. Mages were known for all kinds of tricks, but brothers didn't do underhanded things like this. Brothers protected each other.

Bastien winced, an old pain lancing his heart. At least, they were supposed to.

The gang broke out of the thick trees, increasing their speed. Bastien remembered to hold the reins lightly in his hand.

They were a band of disloyal thieves. He couldn't trust any of them. Trust is what got him here. Bastien spat in disgust. Everything that had gone wrong in his life was because of trust. Why, *why*, did he never learn that lesson? He could only trust himself. And here he was, blindly following three criminals leading him on a path of death and lies.

No lies. He might need the gang for survival, but he wouldn't lie. That, at least, was what he could control.

The gang traveled until nightfall—looking over their shoulders the entire way—when they stopped well off the road. Cold air blanketed the small clearing between the trees, and crickets chirped in the tall grass around them. After rubbing down his horse, Bastien marched up to Tave, ignoring Micah's stare.

"Tave, Micah is using his magic to steal our strength through the marble." He shifted in the too-big boots Tave had lent him. "Last night, he used that marble to drain me and fuel his magic."

Tave dropped his horse's hoof and straightened. He'd shaved off his prison beard making him look younger than Bastien originally thought—maybe late twenties. He glanced from Bastien to Micah and back again.

Micah stood stone-faced.

Tave reached into his pocket, pulling out the marble. "You mean this?" He rolled it in his fingers.

"Yes!" The warmth seeped into Bastien's stomach. "He's doing it now, can't you feel it? Throw it away."

Tave turned a stern expression on Micah and drew his sword. "Is this true?"

Micah edged toward his horse and gripped his staff. The top emitted a low glow. Bastien tensed, preparing to bolt.

"We can't let him get this, Bastien." Tave pivoted to face Micah. "He'll only be more powerful with the other piece of his mage crystal."

Mage crystal? The marble was a mage crystal? Was that how he stole their strength?

Brock cooked dinner over a low fire, watching with wide eyes.

"Here." Tave tossed the marble. It gleamed in the firelight, and Bastien caught it on reflex.

The warmth burst into licking flames in his hands. "Ah!" Bastien shook the fire off, spreading burning globules over the grass. He felt no pain, but the weariness set in, even as his heart pumped adrenaline, and magic filled him unbidden through the glowing marble.

"Acantha above!" Tave stomped on the fires now scorching their campsite. He shot an accusing gaze at Micah. "You didn't say he'd be able to do that."

Bastien brushed the last of the flame from his hand but held tight to the marble. It may sap his strength, but as Tave said, that was better than Micah gaining more power.

Micah frowned, staff glowing in earnest. "I didn't think he could."

Water pulled from the ground and the air around them, condensing on the flames and extinguishing them with a hiss.

Bastien focused on the power of the marble, intensifying the glow until their campsite turned bright as day. He clenched his jaw, widened his stance, and glared at the thieves. He annunciated each word. "What is going on?"

Tave laughed, putting away his sword. "I guess the joke's on us, Micah."

Micah's staff dimmed, and his face resumed its usual scowl. He loped over to the campfire, accepting a plate from Brock.

"Tave?" Bastien didn't lower his offense. The warmth of the marble—mage crystal—churned in his belly, and cold prickles stung over his skin as realization set in. It wasn't the mage crystal draining him, it was the magic. And it was of his own making.

The mage crystal had ignited something from his past he'd never wanted to touch again.

Tave crossed to him, holding his hand up against the light. He slapped Bastien on the back. "Turn off the light and we'll talk."

Bastien focused on the power flowing into him, and the power he'd poured into the light. He slowly, bit by bit, pulled it back until the marble no longer glowed. The warmth was still there, just under control.

Micah stared at him.

Bastien sagged to the ground, no longer able to hold himself up. Soggy, burnt grass smooshed beneath him.

Tave followed him down, placing a concerned hand on his shoulder. "Brock, bring Bast something to eat."

"He needs water," Micah said gruffly, now focusing solely on his food.

Bastien nodded, licking his dry lips. While he drank and ate, Tave talked.

"It's not Micah who's draining your strength. It's you." Tave pulled a log next to him and sat. He pointed to the marble in Bastien's hand. "Turns out I stumbled upon a gold mine in that prison. It was fate. You're a mage, Bastien. You can access magic through a mage crystal, just like Micah. It makes you tired because that's the price you pay for using magic. But it makes you especially tired because you've never learned to use it."

Bastien raised a weary eye to Micah, who glowered into his plate as if it was to blame for all his problems. So he could access magic through a mage crystal? Every mage he'd heard of was rich, but that hardly made up for the price of using magic.

"And, you've earned my trust." Tave slid an extra sausage onto Bastien's plate. "You told me about Micah's plan, even if it wasn't true, and after Micah threatened you, too."

Bastien sighed. "There is so much wrong in my life. I wanted something to be right, even if just for a moment."

Tave smiled. "It's about to get a whole lot better, kid. Despite what Micah would have you believe, we *are* brothers in arms. We bear no secrets nor ill will toward one another, and we serve each other with our lives." Tave stood and faced his partners. "And you're one of us."

Brock dropped his pan and cursed. "What? No way, Tave. You don't know anything about him. How is it that he's a mage and was never discovered and taken to a mage school?"

Bastien kicked at the ground. Those were the most words he'd heard from Brock in the two days he'd known him.

"Doesn't matter, my friend. We need a fourth person, and the Fates have seen fit that Bastien is our man. He's earned my trust and proved himself in rough times. He got me out of Kingsguard. So, he stays." Tave faced the mage. "And Micah here will train him."

Bastien's mouth dropped open as he glanced up. A trainer. That's what he needed. Then he could use his magic with control and leave this band of liars. Maybe it wouldn't have to end in tragedy.

Micah coughed and choked on his food. He rose to his feet using his staff for support. "No. On this, I disagree. He's too old, and his magic too unpredictable. With his gift of fire, he's as likely to roast us as he is the enemy."

Tave crossed his arms. "That is why you should train him. He's already a skilled thief. With even a little bit of magic training, he could be very useful." He paced the clearing. "We'll stop in Maze and get him a crystal and a robe—"

Micah's flat tone interrupted. "They don't sell those kinds of things in Maze."

"—and you can work with him as we travel. Teach him the ways of magic. He'll get stronger and gain better control, and learn his capabilities and limits." He stopped pacing and lowered his tone. All joy fell from his face. "On this, I insist."

Bastien held his breath. If he could get his own crystal...

Micah scowled for a good minute, but eventually nodded. *I'll train you, but don't expect any favors just because you're a mage.*

Bastien startled at Micah's voice in his head. He stared down at the marble. Micah's hate radiated through the crystal, but he hated Micah a little too, after the joke he tried to play, which seemed less and less like a joke and more like a setup.

Still, a small smile broke through his stern composure. He'd see the world and learn to control his magic.

He shoved the marble into his pocket. Tave had declared him a member of the gang without ever asking him if he wanted to be one. What happened to working a few jobs first? Like Micah, he probably had no choice. He was valuable to them now. If he tried leaving, they'd catch him. No telling what Micah was capable of.

He missed Olin. They were supposed to travel the world together.

When you've got nothing, you've got nothing to lose.

The gang rode south, and that's all they could be bothered to tell him about their direction, even if it was already obvious. During their stops, Bastien had his first bath in he couldn't remember how long. His bare feet dug into the mud at the bottom of the fast-moving creek, mud squishing between his toes. The cold water flowed over him, and he shivered at its touch, scrubbing his long hair of the last of rotten food thrown by the townspeople. He finger-combed through the lengths, shaping it to hide his face and retying it in a low tail, just as Miss Bannings taught him long ago. His ruined clothes were left by the creek and traded for an even more ill-fitting pair. Tave, looking fresh after his quick wash, had spared them from his own pack.

After two days, they came to a town. Really, calling it a town was being generous; it was more a small collection of shops along one main street surrounded by more of the monotonous trees and meadows Bastien had seen since joining the gang. The familiar sight of carriages, people milling about, and the smells of animal waste and baking bread gave him a wistful smile for home, as broken as it was.

They tied their horses to a post near a trough, all except Micah, who grumbled something and stalked off. Bastien trailed him with his eyes, then followed Tave and Brock through a heavy door into a tavern.

They picked a round table in the middle of the room. Only one other patron sat at the bar—careworn clothes, flat pockets, no coin pouch. It was doubtful Tave meant to rob him or this dusty tavern.

The barkeep, older and without that hint of suspicion people with valuables to hide usually toted, put down a rag and approached with a smile.

"A round of ale and some of whatever's good, keep." Tave plunked down a few silver coins.

The barkeep scooped them up, pocketing them into his greasy apron. He took a long look at Bastien. "Where ya'll from?"

Tave glanced up. "North."

"You lot traveling through?"

Bastien had never been to a bar, could never afford anything a bar had to offer. Besides, his clothes and often-bare feet identified him as a poor orphan the moment he stepped in the door. Still, the barkeep seemed suspicious. It hung in the air around him.

"Yup. Be gone by nightfall if we're lucky." Tave stared hard at the man.

The barkeep nodded and left for the bar with one last look at Bastien. He returned with three ales and a platter with a loaf of bread, a knife, three fat hunks of cheese, and a small pot of mustard.

Bastien's mouth watered. Tave and Brock leaned forward, grabbing at their share. Tave passed a mug to Bastien, then blew the foam off the top of his own drink, taking a long pull.

Holding the metal handle in one hand, Bastien tipped the liquid back. It went down smooth, filling his belly with spicy warmth.

When he looked up, Tave bit into bread with cheese, smiling at him.

"You've got something on your face, Bastien." Brock rubbed his fingers around his mouth and laughed.

Bastien wiped the thick foam off his lip with his sleeve and grinned.

The food lessened the ache in his stomach, and he felt more relaxed than he had in a long time. They finished the meal but stayed at the table, playing cards. A pleasant buzz in his head had him smiling despite the threat of discovery in such a public place. The hours drew by, and dusk gave way to night. The bar filled with patrons, but his group didn't leave.

Good mood gone, Bastien squirmed in his chair, tired of being in one place when there was a whole world to explore.

Finally, he couldn't stand it. "Why are we still here?"

"We're waiting for Micah." Tave pushed another mug Bastien's way, but Bastien shook his head.

As if he'd been summoned, Micah appeared at the door and nodded.

Tave and Brock stood. Bastien followed. The barkeep came and wiped down the table.

"Thank you for the hospitality." Tave tossed a copper coin down.

Once they'd mounted their horses—something that was becoming second nature—they followed Micah off the main street and down a dirt road until they reached an abandoned barn. Only the moon lit their way. They entered the windowless barn, and Micah slid the door closed. Darkness covered them.

Micah lit his staff, casting white light over the moldering hay scattered around. The rotting barn was empty except for the four of them. Then a second staff lit up in Micah's hands, casting eerie shadows over his deadpan stare.

Tave laughed. "Good job, my man." He took the staff from Micah, and it instantly dimmed. He passed it to Bastien. "Here you go. Just for you."

Bastien held his breath as he took the staff in his hands. The smooth, hard wood weighed nothing at all. The familiar warmth of the mage crystal intensified. What he'd experienced through the marble was nothing compared to this.

They all watched him expectantly.

Bastien gulped and closed his eyes. It was time to swallow his fear and let the magic out. Just what would he be capable of? He concentrated on the crystal, thinking calm feelings—no need to cause another fire. The crystal glowed, just as Micah's had. The glowing intensified until it burned white through his eyelids.

Bastien opened his eyes and grinned. The barn lit up brighter than day. He tilted the staff this way and that; the most valuable thing he'd ever owned. "Thank you, Micah. Thank you, Tave."

Shielding his eyes, Micah huffed.

Tave smiled behind squinted eyes. "I suspect it'll only take you a few years to earn the money back."

Bastien's mouth dropped open. The glow dimmed. "Years?" He should have known. That's how long it took him to pay off Kolb, though Kolb had intended it to be much longer. It might as well have been a lifetime.

Tave nodded, satisfied. "In a few years, you won't want to leave."

Bastien cast him a skeptical look and debated on chucking the staff to their feet and never looking back. Brock appeared unaffected, leaning against the barn door, while Micah had gone back to frowning as if the world insulted him with its very existence.

Swallowing, Bastien lowered his voice. "Look, I've got a friend back in Docimer. He's like a brother to me. He depends on me. I need to get back and find him."

"Don't be stupid, new kid," Brock said. "None of us can step foot back in Docimer. The entire kingdom of Kestrea isn't safe."

Bastien narrowed his eyes. He knew that. But maybe this new gang could help him.

Tave stepped between them. "Brock speaks true, even if he lacks basic manners." He patted Bastien on the shoulder. "In a few years, the heat will have died down and you can try then."

Meaning they wouldn't help, and wouldn't let him leave. Who knew what would become of Olin by then? He could only hope Miss Bannings would find him and take care of him.

Tave chuckled. "I promise, kid. We live like kings on the road."

Like kings? Bastien raised an eyebrow. "Where are we going?"

Tave smiled. "A grand kingdom by the name of Alysies."

PART II

FIVE YEARS LATER

SIXTEEN

Chapel bells rang, sending glorious music throughout the castle grounds. Faelyn stood at her balcony, breathing in the clean air and filling her lungs with the scent of rain. In the courtyard below, servants hopped over lingering puddles, carrying their bundles. Guards clad in blue Alysian livery patrolled the main entrances, studying the faces of noblemen and women as they hurried by dressed in their finest. The clouds had passed just in time, and the birds were singing once again.

Meribeth cleared her throat. "Forgive me, Your Majesty, but it's almost time."

Faelyn turned, her elaborate dress swishing as the heavy, voluminous fabric struggled to keep up with her movements. She smiled at her ladies-in-waiting where they stood in her parlor. "I've been waiting for this moment a long time."

Meribeth exchanged pink-cheeked grins with the others. "As have we all. You look beautiful, my queen. We're proud to have a place in the chapel."

Faelyn gathered her dress, the sparkling crystals pressing into her skin. "I wouldn't have it any other way. Now, let's hurry. We don't want to miss it." She winked.

They laughed as they made their way toward the chapel, the same one her parents had wed in so many years ago. Very few weddings had been held there since they'd reclaimed the castle, but none so elaborate as this.

Harmonious choir music lifted her spirits as she approached the open chapel doors. Meribeth squeezed her hand, then Faelyn entered, head high down the aisle. Carefully arranged bouquets of roses and freesia graced the ends of every pew. Their sweet fragrance perfumed the air. The congregation, piled shoulder-to-shoulder, rose with bright smiles and bowed. Faelyn's lips quirked in return, but her eyes sought what lay ahead.

Captain Nolan stood at the front of the aisle, dipped into a low bow. His crisp blue uniform and polished ceremonial sword made him even more handsome under his freshly cut hair. Candles burned behind him and the priest, creating the perfect scene for such a happy occasion.

When Faelyn reached the front of the chapel, Nolan finally met her eyes. She couldn't help her grin as she nodded and took her place on the front row beside Kian and several courtiers. He bumped her shoulder as the choir changed songs and everyone turned to the back of the chapel.

Amerae, dressed in smooth white silk adorned with tiny pink pearls, walked arm-in-arm with her father down the aisle. She glowed with joy, eyes shining as they saw only Nolan. The aging Lord Calem beamed, every bit the proud father. Faelyn stared as long and hard as she could, never wanting to forget this image of pure happiness.

Amerae stopped just before reaching the front, and she and Lord Calem bowed to Faelyn—something they hadn't rehearsed. Faelyn's eyes welled, and she sent feelings of happiness toward her friend.

Amerae grinned, then hurried to Nolan's side.

The ceremony was beautiful, but not nearly as beautiful as

Amerae and Nolan's first kiss. In that moment, Faelyn remembered all the pain and hardship Amerae had endured when her first love, Michael, died. He'd fought bravely in the battle to reclaim their castle, but lost his life in return. Faelyn thought Amerae would never give in to love again. Now she had, and Faelyn couldn't be happier.

She'd remember these moments and the way love should look when it was her turn.

Amerae and Nolan, being who they were, only allowed themselves a week of newlywed bliss before returning to their posts. Faelyn's gaze couldn't help but be drawn to them as they roamed the throne room, sharing shy smiles. Her courtiers had shown phenomenal patience at her distraction, but they were gone now, ushered out by Kian who'd come with an important update.

Faelyn dug her fingertips into her forehead. "Are you certain, Kian?" Her voice echoed in the long space, bouncing against stone and wooden beams before being absorbed into the tapestries along the walls.

He stood before her on the carpeted aisle runner leading from her dais to the double doors of the throne room. Candelabras and the large windows behind the throne bathed the room in light.

"We're certain. Daltieri is preparing for war." His words didn't fade into the tapestries. They echoed in the room and in her heart. "Two separate units have confirmed. They've been increasing production of salt and storage facilities. They're stockpiling, and they've increased their recruiting." Kian's tone was heavy, but unfazed.

Faelyn looked up. Amerae, dressed in her preferred palace livery, scanned each doorway, including the secret ones behind the tapestries depicting the Rylandor crest. Nolan stood at the main door watching his new wife with worry in his eyes.

Kian's hand gripped his staff, but it was casually propped on the floor.

"You're not concerned?" She shivered from a chill in the air.

He smirked. "Of course not. We have Kestrea tied to us, ready to come to our aid if need be. It'd be folly for them to attack Alysies, and maybe they're not planning to. Perhaps they plan to take to the seas and seek resources elsewhere."

"Their port is only newly completed," Faelyn said. They'd utilized their mages and achieved access through the mountain well ahead of where Kian had predicted. "I doubt they'll use the seas for much. They don't have a strong naval force." She rose, sweeping her gold gown behind her. "We should know, Kian. We should know exactly what they are planning. Why haven't our spies relayed that information?" Her loud voice echoed back to her, highlighting her worry and frustration.

"I don't know, my queen, but I am working on finding out."

"Okay. We've planned for this. I want us fully battle ready. Begin mandatory recruiting. Call in our people. Bring me an army worthy of the name of Alysies."

Kian gave her a wary look.

"When you find out what we're dealing with, we'll hope it's not our worst fears. If it is, we'll be ready. If not, this will be an expensive training exercise. Send envoys to Kestrea and Creadel. They'll heed our call to aid. Daltieri won't get a second chance to take my kingdom from me." *I'm here, and more ready than they know.*

Amerae grinned from the other side of the room. Kian bowed.

Faelyn watched them go, eyes narrowed in contemplative anger. It had to be something else, not preparation for war. As Kian said, Daltieri would be committing precious funds and resources to a fight they couldn't win. Faelyn had spent the last two decades since becoming queen preparing for this. Through trade agreements, she'd made powerful allies. And this was something she'd made no secret of. The only kingdom not in a similar position was Kestrea, and she had the gaudy engagement ring in the vault that proved their alliance.

It was folly. Or a good distraction. Faelyn slammed her hand on her armrest. She shouldn't have to wonder. The intricacies of her spy network were unprecedented and included a list of mages personally tutored by Niri. She should know.

Nolan's eyes trailed Amerae in a hungry way as she left and he allowed the servants and courtiers back in. Faelyn ignored them.

A pair of guards took Nolan's place, and he approached the dais carrying a message. "Your Majesty, his royal highness, Prince Rory, will arrive within a week so you may be reacquainted before the wedding in a few months. His wing is already prepared."

Faelyn blinked. "Acantha above, has it already been five years?" She pressed her fingertips into her forehead again and groaned. The wedding was set to take place that winter, but it had been agreed that Prince Rory would spend some time in Alysies first. She'd rather go ahead and marry now, but that wasn't what was agreed.

"I suppose time passes more quickly for you, my queen." Nolan dipped his head.

"That it does." The years just seemed to blink by. "Thank you, Nolan, for all you've done in service to this kingdom."

His mouth turned up, and his eyes crinkled in a warm smile. "We wouldn't have a kingdom if not for you, Queen Faelyn. I serve gladly, proud to raise my family in such times. Thanks to you."

The genuine gratitude floated through the air and warmed Faelyn's cold heart. She'd had little time for the small moments in between her preparations for Alysies. Even with the assistance of her aides, she was always busy with too many things. There were always fifteen more tasks to take the place of one.

Which reminded her. "Please send a party to ensure the safety of our future king."

"Already done, my queen."

"Good." Her eyes took in her proud captain and smiling courtiers. Nothing would get in the way of this alliance.

CHAPTER
SEVENTEEN

Bastien glared through the rain, using a stick to pick mud from his boots. He'd long ago given up staying dry. Micah wouldn't let him waste energy to make a shield, so their crude shelter beneath the dripping trees would have to do. It rained in Alysies more than it ever did in Kestrea, and he hated the never-ending wetness that, in the right season, made you cold into your bones. This was one of those seasons.

Tave sat leaning against a tree, eyes closed, the picture of ease though a stream of endless water cascaded down on his head. He liked to envision all the possible outcomes before a big job. It'd saved them more than once, so Bastien didn't interrupt.

He looked back out into the rain. Even the wetness couldn't cover the stench of the nearby bog, like a latrine. Live like kings, indeed. Nothing about his life had changed except the scenery. Still the same thieving and sleeping in all sorts of horrid conditions. Even after becoming indebted to Tave, Bastien hadn't meant to stay. The plan had always been to escape and return to Olin, but ever since they'd crossed into Alysies, the desire to head back north had dwindled every day. The gang didn't watch him at night. His magic was strong. He had every opportunity to leave, but he didn't. And it wasn't because he still owed a debt for the mage staff. He harbored a secret hope their jobs would take them to the capital city of Pavora, but in all these years, they hadn't.

Bastien shook his head clear of the guilt. The gang needed him as much as he needed them, and they were still wanted men in Kestrea. The road and marshy ground beyond lightened as the clouds passed. The blasted rain was letting up.

A signal came as a pulse of power from the crystal in his pocket.

"Micah says it's time." Bastien got to his feet, grabbing his staff where he'd propped it against a tree limb.

Tave's eyes opened. He pushed up out of the mud, and together they mounted their horses. Tave led his horse to the edge of the trees. Bastien clicked his tongue, and his horse, Tarten, stopped even with Tave who stayed quiet, focusing on the horizon.

Bastien sighed. "Look, I know Micah thinks I'm ready, but that's a horrible reason to target someone so important. It's reckless. And really, we've already made enough to hole up this winter."

Tave finally broke his gaze from the empty road. "This is the wrong time to change your mind, Bast."

"Was it the wrong time when I said so at the very beginning of this insane plan? This is not just a simple nobleman we're attacking. Let me contact Micah. We can still back out of this." He shifted his staff to reach the marble in his pocket. He'd find some other, less dangerous way to finally pay off his debt for the staff.

"No. This is happening. And we're not attacking anyone. Once the first coach passes, we're only after the goods. Do your part and it won't come to a fight."

Bastien clenched his staff, recognizing Tave's tone; he wouldn't be defied, no matter how doomed the plan.

A lifetime's worth of rapid heartbeats later, Micah spoke to him through the piece of his mage crystal. *The first carriage approaches.*

He's inside as we thought, so let it pass before you do anything. Don't screw this up.

Bastien gritted his teeth. "First carriage."

Tave clenched the reins. "All right, kid. Don't screw this up."

He glared at Tave, then the sound of many horses commanded his attention. Bastien's heart picked up speed; he couldn't help it. Micah chastised him again and again, but no matter how many jobs they did, his adrenaline acted up each time. 'Emotions interfere with the magic.' Bastien took a deep breath.

Second carriage. Make it count.

"Second carriage, Tave." The final carriage.

The first carriage—a flaunty, golden thing—rolled into sight surrounded by many, many guards in green. At least a couple dozen marched by as Tave and Bastien backed into the dripping trees.

"Not yet, Bastien," Tave whispered, staring intently. "Not yet. Almost."

Bastien gripped his staff. Sweat and rain trickled down his neck. His horse pawed the ground. The first carriage passed their hiding spot, more guards trailing behind.

"There're so many." Bastien's heart pounded in his chest, about to explode from his body. "This is insane."

The last of the guards passed by.

"Now, kid. Now!" Tave slapped Bastien's horse, and Tarten bolted into the road.

Precious time ticked by as Bastien struggled to get his horse under control. The guards turned, shouting and drawing their swords. Tave rushed back towards the clatter of the second carriage as it rolled closer.

Bastien raised his staff, mage crystal aglow, and poured magic into his intent. Water rolled toward him, funneled from the puddles of rain. He directed it, and a thick wall of water rose up, separating the first carriage from the second. With shouts of surprise, guards rushed forward, but they were too late. Their horses shied away, rearing back as the guards struggled to control them.

The weariness crashed over Bastien in waves that threatened to weigh him down, but he gritted his teeth and remained firm. Tarten snorted beneath him, sides heaving, but stood his ground. All their practice was paying off. He was actually forming a true barrier. The water rose until it was twice his height and expanded into the thick tree line on both sides of the muddy road.

Shaking, he held the spell.

The yell of the guards behind him meant the gang had advanced on the second carriage. He didn't turn around. The blurred images of wide-eyed guards rippled from the other side of the water. They charged, striking with their swords, but the wall was too thick. Arrows hit and stuck as if it was target practice at an archery range. Each puncture brushed against him with a slight pressure, but his magic held strong.

One brave guard abandoned his horse and leaped at the wall in a running charge. He smacked into the water, submerging his body halfway before he couldn't go any further. With a sucking sound, his companions pulled him out.

Bastien watched him, fascinated, then scanned the wall top to bottom, side to side. He had no formal training as a mage, and Micah said his magic was still unreliable. If the guards found a way through, their plan would be ruined. He couldn't even turn around for fear of failing. But he could hear.

Behind him, the gang attacked the second carriage, the one with the riches Tave was after. The screams of dying men and injured horses terrorized the air. Micah's magic rippled out to him and echoed through the marble; Bastien could only guess what horrors he wrought. Unlike Bastien, Micah only commanded water, but it was terrifying what he was able to do with it. Bastien reinforced his wall and thanked the Fates he wasn't involved with the killing. This time.

In front of him, the guards lined the barrier, some now hacking and attempting to burn the soaked trees to try and go around.

Bastien drew more water, this time from the bog, and extended the wall another few feet into the trees on both sides.

Last one. This was his last job and he'd be free to leave Tave's gang. The debt for his mage crystal would be paid. One more time to survive.

The skirmish behind him drew closer.

Micah, what's going on?

Micah's extreme irritation leaked through the connection in the marble before he closed it again. Bastien wasn't supposed to interrupt. Micah said he'd contact him if necessary, but the job was taking longer than planned. Too long.

Bastien threw more power into the wall and tightened his grip on the saddle horn. He risked a look over his shoulder. Tave and Brock fought back-to-back, each swiping swords at two or three guards. The second carriage hadn't been nearly as guarded as the first, but still more than enough.

Micah's staff lit up like a beacon. Four guards around him grabbed their chests, falling from their horses to the ground. Micah liked to use a person's own water in their body as a weapon against them. But where one guard fell, two took his place.

Movement beyond the skirmish caught his eye. *A third party!* There weren't supposed to be more than two.

Micah!—

A strong thump drew him up short. Bastien whirled to the water wall. Through the wavering liquid, the guards parted and a light appeared. A woman with fading red hair and robed in black stepped forward, waving her mage staff in the air.

Micah! They have a mage. Bastien scanned her robe. There, along the hem, barely visible through the thick water, was the gold embroidery marking her rank. *She's a master. I can't hold against a master.* His heart raced anew.

Micah's panic flowed through the crystal. *What? You have to! That wall can't fall or we all die. You can do it. I can't help you.* He cut off their communication again.

Bastien tensed. *No, Micah, you have to help—*

A force unlike any other slammed into his wall. The water rocked within its tight confinement with the sound of a thunderbolt. The magic penetrated through the barrier. The power of it funneled through Bastien's magic and into his very being.

Bastien cried out and slumped forward in his saddle. Tarten, thank Acantha, was seemingly unaffected by the magic. The pain was like two giant's hands clapping him flat—but the wall held. He doubled his grip on his staff, pushing more magic through it. Panting, he slowly righted in his saddle.

The master mage's crystal lit up brighter, the glow obscuring most of the guards from sight.

I can do this. Nothing to lose. Bastien set his jaw, bracing himself in the stirrups. *The wall will not fall.*

The master mage released a second attack. It lanced through his magic like a knife. The indescribable pain clapped around him, longer this time. He bore down against it and remained upright. When he opened his eyes, water had cascaded down on the enemy's side, thinning the barrier by half. The guards struck, shoving their swords until the tips pierced through.

A whoosh of pent-up air rushed out of him as he focused on reforming the water. With a sweep of her arm, the mage sent the loose water back to the bog. Bastien cursed. Beads of sweat popped out on his face.

Like the back build of a massive storm, magic pooled around the master mage as she readied for another attack.

Bastien poured himself into holding what was left of the wall, diverting just some of his focus to the water in the bog. *I need that back.*

The staff grew heavy in his hand, and his upper body hunched over Tarten's black mane. His energy was gone. There was nothing left to give. With a long exhale, he let go of his tight control over the magic. Instead of the magic funneling through a pinprick of space, it flowed in from all directions until his whole being glowed.

Distantly, he sensed the mage's surprise. Her staff drooped, and her efforts faltered for a precious moment. Under Bastien's command, water rushed back from the bog. Liquid flowed from the remaining puddles. It seeped up from the saturated ground beneath their feet. The wall thickened so fast several guards were caught in it. The master mage stumbled back.

Magic swirled all around him, like warm, invisible specks begging to be directed. He'd never accessed so much before, and he fought to stay conscious. He breathed deeply and smiled behind drooping eyelids.

Pain exploded in his shoulder, and his body pitched forward. Black spots bloomed in his vision. His legs slackened, losing their grip on the saddle, and he slipped sideways. His mage staff caught the lip of the saddle and ripped from his hand as he fell.

He slammed into the ground on his shoulder, vision going black from the pain. An arrow. Tarten screamed and bolted away. Groaning, Bastien poured magic into healing himself. Guards yelled. Water splashed against his face. He opened his eyes to a flood.

Water cascaded down from the top of the thick wall, increasing in speed as it fell. He willed himself to move, but his muscles wouldn't budge. Pain and exhaustion tried to pull him under. Through the screaming of men and horses, the pounding of boots and crashing water, his gaze flicked to his staff mere feet away. He stretched out his good arm. Too far.

Bastien fumbled for the marble in his pocket. He only had time for a gasp before the wall—all the water from their immediate area—crashed over him. He held his breath as it rolled him down the road. The arrow in his shoulder scraped against rock and road, over and over. Bastien screamed in agony, earning mouthfuls of water. Pushing through the blinding pain, he used his arms to right himself and ride the tidal wave down the road on his back. Micah, Tave, Brock, and the entire contingent of guards were charging away as fast as they could, the carriage and riches forgotten.

Bastien's arrow snagged against something beneath the water, twisting him around with a sickening rip. He screamed and blacked out. The mage crystal in the marble pulsed against him. He opened his eyes, craning his neck to the sight of the second carriage, just before he slammed into it head first.

CHAPTER

EIGHTEEN

Bastien opened his eyes to the sight of a dank stone wall. His sandpaper tongue stuck to the roof of his mouth. The room was tiny, with no window except a small latched opening in the thick metal door. No bars, but he wasn't stupid. This was a prison cell.

He smoothed his hair which was somehow still tied in its tail the way Miss Bannings had taught him. What would she think of him now? He pushed up from the bare floor. No mat. No nicks in the wall to mark the passing of some poor soul's life. At least it wasn't Kingsguard Prison.

What had happened? Images of being underwater, terrified and in agony, filled his mind. He'd been shot. He reached around to his shoulder but felt no wound and no pain. The rotten stench of dried bog water lingered in his clothes. The wall of water had fallen. He'd failed. Had the gang got away? Been captured? Were they working on a plan to get him out?

Bastien reached for his pocket, but his leather armor had been removed, as well as his expensive boots. Barefoot in bog-scum-covered clothes, he was that orphan kid again Tave had picked up from prison. Only Tave wasn't here.

The crash of doors opening and closing echoed down the hall. No voices, no whispers, nothing to indicate where he was.

Acantha above, he was thirsty. So small he almost knocked it over, a cup of water sat beside the door. Bastien took it and drank it dry in a gulp, wishing for a hundred more.

He'd been close, so close, to earning his freedom from Tave. Maybe Tave had found what he was looking for in the carriage and would count the debt paid. Or maybe nearly dying was enough. No one could have resisted the master mage, not even Micah.

No gash on his head. She must have healed him. It's the only way he'd still be alive, wound free.

The latched window in the door opened, and Bastien scrambled to his feet. He caught a glimpse of red hair before brown eyes looked in on him.

"You're awake. You've been asleep for days while we traveled back to Pavora."

Pavora. Bastien's heart skipped, but he said nothing. The red-headed master mage had tried to kill him.

Her eyes lit up as if she'd smiled, but Bastien couldn't see her mouth.

"You're too young to be involved in such horrible crimes. Attacking a prince of Kestrea is a hanging offense." There was a note of question in her tone.

Bastien remained still, wishing for his staff. He felt this mage's crystal from the other side of the door, but he didn't sense her magic interfering with him in any way. Micah said some mages could use magic to force information or pry into his memories.

"You're either wise or foolish to keep quiet. Whichever it is, I can't help you until you talk to me." She shut the latch and walked away.

Bastien reached for the door, ready to call for her to stay, but his fingers formed a fist he let drop to his side. She didn't want to help him. She wanted him to help her. Which meant the gang hadn't been captured, and they'd probably stolen the goods.

He crossed his arms and leaned against the rough stone, sliding down until he was sitting. He reached for the connection he'd once felt but had never forgotten. It wasn't there, but there was... something.

The mage would come back. If she thought he could help her, she'd be back.

CHAPTER
NINETEEN

CHAPTER
NINETEEN

Faelyn stood at her window, clutching the soft curtains in one hand. Outside, the leaves were finally starting to turn with hints of red amongst the green. Sunlight twinkled off Pavora Lake. Once, only trees surrounded the water, now tall houses clamored on parts of the shore, each vying for the best view of the lake and castle beyond.

Funny how time changed things. If Daltieri still ruled, the trees might still be there, the people not having a need for expansion in the failing kingdom. A lot of the families who'd moved away during the generations of Daltieri-enforced poverty had returned to Alysies. Of course, many had fled to Daltieri as well.

Faelyn sighed and let the curtain fall over the window. She turned and let out a gasp of startled surprise. Kian stood halfway into the room, brow creased in concern beneath his peppery hair. His light tunic was tucked into loose trousers, a royal blue vest and cape completing the look.

"Kian. I didn't hear you." She smoothed her gown. "Were you using magic?"

"I was not." He stepped forward, polished boots barely rustling the rug. "Is everything all right?"

"I'm fine. Prince Rory arrives this afternoon. Before he does, I'd like to take the time to monitor progress at the compound." Something drew her to the military stronghold, calling to her like an internal signal, distracting her enough she hadn't even heard Kian.

"It is already afternoon. He's here. I've come to summon you to greet his carriage." The worry in his countenance matched his tone.

"Already afternoon? Why did I agree to this, Kian? I should have insisted to Prince Rory that a visit wasn't necessary. The wedding's not for a few months, anyway." She held herself, running her hands up and down her thin sleeves.

Kian glanced at the door, then he crossed the last few steps and wrapped his arms around her.

She leaned against his comforting shape.

"I know this is harder than you let on," he said. "And maybe you don't need me to say it, but you're doing admirably. You were just a girl in a tavern without out-of-control magic when we first met. Like you said, it's not forever."

She rested her cheek against his shoulder. "I know. This was my idea, and it has been the best thing for Alysies. We've already benefited from the increase in trade and less threat from Daltieri." She pulled back and smiled. "Thank you for reminding me."

Kian eyed her smile, looking unconvinced of its authenticity. A haze of anxiety surrounded him. Something worried him.

"What is it?" she asked.

He rocked slightly on his heels. "Prince Rory's party was attacked by a band of thieves on route to the castle."

Her lips parted. "What? Why didn't anyone tell me?"

"I only just learned the full story. Niri arrived this morning with one of the captured thieves. The rest got away after managing to kill some of the Kestrea guards. They didn't attack Prince Rory—they were after a carriage of gifts the prince brought for you. According to Niri, he hasn't accused Alysies of the attack." He paused. "Yet."

Faelyn paced. If he chose, Prince Rory could pin the attack on her and use that as grounds to end the engagement contract. She wrung her hands. That couldn't happen. It was too late to secure another alliance if Daltieri was already preparing.

Kian stepped into her path. "He's here, rested, and in good spirits, I'm told. Niri is handling the thief personally. She thought it best since he is a mage."

She looked up. "A mage?"

"A powerful one, it seems." He offered his arm. "Your prince awaits."

Right, time to play host. She forced an eye roll at his arm but took it. He led her down the halls and stairways until they reached the throne room on the way to the front of the castle.

Faelyn stopped. "I'll wait in there. I'd like him to come to me this time."

Kian nodded and patted her hand, and she went to sit on the throne. A servant offered her water, iced by one of the castle mages, and a chocolate chip scone, but she didn't touch them. Instead, she pulled light from the candelabras and released it, again and again, concentrating on the actions that had become second nature. She didn't have to think about grabbing the light, she really never had.

The throne doors finally parted, and Prince Rory, now twenty, strolled down the aisle. Faelyn breathed in, sensing a wavering confidence despite his haughty appearance. He looked nearly the same, except taller and leaner, outfitted in the Kestrea green. His high cheekbones and square jaw almost lent him the good looks she'd predicted when they'd first met, except for the blonde hair circling his head like an upside-down bowl. Several of his servants and guards trailed behind, along with Kian and Amerae. Prince Rory gave a shallow bow, then snapped his fingers. One of his servants hurried forward carrying a box filigreed in gold.

"A gift for Your Majesty's hospitality." The servant bowed low, offering the box.

Faelyn accepted it with a nod. Though Amerae, having reached the front, leaned forward and eyed the box, Faelyn sensed no ill will from the contents or the servant. She opened the hinged lid revealing a stunning turquoise necklace. Several rows of the polished rocks were inlaid with gold, hanging from a thick gold chain.

"Since you're so fond of this stone, my father and I thought you would appreciate the improvement." Prince Rory's mouth turned up in a confident smile.

Improvement? Faelyn's hand went to the simple turquoise stone at her neck, one of the only possessions from her mother. It had once adorned an intricate wooden haircomb, but she'd broken it in anger long ago. The woman who'd raised her, Mary, said it was a gift from her mother's first love. Nothing could ever be done to 'improve' it.

"Thank you, Prince Rory. Your thoughtfulness is noted." She managed to pass the box along without throwing it in her servant's waiting hands. "I heard about your misadventures here. A very unfortunate situation."

He frowned. "Yes, not the reception I was expecting in your kingdom. Luckily, we managed to recover my personal effects from the flood waters."

Flood waters?

"I'm sure you would like to rest after your journey. I will see you at the feast tonight in your honor." She didn't know what to make of the prince. He'd grown up a lot in a short time, both physically and in maturity. And even though he presented a pleased and professional front, something burned underneath. Anger or resentment so strong as to nearly be hatred. Resentment of what? Having to leave his kingdom and rule from here perhaps. It certainly wasn't customary.

Did that mean he'd find a way out of that fine point of the marriage contract? Or out of their engagement completely? He'd have to be watched.

Prince Rory dipped his head. His entourage followed him out of the throne room. The gifted necklace had already been blessedly removed from sight.

One would think after years of being readied for events, balls, feasts, and meetings, it would become less tedious. Faelyn stood in front of her mirror while Meribeth and her other handmaidens fluffed her green dress—a tribute to the Kestrea prince—and put the finishing touches on her hair and makeup. The end result was stunning, her golden locks curled, cascading into perfection, her curves accentuated by the cut of the dress. The circlet on her brow, inlaid with a diamond, made her turquoise eyes stand out, as did the charcoal drawn on her eyelids.

But it wasn't her. Her true self wore tunic and trousers, surrounded by forests, magic roiling within, blade on her hip. Free to run, to breathe, to love.

She blinked at a knock on the door. Amerae entered wearing her own elegant gown, hair in a braided updo. In her hands, she carried a box with gold filigree.

Faelyn's hand went to her mother's necklace.

Amerae gave a tight smile as Meribeth took the box, placing it on the table. She opened it and brought out the turquoise monstrosity.

"It will clash some with your dress, my queen, but I think it's only fitting." Meribeth held the necklace up for inspection. She'd come from the house of an Alysian lord and knew well of court customs and politics.

Faelyn breathed deeply and nodded.

Meribeth smiled and clasped the necklace around Faelyn's neck without removing her mother's necklace. When she let go, the full weight of the turquoise settled against Faelyn.

"My goodness, this is heavy." The chill in the stones sent a shiver running through her.

They made their way to the newly constructed dining hall, added during a recent expansion. Windows lined the entirety of it, along with ever-burning lanterns her mages had constructed for her.

Instead of the dark gray stone that comprised the older parts of the castle, the dining room was lined with white marble veneer making the room bright and inviting. Kian had given her a warm smile when she'd had it constructed—a little piece of Thomats School of Magery in Pavora.

"All rise for her majesty, the fair and powerful Queen Faelyn Rylandor, the savior of Alysies," the harold said when Faelyn crossed the threshold.

She managed not to roll her eyes.

Lords, ladies, and mages rose from their seats at the long table that wrapped around the room. They bowed and curtsied, smiling and tittering with joy. Prince Rory stood from his place next to hers on the raised table—a place that would be rightfully his in just a few short months. The place of the king.

He wore green silk, loose and opened at the top, along with his ceremonial circlet. In the low lighting, he did look rather handsome with thick brows and dark eyes, watching her.

The significance of this night was not lost on Faelyn, nor any of her courtiers who whispered, casting glances at the prince.

Faelyn smiled, pleased to see everyone dressed in their elegant finery. The tables were adorned with nice cloth and silver platters piled high with food. Per longstanding tradition, they had to wait for her to sit before eating, so she made her way to her chair. Two servants adjusted her poufy skirt and tucked it around her as she sat.

Conversation resumed along with the clack of utensils and plates. Faelyn took a sip of her water—water, never wine—and turned to the prince. "Are you rested after your travel?"

He swallowed a bite of roasted pheasant, dabbing his mouth with a napkin. "I am. Enough so that I was hoping after dinner you might give me a private tour." He stared deep into her eyes.

Faelyn looked away, taking another sip. "In Alysies, our feasts can last all night, Your Highness. Perhaps I can arrange a tour for you tomorrow?"

"All night?" Prince Rory looked at the array of food.

"We don't only eat. There's dancing and musical performances." She felt when his eyes went to her, but she didn't turn toward him.

"Tomorrow, then. May I ask a question of my future wife? What's it like to be so old? To have seen so much history?"

His future wife. The thought sent unpleasant shivers up her spine.

She looked up to see Kian across the room, watching her. Her gaze shifted to the east window and the citadel which abutted the castle grounds.

"It's daunting sometimes, Prince Rory. You understand, a lot of personal sacrifice is necessary to rule. Imagine making those sacrifices again and again. For more than one lifetime."

"My father says you didn't sacrifice for your kingdom until it was almost too late." His tone was polite, but the challenge underneath was plain.

Faelyn finally turned to him, teeth pressed tight together. His clear face feigned innocence despite the calculated insult.

"Just as I've known you since you were a child," she said, "I knew your father as well. You both have much to learn about sacrifice."

Prince Rory narrowed his eyes, his gaze dropping to the gifted necklace. "I'm beginning to learn much, Your Majesty."

What did that mean? There was no need for this animosity; their union was set. Faelyn turned to her food and ate without tasting. The prince was so young. His arrogance and insolence shouldn't affect her.

"How will we divide duties once I'm king?" He interrupted her musings.

If only he'd be quiet and eat.

Her fork stopped halfway to her mouth. "My young prince, now is not the time or place to discuss such things." She leaned toward him, noticing how he watched her lips. "There are too many eyes and ears among my court, as I'm sure there are at yours."

She straightened and fake-smiled at him. He blinked and slowly nodded. "Yes, I see. Perhaps after the feast we might discuss such things in... private." He winked.

Faelyn's fake smile grew bigger. *Acantha above. The prince is a complete idiot.*

A horn sounded from the corner, then a slow ballad filled the air. Conversations ceased, and eyes went to her.

"Would you care to lead me in a dance, Prince Rory?"

He stared around the room, then wiped his mouth with his napkin and stood, offering his arm. Faelyn accepted it, letting him lead her to the middle of the room. He placed one hand on her waist, taking her other hand. Her fingers slipped on his sweaty palm. She smiled, keeping her eyes on him. Surprisingly, he didn't falter. His body held perfect stature and form as he led her around the room, her dress swishing with the movement. The music, at least, was pleasant, strings and flutes playing their sweet notes in perfect harmony.

Her friends and courtiers watched, but she kept her gaze locked on Prince Rory. Did the performance look real enough? Could they see through her act? Not all of it was false, as the giddiness of the dancing lightened her heart. She would learn to love the prince. She could do that for Alysies, and for herself. *And he could learn to have better manners and be less of a pompous ass.*

The rhythm of the song increased slightly with the crescendo of the melody, and she looked at the prince without seeing him. Instead, a thread inside tugged her in the opposite direction, toward the citadel where her army resided.

The song ended, and the spectators clapped. She curtseyed, and he bowed.

Kian approached. "May I have the next dance, my queen?"

She raised an eyebrow at Prince Rory.

"By all means, Lord Kian." He turned, finding the arms of a young, eager courtier as the next dance began.

Kian held Faelyn the way Rory had, but here she found comfort. His callused hand lifted hers delicately, and he gave her a knowing smile. They swept around the room, joined by other members of the court.

"You two look handsome together." His eyes twinkled.

She glared, and Kian let loose a chuckle.

She stuck her nose up. "He's a good dancer. And his shortcomings can be overcome with age."

"I'm surprised he didn't ask about your long ears." He grinned, bracing himself.

Faelyn's mouth dropped open in mock horror. "You were listening from across the room? I knew the magic in the air felt of 'arrogant ass.'"

"Don't worry, I'll make sure Nolan sets guards at your door to ward off any 'private visits' after the feast." He laughed.

She resisted the urge to smack him, then shrugged and hit his shoulder anyway.

Kian held her gaze through the last of the song. He was nearly Faelyn's equal in sensing emotion, but she'd grown adept at masking them. "I'm glad all is well."

Faelyn scrunched her eyebrows together, then the song ended and she didn't dance with him for the rest of the evening. She danced with Prince Rory several more times, along with most of the lords in attendance until it was time to retire.

Blessedly, Prince Rory claimed weariness and canceled their private meeting, though she swore she heard him and the young courtier laughing together down the hall. But maybe not. Her attention remained drawn to the citadel.

CHAPTER
TWENTY

Days passed in the empty cell marked only by the delivery of meals. It was a higher quality slop than Bastien's last prison stay, but still slop—and less of it. By Bastien's count, they only gave him two meals a day, though the intervals seemed to grow longer. Darkness was his only company, continually tormenting him with no distraction from the assault of his past mistakes.

The mage did not return. No one did.

Once, he heard the cry of a fellow prisoner that was quickly cut off. Another time, a pair of soldiers chatted as they passed down the hall, metal armor clanging. The words "battle" and "Queen Faelyn" had him pressing his ear tight against the door to hear more, but they were already too far away.

After that, his mind raced. It'd been so long since he'd seen Queen Faelyn in the streets of Docimer, but he'd never stopped thinking about her. Was Alysies under attack? He'd heard of the great battle Alysies had undertaken to reclaim their kingdom from Daltieri. Talk in the taverns was the townspeople feared retaliation —until five years ago, when the queen's engagement to that cocky prince was announced. She didn't belong with him. The more he learned about it over the years being in Alysies, the more he believed Queen Faelyn had sold herself for a weak alliance.

But what was the talk of a battle? Had something changed? Could the queen be in jeopardy? The compulsion to leave was stronger than ever. Where had they brought him?

Soft footsteps sounded from the hall, then Bastien sensed a mage crystal. The footsteps and the crystal pivoted away from him, traveling down a side hall, while heavy boots drew closer. He considered calling out. He had questions that needed answering, and the redheaded mage was the only one who seemed willing to talk.

The boots approached his door. Bastien backed against the wall. His muscles tensed. This was a guard, and guards only came for one of two reasons: to free you or hang you.

The guard opened the slop hole and threw a pair of manacles into the cell. They skidded across the stone, stopping at Bastien's feet.

"Put those on," a rough voice said.

Bastien scoffed. "Not likely." His voice came out weaker than he'd intended after so many days of not speaking.

"Our master mage wishes to speak to you. Put them on." The guard opened the window latch and peered in. "Don't be a fool."

Bastien raised an eyebrow. It was either a horrible trick or the chance he'd been waiting for.

When you've got nothing...

He picked up the manacles, closing each around his wrist with a locking snap. When he tugged, they didn't budge.

"Okay," he called.

The guard opened the door and entered sword tip first. Bastien kept his shackled hands raised in front of him and his eyes on the sword. The guard waved him forward, grabbing his collar as he stepped into the hall.

"Walk."

Bastien narrowed his eyes but walked. So much precaution for someone unarmed. The guard didn't have to lead him. He walked down the narrow stone hall, turning left where the mage's crystal called to him like an internal beacon, stopping where the concentration of magic felt strongest.

The guard pounded on the door, and it opened from the inside. Two more guards grabbed Bastien's arms and threw him into a chair bolted to the floor. With quick movements, they had his manacles off and his arms and legs shackled to the chair.

When they stepped back, the mage sat in a chair on the other side of the room. Red hair piled loosely on her head bobbed as she nodded. The guards left, shutting and locking the door behind them.

Bastien stared. She stared back. Her staff gave off a subtle glow meant as a warning, but her black master robes were more than enough. She was older than he suspected from what he'd seen through the water wall, subtle lines etched around her eyes, but her faded red hair was unmistakable. It was just the two of them in a larger version of his stone cell. Even shackled, the feel of sitting in a chair was amazing after the hard ground of his cell. He didn't let that show on his face. Let her speak first.

She smiled slightly. "I'm Niri, master mage and former head of the Thomats School of Magic, now advisor and head trainer to her majesty, Queen Faelyn. What is your name?"

Bastien pressed his lips together. Even if she was from the coveted Thomats, he didn't owe her anything.

Niri sighed. "Guards." Her subdued deliverance was carried away, and the guards threw open the door.

Bastien's eyes went wide. "Wait."

Niri held up a hand.

"My name is Bastien."

The guards glanced at Niri, and she nodded. They backed out of the room, casting hard looks at him.

She tilted her head. "Your last name?"

"Never had one." His tone came out harsher than he'd intended.

"Where are you from, Bastien?"

No lies. "Docimer of Kestrea."

Niri smiled. "Thank you for being honest. As a fellow mage, I'm sure you're aware how useless it would be for you to lie. Mages can sense those kinds of things through magic. Trained mages, anyway. Who trained you?"

Bastien frowned. "A mage by the name of Micah."

She leaned forward. "Who are your parents, how did you come by a mage crystal, and why did you attack that carriage?"

He squirmed within the shackles. "It's a long story."

"And I want to hear all of it. To put it in perspective," her staff flared, "your life depends on your story."

"Well, when you put it that way." Bastien started at the beginning, telling Niri of his rudimentary education at the orphanage, joining Kolb's gang and staying for Olin. His setup, arrest, and escape with Tave. Micah's reluctant training and illegal procurement of a staff, then summarized the last five years saying he'd never killed anyone, but stayed with Tave's group robbing coaches and rich people to survive.

"My only job that day was to form the barrier and hold it until Tave could rob the wagon. Then I would have paid off my debt. When I got shot, I lost my hold on the magic." He looked at Niri. "You know the rest. And now I have questions of my own." Sure, he was in no position to make demands, but when had he ever let that stop him?

Niri blinked as if coming out of a trance. Magic fell away. She'd been weighing his words. "Go ahead."

"What is this place and what do you plan to do with me?"

"You're locked away in the special part of our prison for dangerous criminals."

He lifted his arms to cross them, but the shackles held them down. "I'm not dangerous."

"You're a mage without formal training. You showed incredible power holding that wall. Even some master mages never obtain that kind of control." Niri stood. "I've never come across a mage who could withstand the kind of attack I hit you with. And you're not from Alysies." She leaned toward him. "Are you a spy?"

"No, of course not." Bastien's jaw clenched under her scrutiny. "You think I'm lying."

"I know you're not, but you might be omitting. We've found spies amongst our ranks before and cannot be too careful."

"I lost my staff in the flood. Even if I was 'omitting,' I'm useless without it. Not dangerous. And not a spy."

"And that's why we're having this conversation, Bastien. The queen has issued orders that we are to offer criminals a chance for redemption through service in her army. I've deemed that you're not enough of a threat to the crown or the choice wouldn't be in your hands. I'm going to give you a chance. If you prove yourself as a soldier, I may be able to see you trained as a proper mage."

Bastien leaned forward, an edge of panic in his voice. "Is the queen so desperate for soldiers? Why? Is Queen Faelyn under attack?"

Niri eyed him. "What information is pertinent will be relayed by your commander if you make it that far. Don't expect it to be much." She clapped her staff on the floor. "I need you to voice your decision, Bastien."

"And if I choose not to serve as a soldier?"

Her lips formed a thin line, and her eyes turned sad.

Death, then. The choice was obvious. No matter how difficult things became, survival was the answer. Maybe he could find a way to escape and finally return to Olin. Or maybe he'd get to see Queen Faelyn again.

In all these years, he hadn't been able to leave the gang and get close enough to her to feel their connection again. This was his chance to learn about it. And maybe a chance to do something real and right for once in his life.

A slow-building sensation crept over him, starting in his middle and radiating out like pinpricks. He gasped, locking eyes with Niri. He knew this feeling, though it had been a lifetime since he'd last experienced it. Niri stepped forward, eyes creasing in concern.

"I'm sorry for whatever happens next." Bastien blinked and his view shifted into another scene. Niri no longer stood before him.

He overlooked a great battlefield outside of a grand castle. Dead soldiers and felled horses lay all around. Only black and white showed on their uniforms and banners, as if his vision didn't want him to know who'd won or lost. A great beam of light shot from the horizon, and Bastien felt a familiar pull, one he hadn't felt in five years. Queen Faelyn was at the end of that light, and she called for help.

Bastien ran, though his steps found no purchase as his body flowed over the dead. Further and faster he went, but he couldn't catch up. The horizon loomed in the distance, but he couldn't reach it. The pull to her increased in urgency. He cried out with frustration, slipping over blood and bodies.

Bastien's vision vanished. The stone cell reformed in front of his eyes, and he found himself straining against his chains under the scrutiny of a very wary mage, mage staff aglow. He let loose a pent-up breath and slumped back. His wrists bled from the manacles.

"Bastien. What was that?" Niri sat back, voice cautious. She waved her hand, imploring him to speak.

He'd never told anyone about his foredreams, and though he had no reason to trust her, he did.

"Sometimes I get visions. Of the future."

"Fatings?" Niri's eyes opened wide.

He nodded. "And they always come true." His pulse sped. "There's going to be a great battle, with many lives lost. Whatever's coming, whatever Queen Faelyn needs soldiers for, it's going to put her in danger." He looked down, speaking quietly, heart hammering away with the aftereffects of the vision. "She's going to leave the safety of her castle walls, and she's going to need me." As Niri's magic delved into his words, Bastien felt her alarm. "I accept your offer to be a soldier in the army." He looked up, sitting as tall as the chains allowed. "I hope to earn your trust."

"You're telling the truth." The glow on Niri's staff dimmed, then vanished. "There is such a mystery surrounding you, Bastien. Your path will be a hard one. Your unit will know you're a criminal, and you'll have to earn your place every step of the way. But... you know hard paths, don't you?"

He gave a terse nod.

Niri called the guards. "Release Bastien to the army's custody. See that he gets his boots returned." Her voice had turned hard, but sympathy radiated from her as the guards dragged him backward from the room.

Their hands dug into his arms, and they wouldn't meet his eyes. They took turn after turn, the hallways becoming lighter as they approached some kind of exit. Muffled voices increased in volume, and the doors became bars instead of solid metal like his. The prisoners glared as he passed, whispering to their cellmates.

They ascended two flights of stairs, and Bastien squinted as the light of day touched him for the first time in he didn't know how long. The door opened, blinding him, and the guards shoved him out into the waiting hands of more guards.

His eyes slowly adjusted as he walked over packed dirt. The prison looked more like a small castle, a stone fortress with smooth, unscalable walls. Soldiers in blue leather armor gathered in groups, running through individual sword drills or jogging in formation around the expansive grounds within the high outer wall. Trees loomed in the distance, and beyond that, smoke from several chimneys rose skyward. Pavora must be nearby, a city at least as grand as Docimer.

Two brick buildings sat off to the side, and more buildings were being constructed all around them, tall with wood scaffolding. The smell of cooking fires, horses, and metal mixed with the sounds of hammering and captains shouting orders.

"This isn't a prison, is it?" Bastien asked his guards.

"No," the guard on his left said, a tall, burly guy who clearly never missed a meal.

The other guard cleared his throat—leaner, more like Bastien's build—with short brown hair. "Where you were is a prison of sorts. It's where the criminals are held until ready to join the cause."

"Hey, don't talk to him, Chrisso. He's just a common thief." The first guard's stern voice made Bastien bristle.

"It's like I told you, Bear. All these men will be fighting by our side, and who do you want next to you? A friend, or someone you spent your efforts turning into an enemy?"

"Well said, Chrisso." Bastien nodded.

Both guards—soldiers—glared at him.

Bastien walked on like a man without a care in the world. He wasn't about to be hanged, and was finally on the right side of things, joining a worthy cause instead of stealing to survive. He'd been waiting for this moment, his chance to make something good of his life, ever since he'd fated the queen's arrival down the street of Docimer so long ago.

Of course, he hadn't exactly joined more than he'd been enslaved to save his own life. Yet again. But, this was Queen Faelyn's kingdom. This was her war to protect her people, and his fating meant this was his chance to protect her.

The soldiers led him into one of the brick buildings where a man in a blue uniform handed him a stack of blue clothes and a pair of boots. Not his own, but new and well-made of supple leather. Chrisso and Bear led him to a long room full of real beds, each with their own trunk at the end. It was currently empty of people, who must all be out training.

"This will be your bunk," Chrisso said, pointing. "Mine is over there." He gestured to a bed five down from Bastien's. "Get dressed, and I'll show you to your new captain."

Bastien circled his bed, running his fingers over the coarse wool blanket and the small white pillow, clutching his new clothes to his chest and inhaling the scent of soap. A real bed. Even his bed at the orphanage had been only a blanket stuffed with hay. His trunk was made of rough wood that smelled newly cut and looked unused.

He pulled off his soiled clothes, poking a finger through the hole in the back from where the arrow hit him, and dressed in a loose navy-blue tunic that tied with a silver belt at the waist. His tan trousers hugged him, just as they did on Chrisso. The boots fit well, coming up to his calves, though it'd be some time before the leather molded to his feet. He untied his hair, combed through the lengths with his fingers, and retied it in a low tail.

Chrisso exchanged a look with Bear. "Before you meet the captain, there's somewhere else you need to go."

The pair led him out the door and to a busier part of the compound. Here were all sorts of merchants selling wares, blacksmiths forging horseshoes and weapons, trinkets and trifles to be had. No one gave him a second glance as they traveled down a dirt lane that traversed an area more like a market than a war compound. Except for the merchants and some of the women, everyone was dressed similarly to Bastien.

Bear steered him to the back of a line of soldiers. "Wait here, and don't cause any trouble."

"What for? What's at the end of this line?" Bastien peered ahead, but the line curved around the side of a building.

"Haircut, boy. No long hair in Captain Flinn's unit."

Bastien stiffened. They wouldn't be touching his hair. They'd already taken his staff. His hair was all he had left, all he had to remind him of home and the woman who'd been like a mother to him.

Bastien backed away. "You're not cutting my hair." His heart hammered.

Chrisso raised an eyebrow. "Captain Flinn won't like it if you show up with long hair."

"Best listen to him." Bear shoved Bastien forward in line.

Chrisso rubbed the back of his neck.

Bastien stepped out of line. "No." The sternness of his voice left no room for argument. His stance widened instinctively.

Bear raised his fists. "No? You're too green to be telling me no." He pulled back for a swing.

Chrisso jumped between them. "Bear! Bear, it's not worth it. Don't get latrines for this idiot's pride." He jerked his thumb behind him toward Bastien.

Bear glared over Chrisso's shorter shoulder. Bastien lowered his fists, but not his guard. He'd seen bullies like Bear before, and this wasn't through.

Bear stepped around Chrisso, into Bastien's space. "Fine, but you'll learn to listen when spoken to by your superiors." He moved as if to step away, then slammed his fist into Bastien's side.

Bastien grunted from the impact, but he'd been ready and had dodged the worst. Bear kept walking. He'd be a joy to bunk with later.

Bastien rubbed his ribs. "Where to now, Chrisso?" That little scene had drawn attention, and he was anxious to be away from the barber.

Chrisso's face scrunched, looking after Bear for a moment. "Now you meet your captain." He hesitated, then walked away, and Bastien followed until they finally left the market and entered the relative quiet of a training yard.

They walked through a gate to where a group of uncoordinated soldiers practiced sword fighting, clacking wooden swords against each other. Chrisso whispered something into a soldier's ear. That person took in Bastien with wary eyes, then walked away. He stopped beside a man standing in front of the group with his arms crossed. His broad shoulders and white-flecked hair didn't distract from his long mustache. He wore leather armor decorated with ribbons and pins. The man looked up, then strode toward Bastien.

Chrisso saluted with a fist over his chest, so Bastien hurried to copy him.

The captain looked Bastien up and down. "I'm Captain Flinn, in charge of new recruits. We know all about you, Bastien No Last Name, so if you're looking for a fresh start, you won't find it here. You'll join the rest of these criminals to learn enough to pass as a soldier before you're doled out to a permanent unit." He shook his head as if he doubted Bastien would make it out of training. "Go grab a practice sword and join the other cruities."

"Yes sir," he said through gritted teeth. He stomped passed Chrisso and took a practice sword off the rack.

It felt foreign in his hands and not the right width, much too skinny. He swung it a couple times, looking to see who was watching. Everyone. Everyone was watching.

Bastien sighed. This was going to be bad. Tave had never taught him how to handle a sword.

CHAPTER

TWENTY-ONE

Faelyn sat at a large round table listening to the reports on Daltieri. Every chair was occupied. Kian, Nolan, Amerae, and a smattering of trustworthy lords and generals surrounded her. No servants were allowed lest pertinent strategic information be leaked to the enemy. It had happened before, when there were still Daltieri loyalists running around the castle.

Her eyes trailed the room as the generals discussed the latest information. It had taken the length of five blinks to learn there was nothing new. Daltieri still prepared for something, her spies still didn't know what, but it looked more and more like a planned attack. She'd doubled efforts to increase their numbers, and the ranks were swelling. Messages of peace were spread, and Prince Rory's presence and promise of alliance were flaunted, so the people did not fear a war.

But Faelyn did. Everything she learned as queen taught her just how much Daltieri had lost that day, and what they stood to regain in a war. With its multiple sea ports, vast forests, and shared borders, Alysies was a rich kingdom.

152

A knock sounded on the heavy door, silencing the generals. Faelyn sensed Niri and smiled. "Open the door."

Niri stepped in and bowed, red curls falling beside her careworn cheeks. "Your Majesty, I wish to speak with you."

Faelyn nodded and stood. The rest of the room rose with her. "Please, continue." She made eye contact with Amerae, who silently followed them. Kian's eyebrows scrunched, and he quirked up one side of his mouth. Faelyn turned away, smiling out the door. He was just jealous that he lacked an excuse to leave the meeting.

They walked adjacent to tall windows paned with thick glass, stopping at a door not far from the council room. Inside, a fire burned in the hearth. The three women sat in plush chairs and were served cookies and tea. Faelyn studied Niri closely. She was brimming with news. Something important, it seemed, but formalities forced Faelyn to be patient.

As soon as the servants bowed and left, Faelyn used air magic to set a sound barrier around the room.

Niri dipped a buttery cookie in her tea, taking a dainty bite. "See, Faelyn? Being queen is not entirely horrible."

Faelyn smiled. "Your timing was impeccable. I almost fell asleep in there."

"I did fall asleep." Amerae stifled a yawn.

They all laughed, and Faelyn welcomed the release.

"Nothing impeccable about it when you prod my mage crystal practically begging for relief." Niri chuckled.

"True, but now that we're here, it seems you do have something to tell me."

"I do. I'm here to finally report on the thief we apprehended who attacked Prince Rory's carriage. I got him to talk. He's a mage, an untrained, but very powerful mage with the ability to see Fatings of the future."

Faelyn and Amerae leaned forward. "Fatings?" they said in unison. She'd never known anyone to have that ability.

Niri glanced between them. "Yes. He had one while I interviewed him for his release to the army." She looked around the room. "Are you certain we won't be heard?"

"I veiled us the moment the door closed." Faelyn clutched the armrests, her treats forgotten. For once, Amerae appeared more interested in what Niri was about to say than in the room's safety.

"He claims to have fated the aftermath of a great battle. There were dead everywhere, though he couldn't tell which side won. He also said you were in trouble, and that he didn't know how or why, but that you'd need him. When you leave the castle grounds during the battle, you will be in danger."

Need him? "For what?"

"He didn't say." She took Faelyn's hand. "I think it's to save your life."

Faelyn pursed her lips. "And you believe him?" Niri's opinion meant more than most.

"I do." Niri squeezed her hand. "We recovered his staff upon his arrest. He is without it—unable to manipulate his words. I tested his truthfulness myself."

"Did you look into his mind?" Faelyn asked quietly.

"That's still a difficult skill for me, you know." Niri was being modest. She'd been practicing for years now. "But I trust what he said to be true."

"Then war is coming, as I suspected." Faelyn nodded. "And in his lifetime. Where is he now?"

"I released him to the army."

Faelyn raised an eyebrow. "As a mage?"

"As a soldier."

"A soldier?" Her voice came out stronger than intended. "He has the strength to empty a pond into a wall of water all while resisting your attacks, and we give him a sword instead of a staff?"

"He's young, Your Majesty, and obstinate. He's hiding something and has lived a life of lawlessness. I told him I'd train him myself if he can earn my trust."

Faelyn nodded. "That sounds just." She stood. "I want to meet him."

Niri gaped, but Faelyn didn't wait for a response. She swept out of the room. Amerae shadowed her in eagerness. All of a sudden, nothing sounded like a better plan than seeking this young mage out. Prince Rory would understand if she needed to attend to her queenly duties.

The council room's doors were still closed, but Faelyn didn't stop. She walked the castle halls, descending two flights of stairs, then crossed through an inner courtyard full of plants and flowering foliage before coming to the front of the castle. Servants scrambled to open doors for her.

As soon as she stepped outside, the reason she'd been so distracted the past couple of days became clear. That pull, the tug to her middle, overtook her. She hid her reaction, barely missing a step on the way to the carriage that awaited them in the roundabout.

The three of them stepped in, and Nolan rode up behind as they left the castle walls. That feeling had been absent since the day she left Docimer. Now it was strong, enveloping her in a greater urgency to visit the army compound.

She looked up to find Amerae studying her, and realized she was clasping her hands together. Stilling them, she stared silently out the carriage window.

That boy from the market was here.

The barracks beside the castle had grown too small, so a new one had been constructed, pushing out and away from the castle and the city of Pavora. Though nearby, it was a relative closeness. The castle grounds were so expansive, a carriage was the only sensible thing.

The guards atop the outer gate bowed as she passed. Soldiers rode out toward different points of the compound to announce her arrival.

"What is his name?" Faelyn asked, breaking the silence.

"Bastien. He has no last name that he knows of," Niri said from the opposite carriage bench.

"Bas-tea-in." Faelyn tested the name in a whisper. It flowed pleasantly off her tongue.

Her carriage stopped in front of the post where her commander awaited. Her friends stepped outside while Faelyn remained. She detached her skirt, revealing pants, and traded her dainty slippers for the sturdier boots she kept in the command post for her use. Amerae silently passed a belt and sword through the window, and she buckled it on. Her hair was already plated up with a simple circlet, so she kissed her turquoise necklace and left the carriage, giving Amerae a wink.

Commander Rane bowed low. "Your Majesty, you honor us with your presence." He was well chosen to lead her army, a hard, strict man who'd fought well, rising through the ranks in many of the ensuing squabbles after the fall of Daltieri in Pavora. She'd never seen him without armor, which, along with his thick hair and muscles, lent him an imposing presence. He respected her but wasn't afraid to push back. Not always a good thing.

"Thank you, Commander. I will have a look around at my leisure." Faelyn exhaled, tension leaving her body. It'd been too long since her last visit here. The smells of dirt and the sound of clanging swords—this was her world. Yes, she was queen and dealt with the politics and paper required of her, but she was also a swordsman. She caught many eyes, but they took her in, then sidled away, continuing their tasks of training, commanding, or maintaining the army.

They walked toward where the new recruits trained in the back corner of the compound. Forcing herself not to hurry, she turned to Nolan behind her. "Expansion is happening quickly. I'm glad."

Nolan looked to their new barracks, designed to house recruits with some extra room for when the lords' of Alysies individual regiments were called to aid. "Yes, they've done much in a short time. It is its own city now, with family housing springing up and a large market."

Faelyn was only half-listening as he went on. Thoughts of seeing the new recruit, Bastien, went out of her head. Her only desire was to follow the pulling sensation. It was like a magnet, though unlike a magnet, she could turn away if she wished. But she didn't want to. She had to discover where this led.

The worn path took them between buildings—supply shacks, kitchens, and an armory. Faelyn left the path to cut across the grass and walk between the buildings—a more direct route. The increase in the sensation confirmed she was getting closer. A low fence surrounding the training yard stopped her. Placing her palms against the splintery wood, she saw the gate, but it would take her far out of the way.

So, she hopped the fence. Amerae and Nolan sighed, then hopped over with her. Niri huffed like they were all crazy and walked around to the gate. Faelyn continued. The soldiers in the training yard weren't required to bow. Since she regularly came to inspect the troops and freshen up her own skills, it would cause too much of a distraction. So, though they saw her, some even bowing their heads, unable to resist, they continued their drills, instruction, exercise, and fighting.

She bypassed most of them, heading toward the furthest corner where the pull seemed strongest. She quickened her steps down the trodden path, heart racing for an incomprehensible reason. The feeling, this pull, she knew it.

When she reached the new recruits, the last group of soldiers before the outer wall, she slowed, then stopped. So close, she was so close.

"Queen Faelyn?" Amerae asked.

The new recruits were paired up, sparring with each other using wooden practice swords. The clacking and commanding voices of the captains surrounded her. A cool breeze blew through the yard with the scent of distant rain. She took another step forward, earning a glance from the men closest to her. She stared hard, then the soldiers parted. She prepared to scan their faces, but there was no need. Her eyes went right to him, and his were already on her. The palest blue eyes she'd ever seen, set within a handsome, serious face and a youthful, muscled body. He held a practice sword clumsily in one hand, his sparring partner glancing back and forth between them.

Faelyn breathed deeply, focusing solely on him across the ring, ignoring the soldiers still sparring. Magic, he was full of it. How had she not sensed it before? Had the pull to him been of his own doing all those years ago? But he hadn't had a staff then, or a mage crystal. She was sure of it.

As if he felt her testing him, he blinked, and a shift in his essence occurred. She was let into a deeper part of him than just his magical exterior. Whether he meant her to or not, she sensed his deep pain. It felt like her own, born of a hard past.

Yes, she'd seen him before, years ago in the streets of Docimer, as a boy in rags and bare feet. Now he was a man, learning to be a soldier. But there was such great power within him. An untapped potential.

"Your Majesty?" Amerae approached but did not touch her.

"That's Bastien, my queen." Niri panted, having just caught up.

Faelyn blinked and looked to her friends. When she looked back, Bastien was sparring again. Sloppy swings with a heavy hand. A surge of insane disappointment washed over her, but she still sensed his focus on her, the pull to him as strong as ever.

He moved like someone who'd never handled a sword, but the strength of youth resonated in him. He took blows with barely a wince. A fierce determination set in his hard eyes that strayed to Faelyn's at regular intervals. There was no doubt now it was him she was pulled to in some way. Was he doing it with magic? But he didn't have his staff.

The men, especially the new recruits, eyed her in earnest. The commanders looked up from giving directions. She couldn't remain here. Whispers reached her ears. Her attention was being noticed.

"I'm ready to go," Faelyn said without breaking her stare.

Amerae nodded, and they proceeded back to the carriage. Inside, Faelyn closed her eyes, holding her mother's turquoise in her palm.

"Are you well, my queen?" The worry was plain in Amerae's tone.

"I'm all right." Faelyn let loose a breath. Would Kian know something about this pull to Bastien? "Why isn't he with the mages? He should be. I know what happens when you're not trained to handle your magic."

Niri settled herself on the bench. "I'd thought you'd approve of him gaining basic swordsmanship before being advanced as a mage in your army. We haven't returned his staff, Your Highness. And I don't intend to until he proves trustworthy."

Faelyn opened her eyes to see Amerae nodding her agreement. "Did he have a staff when he had his Fating?"

"No."

Faelyn looked out the window as they rode through the compound toward the exit, if not for the buildings, she'd be looking straight at him. The pull told her where he was, lessening only slightly as they went further away. "I think he needs both. Magic and sword." She turned to Niri. "I'd like you to take him aside a few hours each day and work with him. Let him use his staff and learn control." Her voice grew quiet. "His Fating. He said I'd need him. Is he going to save me? I hope it doesn't come to that, but let's prepare him." As an afterthought, she added, "But don't show him the mage barracks. Find somewhere else to train him."

"Yes, Your Majesty." Niri gave a shallow bow.

"May I speak freely, my queen?" Amerae asked from beside her.

"Of course."

"He's a thief. A criminal. From a foreign kingdom." Amerae looked between Niri and Faelyn. "What do we even know about him?"

Niri bristled, but Faelyn held up a hand. "I've met him before. You've seen him, too. Did you not recognize his eyes? He's the boy on the balcony in Docimer. I didn't read any ill intent, but Niri can gauge that as she trains him."

Lips pursed, Niri nodded.

"He's the boy from Docimer?" Amerae asked. "How did he end up here?"

Niri spoke up. "He became indebted to a band of thieves, and they came here to Alysies. We caught him attempting to steal jewels from one of Prince Rory's carriages." She looked at Faelyn. "I tried, but I couldn't penetrate his defenses."

"How did you capture him?" Amerae asked.

"He was shot, and it distracted him from the magic. When I found him, he'd healed the wound around the arrow. I had to cut it out and heal it over again. Luckily, he remained unconscious for the ordeal."

Faelyn stared out the back of the carriage, in the direction of the pull to Bastien, though only buildings filled the view. She'd never had that much control before her training at Thomats. Her emotions always got in the way, either making control impossible or hurling her magic to extremes.

He said he was supposed to save her, and fate had brought him here. She sensed no ill will, but was Amerae right to be suspicious?

"Amerae, I'd like you to accompany Niri during her first few sessions with Bastien. Learn what you can about our newest recruit."

Amerae bowed, pleased. "Yes, Your Majesty."

Faelyn stared unseeing at the passing shops and houses lining the street. They blurred together until a swath of pale blue caught her eye. She honed in on it, seeing a woman in a blue dress holding a basket of bread.

"Your Majesty, I was thinking during your next lesson we should limit you to one element and pair you against the master mage most accomplished with it," Niri said.

They passed the woman, and she blinked, the view blurring again.

Bastien's intense gaze burned in her mind. How did someone with so much power go undiscovered? And how did he end up a thief? So much buried pain. She herself had done deplorable things to survive.

"Your Majesty?"

Faelyn turned to Niri. "Remind me to tell Meribeth that I need a new dress. Pale blue." She ignored Amerae's stare.

Soon enough, they arrived back at the castle. Faelyn was immediately assaulted by courtiers, noblemen with agendas, people needing her to sign off on this or that, or needing funds for some such thing.

"You may find me in the throne room this afternoon, as usual, if you have something worthy for the court." It may be time to rethink her policy on letting people approach her at will, but her father had always been so unapproachable, and the people suffered for it.

Niri said her goodbye, and soon Faelyn entered her part of the castle, where the throngs could not follow. She stopped when she reached her bedchamber.

"Amerae, I need some time alone. Can you have the guards outside field any visitors?"

Amerae's brow scrunched in concern. "Are you well? You've been distant since we left the compound."

Faelyn shook her head. "I'm simply growing weary of war preparations, I suppose." It sounded believable enough. Her time for the past few weeks had been nothing but plans for expansion and recruitment, border security, and fund appropriation. Even her study with Donoven, her old trainer before she'd become queen, hadn't prepared her for the costs or the effort it would take, but they had enough funds. For now.

She closed the door and sagged against it. She didn't have this time to waste. Even now, Kian would be waiting for her to discuss more strategy and proposals. Her four-poster bed loomed in front of her, wrapped in gossamer curtains and fitted with plush silk bedding. What kind of conditions had Bastien endured before given a bed in the soldier barracks? An orphan, Niri said. Which fit with what Faelyn had seen of him. He probably hadn't had the luxury of a bed before. Would anyone come for him? Would he leave with them if they did? He probably considered himself a prisoner here, which he was, in a way. He'd committed a crime, or helped commit one anyway, even if he was better off here than with some lowlife thieves.

Someone knocked on the door. Kian.

"Come in, Kian." She stood just before he entered.

His creased brow mirrored Amerae's next to him. "You looked flushed, Faelyn. Prince Rory is expecting you for lunch."

Faelyn touched her cheek. "I want Donoven to come here and train Bas... some of the troops."

"Your old swordmaster?" Amerae asked.

"Faelyn, he'd be much too old now to train anyone," Kian said.

"He's only... sixty?" How much time had passed without her realizing? "His son, then. I know he passed his skills on to his son." She'd given Donoven the resources to restore their family-run training school, and it had done well, providing some of her best soldiers.

"We'll look into it."

"Thank you. I'll see Prince Rory now." She'd mostly managed to keep their contact to a minimum since he'd arrived.

Their worried gazes abraded her skin as she brushed past them. She'd have to do better and be the strong queen they'd known up to now.

CHAPTER
TWENTY-TWO

Bastien ended his first sparring session with more bruises than he'd ever had. But he didn't feel any of them. Queen Faelyn had come. He'd watched her approach, hoping beyond hope that *he* was her goal, and not simply overseeing her army. Then she'd found him and stared right into him. She'd felt him out with magic, and he'd let her. It was the most intimate thing he'd ever experienced.

Then she'd turned and walked away, taking the force of her with her. She must not feel it the way he did, but he'd seen her again, and that was enough. The warmth from her presence still lingered in his thrumming veins. Had someone told her of his Fating?

"You better get used to it and not gawk like an idiot next time," Bastien's sparring partner said.

Bastien looked toward the wall. "Used to what?"

At Captain Flinn's barked command, they returned their swords to the weapons rack.

"To seeing the queen. I've only been here a few weeks, but she's been here at least a couple times. She's beautiful, but you'll catch heat if you stare, especially at her ears. Do yourself a favor and don't talk about her to anyone either. They respect her here."

He followed his partner, and soon the savory smells made it clear they headed to the mess hall.

"I respect her, too," Bastien said.

"Then don't gawk next time, is all I'm sayin'." He wiped his nose with the back of his sleeve.

"Thanks for the tip. I'm Bastien." He extended his hand.

His partner shook it without slowing his pace. "Dumont. And I know who you are. Hand-picked by a master mage to be here, yah yah yah. You're in my barrack."

Bastien smirked, and Dumont rolled his eyes. "Hand-picked, eh?" It wasn't true, but a handy rumor to circulate. "You beat me pretty solid back there, Dumont. Are you good by sword fighting standards?" They entered the mess hall, a long, dark room with rows of rectangular tables and long wooden benches, mostly full of other soldiers in their matching blue training garb.

Dumont took a place in the back of a line for food. "I'm all right. I fought for Lord Graymer for a bit before coming here. That's where I'm from, small province to the north."

"How did you get here?"

Dumont looked at him, as did a few others in line. "We don't talk about that. Most of us new recruits see this as a second chance and are more than eager to forget what's passed."

Several soldiers around him nodded.

"Sorry. Didn't realize."

Dumont took two bowls and passed one to Bastien. "That's all right, cruitie."

For a long moment of dismay, Bastien envisioned the slop that had been his meals one too many times. He inhaled deeply when the scent of meat stew wafted over him. His mouth watered, and he shuffled forward in line.

Dumont sighed. "I borrowed some money I couldn't make good on. They arrested me, and I couldn't pay the fine." He held his bowl while a cook ladled it full of thick broth with large chunks of meat, carrots, and potatoes. He grabbed a roll off a tray.

Bastien nodded, unsure what to say and too focused on the food to give it any real effort. The stew flowed into his bowl, and a tiny splash landed on his hand. He stared at it, wondering if he could get away with licking it off. The hot liquid warmed his hands through the bowl.

A soldier nudged him from behind, so he grabbed a roll and followed Dumont to a long table and sat at a bench. He licked the drop when no one was looking. The meaty flavors left him aching for more.

Chrisso sat across from him with an easy smile. "Not bad for your first time, Bastien. And don't worry about Queen Faelyn. She likes to monitor progress here. I doubt you offended her or anything."

Bastien dipped his spoon in the bowl and held the savory bite aloft. "Hey, Chrisso. I want to get good at the sword. Really good. And with all I see going on, I don't feel I have a whole lot of time."

Chrisso tore off a hunk of bread and stuck it in his bowl, soaking up the flavorful juices. "Train hard, soldier. You won't be a cruitie forever. Some guys have shown drive and moved ahead of their company." He pointed with his spoon. "That could be you if you work hard enough."

Dumont piped up. "That's how Chrisso did it."

Bastien smiled at the stew in his spoon, then took his first bite. The broth, now lukewarm, ran down his throat in a satisfying blend of meaty goodness. Soaking bread between mouthfuls, he finished the entire bowl, thinking of turquoise eyes and swirling magic.

By the end of the day, exhaustion bogged down Bastien's every movement. He'd sparred, ran, strength-trained, ran, and sparred until he thought he'd beg for death. Never had he worked so hard in his life.

And it was the best feeling.

Even his bones were weary, but they rang with pride for lasting through it all, and for finally working toward an honorable goal. To work so hard for a cause that was just and right, and its queen. He'd be that much stronger tomorrow. Best of all, Captain Flinn hadn't said a word about cutting his long hair. Bear was just having a go at him.

When he got back to his bunk, Chrisso gave him a nod of approval that bolstered his already good mood. His trunk contained a pair of clean undergarments which he put on after a warm shower. Such luxury! He couldn't remember the last time he'd bathed in anything but a cold creek.

Though his mattress was hard, the sheets were clean, and it was still the softest thing he'd ever slept on. The lanterns went out. He pulled his blanket to his chin, and his feet remained covered. He shut his eyes and snuggled down.

But he couldn't sleep. His thoughts, as they usually did at night, turned north. Was Olin okay up in Docimer? Was Miss Bannings looking after him? And what about Tave? Were they planning to rescue him? He nearly laughed at the thought. They only looked after themselves.

Then a vision of jewels danced in his eyes, and he couldn't figure out why. Queen Faelyn, that's why. Her eyes were blue and green like turquoise and emeralds combined. No, more than that. They were like a sunlit forest, the light from a blue sky burning behind the spring leaves whose timeless shadow only made the color ever brighter.

Could she ever see him as anything but a thief?

By the third day, the routine of the compound was second nature. Rise at dawn, breakfast, running, sword fighting, exercise, more running, and more sword fighting until his palms bled. But he worked hard. Harder than he ever had. By the end of day three, Dumont couldn't lay a sword on him, and he was switched to a new partner.

Sword fighting came naturally, like some long-forgotten muscle memory his body was rediscovering.

On the fourth day, he was laying into his third partner when Captain Flinn summoned him. Panting, Bastien tapped his partner's sword and walked to the front. The clacking of weapons resumed, but he felt eyes on him. Soldiers didn't get called out like this, or so the routine had been thus far.

The captain kept his gaze on the trainees, smoothing his mustache with one hand. "Bastien, you're excused from drills this afternoon. Report to the training hall one at once."

Bastien saluted with a fist over his heart, then walked away with trepidation in his steps. He couldn't think of anything he'd done wrong. When he reached the giant warehouse that served as an indoor training yard, he felt her. Niri, the master mage. Her mage crystal gave a distinct warmth to the atmosphere.

His steps quickened. When he opened the door, he was greeted with a smile. Niri stood in the empty space littered with woodchips, probably meant to cushion falls during training.

"I've heard good things from your captain, Bastien. He said you're working hard and are improving at a fast rate."

Bastien closed the door behind him and stepped further into the room. "Thank you. I'm trying, like you said—"

He gasped at the strong tug to his chest and swiveled to the door. Moments later, Queen Faelyn opened it, stopping short. His lips parted as he locked onto her forest eyes. This was as close as they'd ever been, just a few yards between them, and she was even more beautiful than he'd imagined.

Her long ears came to points over her silver crown. Her face was relaxed but closed off, studying him in the bare moments before someone might notice her hesitation. What would it take to make her smile? The intoxicating draw to her nearly tugged him the rest of the way.

She stared at him, and he belatedly dropped into a bow.

"Your Majesty, I was just about to tell him," Niri said.

Bastien rose, never taking his eyes off the queen. From her neck rested a turquoise necklace. The perfectly round polished piece seemed familiar somehow. An image of a girl with brown curls, laughing beside a boy on a blanket in the woods, flashed in his mind. A haircomb.

A fating? But this wasn't like the others.

Faelyn stepped into the room, followed by a woman in soldier's garb, chestnut hair pinned up, a sword at her hip, and a distrustful stare-down on her face.

"Don't mind me, Bastien. I'm interested in your magery so I will be observing you." Faelyn turned. "This is my lady-in-waiting, Lady Amerae Maddux, formerly of Seaside Keep."

Her voice washed over him, filling up his being with music finer than any he'd heard sneaking into the finest opera house Docimer offered. She knew his name, had said it as if they were equals. Happiness, more than he'd ever known, spread to every facet of his being. The grin that formed from ear to ear couldn't be helped.

Faelyn's cheeks reddened.

Bastien recovered his wits. "Pleased to meet you, my lady." He dipped his head. All those years with Tave hadn't been for nothing. He'd learned a few things about court etiquette on some of their more interesting jobs.

And there was something about Lady Amerae that gave him pause, besides the distrustful hostility rolling off her like an avalanche. She wore fighting leathers, rather than a lady's gown. Her narrowed, hazel eyes locked on him in challenge, as if daring him to do something to harm Queen Faelyn. He liked her already.

"Bastien," Niri said.

He reluctantly turned away from Amerae and her queen.

Niri grabbed a second staff—his staff. "We're going to see what you know."

He scanned the ceiling. "Are you sure you want to do it in here?" The wooden building was definitely flammable.

Invisible magic poured from Faelyn in great quantities that thrummed his insides. Bastien gaped, causing her to smile. She performed her magic without a staff or any mage crystal he could see or sense.

"I put a shield within the building. Good luck, Bastien," Faelyn said. The two of them moved off to the side.

His name rolled off her tongue like a caress. He shivered and accepted his staff from Niri. Power instantly flowed to the crystal, lighting it up. The familiarity made him inhale in pleasure. He didn't miss the look Niri exchanged with the queen. Or the way Amerae's hand flicked to her sword.

He examined the ceiling again, unable to see anything, but the magic was there. He reached out and touched it with his own magic, smirking at Faelyn's widened eyes. He'd never made a shield before, but now he could see how it might be done. To make one so big, and with so little effort... the queen was very powerful.

Niri stepped aside and behind her were three buckets. One was filled with water, one with dirt, and the other was empty. "What kind of magic is within your control? Your answer will tell me how to proceed."

He cleared his throat, willing himself not to seek Queen Faelyn's reaction. "Water, as you know. I can also do fire, and a small amount of air and earth."

"Four?" Amerae whispered in surprise.

Niri nodded. "Anything beyond elemental magic?"

He shook his head. She was speaking of mind magic, and other things like spatial manipulation, to transport objects or images. He'd never been able to do anything like that.

"I'm going to test the reach of your ability, Bastien. First, light a fire in the empty bucket."

Bastien raised an eyebrow. Making fire was one of the first things Micah had taught him, and one of the most useful with all the camping they did. He held his palm up and channeled his focus. A small ball of flame appeared, floating above his hand. He willed it to drop into the bucket, and it burned without affecting the wood.

"Good. Put it out with the water."

She'd already seen him use water, but he raised the water out of the bucket and moved it, extinguishing the fire.

"Now use the wind to knock the bucket over."

He leaned forward and tightened his grip on the staff. Wind was not his best skill. A small gust snaked over the ground, scattering the woodchips in its path. The air hit the bucket, but it didn't move. He gritted his teeth, throwing more power into his efforts. The next gust of wind smacked into the bucket, sending it shooting, water flying.

Next, she had him move dirt from one bucket into the remaining bucket, which took more concentration. His shoulders drooped, and his head grew heavy.

Niri picked up the empty water bucket. "Now fill this with light."

"I can't." Bastien wanted to turn to see Queen Faelyn's reaction, but didn't.

"Have you ever tried to move light?"

He shook his head. Except for the water, all his other abilities had been accidental discoveries.

"I want you to try for me. It's just like fire or water, with its own unique energy. But think of it as more opaque, more difficult to grasp. You have to put more into it if you want to succeed."

He'd only been with Micah for five years, and Micah hadn't shown him everything. Maybe there were things he could do he didn't know about.

Bastien reached out with his magic to the glow of the nearest lantern. Like fingers, his magic snatched at the light. It passed through without finding purchase. He tried again, but the same thing happened. A sigh of defeat escaped him.

"You have to be more delicate than that, Bastien." Queen Faelyn's voice washed over him, and his breathing evened out. The staff grew less heavy in his hand, her footsteps light behind him as she drew near. The pull to her increased with each step, and he was overcome with the insane urge to hold her.

His hands would surely be cut off.

He turned to look when she stopped but a pace away. Neither of them spoke for a long moment.

Bastien sensed Faelyn's magic—could almost see it as she drew the light and brought it before him.

Queen Faelyn formed a ball like a large firefly and then cupped it in her palms. "Aether, the ability to control energy and light, is the hardest to master. Because we can't touch it, our minds make us believe moving it is impossible. Think of it like mist in the air which we can pull together and move to our will, except the power of light requires more of yourself, a weight of magic greater than that of the other elements." Faelyn released the light, and Bastien visualized it dispersing back to where it came from. "Try again."

With a great effort of will, he tore his eyes from her and focused on the lantern. He took a deep breath.

"Remember. Gentle, but with a weighty strength."

Such kindness in her musical voice. Such caring. She really wanted him to succeed. And he couldn't let her down.

He reached out his hand of magic again, but stopped before grabbing the light. While paused, he poured more of himself into the magic, adding weight and power that would not be denied. Slowly, his magic approached the light, and instead of snatching at it with gnarled fingers, he cupped his magic into a palm like Queen Faelyn had. Then he dipped down into the light and gathered some. His eyes widened, and with a gasp, he lost control.

"Good. Do it again." Excitement tinged her voice.

He focused, repeating the same steps. His magic shaped the light into a ball and brought it to him. He let it graze the tips of Queen Faelyn's hair before placing it in the bucket.

When he released the magic, the light remained where he'd placed it. The room spun, and he fell to one knee.

"Well done," Niri said.

Bastien panted, head bowed over. It had taken considerable strength, but he'd done it.

"That's five, Niri. He has all five." Faelyn's reverent tone held a hint of the excitement he sensed from her essence.

Bastien looked up, then pushed himself to his feet. Queen Faelyn watched Niri. But she smiled. He'd made her smile.

Niri pursed her lips. "You've done well, Bastien, and I can see you're near your limit, but I have a few more things for you to try." She glanced at the queen, and uneasiness pooled in his stomach.

"I can take it." Bastien straightened. "I want to know my capabilities as well. I can keep going."

"It's not that, Bastien," Queen Faelyn said, concern in her tone.

"No hints," Niri said. "Now, I'm going to do something that might startle you. Resist me if you can."

Bastien blinked, then a magical force penetrated its way into his mind. He cried out, squeezing his eyes shut, as the force assaulted his memories. Images from his past flashed before him. Queen Faelyn's turquoise eyes. Riding behind Tave and Micah. Kolb's fist flying at his face.

He groaned, falling to his knees again. The real world no longer existed. All he saw was his past painfully splayed in quick bursts.

If you don't like it, you have to do something about it, Bastien.

Niri, she was using magic against him, probing for his secrets.

A rotten egg hitting his stomach between the bars of the cage. Holding Olin's hand while he cried one hungry winter.

Bastien focused his magic, willing it to mold into something, anything to get Niri out. Too many secrets needed to stay buried from the world. Magic flowed into him, but he couldn't direct it. He panted, sagging lower to the ground.

A warm hand clutched his shoulder. His magic jolted in response, as if magnified. The draw plunged him out of despair. His eyes cleared, and Queen Faelyn looked deep into him. "You don't know until you try, Bastien."

Niri assaulted him again, and he saw his past.

Digging up the Purple Borahella roots. Kolb's promise of riches if he joined the gang. Miss Bannings stroking his hair just so at the orphanage. Something she whispered into his ear. One of his secrets.

"No!" Bastien's magic shot out of him in a violent wave.

His vision cleared in time to see Niri fly backward only to be caught by Faelyn's air magic. The blast hit Faelyn's shield, stopping it from harming her. The intensity rippled the outer shield along the length of the entire building.

Breathing hard, Bastien's arms gave out, and he collapsed onto a solid wood floor. All the woodchips were gone, blown into a radius around him. She'd entered his mind. The one place he was always safe. The only thing no one could exploit.

"I'm sorry. I... didn't know how else to get you out." He lifted his head. "Queen Faelyn, are you hurt?"

"It's all right." Niri dusted woodchips from her black robe. "We were prepared. It means you are similar to Queen Faelyn, in that your magic is purely elemental."

Joy shot through his exhausted body. They were the same.

Queen Faelyn crouched and placed her hand on his forehead. Her touch sent a thrill radiating through him that wasn't just from the magic. He met her eyes as her whole being radiated with a glow like when he'd first seen her in Docimer. Her magic entered his body, adding strength and energy where his magic had depleted it. He immediately felt less fatigued, and when she removed her hand, he found the strength to stand, though he wished she hadn't stepped back to Amerae's side.

"Don't be disappointed," Faelyn said. "You may not know this, but there are only a small number of mages who can control all five elements. One, in fact. You."

"Is it possible I can do more?"

Queen Faelyn paced away, and Niri answered him. "With training and consistent practice, it is almost limitless what you can do with your five elements. I will test you in other areas after you are rested and have enough stamina to sustain more."

"Niri, Bastien, I am needed elsewhere," Queen Faelyn said.

Bastien bowed, but she didn't see. She'd already turned her back and hurried out the door with Amerae, lessening the irresistible draw between them.

Niri walked toward the door. "I will continue to teach you while you are training as a soldier. After that, your path could take many turns, but for now, expect me every day."

Bastien trudged back to the bunker, stopping only long enough to eat dinner. He fell into bed before any of the others returned, a mixture of emotions warring inside him. Niri had opened his mind and explored it. She did it to push him to respond with magic, but the rawness left behind hurt. His whole life had been nothing but a series of bad decisions, but at the time he'd thought he knew best. He'd come so far from where he thought he'd be, and yet not far enough.

The lingering feel of Queen Faelyn's hand on his forehead and the strength of her magic made him smile. Maybe the Fates were real. Maybe his bad decisions and unfortunate circumstances had to be made to let him end up here. After his Fating, as Niri called it, and the pull he felt toward the queen, he couldn't deny there was a purpose for all this. And they seemed open to teaching him, not holding him back like Micah did—who only allowed him to learn what the gang needed.

Despite that, he hoped Tave and the gang were okay, even if they were another bad decision in a long line of unluckiness. Bastien couldn't allow Niri to look into him like that again. He may not have been able to find a way to push her out, but maybe he could prevent her from getting in.

Over the next two weeks, Bastien had lessons with Niri every day, each day focusing on a specific element. She said once he mastered those individually, then he'd learn ways to combine them, so instead of making it rain, he could make it storm. And instead of a ball of fire, he could make a tornado of flame. He pestered her every day to teach him more and more, soaking it all up.

Though his stamina improved, he was always left exhausted. Luckily, he slept like the dead and woke refreshed for drills and training. They moved him up from the new recruits ahead of schedule. He filed in with more seasoned sword fighters and took solid beatings for a week before holding his own again.

Every time Queen Faelyn visited, he felt the draw to her, but he didn't see her after that first day with Niri. She never came to another session. Still, he threw everything he had into becoming stronger, faster, and more powerful. Next time she came, he'd be someone worth noticing.

CHAPTER

TWENTY-THREE

Amerae left her post beside the throne room doors and walked up the aisle. "Permission to speak, my queen?"

Faelyn narrowed her eyes, and Amerae smirked. Amerae knew she despised the formalities.

"Lord Kian asked that I survey the compound this afternoon and report to you my findings," Amerae said. "I will go now and return shortly."

"Will you be back in time to prepare for the feast?" There was always another feast, especially now that they were entertaining their royal guest, and Amerae's presence comforted her.

"Yes, of course."

Faelyn rose and descended the dais. "Then I'm coming with you."

Amerae frowned infinitesimally. "Yes, my queen."

Faelyn sensed Kian's displeasure as she left the throne room, but he didn't say anything. Her knees bounced the entire carriage ride over, and though Amerae looked pointedly at them, she didn't comment.

They couldn't stay long, but she removed her skirt and buckled

176

on her sword. The more the soldiers viewed her as one of them—a strong leader capable of ruling an army rather than a fawning weakling—the better.

"Faelyn. What do you hope to accomplish by spending so much time here?" Amerae walked beside her, scanning the surroundings.

"You grew up in a land of oppression," Faelyn said, having prepared herself for the questioning. "We fought side by side in the Battle of Pavora. My father may not have been the best ruler for Alysies, but Daltieri certainly was not." She scanned the new buildings and ranks of soldiers filing from task to task, absently following the pull tugging her toward the east side of the compound. "My mind no longer thinks in terms of years, but decades. We were unprepared when Daltieri came before. My memories of that day haunt me. So many people I loved were taken from me, while our guards and small numbers were decimated." She shook her head. "We won't be unprepared again."

But it was more than that now. There was no denying to herself that she went to see him. Bastien. He was a part of her, in a way she couldn't explain.

Amerae remained silent—they'd reached the main training area where too many ears might hear the way Amerae was allowed to speak to the queen. Regardless, Faelyn sensed her pain. Amerae was the daughter of a prominent lord in Faelyn's realm, but Daltieri's reach had been boundless.

After they passed the troops, all doing well, the pull led her to the large clearing before the outer wall, a large field of grass perfect for Niri's lessons. Without Faelyn's help, Niri was forced to train Bastien in the clearing instead of the training hall, lest he accidentally set fire to it. Even from the outskirts, the magic he emanated was palpable.

Niri stood before Bastien in her black robe, red hair bound tight to her head. She nodded, pleased. Bastien gripped his glowing staff pointed above him. He'd formed a tiny rain cloud, which dripped down on his head.

Faelyn's lips twitched. Her fingers tingled with remembrance of the touch on his skin.

"Now, add lightning," Niri said.

"You may want to advise him to move the cloud from over his head first, Niri." Faelyn walked toward them, Amerae by her side.

Niri winked, and Faelyn chortled.

Bastien stumbled forward and looked over with wide eyes. The cloud condensed into thick drops that plopped down on him, matting his long hair to his blue vest.

Faelyn laughed out loud, earning a surprised look from Amerae. Faelyn coughed. She held the laughter inside, and it bubbled through her from head to toe, forcing a smile.

Bastien's eyes softened, and his lips curved into a matching smile.

"Try again, Bastien," Niri said, rather sternly.

Bastien turned away, nodding. His staff lit up, and the water floated up from his hair and clothes, reforming a new cloud that drifted away from him. Niri glanced up in alarm as it approached her, and scooted back several feet.

"Okay, adding lightning." Bastien took a deep breath and closed his eyes.

Faelyn sensed the magic building within him, his face thick with the strain of the effort. He gathered light and energy to form the lightning. It was a complicated trick, especially while continually feeding water into the cloud so it would rain. Bastien continued to master his magic at a much faster rate than Faelyn had.

It wouldn't need much, just a little to create enough lightning for his small cloud.

Bastien collected what he needed, but then he didn't stop.

Too much, too much. Faelyn looked to Niri, who shook her head.

Niri didn't want her to interfere. The magic built. Did Niri realize how much he had?

Amerae's hair rose to the sky, and her eyes widened.

"Niri," Faelyn said in warning.

"It's all right, my queen." Niri stared at Bastien, knees bent, leaning forward.

Bastien's staff blazed, casting shadows that overrode the sun's intensity.

The hair on Faelyn's arms stood. "No," she hissed. Someone was going to get hurt. She pulled her magic forward, forming the beginnings of a shield to contain the coming destruction.

Bastien released his magic. A bolt of lightning as thick as a tree struck the ground between him and Niri. Faelyn threw her small shield around Amerae and braced for impact.

A shield not of her making formed around her.

Bastien and Niri shot backward off their feet from the blast. Deafening thunder crashed outward, rumbling buildings, sending tiles spilling from rooftops. When the rumbling finally ceased, the entire compound—weapons clanging, soldiers repeating orders—plunged into stunned silence.

Faelyn looked down. The force of the blast hadn't touched her. Even the sound of the thunder has been muffled. She looked up right into Bastien's eyes where he lay on the ground. He released the shield he'd placed around her and passed out.

"Queen Faelyn!" Amerae cried out, running to her side.

"Tend to Niri." Faelyn kept her eyes locked on Bastien. He'd shielded her, sacrificing himself to the force of his own magic.

"This was foolish," Faelyn said under her breath, marching to him. It was admirable, a soldier protecting his queen, but he was the one who put her in danger.

She passed the smoking hole his lightning had created in the ground—at least two feet wide and too deep to see the bottom. Footsteps pounded toward the clearing, accompanied by the roar of thousands of soldiers ready for battle.

"Am, head them off," Faelyn shouted.

Amerae left Niri standing next to the hole and ran to meet the army.

Faelyn knelt beside Bastien. His face was relaxed into the restorative peace of sleep, having expended so much energy. Too much. His hair draped over his neck, and his lashes swept his cheeks. Faelyn reached out and placed her hand against his forehead. Just like the first time, the warmth of him—his skin and his essence—filled her palm and spread through her being. Her magic strengthened, as if fed by the pull to him. She'd craved that feeling without realizing it. Pouring magic into him, she found no injury, but sensed the core of who he was underneath the thief—a man with a kind heart and a great capacity to love. She removed her hand, and he didn't stir.

Faelyn straightened and turned her anger toward Niri. "What were you thinking?"

"I'm sorry, Your Majesty. I thought I could contain the blast." Niri approached, panting.

"What do you mean?" The words spat angrily out of her.

"We needed a new well. I tasked him with creating one without using earth magic. That's what he came up with, but I added the cloud as a challenge in combining different elements of magic. I would never endanger you, my queen." Niri bowed low, and the sight stopped Faelyn short.

Her friends shouldn't be cowed enough to bow. Niri had offered her friendship and a warm place to sleep when Faelyn had nearly no one. "Rise, Niri. I shouldn't have become angry. But we cannot continue Bastien's lessons while he is in the compound."

To punctuate her point, she turned to the outskirt of the clearing. The soldiers lined the field, swords unsheathed, faces drawn in a mixture of angry malice and confusion, held at bay by their captains. Amerae gestured wildly, speaking to Commander Rane.

Faelyn stepped toward them and took a deep breath. Every soul quieted, all attention on her.

"My fellow Alysians." Her voice expanded among the ranks, carried by the wind, reaching even the soldiers bottlenecked between the buildings. "You've made me proud today. You've proven yourselves ready to respond to any immediate threat to our kingdom. I couldn't be happier. If this were a real event, our enemies would be quaking in fear." The tension shifted with her words, lessening as the soldiers learned there was no real danger. "We used our magic to create a new water well for our growing numbers, and it created a thunder like no other. All is well. Return to your tasks with my love."

The captains yelled orders, and the soldiers sheathed their swords and filed in line as they were trained to do.

Commander Rane ignored Amerae and approached Faelyn, brows drawn and shoulders bunched. "Your Majesty, this cannot happen again." Words full of anger, he looked at Niri who had her hands on her hips. "The compound is no place for magic."

Amerae stepped forward, mouth open, but Faelyn held up her hand.

"I agree, Commander. Further magic training must take place outside the compound, or within the mage dome." She stepped forward, throwing heat into her words. "But you will not speak to me as you speak to the soldiers, even when tension is high."

Commander Rane's eyes narrowed, but then he bowed. "Yes, my queen. I apologize."

He stayed bowed until Faelyn released him. She and Amerae watched until he was gone, then Amerae approached. "I don't like the way he spoke to you, Faelyn. My father would never, even when he didn't believe you were the queen."

Amerae's father, Lord Calem, had spoken much harshly, and with much more disrespect, but now was not the time to bring that up.

"Commander Rane commands the respect of the army." Faelyn faced her friend. "And mine. He's loyal."

She walked back to Bastien, Niri at his side. "Don't heal him. Let him sleep it off. Amerae and I need to return for the feast. You should be there too, Niri. Have someone take him to his bunk, then join us."

Niri gave a shallow bow, and it was full of apology and guilt.

Later after the feast, though she'd been doing her best to avoid him, Kian finally cornered her into dancing. Prince Rory had danced with her most of the night, but had just departed to rest. Being near him wasn't getting easier as she'd hoped. If anything, her revulsion to him was growing.

"I've heard you had an eventful visit to the compound this afternoon," Kian said. He looked regal in his blue tailored tunic with silver buttons and a blue cape.

Faelyn's heart leaped for no apparent reason. She forced a sigh. "Don't worry, I've forbidden Niri to train Bastien at the compound." Her gaze drifted to the window, seeing only a reflection of whirling colors from the dancers, and blackness beyond.

"So the thief has a name, then?"

She scoffed. "Hardly, though he did almost destroy the compound with his cocky overconfidence."

"Yes, I heard that, too." He squeezed her hand, regaining her attention. "You've been to the compound a lot lately."

"Yes, and after today, I'm confident we will be prepared for an attack, should Daltieri act on their war preparations."

What else could she say? That she was magically drawn to a thief? Maybe even more than magically? The words alone could jeopardize her agreement with Prince Rory and her kingdom's safety. At least the prince didn't question her time spent away. Too busy playing his own games, most likely.

Kian gave a non-committal grunt but didn't comment further. Neither did she.

TWENTY-FOUR

Bastien awoke thirstier and more rested than he'd ever been. The now-familiar snores of the men settled him, reminding him of nights sleeping at the House. He sat up and blinked at the jug of water on his trunk at the foot of his bed. Niri must have known he'd need it. He drank it to the last drop, then headed to the showers. Predawn fog coated the ground outside, chilling the air. He had missed the rest of the day sleeping. If he didn't get an early start, he could only imagine what Captain Flinn would say. He might even get sent back to the new recruits after what happened yesterday. The soldiers had been in an uproar over his magic.

Niri would vouch for him.

Hopefully.

Bastien had been so sure he could contain the force of the lightning he'd called down. It had to be big to make any kind of hole in the earth. He groaned and scrubbed his face. The warm water washed the soap and grime away. *Ugh.* Queen Faelyn had come to monitor his progress, and instead of showing her how good he'd become, he'd put her in danger.

He pulled the lever to turn off the water. After dressing, he headed to the training yard, one of the first to arrive. He grabbed a practice sword and ran through the drills. His feet stepped into the familiar patterns he'd worked on for weeks. His arms swung and jabbed the sword almost by memory. The trainers' instructions plagued his dreams and repeated in his head like a tune he couldn't shake, though he didn't want to. He never would have thought precise foot placement would make a difference, but when he dueled one on one, the motions faded into the background of the fight, giving him room to concentrate on the opponent's next move, or their weaknesses. It helped he was the fastest of the bunch, now that he was in shape and fed regularly.

"Bastien boy," Captain Flinn called from behind. "That was some show you put on yesterday." As nice as the words sounded, the captain's tone begged Bastien approach with caution.

Bastien straightened from his fighting crouch and turned around. He'd never had a problem with the captain before, even when he'd shown up with long hair. As a rule, magic made non-magic folk nervous. Hopefully, being a captain in Queen Faelyn's army, Flinn wouldn't hold what had happened against him, though it didn't look good. The captain's chest puffed out, arms crossing and mustache twitching as the sun's rays lit the sky.

"I'm sorry, Captain Flinn." Bastien avoided his eyes like he did the guards back in Docimer. It was best not to cross people when they acted like they had something to prove, not when he finally had something to lose.

The soldiers began arriving, grabbing swords and eyeing Bastien, avoiding the captain except to say a quick 'good morning.'

The captain's mouth twitched, and it was almost a sneer. "I was informed there will be no more magic training for you. You're just one of us now."

Bastien breathed in through his nose. One mistake, and they'd taken the best part of his day away. "Is that so?"

"You could have destroyed the whole compound. The entire army came running to our queen's aid." The captain shouldered his gleaming blade and approached at an exaggerated drawl.

Bastien mumbled another apology. The whole army? No wonder the captain was pissed.

Captain Flinn acted like he didn't hear him. "You must think you're pretty amazing, I bet. With your magic, and with the general advancing you through the ranks."

Bastien scratched his neck. What could he say? The captain was itching for a fight. A dozen sarcastic retorts came to mind, but he wouldn't be goaded. "I'm just trying to do my best to serve Alysies. It was an accident that won't happen again."

Captain Flinn bared his teeth. He stuck his nose in Bastien's face, poking him with his greasy mustache. "The amazing Bastien interrupted my training schedule and put my queen in danger. And no one endangers my queen." His voice was lethally calm. "Let's prove how good you are. You can fight me." A slow grin promising pain spread over his hard face. "Now."

There was no point in arguing. The captain was in for blood and wouldn't be satisfied until he got it. His big arms and reputation said he was very good, though Bastien had never seen him fight. If Bastien didn't get beaten bloody, maybe everyone would learn to overlook his mage skills and finally accept him as part of the army.

The captain waved Bastien toward a sparring circle, so he walked ahead, carting his weapon. The soldiers who'd merely stared before now gathered around with eagerness, beckoning to those who just arrived. They should have been called to drills by now. The other captains must be in on it.

Bastien tensed, readying for the coming pain. He was used to pain.

He stepped into the white circle and turned to face his opponent. The captain raised his sword, shining steel gleaming in the morning light.

Bastien leaned forward, wielding his wooden practice sword. "You're going to use that in a spar, Captain?"

The men and women around them quieted to mumbles, some shuffling their boots over the dry dirt.

"Surely the captain won't fight him with a real sword," his old sparring partner, Dalton, said quietly. Those around him nodded their agreement.

"Bastien the Amazing can handle it, can't you?" Captain Flinn said.

"No. It's not a fair fight." He'd dealt with bullies like Flinn all his life. Everyone, even the captain himself, knew this fight was wrong. "Get my staff and I'll show you a fair fight."

"Fair is what I say it is for Kestrean spies." Captain Flinn gripped his sword and charged.

The soldiers erupted into cheers.

"I'm no spy." Is that what Flinn believed? Bastien leaned forward, raising his sword. His weight rested on the balls of his feet. He'd have to end this quick, or his sword could be cleaved in two—or worse. Despite himself, his heart pounded.

The captain jabbed. Bastien barely whacked it away on the broad side. Quick as a flash, Bastien struck the captain in his armored torso and then ducked a swing. The captain recovered and swiped toward Bastien's back.

Bastien twisted away and raised his sword. The captain's metal sword sank into the wood. Stuck. Their eyes met for the briefest moment. Captain Flinn had never liked him, but now accused him of being a spy. He had to win this fight.

The captain yanked hard. Bastien yanked as well as he kicked out with one leg, hitting the captain's chest. He gave his stuck sword a slight twist, and the combination ripped Flinn's sword out of his grip. It fell to the ground. Both men lunged for it. Bastien wrapped his hand around the hilt just as the captain reached it.

Bastien scrambled up, pointing both swords at the captain. "I'm not a spy," he panted. "That place is no home to me." He'd gotten so lucky. If he hadn't managed to disarm Flinn, the bout would have ended in pain.

The soldiers went silent.

Captain Flinn rose to his feet, lips pulled back over clenched teeth. "You've made a mistake, boy." The words were low, pulsating with barely restrained rage.

Chrisso stepped to the ring, shaking his head and frowning at Bastien.

He'd won, but something told him he'd lost.

The soldiers around him whispered. "Never touch his sword." "Dead man walking."

Bastien threw down both swords like they'd caught fire. He carefully smoothed back the hair that had gotten loose and held his tongue.

Captain Flinn pointed to two men. "You and you. Grab him."

Two soldiers from the crowd took Bastien's arms. He kept his gaze on the captain and did not resist.

"Let's go," Bear said, grabbing rougher than necessary.

Of course it'd be Bear. Bastien could almost feel the smirk on the big guy's face as his words from their first meeting flashed in his mind. 'He's just a common thief.'

Captain Flinn led them away from the training yard. Many followed until the other captains ordered them back. Bastien sensed Chrisso still trailing them. No one spoke as they eventually came to a busier part of the compound. Not the prison, as Bastien expected. The merchant corner. Here there were all sorts of merchants selling wares, blacksmiths forging horseshoes and weapons, trinkets, trifles, and treats to be had. Bastien had no need to come here as pardoned prisoners didn't get paid.

The captain stopped next to the back of a line of soldiers. "You'll wait here." His voice was eerily calm.

Bear's face split with a crooked-tooth grin.

Bastien peered ahead. He knew this line. Dread dropped into the pit of his stomach.

"I've been thinking, Bastien the Amazing. You'd be much prettier without all that hair the boys say you're so fond of," Captain Flinn said.

Bastien stiffened, the pit in his stomach spreading like ice through his veins. He should have lost that fight. Now he'd be humiliated just like he'd humiliated Captain Flinn.

More than that.

The captain narrowed his eyes, and the soldiers tightened their grip. "Don't let him leave." He stepped closer. "This is an order you will obey, soldier."

Bastien's entire body tensed as the line moved ahead. Four people stood in front of him now, with one man already perched on a stool where a barber took scissors to his dark hair. A sizeable pile of various colors had already gathered, scattered amongst the dirt.

Bastien backed away, but Bear and the other guard grabbed his arms, squeezing hard.

"You're not cutting my hair." Bastien licked his dry lips.

"You'll do as you're told, or I'll have you sent back to prison." Captain Flinn crossed his arms.

Bastien ripped his arm from one soldier, straining against Bear's grip on his other. "You'll have to throw me in prison then, because there's no way in the Hereafter you bastards are coming within an inch of my hair."

The captain placed his fingers in his mouth and let out an ear-piercing whistle.

Two more burly men appeared out of the gathered onlookers. Curious eyes flashed their way.

Chrisso finally stepped forward, alternating his gaze between Bastien and the barber. "We tried to tell you. It's just hair; it'll grow back. The captain will only make your life hell if you cause trouble."

"Hold him steady." Bear shoved Bastien toward the burly men—trained guards meant for unruly soldiers, not ungraduated trainees.

The new men grabbed Bastien on either side, their grips crushing. Bastien twisted and jumped, fighting against their hold.

One of them pulled a knife and held the blade against Bastien's manhood. "Best do what the captain tells you."

Bastien went still. He seethed, teeth clenched and mind racing for a way out of this. He could not allow his hair to be cut.

The men laughed. Chrisso rubbed the back of his neck.

The knife was withdrawn but held at the ready as they walked him forward in line, ahead of the other soldiers. He was forced down hard on the stool, a man on either side of him, the knife pointed between his legs.

Bastien glared at the captain, baring his teeth. He'd never hated a man more.

"If you get any ideas of struggling, you'll lose something far more valuable than hair." Captain Flinn smiled and clapped the soldier with the knife on the shoulder.

Bastien kept his heated gaze steady on him as the barber controlled his surprise and prepared his scissors.

Bastien was going to lose his hair—his shield and the only tie to his past, and to Miss Bannings, the woman who'd been like a mother to him—and there was nothing he could do about it. Though, he couldn't be held accountable for what happened after they were done.

The barber, a slight man with sweat beading on his forehead, held the scissors aloft, hesitating.

"Get on with it, man. He ain't gonna hurt you. Are you, pretty boy?" knife-guard said.

Bastien held his tongue, heart racing in his ears.

The barber stepped behind Bastien, then lifted his ponytail. With a sickening snip and a thump, it was gone, landing in the pile on the ground. Bastien's remaining hair, now chin-length, cascaded down around his face. The men chuckled.

Bastien had seen how short the other men had their hair cut. Just above the ears. He breathed in and out slowly through his teeth. Soon it'd be over, and the captain would realize his mistake.

The barber shot a nervous glance at Bastien, then started on one side, cutting his hair short bit by bit.

When the barber reached Bastien's ear, he gasped and dropped the scissors. They hit the dirt as Bastien's heart raced double.

Bastien locked eyes with him.

"You... you..." The barber's hands shook.

A fierce grin took over Bastien's face. "Get on with it."

The barber's head shook, mouth opening and closing without words.

"What's the problem, man?" Captain Flinn shoved Chrisso aside and came closer.

The barber's hand shook in violent tremors as he pointed. "F-f-f... Fae."

The captain's eyes narrowed, then he grabbed the fistful of hair still covering Bastien's ear, and yanked it up. Bastien kept still, eyes shooting daggers ahead of him.

The captain dropped Bastien's hair like it had burned him, but everyone had already seen.

His darkest secret.

His pointed ears.

Exposed.

The world stood still, and Bastien's heart rate evened out. Shouts of surprise came from all around them. Conversations trickled down both directions of the market street. Bastien leaned down slowly and picked the scissors from the ground. He placed them back into the barber's protesting hands.

"Do it." His words swelled to fill their stunned circle.

The captain, Bear, Chrisso, the burly guards, all had dropped jaws and not a menacing word from a one of them.

The barber gulped and glanced at the captain who stood frozen, staring at Bastien with a hand on his sword. The barber raised the scissors, resuming his cutting while battling his shaking hands.

Now he truly had nothing left to lose. His life, his freedom, his integrity, his promise to Olin, and his deepest secret laid bare for all the world to see.

Bear recovered first, taking a step back. "This doesn't change anything. You're still a petty thief."

Knife-guard sheathed his weapon.

Chrisso shook his head and whispered, "How could this be?"

The barber finished the haircut, brushing loose pieces off Bastien's tunic with reverent-like movements.

Bastien ran a hand through the short tresses. His fingers expected to feel his hair run between them, but it was gone. Gone was the hair the woman who'd loved him as a mother had insisted he keep to protect him from ridicule and persecution. Gone was the shield for his secret.

Bastien stood, strands falling from his lap.

Captain Flinn stared at him with a calculating look. "I found him. He's mine."

Bastien tensed.

"I see you thinking of running. You're coming with me." Captain Flinn launched himself at Bastien, arms encircling him. They landed hard. The captain grabbed for his sword, but Bastien ripped it from the scabbard and threw it aside. He wouldn't give Flinn the satisfaction of becoming his freak prize.

Bastien twisted out of the captain's grip and punched him hard in the jaw. The captain rolled, throwing him off. They scrambled to their feet, circling each other with raised fists.

A group of men surrounded them, but no one yelled or cheered like before. Instead, they murmured and pointed.

The captain threw his weight into a punch to Bastien's ribs, but Bastien ducked and kicked the captain in the knee, knocking him off his feet.

"That's enough." Chrisso jumped between them, but he directed his words to the captain. "How can you fight someone who's fae like our beloved queen?"

Bastien ignored his throbbing hand.

Captain Flinn spat blood. "He's not worthy of the name. Guards, arrest him for treason."

Bastien shifted, fists and shoulders tensed. "Treason?" First, he was a spy, and now he was committing treason?

The two burly guards grabbed him. One of them held his hands behind his back, though they weren't as rough as before. Almost hesitant.

Bastien struggled in their grip. "For the way I look?" He sneered in disgust. He'd been right to cover them up as a kid. It was what he'd always suspected would happen growing up in Kestrea. Their fear outweighed their faith.

The captain straightened, casually dusting off his uniform. "For attacking an officer." His frown spread into a smirk.

Dread washed over Bastien, chasing his controlled anger away. The captain had what he needed to ruin everything, and everyone would know Bastien for the criminal he was. Faelyn would know too.

The guards started to pull him away.

"Wait." Captain Flinn held up a hand. He drew the guard's dagger, grabbed Bastien's arm, and cut it before Bastien could pull away.

"Acantha above!" Burning pain stole his breath. Blood seeped, soaking his new shirt. He cradled his arm against him, glaring at the captain.

Chrisso gaped in horror.

Captain Flinn yanked Bastien's hand forward and shoved his sleeve up, revealing the slice in his arm.

Bastien locked his teeth and stared the captain down, even as he felt the wound begin to knit itself closed.

Chrisso gasped. "He's healing without a mage staff."

The captain gave a satisfied smile and shoved Bastien's arm back at him. "Mystery solved."

Chrisso stepped to get a closer look. "You didn't know. How'd you know he'd be able to heal himself?"

"Intuition, my boy. Every *good* captain's got it."

He'd always been a quick healer. It wasn't until he'd used his powers with Tave that his healing accelerated. The magic worked with or without his staff, allowing him to recover quickly from the brutal training and aiding in his advancement.

It was the one thing his tight rein on the magic that had always been there could not keep at bay.

"Take him to the queen." Captain Flinn said.

The queen? Bastien took a shuddering breath. What would Queen Faelyn do when she found out he'd hidden the truth? What would she think when she learned he'd fought a captain in her army?

Chrisso's eyes went wide. "Captain Flinn. The queen? Shouldn't Bastien be taken to the prison? Or maybe just let him go?" He rubbed his hands over each other.

"After attacking an officer? I don't have to explain myself to a subordinate," the captain snapped.

The murmuring around him grew. More soldiers appeared between stalls and buildings, all trying to get a glimpse. Even from a distance, they stopped to stare. People ran off to tell others. Chrisso, who'd seemed eager for friendship before, remained silent. Bear stood off to the side with his arms crossed, eyes avoiding them.

"Does the queen know?" "I bet they're fake." "Can he do magic?" "Did you see how fast he healed himself?" "How old is he?"

The captain scanned the crowd. "The queen does not tolerate fighting within our ranks," he said a little louder. "She will be informed of this," he gestured to Bastien's ears, "matter at once."

Heads nodded around the crowd.

"At once," the captain repeated.

The soldiers made a path, and the guards hauled Bastien toward the castle.

It was over.

CHAPTER
TWENTY-FIVE

"Queen Faelyn, His Highness Prince Rory understands your position and that your time is valuable," Prince Rory's messenger said, eyes downcast. "I'm simply here at Prince Rory's behest to beg you keep to your appointments with him." The man bowed his head lower.

Low whispers broke out around the long throne room, echoing off the stone walls.

It was a struggle to hold her tongue in front of Prince Rory's representative and her court. The insolence of him to send a messenger to her throne. But, she couldn't argue that she'd allowed herself to be preoccupied from her time with the prince.

"Tell Prince Rory I will see him at dinner." Her words rang flat, but accomplished much. By not reacting to the insult, her courtiers would see she was willing to bend for this union.

Prince Rory's messenger bowed and backed down the aisle, somehow managing not to veer off the path. The doors closed behind him, and Faelyn sagged with relief.

Kian approached the dais and bowed on one knee.

Faelyn pursed her lips. "Please rise, Lord Kian, and there's no need to speak because I already know what you're going to say."

"Oh?" He smiled. "Does your magical repertoire include mind reading now?"

"I'll never tell," she said with humor in her voice. The tension broke in the room, and more people tentatively smiled. The air became easier to breathe.

Kian raised an eyebrow.

Amerae giggled from beside the throne. Even the guards grinned from their posts.

A smile spread on Faelyn's face. There was nothing better than being surrounded by good friends.

"As your top advisor, I would be remiss if I didn't say it regardless." He lowered his voice. "I know you're busy, but you need to spend more time with His Highness. It may never be the relationship you've always wanted, but if you could be friends, you'd be much happier."

A sigh escaped her lips. "I will, Kian. I will. He's going to be here for a while before returning to Docimer. There's time yet. Meanwhile, I can't ignore my people or the needs of my kingdom."

The throne room doors opened, and a guard rushed in.

"See?" She winked at Kian, who scowled and stepped off the runner.

The guard, Colin, made a hasty bow, then walked as fast as he could without running the rest of the way to the dais. Faelyn's smile dropped as Colin's excitement and distress washed over her.

"Tell me." She nodded to Nolan, who nodded back and disappeared through a side door. He would be her eyes and ears if anything was amiss outside the throne room.

"Your Majesty, forgive the intrusion, but Captain Flinn is on his way. He says he brings a prisoner to see you."

Faelyn rose, her heavy gown sweeping against her legs. "And why would Captain Flinn bring a prisoner here? It's almost receiving time."

Colin, young for his position, lowered his eyes. "The soldier attacked him openly, and—"

"Why wasn't he taken to the prison?" She clenched her fists, then gasped at a familiar pull to her soul.

Bastien was near. Bastien was in the castle.

Colin began to reply.

Faelyn raised her hand "No. Let them enter." *What has he done?*

The guard was halfway through his bow when Captain Flinn strutted into the room wearing a smug smile beneath an overgrown mustache. Three people stood behind him. The captain bowed low, and Faelyn's heart stopped. For the length of one breath, her heart was as silent as the rest of the room.

She locked onto pale blue eyes that pleaded for understanding and acceptance. An eternity passed while her gaze moved to his hair, so short, revealing such handsome features in the curve of his jaw, and the strength of his neck.

The point of his elongated ears.

Her heart resumed double.

"Bastien..." Her fists loosened to limp things at her sides. Another fae? Someone else like her? How could this be?

Captain Flinn rose, and his smirk grew bigger as he paced forward. The guards holding Bastien forced him into a bow, then pulled him up and followed their captain.

Bastien's eyes never left hers.

Kian's staff lit up beside her. The room throbbed with conversation.

"Fae." "Fae." "Fae." "Fae."

"He's fae, like the queen!"

Faelyn nearly clapped her hands over her ears. The air was thick with the profoundness of that moment.

At the bottom of the dais, Captain Flinn bowed again. "Your Majesty, thank you for granting me audience."

"Captain Flinn." The words came out a whisper. Faelyn cleared her throat and sat, weakness shaking her knees. "I understand an infraction has been made against you." *His ears. His elemental magic. The invisible pull to him.*

"Yes, Your Majesty." The captain's essence made it clear he was enjoying his little reveal. "I was leading the prisoner in a training exercise—"

"Captain Flinn. What is the procedure for infractions against a leader in my army?"

Bastien opened his mouth, but Faelyn snapped her eyes to him, and he closed it. His gaze captured her, even as the captain replied.

"I wanted to deliver my discovery to you personally, Your Majesty. No doubt something of this importance needed to be made aware immediately. And rumors are that he's a Kestrean spy. Of course, if it was a simple infraction, I would have reported to my general." He bowed his head and stayed there, waiting for her to speak.

This was one of her least favorite parts, being groveled to. People ignoring protocol to vie for her attention and approval. The captain was using Bastien to gain her favor. She gazed into Bastien's soft blue eyes. As much as she burned with questions, she couldn't ignore protocol either. Captain Flinn claimed he was attacked, and Bastien was already on probation as a convicted prisoner.

"Captain Flinn, though your intentions weren't entirely selfless, I am choosing to ignore your breach of protocol. You are dismissed."

"But…" The captain balked.

Faelyn narrowed her eyes, and he bowed and retreated with only a backward glance.

Bastien's smooth, easy smile tugged at the corner of his mouth. He thought he was free.

"Guards, throw Bastien into the castle dungeon to await sentencing. And be careful, he's not a typical mage. He can access magic without a staff." And had pretended otherwise this whole time.

The guards hauled Bastien out of the throne room. His face closed into hardness, as if he wasn't surprised. As if he was used to expecting the worst. She glanced at Kian, but he was already moving to follow.

She forced her breathing to even out when they were gone and resisted the urge to rush after him. He was like her. He'd somehow hidden who he really was from everyone. Did that mean he was truly a Kestrean spy? The sickening sense of betrayal that swept down from her mind was stopped short by the feeling in her heart. That she could trust him. That she could lean on him, depend on him.

But, was his lack of understanding of his capabilities all an act? She was a fool for not digging deeper into his past, but that would be shortly remedied.

Bastien's anger slowly faded, replaced by disappointment. The guards hauled him down several flights of winding stone staircases, tripping him and roughing him up along the way. He'd never wanted to prove someone wrong more than Queen Faelyn. She'd thought him a simple street thief, a common criminal. He'd been so close to proving her wrong, and now he'd ruined it. The connection he felt to her in the throne room, it was real, and for a moment her eyes sparkled like she'd felt it too. But maybe not. He should have told her the truth about himself from the beginning.

The urge to reach up and run his hands through his short hair was hampered by the cold manacles once again around his wrists. Alysies had not been kind to him. Life had not been kind.

A hooded guard met them at the bottom of a dark, torch-lit dungeon. They chose a cell at the back, passing only empty spaces. At least it was bars and not solid metal this time. They tossed him in, and he turned in time to see the door slam closed. The loud echo hadn't stopped by the time the glow of a mage staff lit up the hall and the queen's mage stepped into view.

Bastien had seen him in the throne room, felt the probing of magic, as he did now. The mage had frowned at how long Faelyn's gaze lingered, though it had made Bastien's heart swell with hope.

The guards left, and only Bastien, the mage, and the expectant silence remained. The mage's magic tingled across his skin, then the manacles dropped from his wrists. Bastien rubbed them, nodding his thanks. Something told him not to speak first. The magic trailed up his spine and into his head. He tensed to have his memories assaulted, but it was nothing so deep. Only surface things, such as his emotions, were evaluated.

The mage appeared to be in his forties, with short, graying hair, which didn't mean much since mages lived longer lives. His stern eyes spoke of a man who wouldn't take Bastien's antics and promised pain if Queen Faelyn was in danger. Best to be honest with this one.

The mage wore fine clothes, silks in the royal Alysies blue, but no mage robe. He was more to Faelyn than just a mere mage, then. His stance was aggressive, feet apart, scowling as his magic worked unabashedly. He was protecting the queen, loyal to the queen. She trusted him to be here in her stead, to evaluate the man with her same fae traits.

Bastien's stance relaxed, and his jaw unclenched. He'd get nowhere with Faelyn if he got nowhere with her mage. Her friend.

"I see now we're getting somewhere." The mage's scowl turned to a simple frown of distrust. "Who are you and where did you come from, really?"

Bastien took a small step forward over the dusty ground. "I swear I mean the queen no harm. I understand you have no reason to trust me, but I'm loyal to her, as you are. My only wish is to do good by her and prove my place in her army."

"And you show that by openly attacking one of her officers?" His voice was more dangerous than curious.

"I didn't attack him. He ordered me to a duel and I won." Only a slight omission, really.

A second, stronger magical probing alerted him to Niri's presence. "I believe him." The glow of her staff preceded her as she stepped into view, red hair swept back in a tight bun.

Bastien cast her a timid smile, but Faelyn's mage looked unconvinced.

"Tell me about him, Niri. What do you know?"

"His name is Bastien. He's an orphan born and raised in the capital city of Docimer in Kestrea. He joined a street gang at a young age, but was arrested for assaulting the gang leader. He escaped from prison with the help of a notorious thief and trained in rudimentary magecraft until we captured him attempting to rob Prince Rory's treasury on a caravan."

Well, when laid bare like that, he doubted anyone could trust him, let alone a queen. Bastien crossed his arms. Niri couldn't know all that. He'd maybe told her half. What else had she gleaned while invading his memories?

Niri placed a hand on the mage's tight grip around his staff. Her voice was low, but Bastien heard. "I've worked closely with him for weeks now. I trust him, Kian." In barely a whisper, she added, "He's a Fater. He's seen a glimpse of the future I've verified is true. Our queen is going to need him by her side."

Bastien kept his face carefully neutral. Did she know he could hear?

Kian's frown only deepened. Niri's words had no effect except to piss him off further.

He stepped away from Niri's touch. "You lied about who you are. Why didn't you tell anyone about your fae heritage?" His voice was a challenge that dared Bastien to back down.

"I learned from a very young age to hide my traits. A street thief shouldn't draw attention to himself."

Kian stepped to the bars. "And a soldier shouldn't lie to his queen."

"Deceit was not my intention. Say what you will, but for once I'm sure of my fate." The words had never felt truer. "I must be allowed to train in the army. For Queen Faelyn." He closed his lips. He hadn't meant to say her name with such tenderness.

Kian narrowed his eyes. "Your fate is my discretion. You'll rot here until I know who you are and I'm certain of Queen Faelyn's safety." He turned. "Can he do magic without a staff?"

Niri clasped her hands, quivering her black robe. "I don't believe so." Her eyes strayed to Bastien's ears.

"Yes, I can. But I won't." He could give them that much honesty, at least.

Kian motioned Niri to follow him. "I want round-the-clock watch," he said as they walked away.

Bastien grabbed the bars. Niri glanced back once, a worried expression on her face, then the mages were gone, taking the white mage light with them.

Bastien sighed as hurried footsteps sounded up and down the dungeon—guards no doubt clamoring to fulfill their new orders. He dropped the bars and stepped back. A woman appeared, the outline of her beautiful features twisted into hard anger as she rushed toward him. She shoved a sword between the bars, ramming the point toward his chest. He jumped back, hitting the wall.

Amerae, the queen's friend and lady-in-waiting.

"What in the Hereafter?" His heart hammered, and his magic sang unbidden in the background.

"I knew there was something off about you. I felt it when I first saw you." Her silver armor shimmered in the dungeon torchlight. She didn't withdraw her sword.

Another guard stood by, hands relaxed to his sides, watching her.

The woman stared at his ears, then locked eyes with him. Bastien knew her from somewhere, long ago. Did she hail from Docimer?

He raised his hands. "I didn't mean any harm. I promise." Being threatened by the queen's loyal entourage was getting a little tiresome.

"We'll see." She withdrew her sword, and the pair stormed away, footsteps echoing down the corridor.

He sank down to the floor. No cot, but at least it didn't smell as bad as Kingsguard Prison. What a mess he'd made. If they didn't let him out, he'd have to escape. He couldn't leave Faelyn to whatever Fate had in store.

His ears, just like mine.

"My queen?"

Faelyn looked up at the farmer in his simple dirt-stained tunic and trousers. She hadn't a clue when he'd come before her throne.

"Mr. Rosen from Lord Gilmore's southern holdings, here to plea for an extension on his taxes," her attendant loyally whispered into her ear.

Faelyn smiled. "Mr. Rosen, for what reason do you need an extension?"

He wrung his hat. "Well, Your Majesty..."

What do I do with him now? Where did he come from? Can I really trust him? Acantha above, Prince Rory can't know! Would he recognize Bastien as the boy from the stocks?

She raised her hand, cutting the farmer off. Her attendant stepped forward. "Tell Nolan I need to see him immediately."

The attendant nodded and hurried away.

"Mr. Rosen, I sympathize with your plight and will inform Lord Gilmore you have a two-month extension."

The farmer smiled, and a scribe took notes off to the side.

"Thank you, Your Majesty. You are truly wise and just." He bowed and backed slowly out of the throne room.

Nolan appeared just as the farmer left.

Faelyn stood and, holding her skirt, stepped off the dais. "Receiving is over until tomorrow." Her words reached the right people, and the attendants scurried off to send the remaining citizens on their way.

Nolan and a smattering of guards followed behind until Faelyn reached an abandoned alcove at the end of the hall. The late-afternoon sun filtered through the window's decorative glass, radiating a colorful diamond pattern on the stone floor. She stuck a slippered toe into the light, wishing for distraction in its simple warmth.

"Where is Prince Rory?" she asked.

"He went on a jaunt around the lake, Your Majesty," Nolan said. He couldn't hide the stress behind his words.

"This news needs to be kept quiet from him. Sequester those who know, and make sure they do not spread gossip." If Rory knew there was someone like her, he might feel the marriage contract was in jeopardy.

"I'm not sure that's possible, my queen." He stepped closer. "Most of the army knows already. The rumor spread quickly. Captain Flinn wasn't very quiet about it once he entered the castle. All the dungeon guards know, so all the staff probably know too."

Faelyn groaned. "So it's only a matter of time before Prince Rory hears of it, if he hasn't already."

"I'm sorry, Your Majesty."

She pulled her shoulders back. "That's alright, Nolan. How fairs our prisoner?"

"Amerae and I paid him a special visit in the dungeon." A slow smile spread on his face. "He's fine where he is. I agree an example needs to be made of him and answers found before we can trust him."

Faelyn raised an eyebrow. "Thank you, Nolan. It's so rare to hear your opinion on such things."

Nolan's jaw dropped slightly. "Forgive me, Your Majesty, I'm... Well... Can I speak to you about a personal matter that's been weighing on my mind?"

"Of course, always." Surprise colored her tone.

Nolan glanced at the guards, and they disappeared to a discreet distance. Even still, he stepped closer. Close enough to be past propriety for a captain and his queen, but like the friend he was.

"It's Am, and she'll kill me when she finds out I told you, but I'm worried." The stress behind his words was real.

Faelyn's heart picked up. "Tell me, Nolan. By queen's command, if necessary. What's wrong?"

Nolan rubbed the back of his neck. "Well, she's with child."

Faelyn gasped. "With child?"

"A few months into it, by what the physician says."

Her hand covered her mouth. "Oh, Nolan." Tears sprung to her eyes. "But why hasn't she told me?" Of course Amerae wouldn't say anything. She'd be relieved of guard duty, even if only temporarily. "Amerae! So stubborn." She laughed. "I'm so happy for you both." Faelyn threw her arms around him, taking them both by surprise.

Kian appeared from around the corner. "Him too, huh?" He threw his hands up and didn't slow his angry stride away.

Faelyn let go of Nolan, and they exchanged a happy grin. "I'll speak to her. Don't worry. Keep me updated on Bastien... the prisoner. Excuse me." She left Nolan behind and went chasing after Kian as fast as dignity would allow.

She walked passed her throne room, then rounded a corner, running right into him. She would have bounced off his chest but he caught her wrists. He dropped them a few long moments after she'd righted herself.

"What's the matter?" she asked. He hardly ever got angry. Only exasperated with her lack of attention to her own safety.

He threw a shield of air around them, ensuring no listening ears might hear. She blinked up at him.

"You're legally engaged to Prince Rory of Kestrea, right?"

She put her hands on her hips.

"Then why are you throwing yourself at so many men?"

"Nolan? He just delivered some of the best news I've had in a long time. I care for him like a brother, you know that." She took a deep breath. Kian had never been jealous before. Why would he now all of a sudden decide to act this way?

"And the fae? Bastien?"

"What are you talking about? He's locked away in the dungeon."

"I know you went to the compound to see him. Multiple times. I saw the way you looked at him in the throne room. Almost the way I'd always wished you'd looked at me." His eyes hardened. "I also heard the way he said your name when I questioned him. So, I'll ask again. What is going on?"

Faelyn's cheeks burned, and Kian looked straight at them. She turned away. "I haven't had a real chance to process everything, Kian. Fate delivered a criminal into my hands who just so happens to be a mage with powerful potential we can use." An involuntary smile pulled at her lips. "And he's like me." She turned back to Kian. "Did Niri tell you what he fated?"

Kian's jaw clenched. "He's not stepping foot out of that dungeon or one breath nearer to you until I have answers. I want to know who he really is and why he's been keeping secrets."

"I'll leave the investigation to you, then. But be kind." She patted his cheek. "He might be important to the future of my kingdom."

The banter came easy. She only hoped it had helped mask her confusion and anxiety from Kian's detection. His scowl burned the back of her dress the entire way to her throne room, but it was background to the warmth in her middle. Bastien had said her name in a way that sparked Kian's attention, his jealousy. What could that mean?

CHAPTER

TWENTY-SIX

Faelyn pushed her plate away, leaving most of her roast duck and vegetables untouched. Around her, lords and ladies ate the fine food and danced in excited circles. The musicians played a lively tune from the corner, sending her people smiling and clapping along.

"Are you unwell, Your Majesty?" Prince Rory took a sip of wine. He looked dashing in his green tunic and golden cape, but it was a deceptive beauty. A beauty born of misplaced confidence and the hard labor of royal stylists. Not like Bastien, whom she could feel floors beneath her feet. Was that why she'd kept her eyes down during the feast? His beauty went beyond skin deep, a kind and grounded soul despite all he must have endured.

Faelyn picked at her golden gown. Had her handmaidens chosen this dress to match the prince? She preferred blue. Blue was her favorite color for many reasons. The pull tugged at her middle, willing her down, down, down below.

Prince Rory cleared his throat.

She forced a smile and lifted her face. "I'm just tired. It's been a long day."

"Not too tired for our walk after dinner, I hope?" He leaned forward.

Faelyn nearly cringed. She'd been putting off Rory for too long, and Kian wouldn't be happy if she did so once again. He was noticeably absent from the feast. "Of course not. I'm looking forward to it."

He bit into a forkful of white cake. "Good. With the recent discovery, I worried you might be too busy." His polite words only thinly disguised the bitterness in his voice.

Faelyn hadn't heard how Rory had reacted to the news of Bastien, but so far, he didn't seem troubled. Did he realize Bastien was the one who'd tried to rob him? Not yet, if his subdued reactions were any indication.

Her fake smile grew. "Yes, we are trying to decide how best to deal with the prisoner. He has some magic that could be useful to our cause."

"Part of his fae heritage?" He watched, unblinking. "It's intriguing that there are now two of you."

"I believe so." She reached out and touched his hand where it sat on his armrest. The sliminess of his character coated her fingertips. "Enough about that. Are you ready for our walk?"

He smiled and gulped down his remaining wine. "I'd be delighted." He offered his arm.

Faelyn took it, and together they rose. The gong rang, and all dancing and conversation ceased as the people bowed them out of the room. She'd never felt more like a false queen, pretending to care for this prince. But it would be worth it in the end, when her people were safe with Kestrea's alliance.

She squeezed his arm and led him and their host of guards down the hall. They walked at a slow pace, past burning lanterns, ornate tapestries, and windows darkened with night. Cool air slipped through the stones, washing over her thin slippers.

"What would you like to see?" she asked.

"I've seen a lot in my time here already. My favorite has been the lake. There aren't many lakes near my palace in Docimer, and it's a refreshing change. But I'm curious about what I see beyond the lake. How about we visit your citadel?"

"The citadel? It's much too late to do that now." Rory may have been her future husband, but the compound connected to the castle grounds was an intimate part of her castle's and kingdom's protection. She shuddered. It was as if he'd asked to kiss her.

"I attempted to enter on my walk today, but was turned away." He pulled his arm from her and stopped. "Why would they turn their future king away from any part I wished to see?" He cocked his head to the side, and his light hair shifted off his forehead.

"The citadel is no place for royals, Your Highness. Only trained military may enter unescorted." And they'd been told not to let him enter until he was king.

He smiled as if indulging her. "Then escort me. I do have formal sword training."

"We're undergoing a lot of construction right now. Perhaps when the citadel's finished." She turned and continued walking, holding her breath that he wouldn't push the matter. "Have you seen the observatory? It's one of the first things I added to the castle." Nothing gave her peace like gazing up toward Acantha, and she needed it right now.

Rory sighed behind her. He resumed walking. "I haven't. That sounds lovely." His romanticized words came out reluctant and terse. "My father will be interested to know how well this alliance is equipped to handle our enemies."

Faelyn ignored the threat. Rory wasn't going to bully her into submission by hinting at reporting her actions to the king. This was her kingdom, and would continue to be long after Rory became its king, and hers still long after he was dead. Why the sudden insistence?

Silent and no longer touching, they reached a corner staircase, and she stopped. The pull to go down to the dungeon sped her heart. She forced herself to go up instead, winding round and round to the highest level of the castle, the top of a turret. A guard opened the door, and they stepped out into the open space. Half sheltered by a tall roof, the night air brushed against her, calm and cold. Star charts lined the walls, but Faelyn's favorite spot lay ahead.

She didn't wait for Rory as she crossed out from under the covered area and stepped to the battlement wall. She breathed deeply and looked up. The shining stars filled the dark, cloudless sky in a wondrous display. Peace evaded her, seeming to come from below now, rather than above.

"Refreshment, Your Majesty?" a servant asked from behind.

Faelyn turned to see Rory strolling up, hands clasped behind his back. "No, thank you. We won't be long."

Rory watched her from behind lowered lashes. Faelyn frowned, finally noticing how romantic their surroundings were. This was a bad idea. The observatory had popped into her head, but the feelings emanating from Rory meant he misconstrued her intentions. He stopped beside her, elbows touching, and looked up.

"The view of the sky looks the same from up here as it does from down there." He shifted his gaze down. "This, however, I like." He pointed toward their surroundings.

The castle grounds and city lay around them, houses and street lanterns glowing in the night, highlighting Pavora's vastness and wealth. Thank Acantha the citadel was on the other side of the castle and not visible from where they stood.

"Faelyn, look at me." His voice was low and husky.

She held back a grimace and faced him, looking slightly down to meet his eyes.

He took her hand. "I know why you've been distant. People talk. But I promise it's only rumors."

"Rumors?" The slickness of his hand oozed over hers.

"Yes. You know I wouldn't dare sleep with a lady of your court, or a handmaiden, or whatever those servants claim. Especially not at my betrothed's palace." He squeezed slightly, drawing her gaze from where it'd wandered to the floor. "So you can put those fears to rest and relax with me."

This wasn't the first she'd heard of such rumors, but they'd not been confirmed, and his countenance screamed his lies. She pulled her hand away and didn't bother to be discreet as she wiped it on her gown. She'd never love this vile being. They probably would never even be friends. But none of that mattered once they were married. She didn't need his heirs to continue her line—she could name someone worthy if need be. She just needed his kingdom. Love could wait. Forever, if necessary. History would not repeat itself.

"I have no fear, Prince Rory. I know you wouldn't do anything to break our alliance."

"Never." He moved closer, eyes on her lips.

Could she refuse him now? Handsome or not, the thought of his unfaithful, pandering, slimy lips on hers sent shivers of revulsion through her.

"You're cold." He put his arms around her, raising his face to hers.

She pulled her head back from the stench of alcohol on his breath. His arms felt like an icy cage made of snakes.

"Prince Rory... let's retire for the night." Before she threw him over the side of the battlement.

"Let's!" He shoved his mouth onto hers, forcing his tongue between her lips.

Faelyn gasped and pushed away. Magic rushed in response to her anger. She shook with rage. How dare he take such liberties?

He smiled slyly and wiped his mouth. Her hands balled into fists. Someone cleared their throat. Faelyn glanced over, and Kian stood just outside the shadow of the awning.

"Your Majesty. Prince Rory." He bowed. "Sorry to interrupt, but Queen Faelyn is needed in the council room."

Faelyn's heart raced anew. Only one thing could summon her to the council room at this late hour. A Daltieri attack.

"I'm coming." She turned to the young prince. "Goodnight." Drawing up her skirts, she rushed passed Kian and the gaping Prince Rory. Ignoring the pull to the dungeon, she reached the council room in no time, Kian at her heels.

An attendant opened the door, and Faelyn hurried in. The council room was dark and empty.

Kian's silent chuckles preceded the glow from his staff.

She turned, scowling. "Don't bother." She clapped her hands, and fire erupted, lighting every candle and lantern in the room.

It took three deep breaths before she realized who she was upset with. She slumped into the nearest chair.

"Thank you for rescuing me. Your timing was impeccable." Her voice echoed in the large space despite the cushioned chairs and interspaced tapestries.

"I wasn't rescuing you. I was rescuing Prince Rory. From your wrath." His laughter slowly subsided. "You were doing fine until right at the end." He wiped a tear from his eye. "I felt your magic flare. For a moment, I thought you might toss him over the wall."

Faelyn glared up at him. "Did you see what he did?" She wiped at her mouth with the back of her hand until her lips stung.

Kian frowned. "I jest, but no one should kiss you without your permission. It will get easier, Faelyn. These are just the first steps. Later, when he kisses you, it won't seem so bad."

"Your right. He shouldn't kiss me unless I *want* him to kiss me. And why don't you care about my attentions for Rory like you cared when you saw me with Nolan?" Heat tinged her tone.

"You know why. You're supposed to marry Rory. This was your plan, remember? Your goal. And I begrudgingly agree it's the right one for our kingdom."

Faelyn stood, took a deep breath, and nodded. "Goodnight, Kian." She walked past, trailing her hand over his shoulder. "Thank you."

"Hey, don't be angry. Neither of us has the privilege of marrying for love."

She watched him, and when his eyes turned sad, she turned away and left down the quiet, dark hall. His words and assurances couldn't cover what she sensed inside him.

When she neared the stairs, the constant pull came forefront to her mind. She paused. "Wait for me outside my room," she said to her guards.

Without a word, the footsteps of her many guards continued down the hall, fading as they rounded the corner heading toward her suite. She looked left and right, but the castle was quiet. Lifting her skirts, she stepped quickly down the stairs, crossing through the hall, then down the winding staircase to the dungeon—a place she hadn't frequented since her defeat of Lord Jamison over twenty years ago. Her heart pounded, echoing through the increasing pressure pulling her to Bastien.

At the bottom, two guards stood beside the entrance. Their eyes widened, and they bowed low.

"I'm here to see the prisoner."

One guard stepped forward, gesturing ahead. "Allow me, Your Majesty."

"No need. I can find my way." Even if she didn't know this dungeon so well, the pull would tell her where to go, she was sure of it.

The guards bowed out of the way as Faelyn passed. Her palms grew sweaty, and her magic nudged her mind, urging her along. Why was she so nervous?

Torches lit the bare stone hall. There were only a few rows of cells at the castle, not meant for holding a large number of people, but all of them were empty save one. She rounded the correct corner, cautious steps lithe in her slippered feet. The pull increased as she approached the last cell in the row.

When she stepped into view, he was already standing, waiting for her. A smile played in his light eyes made more handsome by the glow of the torches. His short hair hit above his pointed ears. Now that she took the time to study him, there was a familiarity about him that went beyond the ears and soldier's uniform. Of course, she'd seen him before, but this was something more.

He broke eye contact to dip his head in greeting. "Good evening, Your Majesty."

"How did you know I was coming?" She dropped her skirts, and they rustled against the floor.

He pointed to his ears. "I have excellent hearing."

Like me. But does he feel the same pull?

She extinguished nearby torches with a small push of magic. "And can you see in the night?"

He stepped toward the bars, staring intently. "Very well."

Electric tingles seemed to run between them in the darkness. Could he feel them too? She brought back the light. "My advisors believe we don't know enough about you to trust you."

"What do you want to know?"

"How old are you?"

"Twenty. How old are you?"

She blinked. No one asked her that. "Over a hundred," she said slowly, gauging his reaction.

His lips pulled into a smile, highlighting smooth skin. No facial hair. Not even hints of shaved stubble.

She reached out with her magic, needing to dig deeper into the essence of him, of who he truly was. Invisible, it touched him, enveloping his body. His smile parted into surprise. Faelyn breathed, staring. If he were a mere mage, he wouldn't have noticed her there. Would he forbid the intrusion?

He closed his eyes, and a sigh escaped him as he relaxed his being into it. Powerful magic swarmed inside him, withheld like a perfect master mage, yet he held no staff to channel it into him. He wasn't aware of his true capabilities.

Beneath the layer of protective magic was a raw, but resilient man. Above his feelings of nervousness, curiosity, and eagerness, lay a much stronger emotion. His desire to be loved and to love in return —the unquenchable need born of a hard life.

Like her own.

With her magic wrapped around him, the intimacy of the moment overtook her, yet it didn't feel wrong. She longed to understand his pain and to heal him of it, so she sent more of her magic into him. Her gift wasn't like Niri's. She couldn't see his memories, only his emotions, his essence, yet he let her in, giving her his trust. Trying to prove he didn't need to be locked away.

His magic, the flavor and feel of fresh-picked roses, caressed her like soft fingertips to her cheek, asking for permission past her barriers.

Footsteps sounded from a few halls over. Faelyn opened her eyes —when had she closed them? —and found her hands wrapped around the bars of the cell. She lifted her head from where it rested against the cold metal, her breathing ragged. Bastien stood but a handspan away.

The footsteps grew closer. Kian was coming.

Faelyn locked eyes with Bastien. His breathing was pitched, his eyes knowing, but he didn't say a word. He gave a low bow. She unlocked her grip from the bars and stepped back just as Kian appeared down the hall.

Her heart was racing.

She spoke in a low whisper. "You don't really need a staff, and yet you haven't tried to escape."

His jaw clenched, but then Kian approached.

"Your Majesty, I've been looking for you." He bowed, maintaining the formalities in front of the prisoner, but underneath, Faelyn sensed his fury. Everything he wanted to say burned in his eyes, but he wouldn't do it here. Just like she wouldn't question why he'd followed her.

"I was just finishing. Let's go." She picked up her skirts. Her head turned for a last look at Bastien but caught Kian's scowl and stopped. She hurried past, and he followed.

Though her head was heavy with guilt, she held it high as she ascended the castle back to her suite. There were always eyes watching. Besides, she hadn't done anything wrong. Questioning the prisoner to assess the security and well-being of her castle and kingdom was her top priority.

Right.

Her guards were waiting by her door, eyes downcast, looking abashed. Kian must have given them a good tongue-lashing before he found her.

She turned to him. "I read the prisoner's intent, and it's not malicious. I believe he can be trusted." She hadn't meant to speak so formally, as if delivering a rehearsed excuse to her childhood nurse, Mary.

He stepped closer, whispering. "But can you trust yourself around him?"

She inhaled.

His staff lit up as he cast a sound veil around them. "I felt your magic. I felt the desire in it." Anger colored his tone and essence behind narrowed eyes.

"Desire for truth! Nothing more." She backed a step. "Don't assume to know anything, Kian." With a thought, she dissipated his veil. "Goodnight."

She paced to her room, and he didn't stop her. If she could make it through the door, she could block him out. Block out her burning cheeks and racing pulse. Block out the doubt he'd put in her heart.

Her guards opened the doors.

Doubt about what? She'd questioned a prisoner in her castle. Nothing more.

Or was it Bastien affecting her heart?

She crossed the threshold and down the hall to the still-lit sitting room. Two of her handmaidens had waited up to help her change. One gown for another, but at least this one didn't crush her ribs.

She slipped into her fluffy bed, finally alone, but sleep evaded her. The pull, ever stronger, forced tingles over her skin, and her mind raced well into the night.

Bastien knew the moment Faelyn fell asleep. The draw to her became less zinged with electricity and instead became a low hum. His lids drooped, heavy, but his heart soared. He'd never felt anything like it before. She'd pushed her magic, searching and exploring his soul, and he'd embraced it thoroughly. No distrust, no second thoughts, and when she'd been interrupted and retreated, it was like she'd taken air from his lungs. But she was the one out of breath.

Amazing. She was amazing.

TWENTY-SEVEN

Faelyn awoke with a smile on her lips that quickly turned into a frown. Behind her closed eyelids, the heat of anger radiating from Amerae nearly glowed red. She opened her eyes.

Amerae stood at the foot of the bed, expression relaxed, but fire burned in her essence. She'd pleated her chestnut hair into its usual braid, but instead of a soldier's uniform, she wore a simple cream-colored dress. The sleeves flared at the elbows, and the cotton hugged her curves, highlighting the obvious bulge of a pregnant belly.

"Oh, Amerae. I haven't had the chance to congratulate you." Faelyn threw the covers aside and hurried around the bed to her friend.

Amerae took a step back from the embrace, her anger finally slipping through her calm demeanor. "They took my uniform. My breastplate. My leathers. They probably would have taken my sword if I wasn't threatening their lives with it."

"Who?" Faelyn had given the indirect order that Amerae wasn't to be on active duty, but she hadn't wanted them to take her things.

"Rupert. The master of arms." Amerae clutched her stomach. She struggled for words, and her eyes shone. "My queen, have I done something to displease you?"

"I'm sorry about your armor, Amerae. We'll get it back. But, why didn't you tell me you're expecting?" Her fingers itched to touch Amerae's belly, connect with the soul within, something she'd never experienced before, but she withheld. Now wasn't the time.

"I didn't want to be relieved of my duties." Amerae gave a flat stare.

"I still need you, but I don't need you fighting or putting yourself in harm's way. I'd like you to coordinate the efforts of our spies. Gather information to make strategic decisions about where we should focus our time and attention. These peaceful times cannot last. Will not, if Bastien's Fating is to be believed." The corners of her mouth quirked into a brief smile.

"Who will protect you?"

Faelyn could feel Amerae's anger cracking. Her need to be useful had been given direction. "Nolan, and Kian, and the other guards." She put a hand on her shoulder. "And you, once you're ready to don the uniform again."

Amerae nodded and wiped her eyes.

Faelyn smiled. She stretched out a hand and gently placed it against Amerae's stomach. Amerae gave a quick intake of breath. Reaching with her magic, she sensed the infant inside. Sensed its fluttering heart. The warmth was more than Amerae's skin, but a feeling of comfort from baby and mother. And love, pure love.

She looked up into Amerae's wide eyes. "I'm very happy for you, my friend."

Amerae finally smiled. "Thank you."

The ladies in waiting took that as their cue to intrude, bustling over with the day's gown, circlet, shoes, and makeup. Faelyn sighed and stepped to her mirror. The pull of Bastien beneath her feet increased. Her heart leaped. He was awake.

The bristled brush tugged through her long hair.

"You're smiling." Amerae caught her gaze in the mirror. "Normally you scowl through this entire process."

Faelyn lifted her arms as the nightgown was tugged over her head. "What are Kian's intentions with our *prisoner*?" She nearly rolled her eyes on the last word.

Amerae's countenance turned dark. "Hopefully to hang him."

Faelyn's hand shot to her chest. "Amerae!"

Amerae's eyebrows rose. "What? He compromised the safety of our army. More than once. He's an outlaw refugee from a foreign kingdom and he lied to us, concealing important information. And, he's fae." Amerae met Faelyn's eyes. "He's fae, like you. With pointed ears, magic, quick healing, and... he never told us. Did anyone find out how old he is? What do we know about him? How do you know he's not a spy sent to destroy you?"

Faelyn opened her mouth to defend Bastien, but Amerae wasn't done.

"And what's more, he gives me a strange feeling." She lowered her voice. "I feel I can trust him, like I'm totally safe by his side. Like he's dependable—an old soul I've met before—and that's not right. I don't know anything about him except that he's untrustworthy, which means magic could be involved. Do we even know what he's capable of?" She took a deep breath. "If Kian asks my recommendation, I know what I'll tell him."

Faelyn gritted her teeth. What could she say? Everyone was right to be cautious, but she *knew* him, even without ever really having spoken to him. He wasn't a spy. He just had to prove it to the others.

"But of course, the final say rests with you, my queen."

"So, it's his secrets Kian wishes? To ensure he's not a threat? Fine." The last pin was pushed into her hair. She held up the long skirts of her gown, emerald blue like her eyes, and swept out of the room.

A court aide met her at the door, rushing to keep up as he prattled off a list of things that needed her immediate attention. Nolan waited beside the usual staircase down to the throne room, but she burst by him. He stepped in line behind without a word.

"Your Majesty, you can't delay. You're to receive Lord Gilmore and then you have breakfast with Prince Rory," the aide said.

Faelyn stopped, her entourage halting behind. "Have Lady Amerae send my regrets to Lord Gilmore. I will be on time for breakfast with the prince."

The aide nodded and took off. Faelyn reached the winding corner staircase and descended. A giddiness she hadn't felt in a long time quickened her steps.

"Nolan."

"Yes, my queen?" His pace matched hers.

She'd never be able to repay his loyalty. "I'm going to question the prisoner, put an end to this waste of time. I appreciate everyone's concern for my safety, but I wouldn't place the kingdom at risk. I'll seek answers and then set Bastien free to resume training. See to it that no one interrupts me."

"Yes, Your Majesty." Nolan might not like it, but he didn't utter one word of disagreement.

She reached the bottom and passed the guard station where Nolan and her personal guards took up residence. Two rows over and down the hall came the scraping of boots as Bastien scrambled up. She stepped into view of his appreciative grin and couldn't help the smile that overtook her.

"Good morning." His baritone voice echoed down the stone, vibrating her bones.

"Good morning, Bastien." His name flowed off her lips, shy and sweet.

He stared, his grin growing wider. It wasn't until he quirked an eyebrow that she realized she was supposed to speak. Her eyes swept over his muscled arms and chest, no longer hidden under the soldier's leathers.

She cleared her throat. "My court doesn't trust you." Was that it? Was that going to be her grand way of starting this conversation?

"But you do?" He took a half step forward from the middle of his cell.

"I... do." She had no reason to, but she did. She shook her head. "I don't believe you mean me harm, or more importantly, my kingdom."

"A thousand mages could test the truthfulness of my words and not find them wanting." He stepped forward and gripped the bars in both hands. "I mean to stand by you and protect you, and so protect your kingdom."

The depth of sincerity blossomed something within her heart, burning all the way to her cheeks. He truly meant what he said.

She took a step closer, close enough to touch him. "But why? What allegiance do you owe me or my kingdom?" She was queen, and soldiers had said more words about serving and protecting before, but this didn't feel the same. She wasn't *his* queen. This wasn't *his* fight. Every ounce of her waited for his next words. She didn't want another blind follower to command. She wanted him to be something more.

His eyes cast downward. His grip relaxed to his sides. "I saw you when I was a child. I had a vision, a Fating. You came down the street and my life was changed forever. All of a sudden, I wanted for better, even if it's taken me this long to be able to achieve that goal. It was magical, the peace and awe that Fating brought me." His light eyes raised to hers. "I never imagined it would be even more so when I finally met you."

Faelyn's heart raced with the truth of his words.

He paced the small cell, watching her. "I thought I was alone until I heard of you. Your beauty, the respect and love your people have for you, all while you never hid who you truly are. I wasn't as brave as you." He stopped and touched his long ears. "I... was brought up to hide this. Who I am. It was safer that way, but I don't want to hide anymore. I want to be part of your world. A better world."

She placed her hands over the same bars he'd gripped, still warm. "I remember you. Even then I felt..."

He glanced up sharply. "The draw. You feel it too?" He approached, his body just a few inches from touching her hands. His scent—wood musk and springtime—blanketed her like coming home.

Her heart stuttered with surprise. They both experienced the same thing. Her grip slacked on the bars. He reached up and slid his hands around hers. Magic swarmed to her surface. Its heat gathered in her hands, multiplying and shifting into him. The magic within him stirred in response like a buzz of humming electricity she felt to her toes. He blinked, but showed no surprise that he gathered magic without a crystal.

The warm touch of his skin felt delicious, easing an ache within, yet awakening new ones she hadn't known existed. He stared into her eyes, letting his hands rest over hers, sure and confident.

She breathed deeply and stepped back. His calloused fingers slipped over her skin, but he didn't protest, simply reclaimed his former hold on the bars.

"I want to let you out, but my court seeks answers first." She straightened her shoulders. "Why did you hide who you really are?"

"You're much older than I am. Have you ever hidden your identity for your own safety?"

If he knew anything about her past, he would know she had. "It was my greatest shame."

"Then, like me, it's probably not something you like to talk about?"

She winced in remembrance of black smoke rising in the distance as she fled toward a foreign kingdom, hiding away as her people were overrun by the enemy for decades. "No. The memories are best lost to the depths of time."

His face hardened. "My memories will haunt me forever." A profound sadness lanced out from him, and his jaw clenched.

"You can tell me, Bastien. You have to tell me, if you want to be free."

He huffed through his nose. "So that's the price, Faelyn? My deepest secrets and darkest fears."

"That's the price, prisoner." Kian's biting words preceded him down the hall. "And you will address her as 'Your Majesty.'"

Faelyn jumped back. She'd been so close to Bastien, too close for proprietary's sake. "How did you get past Nolan?"

His eyes widened in surprise, and she instantly regretted her words. Kian outranked Nolan, and she'd never kept Kian from her confidences before.

"Your Majesty has placed me in charge of the prisoner, and since you are late for your date with your betrothed, I've come to be of assistance." His emphasis on the word 'betrothed' was not lost on her, nor his gritted teeth as he delivered the seemingly harmless words.

Bastien quickly smothered the flash of hurt that escaped his impressively tight control over his invisible emotions.

"I must have lost track of the time. Bastien, I believe you've met Lord Kian Foster, my master mage and head advisor. It is he whom you'll have to prove your trustworthiness." She glanced back, and Bastien looked straight at her, while Kian stared straight at him. The tension rising between them almost shimmered in intensity. "I'll be back, if time allows." Whatever Bastien was hiding, he'd have to confess before she could secure his release.

Kian stiffened, and Bastien relaxed. Faelyn turned and walked away. Time to pretend niceties for the untrustworthy prince.

The swish of Faelyn's dress against the stone was long gone before Kian turned his slow, steady gaze. Bastien crossed his arms over his chest, magic still thrumming through his veins.

"I'm not blind, prisoner. I see more than just with my eyes." He tilted his staff forward. "You think you're the same, that you can somehow win her over, make her trust you. I feel what rolls off you both in waves. She's so desperate and deserving of love that she'd cling to whatever shred of it someone offered." He stepped forward, a heavy, threatening step. "I won't allow you to play games with her heart."

Bastien scratched his neck. He didn't know what he felt for Faelyn beyond a fierce need to protect her and an indescribable draw to be near her. This Kian had read more in their interactions than he'd been able to give voice to. The direction of the mage's thoughts, the heat in his tone, spoke volumes. Kian was jealous.

"I play no games, Lord Kian. Like your queen, I've seen too much hardship not to take things seriously when there are bars between me and my freedom."

"If Queen Faelyn's life is the measure of hardship, none can compare, least of all your insignificant existence."

Bastien's arms slowly dropped to his sides, hands curled into fists. "Then you must know enough about me to be satisfied and let me go."

"You came from Kestrea, did you not?"

"Yes."

"How old were you when you fled with that band of outlaws?"

The bite in Kian's words was lost as Bastien remembered Tave. What had become of him? On to new places and people to rob, he was sure. Tave certainly hadn't bothered to come after him.

"I was fifteen."

"And before that?"

Bastien gritted his teeth. "Like Niri said, I belonged to a gang of orphans, banned together by an arrogant man called Kolb."

"And you robbed people for a living?"

Bastien nodded, not quite meeting Kian's judging gaze. The shame of his past choices bled through his chest, but he wouldn't offer excuses to this mage who thought himself so superior. He'd been a kid trying to survive what the Fates had handed him.

Right?

"How did you hide your identity?"

"I didn't. Everyone knew who I was: the best thief in the city." At Kian's deepening frown, Bastien continued. "There was a woman at the orphanage I lived in until I was seven. It was her idea to keep my hair long, shape it in such a way it would hang over my ears if I wore it back."

Kian shifted his stance. "Queen Faelyn had already established trade with Kestrea around the time you were born. The people accepted her fae heritage, revered her for it, in truth. Why hide that you shared similarities? Surely you only did yourself a disservice."

Bastien took a step back, sweat slicking his clenched fists. This was dangerous territory. "Her faeness was not so revered as you like to think. Besides, I couldn't have anyone on the streets able to identify me as the boy who'd robbed them."

"The woman at the orphanage was helping you be a better thief?" Kian's lip curled. "No. What's the real reason?"

"You know how cruel people can be to those who are different. I'm sure your queen can testify to that truth." Bastien crossed his arms.

Kian scoffed. "I thought she was your queen as well. Or do you not see yourself as someone in her service?"

"Of course I do. I'm duty-bound to her. It's written in the Fates." Damn this Kian; he was quick on his feet.

Kian pointed a finger. "You're distracting me. Evasion is a notable tool for a thief. Why did this Miss Bannings help you hide your identity?" Kian's staff glowed.

Had Kian talked to Niri? Of course he had, and she'd not kept his secrets. The weight of Kian's magic, full of distrust and hostility compared to Faelyn's sweet flavor, settled over him. With a nervous heart, a sliver of power slipped through Bastien's tight control and took shape.

Kian's eyes narrowed.

Bastien took a deep breath, allowing the sliver to blossom. He pulled at it, as he would the magic through the mage crystal on his staff. It came willingly, but he held it at bay. "I've already answered your question."

Kian looked up from Bastien's chest. "Fine." He turned and left, stopping only to whisper hurried instructions to the guard at the end of the hall.

Bastien slumped against the wall. That had not gone the way he'd hoped. Kian's jealousy was pushing him to extremes, demanding more of Bastien than should have been reasonably required to prove he could be trusted. And what did *Lord* Kian have to be jealous of? He was a master mage, Faelyn's most trusted advisor. He'd probably never committed a crime in his life. And he was clearly in love with Faelyn. Did she love Kian back? Bastien kicked his empty plate across the cell, sending it crashing into the wall. If Kian hadn't married Faelyn, what chance did he have?

He straightened. Marry? When had he ever thought about marrying anyone?

The draw lessened as Faelyn traveled further away. If he could wrap his hands around the invisible thread between them and pull her back to him, he'd never let go. She wanted his secret, the thing he'd hidden away and didn't dare think of. But he'd do it. For her. No one else, but her.

Already she'd pulled some of it from him. His magic, without a mage crystal to conduct it. He'd sworn never to touch it again, after...

His brow creased, and he slowly brought earth magic forward, pulling from within him versus channeling it through a crystal. The magic hovered in his core, and he concentrated on the lock. The entire door was made of metal bars. It would be nothing to bend them to his will, and hardly much more to escape this dank dungeon.

But he couldn't. He'd be no closer to his goal, however extraordinary it might be. He had to be by Faelyn's side, one way or another. Apparently, he'd have to go around Kian first.

TWENTY-EIGHT

Prince Rory's impatient sighs set Faelyn's teeth on edge even before she entered the dining hall for their breakfast. He sat alone at the end of the long table piled high with food. Her internal dread filled the usually bright and airy room despite the fresh flowers in hues of purple and white interspaced on serving tables manned by castle servants.

A place had been set next to his—on the side of the table rather than the head. His idea, no doubt. That would explain the sweat dripping down the head attendant's brow. She loosened her jaw and sat without comment. Her plate was immediately filled with her favorites—an array of fruits, a chocolate chip scone, and a side of porridge.

Rory bit into a thick piece of sausage, grease dripping down his chin, then placed a hand on her thigh beneath the table. "Busy morning, my dear?"

She choked on a gulp of water and swatted his hand away. "You shouldn't take such liberties." The words were out of her mouth before she'd thought twice. She lifted her chin.

He slowly pulled back his arm, face turning red and eyes narrowing. "Are we not betrothed to be married? Am I not to be king of these lands? Did you and my father not sign a contract ensuring safety for your people in exchange for marriage? We'll need heirs." He leaned closer. "You must loathe me not to accept a simple touch from your future husband. Or is there another who's captured your attention?"

Faelyn stood, scraping back her chair. Fury threatened to bubble up, but she kept it in check. "I would never think of breaking our contract, Prince Rory, and though it doesn't explicitly specify no infidelity, to me, it is implied. Though, I can't say the same for you."

The servants gasped around the room.

Rory stormed to his feet, tossing his napkin to the table. "You dare to—"

"I'm not finished. While I may entertain the formalities of an engagement period, I won't pretend to care for you, and I won't allow you to take liberties as to place your hands on me without my permission. Perhaps the blame is mine for not explaining myself more fully upon your arrival, but I do not enter this union blindly. I'm not some simpering fawn waiting to bend to your will and wiles. I may hope to one day care for you, even love you, but that is not the purpose of me and you, and you well know it. We don't have the luxury of being guided by our hearts." Her eyes dropped to the ground beneath her feet. The pull felt especially fine, as if Bastien was looking straight up toward her.

Rory remained silent, only the grinding of his teeth reminding her he still stood there.

"My father has done me a great disservice." He stood there for a breath more, then turned and blew out of the room.

Faelyn sat slowly back into her chair, which a servant pushed up. Those around the room stared straight ahead, muscles twitching with their likely need to rush and spread the latest gossip. She let out a long, slow sigh. She'd spoken the truth to Rory, but perhaps it was unwise. While breaking the engagement contract would be near to impossible, King Bautamin could find a way if his son was truly unhappy.

Was it worth all this? Sacrificing her heart for such a man?

Of course it was. She would not become her father, putting herself before Alysies. She stood, discarding her meal. "Where is Lord Kian?"

An attendant stepped forward. "He's in the council room, Your Majesty."

Faelyn swept out of the room and traversed the castle. The council room guard barely got the door open before she burst through. Kian sat alone at the long table, poring over reports. He stood and bowed while she eyed the guards. They retreated, shutting the door behind them.

"You're right, Kian." She sniffed. "I feel a pull to him unlike any other. It's more than just knowing he's fae. There's something there, something about him that draws me to him. I... I feel like I'm falling for him, but I hardly know him."

The parchment slipped from Kian's fingers and fell to the table.

Faelyn stepped toward him. "It's more than magic, it's something else. More powerful." She looked down.

"He's making you lose sight of your goal." Kian's statement rang hollow but without surprise.

She nodded. It was hard to admit she'd need Kian's help to move past this and aim for the greater good—even harder to do what she must and stay away from Bastien. But what choice did she have?

"This pull to him you feel, it is not magic, or I would have sensed it. But it doesn't take magic to see your growing affection for him." Kian took a deep breath. "Which is why I've ordered to remove him from the castle."

Faelyn gasped. "What? When?" Her eyes narrowed. "To where?"

"He's moving as we speak to a location I will only disclose if you command me to." His voice softened. "I won't deny you happiness, Faelyn, but I know you. You've always done what was best for your kingdom, and Bastien isn't it. A queen can't marry a commoner, and we need Kestrea as an ally."

She breathed in sharply through her teeth. Hands trembling, she bit back every foul thing she wanted to yell at Kian and focused hard. The pull had indeed moved. Instead of below, it was angled toward the back of the castle. A thin line of distress was buried within.

She squeezed her eyes shut and took a deep breath, letting it out in a gust. "Why is this so difficult? I know this is the right thing. I know it. But I'm so angry at you for taking him away from me."

Kian rounded the table and placed a comforting hand on her cheek. "I know how you feel, Faelyn. If you truly love him, his absence will always burden you. If I can let go for the greater good, so can you."

She blinked to hold the tears from spilling and wrapped her arms around him. "I'm sorry for what I did to you. What I'm still doing to you. I've never deserved your love." The pull to Bastien drew further away. He must be near the docking area. They wouldn't make a scene by loading him in the front. The barred prison wagons collected people where the masses wouldn't see. "I have to say goodbye to him."

He let her go. "I wouldn't. It will only make it harder."

"I know. I just... If you'd had the chance to say goodbye to me before you left Thomats, wouldn't you have taken it?"

His jaw clenched, but he looked at her with pity. "I'll come with you."

She spun on her heel and rushed out of the room. The back of the castle was far away. The thin line of distress grew the closer she got, and she held it tight in her mind until she was running down halls, corridors, staircases, and courtyards. Kian just managed to keep up as courtiers and servants dodged out of the way.

She blew through the loading dock door to see Bastien being led to a wagon. His wrists were bound behind him, surrounded by a half-dozen guards. His bright blue eyes tracked her progress down the stone stairs leading to the cobbled street. This was wrong. He was innocent and being punished for nothing more than her feelings.

"Stop!" She rushed forward, halting halfway to the wagon. She panted, only half-caring she was making a scene. Behaving ridiculously. "Remove his manacles."

The guards glanced toward each other, uncertain. They had stopped just short of hauling Bastien into the wagon. One of them unlocked the manacles. Bastien gaped in surprise.

"Leave us," Kian barked.

The guards' eyes went wide, but they didn't hesitate. They let go of Bastien and filed two-by-two back into the castle.

When the door shut behind them, Bastien took a step toward her, arms slowly raising. His face held only a grim understanding, but his essence mingled pain and hope.

Faelyn ran to him, throwing herself into his waiting embrace. Their bodies slammed together, the warmth and nearness of him filling her up. Her magic leaped, as if magnified.

"Oh, Faelyn," he breathed. The heat of his breath washed through her hair, and she snuggled into his neck.

"I'm a fool. I don't know what I'm doing here. But I couldn't let you leave without saying goodbye." Tears leaked down her cheeks. "I don't know what's wrong with me."

He squeezed her tight, the feeling like coming home. Like a piece of her she'd never known she was living without had been found.

"I can't begin to hope I've captured your heart, but you have mine. I give it to you freely for it's all I have to offer," he breathed.

She pulled back far enough to look up into his kind, smiling face. He brushed tears from her cheeks with a calloused thumb.

"I'm sorry, Bastien. There's so much more to this than you and I." The words burned her throat.

"I know, my love, I know." His magic swirled within, but he didn't unleash it. He could escape if he wanted, yet he stayed.

She didn't dare encourage him. It would only make things harder.

He must have felt her true intent because his sadness became a weighted thing in the air around them. "So this is really goodbye?"

She squeezed the sleeves of his tunic. Why did the Fates mock her so? "I know you're innocent, that you mean no harm and only wish to serve Alysies. Wherever he's sending you, I'll make sure you're free, but..."

Bastien's eyes snapped up to Kian behind her. "But I can never come back."

Fresh tears filled her eyes. Would Bastien have long life like her? Would he outlive Prince Rory? She could manage no more than a whisper. "I'm sorry."

"Queen Faelyn." Kian's voice came as a warning, his essence laced with sadness. They were out of time.

Bastien didn't falter. He gazed into her and placed his hands on either side of her face. "I've fated you. My fatings always come true. We will be together again."

His Fating. What if sending him away disrupted it somehow? What if he wasn't there when she needed him?

He dipped his head, eyes intent on her lips. She should stop him. Stop this before it became more than just spoken intentions and trapped her in her misery. As true as that was, she knew she wouldn't. Her body and soul needed and wanted his love as much as he needed hers.

She stood on the balls of her feet and tilted her face to his. Their lips met, fitting softly and sweetly together, claiming each other. They moved and breathed in the most intimate dance she'd ever experienced. The taste of him was surreal, the most intoxicating flavor, making her want more. That wanting didn't stop at the touch of his skin or the feel of him against her. It delved deep, beyond her body and her magic and her essence.

Her soul called to his.

He moved a hand to the nape of her neck, pulling her closer. Her hands slid up his muscled arms, feeling his strength with her mind and magic. From his broad shoulders up his smooth neck, to his pronounced jaw, and finally to the shape of his pointed ears.

Those ears, as familiar as her own, which they both spent their youth trying to hide from the world.

He gasped, one hand winding around her waist, lips moving with desperate need, just as strong as hers. More, she needed more. She parted her lips, and he acknowledged the invitation eagerly. His tongue slipped in and collided with hers. Tasting, tangling—a wanting that sent her shivering and set her on fire from the inside out.

"Faelyn!" Kian yelled the moment before the docking door crashed open.

She jumped and swiveled around, still encircled in Bastien's arms, panting.

Prince Rory stood at the top of the stairs, flanked by his personal guards.

CHAPTER
TWENTY-NINE

No, no, no. Cold horror washed over Faelyn's heated skin.

Prince Rory's face turned red as he sputtered at the top of the docking door stairs, fumbling for something to say. His lips curled back in a snarl, and he reached for the sword at his side.

Faelyn stepped away from Bastien, but he grabbed her hand and didn't let go. Right before her eyes, her carefully laid plans were crashing down around her. "Prince Rory, put the sword away."

He finally found his voice. "You hag! You harlot." He stormed down the stairs brandishing his sword. "How *dare* you?"

Bastien tugged her behind him. "You will not touch her!" His magic blazed within at the same time Kian's staff lit up the stone dock.

Rory's guards jumped from the stairs, drawing their swords and rushing to place themselves in front of their prince. Faelyn's guards charged through the open door with cries of alarm.

Panic seeped through her magic. "Enough!" Her voice boomed through the street, carried by the wind. The volume shook the castle foundation in a low rumble. She stepped in front of Bastien.

Rory's guard stopped short of swinging at Kian. Her guards halted to an immediate stop, awaiting orders.

Prince Rory shoved passed his stunned guards. "I want him gone! Beheaded by dawn." His words were iron rage, and he pointed his sword straight at her heart.

Rory wanted him gone. Not gone, but killed. She wouldn't let that happen. If she chose her words carefully, there would have to be a way through this.

"He's leaving, Prince Rory. Before you do anything rash, remember Kestrea needs Alysies as much as we need you."

Rory lowered his sword and paced forward, head down like a slow-moving bull. Kian let him by, knowing better than to attack the prince. Bastien squeezed her hand in warning. Rory's boots ground the loose dirt against the cobblestones until he stopped one pace away. He looked up through narrowed eyes.

Faelyn's heart pounded. She sent calming magic sweeping across him and the glaring guards. Kian watched, jaw clenched. He knew exactly what was at stake in this moment. Bastien's magic swirled behind her. The tension rolled through his palm to her. She was still holding his hand.

Rory took a deep breath. Then spat in her face. Before the revulsion of the slimy spit had completely registered, a burst of power escaped Bastien. She couldn't stop it. A blast of air magic shot past her. It hit Rory square in the chest and sent him flying backward. He crashed into one of his guards, sending them both sprawling to the ground.

Time stood still. Her eyes drifted until they locked with Kian's. He shook his head.

It was done.

Rory's guards yelled and attacked. Faelyn's guards awaited her nod, then rushed to surround her, raising their swords to deflect and defend. There was no need. Bastien pulled her behind him, shielding them both with a bubble of air. She nearly dropped to her knees from the anger that raged within.

How could she have been so careless? Why now did her heart decide to take over all rational thought?

Two of Prince Rory's guards assisted him into the castle as the fighting erupted. The Alysian guards quickly disarmed the rest, and with very few injuries.

Faelyn turned to Bastien, knowing they couldn't be heard within his shield. She took a deep breath, ignoring the chaos around her. "You can't come back, Bastien. I gave up my right to live my life for love a long time ago."

His lips parted, eyes creasing in pain. "You need me." He squeezed her hand. "I need you."

She lifted his hand, placing the side of her face into his palm. Nuzzling the sure warmth, she kissed it. "I'm sorry."

She let go and stepped through his magical shield, dissipating it. The chaos of the fallout greeted her.

"Kian, see the prisoner removed from my castle. Guards, ensure Prince Rory's safety and see to it he's provided what he needs for his likely departure. Take his guards to the dungeon until they've calmed."

Her people rushed to follow her orders. Kian and two guards approached Bastien where he still stood beside the barred wagon, a look of miserable acceptance distorting his beautiful face. The guards placed their hands on his shoulders and shoved.

"Faelyn, is this truly what you wish?" Bastien reached toward her, peering between the guards.

No, not at all. "It is." She turned away to hide her tears, fearing she might crack under his penetrating and accusing gaze. "I'm so sorry, Bastien."

The guards shoved him again. "All right!" He pushed them back, holding up his hands in defeat, then climbed in the wagon of his own free will.

Faelyn stepped toward the castle as the wagon door slammed shut. She ascended the stairs, one slow step at a time, as the guards took their places on the driver's seat. They flicked the reins sending the horses into a steady walk.

"I'll find you," he said to her. His voice rang loud with pain. "I'll crawl on hands and knees to the Hereafter if that's what it takes. I will see you again."

Faelyn gasped and spun around. The words shook her to her core, igniting something so close to a memory, it might have been real. *Arden.*

Arden?

"Wait!" she called, rushing back down the steps.

Bastien stood, gripping the bars as the wagon sped up.

"Stop!" She ran toward him, but the wagon passed the wall out of sight.

Kian lunged in front of her, and she slammed into him. His strong frame held them upright.

"Let me go, Kian!" She beat her fists against his chest, calling her magic forward.

"Don't!" His words were harsh, commanding, then softer. "Don't. Let him go. Remember your people."

Racking sobs burst out of her, and she collapsed against Kian's chest. Not in decades had she allowed herself to break down like this. Half of her had just been sent away in a prison wagon. The echo of a familiar pain lanced through her, as if she'd been here before, losing him to an unknown future all over again.

But none of that made any sense. She'd only just met him.

Kian's concerned gaze bore down on her.

"I'm sorry, Kian. I don't know what's wrong with me." She lowered her voice. "I'm losing control, aren't I? I'm failing."

"Shh, it's okay." He caressed her long hair. "Talk to the prince. The prisoner is gone. It might not be too late."

She shook her head, and an irrational laugh nearly bubbled out of her. "I'll do whatever it takes, but there's no coming back from this."

"We don't really need Kestrea. We can find other ways to fend off a Daltieri attack." His words weren't entirely true. With the alliance with Kestrea, they wouldn't have had to fend off a Daltieri attack. They'd be too powerful for Daltieri to even consider it. Now...

"This way would have been easier." A premature hope bloomed in her heart. If Rory truly called off the engagement, she'd be free to marry another. "Do you think—"

"No, Faelyn." He let go and stepped back. "Forget about him. And don't ask why. You know very well why."

For Alysies.

Kian walked past, not looking back as he entered the castle behind the last of the guards. Hiding his expression from her couldn't hide the pain cascading behind him like a sweeping train. She'd learned to love another, her first since Kian, and he felt the pain of her decision anew.

She stood alone at the back of her hard-won castle, staring at the space where Bastien had held her and she'd known love for just a moment. The line connecting them thinned, his desperate pain becoming faint, until the connection snapped. It rebounded to her, crashing against her soul, nearly doubling her over in pain. She cried out and clutched her heart, like in Docimer when she had thought she was under attack.

This wasn't an attack. This was torture of her own making. She breathed in deeply through her nose, steeling her resolve. He'd promised to see her again. Should she let him? She shook her head. Now was not the time to be making any decisions, when she'd be more likely guided by her heart than her head.

She turned and walked up the cold stairs to face her punishment for allowing a moment of weakness. A moment where happiness was within her grasp. She'd found someone she could truly love but couldn't have.

The Fates had denied her yet again.

When the draw to Faelyn shattered and the pain washed over his insides, Bastien slumped to the splintered wagon floor. It was nothing compared to the pain in his heart.

The horses clopped through the streets, bumping the wagon over the stones until they transitioned to a smoother dirt road outside of town. Only the occasional rut or divot rocked his numb thoughts.

He should have known Kian would separate them. Of course Faelyn couldn't be his. He didn't deserve her, and she could never choose him. That didn't mean he wasn't meant to help her.

He'd been so close to earning his freedom, proving to Faelyn and her court his trustworthiness. Kian ordered him away, and Bastien had tugged on the thread to her so tight. Just when he'd lost all hope of ever seeing her again, she'd come rushing out.

She fit into his arms so perfectly. Had she even noticed their magic dancing together? He smiled, recalling every detail of their passionate kiss. She'd kissed him back, unashamed and eager. He never wanted to let her go, but of course, it couldn't last. Nothing good in his life ever did, but even the pompous prince couldn't ruin the memory.

Prince Rory hadn't recognized him, but Bastien had recognized the Kestrea prince—the same rich noble he'd collided with in the alley that day his life had changed. No one must have told the prince who Bastien was, or things would have gone a lot differently. Rory could have made good on his threat to behead him, and no one could have stopped him. The prince wouldn't blink an eye as the axe fell.

Bastien kicked at the floor. So the scheming prince will marry the queen and become a king. It was good he was leaving. This was what Faelyn wanted, and he wouldn't stand in the way. But he would keep his promise. He'd see her again, no matter what happened. His Fating had yet to come true.

"Where are we going?" He sent his voice on the wind with the magic that had come easier since Faelyn had searched him with hers back in the dungeon.

The guards ignored him. Again.

They'd crossed into a dense wood on the outskirts of the city, heading west, passing fewer and fewer travelers as the sun moved through the sky. There had to be a prison out here somewhere—a place he could expect to be beaten and tortured.

How would they prevent him from defending himself? If Kian was paying a shred of attention, he'd have seen the pompous prince tossed across the courtyard by Bastien's magic, and without his mage staff. Kian was likely changing his plans even as Bastien rolled to his fate. Maybe they'd ensure he didn't survive .

He glanced at the locked wagon door. He could leave now, flee back to Docimer, find Olin, and learn what had become of Tave. But, no. He couldn't leave Alysies and Faelyn behind. Maybe he'd live a long life like her, and maybe his Fating of her needing him was far off in the future, but he couldn't leave now. Whatever ambitions or goals he once had no longer mattered.

She was his purpose now.

He and Olin had always said, 'When you've got nothing, you've got nothing to lose.' Well, he had something now, and losing it would mean losing everything. He'd do anything to keep it, even if it cost him his lifelong goal.

Survival.

THIRTY

Faelyn's best attendant mopped the sweat from his brow with a sodden handkerchief and leaned toward her throne, whispering, "I've summoned him, Your Majesty, but his servants sent me off. His transport is already preparing for departure." Worry coated his essence.

Faelyn glanced up, eyes sweeping the multitude gathered before her. Farmers, peasants, minor lords and ladies, all looking to her for guidance and protection, trusting her to lead them and continue toward a stronger, free Alysies. They spoke in low tones out of respect, waiting for their turn with her or simply observing the spectacle of a receiving session in the majestic throne room. The sound filled the area from rafters to marbled floor.

How could she have let them down? What would Daltieri do when word of this failed alliance reached them?

"Inform Lady Amerae she is needed in my stead. She'll know how to answer according to my wishes." Faelyn stood.

Her attendant bowed at the same time a young runner rushed off to find Amerae. "Yes, Your Majesty."

Faelyn stepped down the short dais, smiling and walking calmly out of the room. Inside, anger melted her veins. Rory had refused her entreaties too many times to count, and now he was leaving without even a word passing between them.

Once out of sight, her pace picked up, her personal guards following close behind. A servant in Kestrea green livery sped past carrying a small trunk. The fool prince was wasting little time in making the biggest mistake in Kestrean history. Alysies might be newly reborn, but it was fast again becoming the most powerful kingdom in the northeastern hemisphere.

At the double doorway to Rory's temporary wing of the castle, two of his guards stood across the entryway from two of her guards. Both pairs eyed each other warily, hands clenched around the hilts of their sheathed swords.

Faelyn gathered herself and headed toward the closed doors. Rory's guards sidestepped in unison, barring her entrance. She bared her teeth. Her guards' swords sang their threat as they drew them from their scabbards. She held up a hand, halting whatever they'd planned to do.

"You do not bar me from sections of my own castle." She could cut off their air if she wished, send them sailing out the windows, perhaps. But the piled tinder needed only a spark to ignite, and she wouldn't provide it if it could be helped. "Move, or I'll have you arrested."

The guards didn't blink an eye.

Faelyn barely held her temper at bay. Magic seeped through her until a low white glow outlined her figure. She sent fear into the guards, hoping to play on the nervousness she already sensed from them and shape it into action. "I won't ask again." She enunciated every word. "Move out of my way."

Sweat rolled down one of their faces. The guard on the left. His hand trembled at his side. Her gaze snapped to him. He caved, side-stepping and even bowing, followed shortly by his companion. She let herself into the long hall of the wing.

More servants in green bustled about, collecting silver candelabras, pottery, and artwork not theirs to collect.

"What in the Hereafter?" The angry words burst from her.

The servants within earshot gasped and threw down their spoils. Glass crashed to the floor in a nearby room.

"Guards!" Her personal guards rushed up behind her. "Get Captain Nolan," she ordered. They hurried off.

"I need to speak to Prince Rory, immediately." She summoned a bit of magic, using wind to shoot her words down the long hall. The sound boomed off windows and walls, and the scuffles of Rory's servants abruptly cut off.

Fifteen Kestrea soldiers appeared. They wore battle armor of metal breastplates over dyed-green leathers and marched down the hall toward her.

Faelyn called the full force of her magic, wishing she had her sword. Who would have thought to bring it? Never did she imagine Rory would be reckless enough to attack her openly in her own castle.

Her hot rage channeled into a sword of blue flames. She held it up, spreading her feet apart beneath her queenly gown. Enough playing nice.

The guards halted, eyes wide. Their ranks parted, revealing Rory behind them. His green travel clothes, accented by a sweeping cape and a gold crown on his head, made his intention clear. He eyed her sword.

"You dare move to attack me?" She practically spit the words.

"I'm leaving, Faelyn, and no amount of threats or magic can stop me. You can consider our marriage contract void. A messenger rides ahead of me to inform my father." He smirked.

Faelyn released her sword. The flames dissipated into shimmering heat waves. "No one is trying to stop you. I only implore you to see reason. Your father will be most displeased if our two kingdoms do not unite. Or if your behavior makes us enemies."

The pounding boots of her guards arriving filled the corridor behind her, at least a couple dozen.

"I think my father's reactions may surprise you."

"My queen?" Nolan called.

"Prince Rory's servants have pilfered valuable items from this wing. Retrieve them with as little force as possible."

Nolan bowed, and the guards dispersed, filing down the hall and into the adjoining rooms.

Rory and his soldiers glared as they passed. "When your kingdom falls, you'll have no one to blame but yourself."

Her jaw clenched. Alysies would not fall. "The measure of a true leader is knowing when to hold your tongue, my young prince. If you continue, I may decide to take your threats seriously."

Rory's mouth snapped closed. "Bah." He shook his head and turned his back to her. "Get me out of this forsaken castle. Immediately."

Faelyn sighed, suddenly weary. She left the damaged wing with heavy steps, leaving the chaos behind. Why hadn't Kian come? She crossed the castle to the council room, but it was empty. A nearby guard bowed when she caught her eye.

"Where's Lord Kian?"

"He told me not to tell you, but I believe he was heading toward his room, Your Majesty."

Why would he want to keep his location from her? "Thank you."

Kian's room was near her wing of the castle, and she hurried that way, a sinking feeling in the pit of her stomach. She knocked on his door. Rustling sounded within, then footsteps. The door opened to Kian's flat stare before he turned. He crossed through a small sitting area and into his bedroom. A trunk sat open at the foot of his four-poster bed, half filled with clothing, more strewn on the silky bedcover.

He was in the middle of folding a black mage robe, but he didn't line the seams and it turned into an uneven mess. Kian crumpled the robe into a ball and tossed it into the trunk. He glanced up at her, then turned his back, standing in place atop the expensive cream-colored rug she'd ordered just for him. Her fae senses drowned in the sadness and betrayal emanating from him.

"You're leaving?" The shaky words felt surreal on her lips. Kian had never left her side. Not once.

"With this new blow to our kingdom, I feel it's necessary to renew our ties to Creadel. I've sent a message to King Wesli to expect me." He still didn't turn around.

There was truth in his words, but it was only a partial truth.

"We can do that through an emissary. Why go in person? I need you here, Kian." He was her trusted advisor, her best friend. Though selfishly, she needed his love and support to see her through the pain of losing Bastien. The ache burned her insides raw.

"You won't need me unless there's a fallout of this mess, and I hope to be back before that."

"So, you will come back?" She glanced at his trunk. Nearly every article of clothing he owned must have been shoved inside, too much for a quick journey. "Look at me."

He turned, then sketched a subservient, low-sweeping bow. "You command. I obey." His eyes shone when he rose.

Faelyn's hand rose to her chest. She'd hurt him. Deeply. "Why? I didn't think... I mean—" She stopped. This was about Bastien, and Kian's constant affections for her. "You didn't care when I was supposed to marry Rory. What did I do wrong? How can I make it better?"

"Don't trouble yourself, Faelyn. Sometimes it's not about you." His words lied.

"It is though." She stepped toward him. "Why?"

He held her gaze for a long moment, expression empty though she sensed him warring with indecision. "Nothing. It's nothing." He grabbed a blue tunic off his bed and proceeded to fold it unevenly. "I should return in no more than two months." He tossed the balled tunic into his trunk and reached for another.

Faelyn grabbed his arm, stopping him. She drew closer and

placed her forehead against his. "You can't go and leave unspoken words between us."

He slumped onto the edge of the bed. Eons stretched on before he spoke. "You didn't love Rory. All those years we planned your engagement, picking out which future prince you'd marry, it was hard knowing you wouldn't marry me, but I understood. Your priorities are different from when we were at Thomats together." He groaned. "I keep picturing you locked in the arms of that *thief*, and it makes me sick."

She placed a hand on his shoulder, but he shrugged it off. She pretended it didn't sting.

"I know I should be happy for you," he said. "My logic says this might be what the kingdom needs more than a political alliance—a queen who's happy and thriving and has found someone to share her long life with. But my heart does not agree." He shook his head. "The emotions have mixed so much that I can't discern the difference anymore. So I will go away for both our sakes. I need to come to terms with the reality of your feelings for me, and you need to decide for yourself what's in Alysies's best interest." He met her eyes. "I sent Bastien to—"

"No." She held up a hand. "Don't tell me. Like you, I don't know what's what anymore. It's best if I don't know until I'm sure again."

He closed his eyes and nodded.

She took his warm hand, and this time he didn't pull away. "You'll come back?"

He squeezed her hand. "I will. Damn me, but I will."

She took a deep breath. Her next question was too much to ask, but she had to. "And the ring with the piece of your mage crystal?" He'd given it to her when he'd asked her to be his wife. In her grief, she'd kept it, and it'd since been a convenient way to communicate with him over long distances.

He smiled and opened his eyes, staring at his lap. "Awaiting you in Amerae's keeping."

She didn't know what else to say. If she could have chosen the path of her heart, her life would have looked a lot differently. But her path was set, almost as if preordained in Acantha above.

"I'm sorry, Ki—"

"Don't apologize. You can't help whom you love any more than I can." He took her chin gently between his thumb and forefinger and dipped it, kissing her on the forehead. His endless love flowed through that simple goodbye, and it nearly broke her heart.

She stood, knowing he wanted to be alone, and backed out of the room, closing the door softly behind her.

Rory's entourage rolled off the castle grounds that afternoon. Nolan reported most of the stolen items had been recovered, and the servants were already hard at work restoring the damage. Faelyn gritted her teeth through his report, halting him before he'd finished. She didn't need any more proof of Rory's vile character.

Kian left at dawn the following day. Faelyn had barely slept that night, her mind bouncing between wondering where Bastien had been taken, and wondering if she could still convince Kian to stay. Maybe Kian hoped she'd beg him to, but he was right. They both needed to sort themselves out, and strengthening their southern alliance wouldn't hurt. After all, Kian was from there originally and was still considered lord of his lands.

She glanced at his ring before shutting the door to the safe in her room. An advisor loomed in the door, reminding her she had a kingdom to run, without Kian, and without a betrothed.

THIRTY-ONE

The wagon rolled on for several days, vibrating Bastien's teeth with each rocky mile, jolting him from sleep with each dip into a rut. They stopped only at night and to rest the horses. By the sun's location, they always headed west. Bastien stretched, changing positions often, but his butt had gone numb somewhere around hour two, and it was officially a lost cause. It didn't help they never let him out. Not once. They slid infrequent bread and cups of water between the bars. He relieved himself as they traveled, cursing each time for not having the sense to escape.

Tomorrow. I'll leave tomorrow.

The guards were too busy grumbling about the journey to pay him any attention. He breathed in deeply, feeling his power rise within. The scent of damp trees and earth couldn't mask the magic of the world, but he didn't direct it, not even to escape whatever torture Kian had waiting for him. Escaping wouldn't help him, only give Kian and Faelyn's court more reason to distrust him.

They ascended a steep hill as night fell, a welcome change from the flatlands and woods they'd crossed for days. Bastien's sore back pressed against the metal bars. His head drooped, nodding off. Street thieves learned to fall asleep in worse conditions. The wagon jerked to a stop, jarring him to look up. They'd reached the back of a tall white-painted building. The walls stretched wide, interspaced with ordinary windows. His guards hopped off the wagon, and he sat up. He couldn't begin to guess where they were.

They opened the door for the first time since leaving the castle in Pavora. The hinges squeaked in protest. Bastien stared at them. The guards exchanged a look, then stepped into the wagon, grabbing him by the arms. He landed on hard-packed dirt before they hauled him up. His numb butt reveled in the movement of walking again, even if it was between two silent-as-the-grave guards.

"Finally going to tell me where we're going?"

Two lanterns burned beside an open door—a simple white with a screened window.

"Shut up," one guard said, grunting as the pair hauled Bastien through the doorway.

The inside hallway was dark but clean—no blood or scuffs. The air smelled of stewed vegetables. *What is this place?* The only noise was the night insects he'd left outside and the sounds of movement somewhere in the building.

Polished floorboards led them to another door. The guards dropped his arms and shoved him roughly inside. His boots hit a door jam, sending him sprawling over the empty space, but he caught himself after stumbling a few steps. He turned in time to see their sneers before the door slammed closed and a lock clicked in place.

Wonderful. He flipped the knife he'd pulled from the guard's belt and smirked. *At least I got a consolation prize.* He patted the new money pouch in his pocket. The coins jangled.

The guards' laughter followed them back out of the building. The wagon creaked as they drove away. No other sounds reached his ears. Not the pacing of a watch guard—or the snoring of one. No sound of the usual prison activities.

He tucked the knife in his belt and surveyed his room. It was twice the size of his cell at the castle, but completely bare, without even a blanket or chamber pot. The floor was more of the hard wood, but scuffed and worn like heavy objects had been dragged across it. He jiggled the handle of the door. It turned freely, but when he pushed, the door wouldn't budge. Latched from the outside.

Bastien scratched his neck, still surprised by his missing hair. It would take forever to grow it back out. He sat on the hard floor. Maybe he would have forever. He smiled. And maybe that forever could be spent with Faelyn.

He lay on his back, staring up at the white ceiling. He was too keyed up to sleep, but he'd need his wits about him. Who knew what was in store when the sun came up? He closed his eyes and was out in moments.

Bastien jolted awake at the first hint of noise. Blue light seeped under the door. Dawn. Voices drifted through the wall. Two men and a woman conversed, but he couldn't make out what they were saying over the constant banging and the distinct, slow grating of knives or swords being sharpened—big, long ones by the sound of it.

He hopped to his feet, smacking his dry mouth. Was this part of the torture? They'd deny him food and drink, give him no information, then eventually hurt him until he talked? What more could he possibly say? Besides the one thing he'd go to his grave with, of course.

The knife sharpening ceased. More people joined the others, followed by more banging. Water boiling.

Bastien called his magic. He was willing to cooperate to a point, but he'd go down fighting if they planned on harming him.

Not much later, delicious, mouth-watering smells floated from under the door. Bacon. Sausage. Bastien hurried over, pressing his nose to the seam. His stomach rumbled. He banged his fist on the door.

"Hey!" he yelled at whatever guard was listening. "You won't get anything from me if I die of starvation!"

All activity in the next room halted. Completely.

Footsteps slowly approached his cell. Bastien backed nearly to the wall, hand hovering over his knife.

Someone fumbled with the latch. It clicked, then the door slowly opened. A man dressed in cotton trousers, a simple tunic with the sleeves rolled up, and a flour-dusted apron stood wide-eyed in the doorway.

"What are you doing in the pantry?" The man swallowed. "We feed the hungry every day at eleven. No need to steal." He had short black hair and a shiny, friendly face with red cheeks.

"Huh?" Bastien tilted his head. What in the Hereafter was going on? "I'm not a beggar."

"How did you manage to get yourself locked in here?" He opened the door a little further, and Bastien saw two women, hands over their mouths, peeking from behind. They wore white aprons as well.

"What? I didn't lock myself in here." His tone was incredulous. He held his magic back. The man's brow furrowed, making him look as confused as Bastien felt. "Your goons locked me up without food or water!"

"Goons?" He glanced to the women behind him, whispering, "Get Master Cinda."

They nodded and ran off.

"Why don't you tell me your name?" The man took a step into the room, hands raised.

Voices sounded from the adjacent room. Bastien glanced at the wall.

The man gasped, his mouth gaping open. "Your ears, like the queen! You're Bastien."

Bastien's eyebrows scrunched. "Of course I am. Haven't you been expecting me?" He'd never guess a prison transfer coming from Faelyn herself would be handled so sloppily. Something was definitely going on.

"Yes, we were, but... why are you in the pantry?" The man paused a beat. "Forgive me, you must be famished after your travel. Come to the kitchen. We have plenty to eat." He stepped back into the hall and motioned Bastien to follow.

Hand still hovering over his knife, Bastien took cautious steps. He rounded the corner of his cell—or pantry—and indeed entered a kitchen. The space was large and white, with sinks, tables, cabinets, and cooking fires that lit the room. Several more people stared at him, paused in the midst of chopping vegetables. And sharpening butcher knives.

"Everyone, this is Bastien." The man clapped him on the shoulder with a strong hand, making Bastien jump. "I heard he wasn't due until this afternoon, but here he is! Let's get him some breakfast, eh?" The man moved past, grabbing a plate from a shelf.

Bastien gaped as people rushed to pile it with food. "What is going on here? Will someone tell me where I am?"

A woman stepped into the doorway dressed in black mage robes, a sharp contrast to all the white. "You are at Thomats School of Magic, and we are pleased to host someone who shares our fair queen's unique attributes. I am Master Mage Cinda, head of the school." She dipped her head.

Her magic fell over him like spider's thread, testing and studying him.

"Thomats?"

The cooks exchanged glances.

"None of this makes any sense." He shook his head.

The man cocked an eyebrow, placing the plate in Bastien's hands. He set it down on a nearby carving table.

One eyebrow raised, the mage stepped further into the room with her staff in hand. She looked to be maybe in her thirties, red hair braided and rolled into a low bun at the back of her head. "I was told you were locked into the kitchen pantry."

"Yes!" Bastien jerked out a nod.

"I apologize, Bastien. It sounds like someone was having fun at your expense. Lord Kian sent a rider ahead explaining who you are and when you'd be arriving. He said we are to train you. That it is of the utmost importance."

"The wagon guards, they locked me up..." *Bastards!* They'd let him believe he was a prisoner. But instead he was at the best magic school in the continent, possibly the world, and they'd been ordered to train him by Faelyn's right hand.

Kian must have finally believed the Fating was real. Bastien had dreamed of seeing this place ever since he was a kid, picking pockets with Olin on his heels. He looked at the steaming plate of food. His anger slowly melted away, and a slow smile spread over his face. He was free. No torture. No prison.

He looked up at the mage, Cinda. "When do we start?"

She smiled. "Eat quickly, then follow me."

He grabbed the plate and took a fork from the cook with a nod of thanks. The warmth of the savory food filled his belly and soul. A tall cup of fresh milk washed it down.

"Thank you all. I'm sorry we had to meet in such a way." He set his dishes down in the sink.

The man who'd discovered him laughed. "That's a foul trick to play on someone. I'm Gus. I run this kitchen. You're welcome anytime."

"Thank you, Gus." Bastien beamed. These people treated him with respect. Did they not care that he was different from them? Did they not know his past? Cinda did, probably the worst version of it, coming from Kian. Yet she too treated him as an honored visitor.

So far.

Morning sun lighting the way, he followed her through a long hall lined with closed doors until they reached outside. He followed Cinda and jerked to a stop.

Thomats.

He'd only seen drawings in books at the orphanage, but the scene before him was unmistakable. A flat, sprawling lawn stretched beyond, interrupted by a courtyard connected to a tall building maybe three stories high. Marble columns surrounded the structure, wrapping all around until it connected back to where they stood. He'd never seen a building like it in all of Thera. Students in black robes hurried this way and that. A three-tiered fountain sprayed water from the mouths of fish, complementing the sounds of students conversing in the large space.

His wide eyes took it all in. "I've heard of the beauty of this place, but never could have imagined."

"Queen Faelyn provides for us very well. She studied here for a time, and my mother has trained her personally since the fall of Daltieri."

Bastien studied her red hair and rounded chin. "You're Niri's daughter."

"I am." She smiled and walked ahead. "She wrote to me too, singing your praises. Based on her recommendations, we've already selected which master mages to start you with. You need to become comfortable casting your magic without a staff, and of course, we'll focus solely on elemental magic."

"And what did Kian say about me?" He couldn't help himself.

Cinda glanced at him. "He said the queen is not to know you're here, which is strange, but I don't question my orders. He also said it was important to Queen Faelyn's safety for you to learn as much as possible quickly. I apologize, but due to his recommendation, we're forgoing our entry courses. We're also not placing you in classes with the other students. My mother indicated you haven't had much education, though you're very smart. Students come to Thomats already educated in basic non-magic courses. If you progress as steadily as I suspect you will, I'd like to bring a tutor to fill in any gaps."

Nearly to a door across the courtyard, Bastien stopped again. His mouth spread into a wide grin. "Thank you. Thank you so much." Maybe he could finally make himself worthy of Faelyn.

She smoothed her robe. "Don't thank me yet, Bastien. Lord Kian has set one condition to all of this." Her mouth formed a grim frown.

Bastien's spirits deflated. Of course the Fates wouldn't just hand over everything he wanted.

"I'm required to discover your past, your secret. Whatever you hid from my mother and denied Lord Kian."

Bastien stepped back from Cinda and the white door, studying her with new eyes. She must have inherited her mother's magic ability. His jaw clenched. His first instinct was to curse her to the Hereafter, steal a horse, and never look back. Luckily, he'd always had great control over his emotions.

His old goal was to survive. Now, he'd do anything to return to Faelyn, and the only way to do that was through Cinda.

"Do you have to tell anyone what you discover?"

Her frown deepened. "If it's a threat to the queen, yes." She fidgeted.

"What else are you to do if the secret's a threat to the queen?" He took a step closer.

She placed her staff between them. "I cannot say."

He watched it, feeling the thrum of magical potential in its crystal. "And if I'm not a threat to the queen?"

"Then it will be a secret only between you and me, unless Queen Faelyn orders me or I deem it information important to her rule."

"I give you my word, I'm not a threat to the queen or the kingdom. I would never do anything to harm her." He held his breath.

Her head shook softly. "I still have my orders. I still must look for myself."

Bastien nodded. Though not easy, his choice was clear. "Okay. I'll let you in." *When you've got nothing, you've got nothing to lose.*

Cinda's shoulders relaxed. "Thank you. I hope this difficult beginning doesn't sour our relationship. I want to help you, and in turn, help the queen."

His palms grew slick. "Let's do it now, or I might change my mind."

Cut me open, take my soul. Bleed me 'till I'm no longer whole. I will remember my goal.

THIRTY-TWO

Faelyn sat on the velvety cushions of her large window seat, head resting on her arms, staring westward as the rising sun unhurriedly bathed the town. If she squinted, she could barely make out where the forest began. She'd done as much as she could to prevent cutting further into the woods, but the town was growing too fast. They needed the space.

Why had she chosen this window to mope? The shrinking forest always depressed her. West just felt right today for some reason. Maybe Bastien had gone west. She let out a long sigh as Amerae's footsteps sounded behind her. It was good Kian was gone. She'd have forced him to tell her Bastien's location.

"A scout report came in, Your Majesty. Prince Rory has crossed into Kestrea."

Faelyn sat up. "In two weeks? That's outstanding time."

Amerae's hand drifted to her belly, bulging beneath a loose burgundy dress. Her dark hair spilled down her back. She looked radiant. "Yes, they pushed their horses hard, switching out for fresh ones often."

Faelyn looked toward the window. "I'm sure we'll hear from King

Bautamin soon." Her chin rested on her fist. In a few short minutes, she'd have to face her duties again. For now, she could spare her infallible reputation in front of Amerae. She didn't have the energy to care.

Amerae's steps retreated, followed by the sound of the bedroom door closing. To Faelyn's surprise, Amerae hadn't left. She padded back, easing her body down onto the cushions.

"Faelyn, I'm going to speak freely, and I ask the same of you." Amerae took a shallow breath. "Please tell me what's wrong. If you don't, I will guess and you probably won't like what I say."

"Go ahead and guess, Amerae. I'm saving my strength for what's ahead."

Amerae tsked, her essence growing irritated. "All right, you miss Kian and having his help and friendship. He understands you better than most, better than even me. You're upset things didn't work out with Prince Rory, even if he's a worm. You feel you've let your kingdom down by failing in this alliance."

Faelyn faced her, offering a small smile. "You're very observant, my friend." She patted Amerae's knee. "Don't worry. I'll shake this off soon."

"I wasn't finished, and this last reason overshadows all the rest." She looked at Faelyn with knowing eyes.

Faelyn's pulse sped up. How much did Amerae know?

"You've found the love you've waited a hundred years for, but everything is all wrong. Your court doesn't trust him. He's much younger than you. He's uneducated and a commoner, while you're royalty. And more than that, he's a criminal." Her words weren't harsh or judgmental, but they stung nonetheless.

Faelyn turned away, hiding the traitorous tears stinging her eyes. She wanted so much to be able to confide, to share her love and longing for this beautiful soul who was just like her, but it wouldn't change anything. Bastien would be just as out of reach as before.

She blinked a few times and stood. "Yes, that too, Amerae." She shook her head, and with it shook away all the things she wanted to say. Instead, she simplified. "You know me well. And despite all that's stacked against him, he's everything I could ever hope for, and everything I can't have." She nodded to herself and swallowed, not quite meeting Amerae's worried eyes, then hurried out of the room.

"Faelyn, come back," Amerae called.

Her protests faded into the background as Faelyn met a court clerk in the hall where he waited with a new list of items needing her attention. The beginning of one more day in what had become her monotonous existence. She needed to find a new alliance now, some other prince to marry before she gave in to her instincts and left her duties behind to track down Bastien.

THIRTY-THREE

Cinda led Bastien to a different section of the white-columned building which still boasted polished wood floors and smooth walls. Though empty of students, there were portraits of various men and women, posed in decorated mage robes, holding their staffs. A few hallways later, Bastien felt the presence of the mages before they turned the corner. Six mages stood lining the hall. They looked up, and he resisted the urge to hide his ears.

"This is the contingency, isn't it? In case I'm a threat?" Bastien's fists clenched.

"These are the members of the school council." Cinda gestured toward them but kept going, opening the door and ushering Bastien in.

They each nodded to him as he passed.

Cinda closed the door. "Because of the ridiculous manner of your delivery, word of your arrival has already spread. The board is concerned for the safety of the students. They are here as a contingency, as you put it. But also, they are curious and more than a little awed, like the rest of us. Queen Faelyn was thought to be one of a kind, but here you are." She gestured to a velvet couch with a red pillow. Besides that, the windowless room had only a simple chair.

Bastien sat on the couch and wiped his palms on his dirty trousers. His heart sped, and his magic sprang forward.

"You need to calm down." She patted the pillow indicating he should lie down. "I won't hurt you, but I also won't stop until satisfied. Whatever you've held back from my mother, it's best you get right to it. I'll find it either way. I'm the one who taught her, after all."

He gritted his teeth and lay back. The cushioned softness of the couch and pillow welcomed his weary bones, but his pounding heart betrayed him.

Cinda's staff glowed, the light overtaking the weak lanterns in the room. Bastien's magic rose up in response.

"No, no, Bastien. No magic. You might react defensively, and I don't want to be injured."

He nodded and forced his magic back, shrinking it smaller within himself, easy after suppressing it for so much of his life.

"Good. Your control is amazing." She placed a warm, dry hand on his forehead. "Close your eyes, and we'll begin."

He held them open, not even closing to blink for as long as possible, but there was no getting around it. This was his path now. Acantha forgive him.

He shut his eyes, and Cinda entered his mind. He slipped into a place between dream and awake, aware of everything she explored, yet unable to control or stop it. His mind knew he wasn't supposed to stop her, but his heart shrieked.

She started slowly, with pleasant memories, and he didn't resist, letting them and how they made him feel flow freely—as if he had a choice. He remembered Faelyn, the love in her eyes, the touch of her lips, the empowering feeling when he'd protected her from Prince Rory, knowing he'd live to defend her. Some of Cinda's emotions slipped through to him: her genuine shock at her new discovery. Her new understanding of why Kian had forbidden her to tell Queen Faelyn where Bastien was.

Cinda moved back to his time training as a soldier, proud and driven, and studying as a mage with Niri, then further back to his time with Tave and the House with Kolb and Olin. Those events were all well-known and not what she was looking for, Bastien knew, so she did too.

Images of a woman flashed in his mind, cradling and smiling down on him. The warmth of the blanket he was bundled in filled him with peace. She was pretty, with kind eyes. Her pleasant gaze averted at the sound of a cackling voice.

"What's it still doing here? I said get that thing out of my sight." The woman wailed, carrying on about her child being switched by a demon.

The kind woman lifted Bastien to her shoulder, giving him a view of a dilapidated shack lit only by a candle. "What would you have me do with him?" She patted Bastien's back in a comforting rhythm.

"Throw it in the river," the woman snapped back. She paused, then began wailing again.

The kind woman gasped, rushing outside the shack to a forest lit by the moon. "I'll protect you, little one. I'll find you somewhere safe. Tales of the fae queen of the south cannot be false, not after what I've seen this night. The Fates are at work here."

Bastien and Cinda came to a realization at the same time. That cackling lady had been his mother, and the woman, whoever she was, must have taken him to the orphanage. Cinda had delved into a past even he didn't remember. But that's not what she was after.

What she wanted was further ahead. As soon as Bastien thought it, Cinda latched on, prying his memories open even further, digging way, way deep. His magic spiked, filling him from an overflowing reservoir. The world glowed. He'd failed to protect Olin. He wouldn't fail to protect Eliot.

Eliot.

She'd made him think his name. He'd nearly forgotten it, had forced himself to, just like he'd forced his fae magic into hiding. *Eliot, my brother, I'm so sorry.*

No!

Fire, and earth, and light. Lightning, and water, and wind. His mind was a storm, and he could stop Cinda. He would stop her.

Bastien. Cinda eased back, drawing her prying grasp away from his brother. *You're hurting me, Bastien. Remember, you must let me in. Let me through the layers of heartache and hardship.*

"No!" He blinked awake and pushed up to his feet, stumbling. He gaped at his surroundings. The velvet couch had been reduced to ash.

His vision blurred through dizziness and tears. The mage council stood in a circle around him, faces intent and staffs glowing. A shield of air enveloped Bastien, trapping him. Steam rose from the blackened floor, holes in spots. He'd made it rain and had called fire. Cinda cradled the palm she'd held to his brow, blistered and raw but already healing.

He looked down. His clothes had been burned away. He was naked but for the ash he'd smeared thrashing around.

He lifted his chin, breathing heavily. "I'm sorry, Cinda. I cannot allow you in."

The shield around him dissipated. A student mage entered the room carrying a spare mage robe. Bastien took it, shrugging into the black folds.

"I told you that I would get in rather you let me or not. Please don't force my hand." Cinda took the staff from the crook of her arm. "I want to be friends. I want to help you."

She spoke the truth. He felt it in her essence and saw it in her earnest eyes. He could go far if he cooperated, and it probably meant death if he didn't.

"I don't know if my magic will allow you to pry so deep." Had it been him who wreaked such havoc, or his lack of control?

"If that's all it is, we can help you." She gestured to the other mages.

Bastien shifted his stance, glancing left and right. "I don't know if that's all it is," he said through clenched teeth. Death was better than the pain of reliving his past.

"Will you lie down?"

Bastien looked to the ashy floor. "I will not."

"Then we will help you to complete this difficult task." Her staff lit up. "Remember, only I will see your past, and I'm trying to help you."

Bastien tensed. "Help Kian, you mean."

Cinda nodded to the mage at her right. Bastien called his magic and lunged for the door.

His limbs locked in place. He slammed face-first into the door, forehead scraping wood as he slid to the floor. His mind screamed, body fighting to move. His eyes roved, but all he saw from being face down on the ground were shuffling feet. White light burst from him. Snarling and feral, his magic struggled for any way to combat the spell.

"None of that now." Cinda's words came faint beneath his panic.

The power of multiple master mages was upon him like heavy ropes weighing him down. A shield. A spell to calm his mind. Darkness to dampen his white glow. He struggled harder, pushing against the force that would resist him. His magic bubbled out, nearly bursting the bindings of the mages' combined efforts.

His eyes, the only thing he could control, drooped as another rope fell into place, a spell to make him sleep. *No, Eliot. No...* A warm hand on his forehead. *Forgive me.* Then nothing but memories.

The images flooded against Bastien's will. He had a brother, Eliot, who was one of his very first Fatings when Bastien was four years old. He'd seen him coming, a knock at the door in the middle of the night.

Days later, the infant Eliot was left at the orphanage. Miss Bannings knew right away they were brothers. They had the same eyes. And the same ears. Except for the age difference, she'd said they could have been twins. Bastien took one look at the tattered blanket and ears just like his and knew he'd forever love that crying infant, his brother.

Bastien showed Eliot everything. He helped him learn how to walk, then talk, and even some of his letters. Bastien's hair was long enough to hide his ears, but Miss Bannings said it was best to keep Eliot out of sight until his grew out. They didn't play outside much, except when it was dark and their eyes could see where humans could not. They even slept in a separate room—the back storage room, which was out of sight of the other boys in case their ears were revealed in their sleep.

Eliot followed him everywhere. He loved his big brother and copied everything he did.

One night, they lay in their shared cot when Eliot decided to make fire dance in the palm of his hand, practicing a trick Bastien had shown him.

Bastien smiled. "Put that away, Eliot, and go to sleep. You know we can't do magic here." He snuggled next to his brother, eyes drooping, silently promising to always protect him.

He awoke to the room ablaze and Eliot's screams from the corner near where they sometimes snuck handfuls of sugar. Bastien threw himself off the cot. Smoke was thick in the air, but fear choked him. He summoned every ounce of magic in his control, trying to counteract the blaze. It wouldn't respond to his call. Panic blinded his efforts.

Desperate, he charged through the fire, choking and coughing as the heat entered his lungs. His skin burned in searing pain, healing itself and scorching in tandem, driving him back. He was about to leap again when Miss Bannings caught him by the arm. He fought against her, but his tiny, seven-year-old body wasn't strong enough to break free.

All his love and protection couldn't keep Eliot from harm. He'd been three years old.

Bastien had failed his brother and joined Kolb's gang within days. His biggest shame followed by his biggest mistake.

After that, he'd sworn off magic forever—buried it and his memories deep inside—and vowed to never reveal his true self.

Cinda's warm hand, now clammy, left his skin. The spells lifted one by one, and when awareness resurfaced, Bastien found himself crying, curled into a ball on his side. His body shook with sobs. His full magic returned, but it couldn't heal this kind of agony.

Someone rubbed his back, startling him to awareness of his surroundings. The mages were gone. Only Cinda remained.

"There's no shame in this, Bastien. Everyone bleeds tears when their souls have been scraped raw." Her voice was gentle and full of infuriating understanding.

He shook off her touch, taking deep breaths to control himself. She sat back and waited. Eventually his crying stopped, but he did not move. She held a cup of water in front of him. His sandy tongue scratched his mouth. He took the water and sat up to drink the entire cup.

He wiped his face with a handkerchief she'd placed on the floor, likely knowing his pride wouldn't allow him to take it from her and acknowledge the tears. She probably knew him better than he knew himself now. He shuddered.

"So you admit you've hurt me enough to make me bleed?" His voice was hoarse, as if the screaming in his mind had been real.

"I do, and I'm sorry." Cinda paused. "It wasn't your fault. None of it was. And it's okay to forgive yourself." Her voice broke.

He peeked over his shoulder, looking at her for the first time since awakening. She sat, shoulders slumped and head bowed.

When she glanced up, fresh tears spilled down her cheeks. "You've had a hard life, Bastien, harder than most. Yet you've persevered and are truly here for the right and good reasons. Don't hold on to your anger and forget what those are." She took his hand where it rested on the ground.

He pulled it back, turning away. "I don't think I can stay here."

"I know it hurts, and I know you think I know too much about you, but I promise, that will only help me teach you. You could be great here. We were almost unable to contain your magic. If you'd had formal training, we couldn't have. Already, I have a love for you, as one can only have when one has seen the true essence of another. I wish I could explain it." She sighed, long and weary. "The other mages left before you came to. They don't know what I found, only that I've deemed you not a threat, and that you are very powerful. You are free to go so long as you don't return to Pavora, but I wholeheartedly encourage you to stay."

He pushed to his feet, catching himself against the wall during a wave of fatigue. He could barely think through his tiredness.

"We both must rest now. You've spent much of your magic and energy, as well as the emotional exhaustion. There is a room prepared for you right across the hall. I imagine you'll sleep the rest of the day and night, but food and water will be brought to you at regular intervals."

"Do you have to tell Queen Faelyn?" He regained his footing and reached down to help her up.

She accepted the offer with a grateful smile, standing. "Only that you aren't a threat to her or the kingdom."

He nodded, reaching for the comfort her words should have brought, but finding none.

"Your love for her is great, Bastien. Memories through my gift don't lie. I can see the truth from the imagined. There is a bond, a connection, that goes deeper than any human love I've seen, and I'm not referring to the inexplicable draw you felt. It's real. I'm sorry it's not to be." She patted his arm, and this time he didn't reject her.

"Yeah. Me too." He leaned against the wall, exhausted anew.

"Come, I must rest too. I'll show you to your room." She opened the door. New, younger mages stood outside. They didn't seem surprised by Bastien's state, though a couple surveyed the ruined room with wide eyes. They hovered as if expecting one of them to drop.

Thinking it was entirely possible, Bastien made his way across the hall to his prepared room. His vision blurred if his eyes moved too fast. Magic lit a lamp, revealing the cozy space—a small rug and an inviting bed, a simple dresser topped with a basin of water, and a platter of food. He nearly groaned with hunger.

"Goodnight Bastien. Don't make any decisions until the morning. Best not to think too hard right now."

"I just want to sleep." He gazed longingly at the bed. It was a clear indication of his exhaustion that sleep was winning over food.

"Good. I'll find you in the morning." Cinda smiled a weary smile, not quite masking her worry.

Bastien was halfway to the bed when the door shut. He fell in, not wasting time undressing or getting under the blanket. His raw emotions needed a place to hide from the pain. Sleep was a welcome relief.

Bastien awoke with his eyes crusted shut. He rolled over, kicking at his tangled mage robe and rubbing his face. Breakfast sat steaming on a silver platter. The smell of fresh bacon and eggs enticed him to sit up, only slightly dizzy. He smacked his dry mouth and then drank the cup of cold water on his bedside, unnerved someone had been in the room while he slept.

He wolfed the food down, bacon burning his throat. The crunch of fresh, toasted bread with butter eased the ache in his belly. He breathed in deeply. His heart still felt the sting of the memories and the bitterness from the intrusion, but he felt lighter, almost freer. The weight he'd carried had been lifted slightly. Cinda had done that for him, even if against his will. She was a powerful mage, and Niri's daughter.

He missed his brother fiercely, but it felt right to finally think of him. He deserved to be remembered.

A knock sounded at his door. It was her.

"Come in." He smoothed back his short hair, his hand coming up ashen. He glanced at the bed, cream sheets turned black, and shrugged.

Cinda entered with a fresh pitcher of water, cool drops beading its sides. She'd bathed and wore a fresh robe. "How are you feeling?"

"I'm angry with you," he snarled half-heartedly. "You betrayed my trust. But I feel better after resting and eating."

"Anger is good. You have every right to feel that way." She set down the pitcher. "Have you reached a decision?"

He hadn't given much thought to staying or going, but the answer broke free anyway. "I'm staying. I want to do what I can for Faelyn."

Her initial grin of excitement faded. "Yes, I saw your Fating. I know it is real. I believe Lord Kian does too, which is why he asked me to train you quickly, and I agree. If you're well enough, we begin today."

"Good. Let's get started."

THIRTY-FOUR

Faelyn took a small bite of roast chicken, grateful for the brief respite from her duties. Her courtiers sat around the long dining table, chatting pleasantly with each other. The ladies wore fine gowns of silk, corseted at the waist, ruffled at the neck. The colors varied. Some wore blue because they knew she favored it on herself. The men wore tailored tunics in earth tones but heavily embroidered in bold patterns. She listened to the words they didn't say—the currents and emotions behind seemingly innocuous conversation. It paid to be up to date on the kingdom's holdings, and these were the ladies and lords who helped her do that.

She took a sip of water, staring unseeing down the table. The dark wood boasted a lace runner, fresh flowers, and dainty displays of the usual lunch fair. At least it was only lunch, and there was less of an audience to smile for. She'd hidden her melancholy well, she thought, but a letter had arrived from Kian admonishing her for moping. It wouldn't last forever, Amerae said, but a month had passed since Bastien left, and things weren't getting easier.

Nolan's most trusted guards stood around the room, at attention, but just as bored as she was. In fact, most of these people were bored. The feeling hung in the air. They smiled and feigned delight in politics and trade, matchmaking and matrimony, but it was an act. This was a job to them, as much as socializing during meals was a job for her.

Faelyn tilted her head, earning a few smiles. She turned, looking left and right. Something else was in the air.

Panic. Fear.

She shot to her feet. The room went silent. Steps. Thundering steps of two people running down the hall, coming her way. She called her magic.

"Queen Faelyn, is anything the matter?" Lady Williams was the brave soul to speak up.

None of them felt or heard what she did.

Two guards burst through the open doorway, wide eyes locking on Faelyn. She tensed.

"Your Majesty, Lady Amerae sent us." The guard panted, struggling to catch his breath. "There's news. From Kestrea."

"You're needed in the council room, Queen Faelyn," the other guard, Cas, finished for his partner.

She ignored the excited whispers behind her and hurried past the guards. They followed, along with several others, stepping quickly to keep pace.

Riders from Kestrea. This wasn't a simple visit. The guards were afraid. She'd have to tread carefully. She'd fallen into the trap of using peoples' emotions to interpret the situation before, rather than her own judgment. They often misconstrued the information, leading Faelyn to believe a false reality.

Only one thing came to her that explained why they might be here, but she wouldn't even think it.

"What's the news, Cas?" she asked.

Servants and guards buzzed around them. The news was spreading quickly.

"They've crossed into our lands, my queen. Prince Rory and a legion of one thousand riders."

Faelyn stumbled, rounding on Cas. "How far away?"

Cas swallowed. "Lady Amerae said she has the answers you seek."

Faelyn ground her teeth and took the stairs two at a time. Once in the council room, she sat at its head. Only Amerae and Nolan were in the room, but more lords filed in.

Amerae stood. "They are a week away, Your Majesty. Our border guards witnessed them cross, then hurried to return the message. There's been no report of an attack. They aren't trying to hide, and we haven't found any more crossing. They know that's not enough to be a threat, so my only thought is it's a warning. They've brought enough to get our people's attention, and protect themselves against small skirmishes."

Faelyn clenched her hands into fists, longing for a sword to swing. "Have they sent a messenger? Have we tried to contact them?"

"No messenger, and they refuse to see our messengers. Their only reply is that they will speak solely to you."

Faelyn paced, eyes on the mosaic beneath her feet. King Bautamin of Kestrea had only ever desired peace for his kingdom. Kestrea hadn't been part of any conflict in her living memory. Prince Rory couldn't be in Alysies for malicious reasons. Still...

"We can't let them reach the town," Faelyn said. "We don't need panic or Kestrea soldiers nosing around while we negotiate whatever terms Rory's pretending to offer for this so-called affront." She turned to Amerae and Nolan. "He will not enter Pavora. I will not have a potential enemy legion enter my peaceful domain."

"I've already called the citadel to action, one-thousand troops to match his," Amerae said.

Faelyn nodded her approval. "Good. No need to make a show of force. I will ride out within the hour. Nolan, you'll accompany me ahead of the army. Send word to Kian."

"Already done, my queen," Amerae said.

The lords sat mostly silent, watching the exchange. They trusted her to make the best decisions for Alysies.

"I'm giving Lady Amerae authority to act as steward in my absence, but I don't suspect to be gone long. Nolan, make your preparations and meet me at the stables in one hour."

If Kian were here, he would have spoken up, reminding her she was needed more at the castle than to intercept a childish prince. She smiled. He wasn't here, and her friends who were wouldn't speak up unless they thought she was endangering herself.

Amerae and Nolan bowed, as did the lords, and she swept out, issuing orders for her armor and horse to be readied. For an entire quarter of an hour, she hadn't thought about Bastien, and now her mind had other things to keep itself occupied. Her blood sang, anxious for the coming conflict. She'd been polite and pleasant to the pompous prince for as long as she could stand it, but they wouldn't march troops onto her soil and get away with it.

Half an hour later, armored in a fine blue leather vest with the silver Alysian crest and a short attached skirt over riding trousers, she paced. Her blue cape fluttered with each turn, and a less valuable, but no less ornate, circlet shifted on her brow. Her horse, a hearty white and gray spotted mare, waited saddled and ready. Servants rushed to fill the saddlebags with needed supplies. Extra water bags were hung to combat the side effects of expending magic.

She thought she'd go mad with impatience when Nolan finally showed, similarly armored, but for the lipcolor smeared across his lips and cheek.

Faelyn grinned. "Let's go."

They mounted their horses and left ahead of her preparing army. She wasn't worried about approaching Rory's legion alone, only preventing him from reaching the city. Whatever this new threat was, she'd meet it head-on.

THIRTY-FIVE

After three days of hard riding, they spotted Prince Rory's legion across a distant field. Faelyn stood beside Nolan, reigns locked tight in her fist. From the cover of the trees, they watched the Kestrea legion break camp. There were indeed a thousand of them.

The sun was rising, making the crisp white tents orange. Some of them were already being taken down in preparation for departure. The soldiers went through the morning routine of doling out food to long lines. Several ranks spanned across the field, and she sensed mages amongst them before spotting their staffs. Of course Rory would bring some. It'd be foolish not to. In the center stood a large tent edged in green with double Kestrean flags fluttering atop.

"Wait for me here, Nolan. Retreat if things go awry. You know what to do." She handed him her reins.

He opened his mouth, closed it, then sighed through his nose. "Yes, Your Majesty."

Faelyn removed her cape and then stepped forward through the trees, taking the two sentries by surprise.

The men jumped at their post. "Halt!" They drew their swords.

Faelyn ignored them, continuing on toward Rory's tent through the masses.

"Sound the alarm!"

Shouts rang out around camp. The ringing sound of swords being drawn accompanied the neighing of panicked horses.

She stepped through the ranks of drilling soldiers, calm but steady. They eyed her incredulously, grips tightening on their swords. No one dared attack, but her magic lay in waiting. They parted before her until she reached Rory's tent. The guards moved to block her way, neither speaking nor meeting her eyes.

The feel of magic seeped into the air behind her. The mages were trying to hide their presence, but they were there. At least a dozen. She sensed Rory seething inside the tent, throwing a tantrum like a child. King Bautamin, being the reasonable and peaceable ruler he was, must have talked sense into his son and convinced him to beg forgiveness. Well, they could have picked a better way to start than this ridiculous show of force.

She addressed the guards, loud enough for Rory to hear. "Your presence is an act of war that I'm currently choosing to ignore. However, if you don't move out of my way, I will gladly use force."

"Acantha's sake, let her in." Rory's gruff voice came muffled from inside the tent.

The guards stepped aside, and a servant held open the tent flap. She ducked inside, eyes immediately adjusting to the dark space. The sour scent of tanned animal hide and furs assaulted her. Rory sat upon a makeshift throne—a thick wooden chair set atop a moveable platform. He lounged as if bored by her presence, but his anxiety could not be hidden from her fae senses.

Faelyn stopped in the middle of the tent. Fur rugs carpeted the stuffy space. Servants and guards eyed her warily. Rory yawned.

"Welcome back to Alysies, young prince. You left so suddenly, I thought we might never see you again."

He frowned, sitting up a bit taller. "It wasn't by choice I've returned to these forsaken lands. My father sent me."

Faelyn suppressed a smile. So, King Bautamin could see reason after all. He needed Alysies as an ally. "Then why the soldiers? Surely you didn't fear an attack."

"They're for my protection, naturally." He snapped his fingers.

An overdressed aid, with puffy sleeves and a feather cap, stepped forward. He bowed to Rory and passed him a sheet of parchment. Rory unrolled the paper and held it up. Their engagement contract. Did he mean to renegotiate the terms? Well, that wasn't going to happen.

Rory snapped his fingers again, and a servant proffered a tray with a lit candle and a large empty bowl. Rory took the candle and held it to the corner of the contract. It caught fire, flames spreading quickly before he dropped it into the bowl.

Faelyn tensed, stretching her senses for the presence of the mages. They surrounded the tent but held their ground. *Don't do anything stupid, Nolan.*

Rory smiled as the servant carried the ashes away. "I feel freer already."

She didn't know what to think. Was he acting against his father's wishes?

"I have one for you, though I would advise against burning it." He waved his hand, and a document was brought to her.

She unrolled it, quickly scanning the contents. Her blood ran cold. She blinked and reread, not quite believing the words.

"You've gone pale, Your Majesty. Do you like my father's signature at the bottom?" He leaned forward.

"Kestrea is declaring war on Alysies under the false pretense of a broken marriage contract? This can't possibly be legitimate." Her fists clenched around the paper.

Rory sneered. "You can't possibly be so stupid. Your act of infidelity voided the contract. Kestrea is now denied land, resources, and certain rights our union would have secured for us. You've left us with no choice."

"Your father would never declare war with no negotiations, no warning or chance to make amends." The pompous ass was up to something. Rory's words were layered with the feel of hidden lies and half-truths, but nothing clear. She snarled her next words. "You've damned your people."

Rory shot to his feet. "Your actions caused this, Faelyn, not mine."

Her magic flickered white light in anger. "Alysies will bury you. Why would your king wish for this? Why would he send his heir here to declare war?"

"Believe me, my presence is worth it just to see the look on your face when I tell you this next piece of information." He paused. The side of his mouth curled up. "We have a new ally. They were all too eager to join with us."

No! The room spun, but Faelyn gritted her teeth and planted her feet.

"Alysies will fall, and Kestrea and Daltieri will reap the spoils. Our soldiers are already mobilized." He smiled in immense satisfaction, then glanced meaningfully to his left and right.

A soldier banged a gong. The mages surrounding the tent attacked. Bursts of invisible magic shot toward her, seeking to bind her in place. She bared her teeth at the watching prince and doubled the strength of the shield she'd put up the moment she'd stepped into his camp.

The prince grinned, anticipating her fall, not realizing she was already under attack. Eight mages. Not all Rory had with him. She sensed their fear of her, their meticulous efforts to find a way through to her. Their magic struck against her shield like painless pinpricks. The building fury and shock broke through her tight dam. She raised her arm, fingers curved upward.

Rory's smile dropped. He cowered further into his throne as his guards drew their swords.

Concentrating, she traced the magic back to the mages, latching onto the crystals of the four behind the tent so they'd be more out of sight of the army. They panicked, trying to cut off the attack. She clenched her fingers, and as if she held their crystals in her grip, crushed them all at once.

Their agonized screams pierced through the tent walls, bathing the room in more fear. The pinprick attacks from the remaining mages ceased. Rory's eyes went wide.

Faelyn shook her head slowly. "Why? Why would you do this? For your pride?"

"Seize her!" Rory leaped behind his throne, pointing.

The rest of the guards in the tent drew their swords and charged. The two closest swung. In an instant, Faelyn had her sword out and thrust up, catching their swords. She threw out her hand, channeling magic into a burst of air that tossed the two into more approaching guards. Limbs flailing, they all tumbled into the tent wall.

She straightened. With a thought, she stole the breath from the remaining guards. They struggled, choking and writhing, until collapsing to the ground.

Slowly, she stepped toward the prince who stood, eyes wide, clutching the back of his chair like it might protect him. How dare they ally against Alysies? What had he told the king?

Rory's furious face turned to panic, and he drew his sword.

"Your king didn't want this." She held her sword up in warning. There'd be no stopping this if she killed Kestrea's heir.

"You've forced my father's hand. We will have these lands." He looked over her shoulder. "Where's my legion, you idiots?" he shouted.

A servant beside the entrance placed a horn to his lips and ran out of the tent, blasting the instrument.

The document had been signed and served. Rory's life or death wouldn't stop what was already in motion.

She sheathed her sword as the horn blared behind her. "Since we are now at war..."

The legion's uproar was deafening, but she didn't give it a thought. Her white magic filled up the space, and she focused on the dirt beneath the horrid animal furs. The earth beneath Rory's throne trembled. The rugs shook up and down. Rory glanced down, hate and fear in his eyes.

"My queen!" Nolan called from outside. Curse him—he hadn't waited with the horses as she'd told him to.

A heartbeat later, a sword whistled through the air outside the tent, followed by a thwack as it met its mark. The canvas sagged on one side of the tent.

Rory glanced side-to-side. Two more thwacks of the sword. Servants screamed. In no time, the throne had sunk several feet. Rory lunged for the edge, but she knocked him back with wind. She would bury the bastard alive.

Soldiers piled into the tent, but with a final thwack, Nolan finished his task, and the tent collapsed. Faelyn crouched, but the poles toppled, and the weight crashed on top of her. The screams went muffled, and the world went dark. She tried to push to her feet, but the heavy fabric wouldn't budge, trapping her against the fur rugs.

There were too many reasons to panic, but her wits stayed razor-sharp. She directed the magic to in a weak burn, and slowly, a hole opened above her. Sunlight streamed through, along with a breeze of fresh air. She pushed to her feet, finally free. Around her, the collapsed tent covered squirming, screaming bodies, and beyond it, Nolan had engaged three Kestrean soldiers while more pressed closer, trying to find a way in.

"Get her!" a voice yelled from behind.

Faelyn swiveled. Her eyes went wide. An entire legion had surrounded the tent. They roared and charged. Her heart, already thrumming, went racing.

Sorry about this, Nolan.

Air whistled into her lungs as she inhaled, building her magic up and adding it to her already stocked reservoir. The soldiers reached the downed tent. She threw herself down. Air blasted out in a circle around her with the force of a hurricane. The soldiers cried out, their bodies hurled backward in a crash of armor and bone.

The world spun as Faelyn stood—she'd expended too much magic. The Kestrea army lay scattered about the trees and grass. Orders were shouted to regroup. She turned and leaped over the people still struggling beneath the tent, nearly falling as she pitched to the side.

"Nolan!" she shouted.

Among several downed Kestrea soldiers, Nolan pushed himself up, using a thick tree for support. Blood trickled down his forehead.

"Don't let them get away!" a soldier shouted.

Pinpricks of pain raked over her shield as magic assaulted her from the remaining mages. The foulness of it coated her tongue—her shield was failing. She'd pushed herself too far.

Nolan's eyes went wide. His limbs locked stiff, and he fell over into the brush.

She rushed to his side and extended her thinning shield to him. Placing a hand on his forehead, she healed the shallow gash. His limbs unlocked, and she pulled him to his feet. He nodded a quick thanks. Boots pounded behind them.

They ran into the trees, Faelyn in the lead. Their horses were all the way on the other side of camp. The trees here were young and thin, not much cover, but with no better options, they stuck to them, running as fast as they could.

Soldiers crashed into the trees behind and next to them. Neither had breath to speak. If she did, she'd scream. Her plan to ensure the safety of her people had rebounded. This was the kind of thing Daltieri had been waiting for all along.

Rory's shouts competed with the snapping of sticks and rustle of brush. He'd survived.

Faelyn and Nolan reached where they'd left their horses. The horses were gone. They panted for breath, hands on their knees, and exchanged a long glance. The magic from the mages hammered her shield. The roar of the army crescendoed.

Faelyn straightened. Was this the moment Bastien had fated? Was he coming for her now?

"Let's run, Your Majesty." Nolan's jaw clenched. Neither of them were cowards, but they weren't fools either.

She nodded. "Let's go."

They took off running just as the first soldiers trampled through the brush. Bows twanged, arrows landing all around them. One hit its mark on her back. Her shield gave. She cried out, stumbling as it bounced off her armor. She caught herself on Nolan's arm and pushed on, throwing more magic into their shield.

They couldn't hold out like this. Already the sound of hooves rounding the trees was overtaking the cry of the foot soldiers.

"Nolan." She stopped and turned, drawing her sword.

Adrenaline rushed through her veins. The cavalry was coming. If they could fell the first couple of soldiers and secure horses, they could escape.

Nolan, in his bravery, didn't question or hesitate. He stepped to her side, eyes focused ahead, likely seeing his end storming to meet him in the form of a hundred horses. Dirt flew as hooves ate up the short distance of the field.

Another sound drifted underneath her panting and the pounding hooves... coming from behind, pushed away by the wind, but there. She planted her feet and sent her senses toward Pavora. Thunderous hooves. Crisp banners flapping.

She breathed deeply with the hope blooming in her heart. "Change of plans. Run."

She took off again, Nolan close on her heels. The horses charged closer, but all she needed was a little time.

An involuntary cry fell from her lips as the tips of the blue Alysian banners crested the shallow hill. Pride sent her legs flying. The front line came into view. Her people had arrived.

The Kestrea cavalry slowed, then stopped as orders came to form lines and regroup. Her army rushed to meet them, eyes angry and faces eager. They reached her, and she was blissfully, gratefully engulfed into the ranks. Relief immediately surrounded her, providing water and aid. Soldiers formed a protective barrier as the captains and their general filed in. Two fresh horses were brought to them.

Faelyn took a long drink, then a deep breath. She locked eyes with her general. "Bury them."

Excited shouts rang out. The general issued orders, and the captains rushed to rejoin their companies. Faelyn and Nolan mounted their new horses. With practiced speed, their lines reformed, her at the head beside Nolan.

Her one-thousand troops were all mounted, superiorly trained, and eager.

Faelyn nodded, and the general gave the order. As one, her army charged, screaming in defiance. Her horse bolted forward, its powerful muscles rippling with the strike of hooves. Faelyn screamed along with them. Their victory would be sure, but this was only the beginning.

Kestrea had regrouped, infantry in front of cavalry. On a command, they released arrows. Faelyn cringed. Her soldiers would raise their shields, but some would die. She sent a blast of wind toward the volley, knocking the center portion off course. The rest found their marks. Horses screamed and fell, but she couldn't think of that.

Soldier and horse converged into the Kestrea lines. Her horse trampled troops as she swung, plunging ahead without shying. Men screamed as her sword struck true, seeking weak spots in the enemy armor, again and again until the battlefield turned into a blur of motion, blood, and unending uproar. No mages attacked. She didn't sense any magic.

At a break in the bouts, she scanned the masses. Swords arced through the cloudless sky as their masters aimed for blood. Horses reared. Bodies littered the ground. He horse huffed and stomped beneath her. Prince Rory was not among his troops.

She turned to the soldiers at her flank, each engaged in combat to keep the enemy away from her. "Follow me."

They broke from their fights as she led them toward the back of the enemy ranks, racing past infantry swinging to hack at their horses' legs. They'd almost reached the outskirts of the battlefield when a squad of Kestrean cavalry charged, cutting off her path. They were protecting their prince, the coward.

The enemy swarmed her small group, swords ready. Faelyn swung at the first attacker, the metal-on-metal vibrating down her arm. Around her came the clangs of her soldiers engaging the enemy. Her opponent pivoted his horse to attack her from the side, eager eyes on her crown. Rage ignited her magic, and she hit him with a gust of air. He tumbled screaming off his horse. She charged through the opening he'd left. The field beyond was empty. She scanned the horizon, but there was no one.

Rory was gone.

She turned back to her army. More of her soldiers had joined the fight against the Kestrea cavalry squad. Barely any green remained upright amongst her blue. It was over almost as quickly as it'd begun. She sheathed her bloody sword as a victory cry rang out from her army.

Hands and swords pumped into the air, but she couldn't join them. What if it was a trap? A diversion to draw her from Pavora. They had to get back.

"Nolan," she called.

He trotted to her from a group of leaders, sweat pouring down his face, but no blood.

"My queen." He bowed in his saddle.

"I must return, but Rory has fled. Send a squad of our best, but tell them not to be seen. His mages are with him, and they'll bind them if discovered."

"I'll see to it personally."

"No!" Her heart raced. At his surprised look, she lowered her voice. "I need you back at the castle." The men she sent might die for their efforts, but they had to try.

He bowed and issued orders. In no time, their dead were gathered, she'd healed the injured, and they were marching back to Pavora, exhaustion finally seeping into her bones.

"Is Pavora okay, Nolan?" Her fierce worry leaked into her tone.

He nudged his horse closer as they galloped, speaking over the wind. "No riders from the city have reported any attack yet, Your Majesty, but I sent our fastest ahead. We'll know for sure within a day."

It'd been the longest day of her life. With a single blow, they'd gone from hope for a prosperous future to a state of war.

She prayed to the Fates to keep her people safe. *Where are you, Bastien?*

CHAPTER

THIRTY-SIX

For the fifth time that morning, lightning penetrated Bastien's shield, hitting him with blinding pain until he fell to the grassy ground.

His limbs twitched from the after-affect, and he groaned. "Acantha above, Pinea!" He pushed up to all fours, glaring up at his aether tutor.

She rushed to his side. "I'm sorry! I'm so sorry, Bastien." Her unique accent elongated the r's. She bent over him, and her blonde hair whacked him in the face. Pinea was young as far as master mages went, but very talented. She hailed from an island east of Kestrea.

"Don't apologize to him. He's sloppy. Distracted." Cinda paced around him, one hand behind her back, the other using her staff like a walking stick. She'd overseen every training session this past month and had adopted tough love as her preferred teaching method.

Whatever. He'd known worse.

They stood on a hill outside the school grounds overlooking the trees and valley below. He glanced eastward, slowly rising to his feet. Inexplicable worry had eaten at him all morning.

"Something's happened with the queen," he said softly.

The two master mages exchanged glances.

Cinda stopped in front of him. "Possibly, but you can do nothing about it from here, except to continue training and preparing." She waved her staff toward Pinea. "Again."

Bastien snapped back to the moment, throwing magic into his shield. He'd learned to use air to fend off objects such as swords and arrows, combined with aether to repel magical attacks, but he hadn't yet been strong enough to keep Pinea out, only dull the strike. If his attention slipped again, he'd be roasted.

Magic built around Pinea, electricity pooling in the air. His short hair stood on end. He clenched his teeth and braced himself, eyes on the horizon. The bolt, thicker and faster this time, struck his shield in a continuous white beam. He raised his hands, yelling through the effort to hold it a bay. The force increased. He pushed one final time, praying it'd be enough.

It wasn't. His shield shattered into blinding pain.

Pinea cut off the magic, but not before he fell, writhing on the ground.

She winced. "I'm sorry, Bastien. Cinda told me to increase. I thought you could take it."

He rolled over face down in the dirt, breathing heavily. Scents of grass and burnt hair assaulted him.

"That was about the extent of my ability, if that makes you feel better." Her voice was apologetic. She was barely winded. He'd built up his stamina significantly, but the day had been long.

Bastien couldn't spare a thought to easing Pinea's guilt. He could feel the smoke rising from his singed mage robe. His healing magic took over automatically, thank Acantha, because he could hardly move.

"You say you want to be a soldier?" Cinda shuffled closer.

Here we go.

"You say you want to be ready to help our queen and defend our kingdom? Soldiers don't have the liberty of napping in the grass when they're tired or hurt. Get up and try again."

He mentally shook himself. Cinda was right. He pushed to his feet, angry with himself. This wasn't the moment for his dumb antics. He'd come so far since arriving at Thomats, but this attitude wouldn't help him go further. His pain and suffering now could be Faelyn's salvation another day. He squared his shoulders.

Cinda smiled. "Good. Again."

The distress coming from the horizon lessened. Hopefully Faelyn was okay. For now. He pulled his gaze to Pinea. He'd been wrong about her endurance. There were bags under her eyes, and her pale face showed the toll this training was taking. He was sure he looked the same—besides his scorched robe. His quivering legs barely held him up.

Invisible magic streamed into Pinea's glowing staff. Cinda's gaze singed his back. Breathing deeply, he raised his chin, building up his own magic once again. He funneled it into his shield, making it thicker and stronger. Not that it would do any good—just more energy for the same painful result.

But what if he could do something else to his shield?

He shifted some of his magic to conjure lightning, even pulling some from the electricity Pinea gathered. It sectioned off into tiny spheres of blue sparks, which he distributed into the shield of air around him. It actually stuck. Perhaps Pinea's aether striking his would counteract each other somehow.

Cinda's curiosity radiated from behind him, but she kept silent.

He planted his feet. Pinea unleashed her bolt, stronger than all the rest. It struck his shield and penetrated halfway through before he panicked again, throwing up his hands and hurling his own sparks into the solid beam. They pushed the beam back. His eyes widened. It worked! He filled in the hole with more air, conjuring more electricity from all around him.

Sweat trickled down his face. Pinea fell to her knees, face

scrunched in intensity, giving everything she had into her continuous lightning.

His legs wobbled and arms drooped with weariness, but he threw lightning into her beam. A bubble of blue light expanded at the sight, then exploded. White light and the sound of a thousand claps of thunder overtook his world. Bastien flew backward and crashed against the hard ground, his shield cushioning him from severe injury. He pushed up on his elbows, ears ringing.

"Cinda! Pinea!" The two mages lay on their backs several feet from where they started.

Flames burned across Pinea's robe. He rushed to her still form. She moaned with her eyes closed.

He grabbed at his hair. "What do I do?" Water. He needed water.

Magic burst into him, responding to his panic. He held his hands over the ground.

No. He didn't need water. With little effort, he took hold of the flames searing Pinea's flesh and vanquished them.

She opened her eyes and screamed. She clutched at the grass, tears streaming down her red-rimmed eyes. Her staff lay charred and forgotten by her side.

Bastien stooped beside where she lay screaming and writhing in pain. Her robe had burned away over her chest and stomach, revealing raw, smoking flesh. He grabbed her staff and thrust it into her hand, but she jerked, still clawing at the ground. If she couldn't hold her staff, she couldn't heal herself.

He didn't know what to do. He'd never healed anyone else before. Cinda stirred but didn't rise. Students poured from the buildings, but they were so far away. Could any of them do better than he could?

"Help! We need a healer!"

"You, Bastien," Cinda rasped from behind him. "Hurry. She's dying."

He threw a panicked look at her. Cinda's head fell against the grass, eyes closed. Pinea ceased screaming. Her thrashing turned feeble. Blood seeped from many of the deeper burns.

No choice.

He channeled his magic over Pinea's body, but it wouldn't heal her. It rolled and tumbled ineptly. *Damn it! Save her!* He poured more of himself into the magic, but couldn't shape it to his will. If only he could figure out how it works—

An idea took hold. He drew his knife and sliced it across his palm. Stinging pain and welling blood hit for just a moment, then his own magic took over. Like faint tingles, it swarmed to the surface of his skin, pooling into his palm. Where it found injury, it rebuilt skin as if the wound never was. He latched onto the essence of that magic, focusing on what it was doing within him and projecting it to Pinea.

His palms glowed white as the magic left him. She'd stopped moving.

Please work.

Groaning with effort, he threw himself into healing her. His palms hovered over her injuries, afraid to touch. The light and magic seeped into her. The blood stopped flowing, and the bubbled skin slowly smoothed out, losing its red rawness. The open wounds closed themselves, healing over with new skin.

Bastien's head drooped, arms growing heavy. He shook with the effort to hold them over her. His tongue grew sandy. Pinea's eyes snapped open and she gasped, reaching for her staff.

"Bastien, stop. You must stop or you'll burn out." Pinea pushed his hands away as her staff lit up, completing whatever healing he'd missed.

He looked down at her healed, but naked chest. Heat rose to his cheeks. He averted his eyes and shrugged out of his robe. He thanked Acantha he hadn't adopted the practice of going nearly naked underneath—he wore trousers, at least.

She blinked up at the robe, then looked down and snatched it from him, drawing it over her chest. He crawled to Cinda. Her eyes were closed, robe twisted around her body. The heat of the blast hadn't touched her. She must have shielded herself.

"Cinda." He touched her forehead with a glowing white palm.

She gasped, breath rushing into her. Her eyes fluttered open, and she coughed.

She's okay.

He collapsed to the grass beside her as the first students finally reached them. Their footsteps thundered in his ears through the ground. The cold grass prickled against his disrobed skin. The blue sky swirled with wispy white clouds above.

What had caused such a reaction?

Cinda leaned over his view of the sky, upright with the support of a young mage. "I like how your mind works, Bastien. You lack the formal training you would have received if you came here young as most of our students. Your mind fills in the gaps with creative ways of solving the problem. Effective against enemies, but don't try that one again."

She hobbled off with the assistance of the mage. Bastien breathed deep, restorative breaths, filling his lungs to capacity and letting it out slowly. Someone brought him a waterskin, and he drank it dry.

"Do you need assistance, my lord?"

Bastien tilted his head toward a trio of mages looking down on him. He hadn't interacted much with the students on campus, but they'd never addressed him as lord.

"Um. I'm all right. Just need to rest a bit." He glanced over and met Pinea's gaze. She walked carefully toward campus now wearing his robe. Students surrounded her. They shot questions, hands waiving excitedly through the air.

The trio dipped their heads and retreated after the rest. Then he was alone. He sat up slowly, facing the horizon once again and massaging his healed palm.

That was too much. Maybe no more experimenting. Pinea had nearly died.

A slow-building sensation began in the pit of his stomach. He shook his head. *No.* He wasn't ready for another ill-fated vision of the future. Dread accompanied the magic as it worked its way up despite his wishes. He held his eyes open as long as he could, until they were dry and aching. He blinked involuntarily, and the trees and hills of the eastern horizon were no longer before him.

Stone houses and shops wound around the slow incline of a gray mountain. His hometown of Docimer. Snow drifted down, dusting the few orange and red trees like powdered sugar. He followed behind a parade of horses, green and gold banners flapping as they trotted through the palace gates, too hurried to be a celebration.

A man dressed in battle armor led the front of the pack. His helm had a golden crown soldered to it, meaning he could only be one person. Prince Rory. He rode nearly to the front entrance of the palace and dismounted. Ignoring the greetings of those around him, he rushed inside.

"Where is my father?" Rory threw his gauntlets and sword into the arms of a hapless servant, nearly toppling him. He removed the helm and shook blonde hair from his eyes.

"In the throne room, Your Highness." The servant bowed.

Rory sneered and took off down the marbled hall. Bastien followed, fascinated. He'd never seen the inside of the palace. Green marble lined the floors and covered the columns all the way to the tall ceilings dripping with antler chandeliers. Servants in green livery flitted down the halls, dusting, or carting silver trays bearing various covered dishes. He imagined they contained the fanciest food. He inhaled deeply but couldn't smell anything except the faint scent of grass.

He shook his head. Though the inside of the palace was as lavish as he'd expected, it was ugly. Too much green in one place, and what was the purpose of all the fur carpets?

Eventually, Prince Rory arrived at the throne room and hurried through the open doorway. Two men sat upon the dais. The one in the center, King Bautamin, wore a silk cape and a fur wrap at his shoulders. A gold crown sat upon his head, and a gold necklace hung from his neck with the green emblem of the royal crest. He nodded as Rory bowed before him.

The man to the right of the king was much older, with long gray hair and age spots. The crown on his head showed he was a foreign king, yet he commanded the room. The servants and guards kept their eyes on him, tracking his movements, whispering among themselves. The man sat tall, looking around as if he were the ruler instead of King Bautamin. Indeed, the crown upon his head was a fraction larger. His black attire along with his dark flowing cape made his smile all the more sinister. Gold fringed his clothing, adorned his fingers, and gleamed upon his heavy necklace. The emblem featured a golden mountain behind a black raven.

Daltieri.

"King Seber." Prince Rory bowed and kissed the king's extended hand. "I did as you said and returned as swiftly as I could."

King Bautamin blustered. "What reason did Queen Faelyn give for denying our terms?"

Rory glanced sideways at the Daltieri king. "She gave none, Father, merely attacked my mages."

King Bautamin shook his head in sadness, eyes drifting to the marbled floor. "I never would have expected this of her. I thought she'd forgive a young prince's insolence and renew the marriage contract." He turned to Prince Rory, eyes narrowing. "You never should have left in the first place. A kiss is nothing that can't be fixed." His tone changed to one of disbelief, almost desperation. "Did you apologize exactly as we'd discussed?"

Bastien inhaled. Queen Faelyn's betrothal would come to an end? Had he ruined things for her? She'd never forgive him if that was true. But why was Daltieri here?

Prince Rory glared at his father.

King Seber cleared his throat. "You did well, Prince Rory." His voice rose as he addressed King Bautamin. "You sent too few. I warned you she'd attack when your heir came seeking my counsel." His chin lifted. "I suppose Kestrea's isolation is to blame for allowing history to repeat itself."

Rory's lips pulled back. "You think we weren't aware of what she did to you at Pavora? We're also aware that you did nothing to check her from driving the rest of your forces out of Alysies, and nothing in the years since."

King Seber shot out of the throne, his aged face contorted with anger. "You dare to—"

King Bautamin grabbed Seber's arm, glaring at Rory. "That's enough, foolish prince. Since our so-called isolation didn't keep you from your expensive education, you know very well Daltieri fought for years to regain their foothold in Alysies. The war and sudden cut-off of their resources took its toll."

Prince Rory looked away from his father's warning stare. "How right you are. My apologies, King Seber."

The wide-eyed servants lining the room did not release their breaths.

The redness of King Seber's face faded only slightly. "You're lucky this is not my throne room, Prince."

Damn. Too bad they couldn't have taken each other out.

King Bautamin shifted in his throne. "Tell my son the good news, at least."

Seber slowly sat and placed his hands on his knees. "My scouts report the fae queen isn't prepared for a coastal assault. Her strength lies in the middle of her kingdom, protecting her precious capital. My fleets will arrive in Caprina inside a month. We'll take it by storm and control one of their biggest trade ports. At the same time, the Kestrean force will join us in an attack on the northern border. The rest of the army will move to the capital as she suspects, giving her false numbers. She'll have no choice but to spread her forces thin. The capital will be overridden."

"And the other news?" King Bautamin prodded.

King Seber leaned toward Prince Rory. "Also, your actions in this manner have earned your reward. My daughter, Princess Cassia, whose beauty is well known. Despite your insolence, your father and I arranged your engagement. Once you win this war with me, you can rule here with a proper *human* wife at your side."

Rory's lips turned up in a slow smile, and he nodded eagerly. "I'm honored, King Seber. They sent the male fae westward. I want him found and killed."

King Seber harrumphed. "You do with your resources what you will, *after* we win the war. I've no time for petty squabbles now."

Rory narrowed his eyes. "So long as the fae queen dies."

Bastien's Fating ended with a strangled gasp. He shot to his feet, stumbling under the weight of his exhaustion. He looked to the darkening horizon, and shouted, "One month! From when? From now?" Rory had left the kingdom last he heard. Had he returned and then fled again? When did the vision take place?

Snow! It was snowing in the vision. It was only just now autumn, but snow often came early in Kestrea. And the leaves hadn't completely fallen from the trees yet in his vision. Bastien paced, pulling at his face and stumbling every third step. His visions were always of the future, so they had a month, but more than that couldn't be guaranteed.

He spun around. Cinda stood halfway across the field from him, lips parted in horror.

"A month?" She panted. "The queen must be warned."

He'd been so wrapped up in his own shock, he hadn't noticed her watching, seeing what he saw. He wanted to be angry, but the reality was that it saved them time. "I'll leave immediately." He rushed toward her.

Her mouth snapped shut. "No. You cannot leave. I cannot allow you to return to the queen." She followed as he hurried past. "Someone else can pass along what you've seen."

"I don't care what you say, Cinda. Just try and stop me. You saw my Fating, and you've seen the one before. The one where I'm searching for her to help her. You know I can be trusted. I won't harm her, and I've delayed my return long enough." Exhaustion pulled at his eyelids.

"Bastien, stop!" The commanding tones were so desperate, he had to obey.

He turned around slowly, and she caught up, panting. She placed a hand on his shoulder and pressed her lips tight together, eyes beseeching his.

"What?" he barked.

She swallowed. "I shouldn't tell you this." Pausing, she glanced around. "I know you're trustworthy, and that you will do what you can to protect our queen. That's not the real reason you can't return. Doubt in your trust is not the real reason you're here." Cinda took two deep breaths, and Bastien thought he might explode with impatience. "She cares for you, Bastien. She cares for you and it puts the kingdom at risk. She can't be with you. Can't marry you. You offer no political alliances or financial gain..." Her voice trailed off, and Bastien forced the wince from his face. "Only love, and that's not enough to win a war."

He jerked from her touch, eyes stinging, breathing heavily. His hands balled into fists. "Maybe we can't be together. Maybe she'd be better off marrying a foreign prince. But I *can* and I *will* do whatever's in my power to protect her. It's written in the Fates, Cinda. It's done."

He turned and stormed away.

She didn't follow. "For what it's worth, I'm sorry Bastien. I've seen the perfect love in your heart and marvel at how it came to be so quickly in your brief acquaintance."

He didn't look back. "It was always there."

THIRTY-SEVEN

Bastien ignored the curious stares of the student mages as he entered the Academ's dorm, his home for the past month. Cinda knew his intent and was bound by royal decree to prevent him from leaving. It was only a matter of time before they came to stop him, and he didn't want to have to hurt anyone. The master mages who'd trained him in all five elements had become his friends, in a way. But they'd be the ones to try and keep him from leaving, and nothing would stand in his way. Faelyn needed him.

Up one flight of stairs and down the hall, he entered his room—small with a single bed, tiny writing desk, and a window. It was devoid of any personal touches. He hadn't had the time or inclination to make the space his own—though it was the first place he could ever really call his.

He grabbed the book bag he'd been given for his studies and dumped the contents on his bed, then after dressing in travel garb, crammed it full of clothes. Money would have been nice, but he had no need or way to earn it. He carefully placed his remaining mage robe on top of the pack. The books, papers, ink, and quill were left on his bed and desk. There was simply no room. He ran his fingers over the pile of books. Perhaps when his task was done, he'd return. The world of learning and magic had been opened to him. Thomats had been a taste, just enough to know what he'd been missing. He'd give it up a thousand times over for Faelyn.

He threw the strap of his bulging book bag over his shoulder so it hung at his side just as a knock sounded at the door. He tensed, reaching internally for what little magic had built back up.

From the other side of the door, the person seemed nervous, but also apologetic. They were alone and without any intent to attack he could sense. It could only be Pinea.

"Come in."

The handle turned, and Pinea stepped through the door. Her red-rimmed eyes were hallowed with exhaustion. They swept the room, touching upon his upended wardrobe, discarded books, packed bag, then finally him. Her blonde hair, once hanging to her waist, had been burnt away to her shoulders.

She held out his mage robe. "It wasn't your fault, Bastien. I'm not sure what else you could have done to stop me. Please don't leave on my account." She offered a small smile. "I've come to tell you that you passed your aether requirements."

Bastien took the robe and draped it over his bag. "Are you all right? I'm so very sorry. I didn't expect you to get hurt."

"I can't shield myself the same way you can. I can only control aether. I should have made my own shield of energy, but I was sending you everything I had. Anyway, I'm fine, thanks to you."

Relief washed over him, though guiltily—Pinea's wellbeing had not been on his mind. "Thank you for all you've done for me. Now, I must go." He moved toward the door.

She half-stepped into his path. "You have amazing potential, Bastien. Don't throw it away because of one accident."

"I may be back someday, but right now I am needed elsewhere. Soon enough, we all will be needed elsewhere." He gave her a sad smile. "Cinda will tell you more."

She nodded, still confused, but accepting his answer.

At the door, he turned back to her. "If you're ordered to try and stop me from leaving, please find a way to stay out of it."

Her brow scrunched in confusion.

"Please." He left her in his room and quickly exited the Academ's dorm—the same place Faelyn had lived during her training as a mage, he'd discovered. He'd also spent time reading about her in the library, about the state of Alysies under Daltieri rule: a land of slaves, breaking their backs for Daltieri gain. He'd read about the battle at Pavora when she'd defeated the Daltieri lord, beginning the process of driving them out. Alysies was a different kingdom now because of Faelyn. Because of the sacrifices she'd made along the way.

The sacrifices he'd interfered with.

The sun was truly setting now, casting a glow that made the buildings shine. Good, maybe Cinda wouldn't risk sending a messenger to warn Kian so close to nightfall. Bastien stepped into the kitchen, where his adventure at Thomats had begun. Gus looked up from the cutting board with a broad smile.

"Lord Bastien! We're preparing supper, but I heard of your ordeal." He gestured to the counter beside him.

Bastien followed the motion until his eyes set upon a platter of cheese, bread, coldcut meats, and grapes. His mouth watered.

"Thank you, Gus." He smiled appreciatively and headed to the food. He talked as he munched on a hunk of cheese. "What's with everyone calling me lord? I'm no lord." He stuffed the bread in his bag.

Gus paused in his chopping. "There's no need to save some for later. We have plenty. And Lord seems only proper, seeing as how you're the same as our beloved queen."

Bastien paused in his chewing. "I'm going away for a little while. To help our queen."

Gus glanced out the window in the door. "Now? But it's nearly dark."

"Yes, now. I can see just fine in the dark."

"Well, of course you can." Gus laughed. "Tafity, pack some provisions for our friend."

Tafity, one of the cooks who'd first discovered him in the pantry, rushed off.

"I'm in a hurry. I only stopped by to thank you for all your kindness." He rolled up a slice of ham and bit into it. The food restored more of his strength. He hadn't realized how famished he was.

"We are used to this, young mage. People are always coming and going. We know how to pack quickly." Gus finished chopping onions and tomatoes and then placed them into a large pot.

Sure enough, by the time Bastien finished his meal, Tafity had returned with a knapsack bulging with provisions. He took the strap, tossing it over his shoulder.

"Thank you. All of you. I hope we meet again." He headed out the door.

"Travel well, Lord Bastien." Gus flashed one more red-cheeked smile before the door closed.

Bastien sent out his hearing, but no one was in pursuit. He skirted along the edge of the building, heading to the north side of campus where the stables were. The large barn lay down a short dirt road. He walked quickly, but no one seemed to be about.

He sensed her before he saw her.

From the glowing lantern light within the barn, Cinda emerged, staff in one hand, and the reins of a saddled horse in another. Bastien stopped and called his magic.

"No need for that Bastien. I'm here to help." She brought the chocolate gelding forward and handed him the lead.

He eyed her warily. "Why aren't you trying to stop me?"

"I'm giving you a day's head start before I tell the school council of your Fating. Queen Faelyn needs you, in more ways than one. And even if she chooses politics over love, I'll feel better knowing you're there to protect her." Her reassuring smile crinkled her eyes.

Warmth flooded from his heart into his bones. He wouldn't have to skulk away, fleeing from authorities and feeling like the criminal he used to be. Here was someone who finally saw the good in him. She'd seen inside his mind and knew he was decent and honest.

He threw his arms around Cinda, knocking her off balance. "Thank you. That means a lot to me."

She gave him a quick squeeze, then stepped back and peered up at him. "Trust in yourself, Bastien. Trust in your magic and in what you've been taught." She placed a hand on his cheek. "You're better than your past. It does not define you, only your actions, and yours are the actions of a hero. Eliot would be proud of you."

He looked away, hand clenching the reins. Words failed him, so he nodded and mounted his horse.

Cinda stood back and smiled. "Take it easy tonight. The moon will be bright, but you overdid it today. No one will follow you, so rest when you're tired. And come back. You'd make a great master mage someday."

He gave a tight smile, emotions threatening to break through his composure. Cinda knew him so well, every part of him in and out. She knew his desires and his love for Faelyn, his past regrets and failures, and was helping him despite it all. Or because of it all.

"I will. Good luck to you in the coming future. I'm forever grateful for all you've done for me."

"And I for you."

He kicked his horse into a trot, only slowing when he'd descended the hill away from the school and into the valley below. Full night had set in, and he and his new travel companion had a long way to go.

I'm coming, Faelyn. We'll be together soon.

THIRTY-EIGHT

An odd feeling of happiness swept over Faelyn as she sat sipping warm cider by the low campfire. She tried shaking it off. Her kingdom was in a state of war with two powerful enemies. She was two days away from home and being thrown into complete chaos of preparation and strategizing. And they would arrive with fewer soldiers than they left with. The last thing she should feel was happy.

"Queen Faelyn?" Nolan looked at her askew from where he sat across the fire, polishing his blade. "Everything all right?" The other leaders watched her from the sides of their eyes.

"Not really, why?" Her statement gave the leaders permission to acknowledge their very real situation.

"Your mouth is smiling, but your eyes are narrowed. It gives you a menacing appearance I'm not accustomed to. If you're planning something, let me know how I can help." He grinned, but his words were more than earnest.

She frowned and drained the last of the cider, passing her cup to a servant. "You can help me by supplying a list of those we've lost. I wish to visit with their loved ones personally." That was one of the hardest things she'd encountered as queen, knowing that every decision she made could lead to her people's deaths. She rose. The rest of the leaders around her did as well. "Goodnight."

They bowed, and she crossed the field into her tent—less lavish and more practical than Rory's. There was a desk and stool, as well as her cot piled with soft pillows and blankets. During bigger battles, a council room was required, but none of that was necessary now. A servant offered to help her into a nightgown, but she preferred to sleep clothed. Though they had scouts and spies on patrol at all hours, she wouldn't be caught in her nightgown during an ambush.

Her head hit the pillow, and her thoughts turned to Bastien. Was he okay? Had he been harmed? Was he still in Alysies? Her heart told her he was. She rolled over, fluffing a pillow beneath her cheek. She'd done her best to try and forget him, but it was impossible. The memory of his soft lips tangled with hers, his iron-strong arms wrapped around her waist, sent heat flashing across her skin. His magic, his faeness, felt like coming home. Like she'd known him her whole life. Maybe even longer than her whole life.

She slapped her arms down beside her. *Focus. Bastien is gone, as well he should be.* It would take Rory a few weeks to get back to his father, less if they'd planned this the way she would have and met with Daltieri's army at a more strategic location, perhaps where their three borders met in Crosston.

Seething, she kicked the covers off her despite the chilly air. Had this been their plan all along? She sat up. King Seber had ignored any implore for peace, yet hadn't attacked. He knew he didn't stand a chance against a united Alysies. He needed an ally. How fortuitous he'd caught word of her blunder and Rory's hasty retreat. His spies worked quickly. Had King Bautamin contacted him? Or was Daltieri quick to poison the mind of a peaceful king, no doubt planting the vile seeds of greed and revenge?

Faelyn fell back onto her pillows. No matter. It was done. Now she had to decide how to move forward with the least casualties and the best chance of victory. Thank Acantha Kian had the foresight to solidify their alliance with Creadel. They'd need their help. Again.

She touched the turquoise stone at her neck. Crickets chirped in the field around her, not quite drowned out by the crackle of fire and whispered conversations outside her tent. Heavy lidded and heavy hearted, mind jumping between strategic possibilities and Bastien, Faelyn fell asleep.

CHAPTER
THIRTY-NINE

Faelyn pushed the legion hard the next two days. They rode back into Pavora hailed as heroes, waving their blue banners with chins held high. People came from shops and homes and lined the street clapping and cheering, clamoring for a view of the victorious queen.

She put on her best brave, smiling face, but every child they passed, every portly old woman, or hardworking shopkeeper greeting her as their most beloved queen, was like glass shards to her heart. Together, Daltieri and Kestrea doubled Alysies's troop numbers, and Pavora was exactly where King Seber would come. She knew it without a doubt. This was where he lost his slaves. This was where he'd come to reclaim them.

How many strapping young men and fair ladies would survive Daltieri's wrath this time?

"We'll have to evacuate the town, Nolan," she whispered as quietly as she could and still be heard over the noise of the horses walking the cobbled street and the clamoring revelers. "Save as many as we can."

"We will, Your Majesty."

She smiled through the tears pooling in her eyes. *Okay. It's going to be okay.*

They marched up to the palace, the royal party breaking off from the soldiers who would return to the citadel as conquering heroes. They traveled through the gates and the tunnel through the thick wall surrounding the castle. Faelyn studied it as they crossed beneath. It had been repaired of the damage she wrought during the last battle. The finest master mages Alysies had to offer assisted her in imbuing it with magical properties, ensuring its protection. They had renewed and strengthened the spells every year since, but was it enough?

Patrols lined the top of the wall, pacing. They all looked sharp and aware, scanning the horizon and the town. The guards higher up in the towers waved the blue flags that all was right. She breathed a quiet sigh as she dismounted near the stable. The horrors hadn't touched her people yet. Her soldiers would be ready when it did.

A swarm of generals and advisors surrounded her, carrying parchments and shouting questions over one another. Apparently, Nolan's messenger had returned and relayed the news. They matched her brisk pace into the castle.

"Daltieri and Kestrea have joined forces and declared war against us," she said as she hurried through the castle. "Send for Lord Kian to return immediately. Advise all lords to send a representative here in two weeks' time to receive instruction." Advisors and scribes darted off as she spoke. "Issue the draft for all men sixteen and older and any women who wish to join. Prepare the citadel to receive the new recruits and the land eastward to support the lords' forces."

She stopped beside the stairs leading up to her suite. "We will meet in the council room this afternoon, and I will give you the details."

Mouths opened to fire more questions but quickly closed with one look from her. The leaders bowed and scattered to carry out orders—and gossip, no doubt. They knew as much as they needed to in order not to cause a panic. What was spoken in the council room was not to be repeated, so the true disaster wouldn't be made imme-diately known to the rest of the kingdom like the rumors spreading now.

She ascended the stairs, only Nolan and her regular guards following behind. "Send Amerae as soon as you're done with her."

Nolan flushed. "Yes, Your Majesty." He hurried back downstairs, his steps flying.

Once in her rooms, her maids met her, gushing over her and telling her how much they'd missed her. She hugged Meribeth, who led her into the bathing room. Lavender-scented steam rose out of the large tub set deep into the floor. Blue floral tile ringed the room, complimenting the white-marbled floor. It felt cool on her warm toes until she stepped onto the soft carpet beside the tub. With assistance, she peeled off her battle garb. Luckily, these were clean compared to her other set, still stained with the blood of those she'd slain.

The intoxicating scents filled her lungs, and the warm water splashed over her feet as she stepped in. She settled down into the tub, water up to her chin and her arms and legs floating weightless, but the tension remained in her shoulders.

She allowed herself to be scrubbed, something she'd come to enjoy rather than simply tolerate. Meribeth lathered rose soap and massaged it into Faelyn's scalp with her fingertips. Faelyn closed her eyes, and for just a moment, tried to forget her problems. Too soon, she was clean and stepped out of the tub. A large, warm towel was draped around her. When she was dry, the ladies brought a blue dress with poufy skirts and a tight bodice.

"Something simpler, Meribeth. It's going to be a long afternoon."

"Yes, my queen." She hurried into the closet and chose a straight light-blue dress with thin sleeves and none of the layers of skirts that were fashionable these days.

"Much better. Thank you." Faelyn flashed a warm smile.

She dressed, and her ladies did her hair in an elegant braid twist and pinned it up. They placed the circlet on her head just as a knock sounded on the door.

"Lady Amerae to see you," Meribeth said upon returning from answering the knock.

Faelyn patted the delicate circlet in place. "Send her in and give us some privacy."

Moments later, the room was cleared and Amerae entered, smiling broadly. Her enormous belly protruded, moving side to side as she waddled into the room.

"Goodness, Amerae. I should have come to you." Faelyn hugged her friend. "How much longer?"

Amerae puffed, out of breath, and sat on the settee. "Any time now. The physician says walking's good for me, that it will help induce labor." A look of deep concern crossed her face. "I hope the baby comes quickly. I need to be ready when the battle reaches Pavora." She held her stomach.

Guilt wormed its way through her, but Faelyn spoke her thoughts aloud anyway. "Yes, you will." Amerae was too valuable to send away. "Don't worry. He or she will have only the best protection and nurses until you can be reunited. I intend to evacuate the city as soon as necessary."

Amerae's lips formed a thin line, her hold on her belly tightening. "Your thoughts are in line with mine, then. I've gathered what I can from our spies. Some have not returned. Prince Rory heads for Kestrea, and there's no movement at the Daltieri border. Two different sources confirmed that King Seber is in Docimer."

Faelyn looked up sharply. "Part of me had hoped that pompous prince was bluffing."

"He's not bluffing. Nolan showed me the declaration. It's authentic. Though, there was something off about King Bautamin's signature. It is slightly different from those on previous trade agreements."

Faelyn frowned. It could mean nothing but a show of nerves for the king making such a bold move. She dropped into the settee next to Amerae. "It's so much more complicated now. Last time they were on our land and we had to drive them out. We stand to lose so much more if I don't make the right decisions."

She glanced into Amerae's widened eyes and opened her senses. Amerae was scared, not for herself, but for her child. Faelyn sat straighter, feeling a fool. She didn't need to unburden herself on Amerae. She was her queen first, friend second, and Amerae trusted her to lead them through these times of trouble.

"We are much stronger and more prepared this time." Amerae sounded as if she was trying to convince herself as much as Faelyn.

She patted Amerae's knee. "You're right. We are ready for them." She stood and offered Amerae a hand up. "Come, we have a meeting in the council room to attend. I'll cast a sound veil so we can continue our conversation without being overheard."

As they walked Amerae filled her in on what she'd missed while away. "Mostly the people had the usual complaints: land disputes, tax payments, requests for more grain. But once word got around that the troops had left, more people showed up, and they all wanted to know if you were all right and if we were under attack by Kestrea. We did our best to reassure them, but soon everyone will know of our state of war."

"Yes, the matter will need to be handled with delicacy." Faelyn stopped suddenly and scrubbed at her face, groaning. "Why did I give in to him, Am? Why? Are people going to lose their lives for my folly? Is my kingdom in jeopardy because I allowed myself one moment of happiness?" She shook her head. The weight of the circlet on her head moved with her. "I once said everyone I ever love dies. And I love my people, Amerae, more than myself. More than anything. Even more than Bastien." She ignored Amerae's keen gaze. "I vowed not to become my father, choosing myself before my kingdom, and that's exactly what I've done! And now look what's happened." She backed nearly to the wall as her magic flared, trying to find an outlet for her emotions. The candelabras and chandeliers flickered and flashed.

She buried her face in her hands, breaths more like sobs.

Amerae's warm, steady hand rested on her shoulder. "You love Bastien, my queen?"

Faelyn peeked up from the tips of her fingers. "I didn't say that."

"You did, though."

Faelyn dropped her hands. "I'm sorry, Amerae. I don't mean to diminish myself in your eyes this way." No one needed to see her brokenness.

Amerae gave her an understanding smile. "We've been friends for a long time. I hope you don't feel the need to pretend with me. Let me be the person you trust to talk to when you need to unburden yourself. And in this, let me provide some measure of comfort." She patted Faelyn's shoulder. "King Seber was in Docimer even before Prince Rory left here. Our informants confirmed it. We have a strong reason to believe they planned this no matter how things ended here. Either they'd take the kingdom once Prince Rory was king of Alysies, or find another way to take it by force. You did not fail our people by giving into happiness." She gave a sly smile. "And for what it's worth, *should* you give in to happiness again, I believe our people will be fine. Why shouldn't a fae king be as good as a fae queen?"

Faelyn held her breath. A premature hope threatened to open up impossible conclusions. She didn't need anyone's approval to love who she loved, but there was more than just herself to think about. "You hate Bastien."

"I don't trust him. But if you do, I can learn to."

Faelyn squared her shoulders. "I'm grateful for you, Am, but he's far away now, out of my reach and out of the realm of possibility." She continued walking arm-in-arm with Amerae.

"If there's any one person who could change that, it's you." Amerae squeezed her arm, leaning her off-balanced weight against Faelyn.

"It's Kian, actually. Only he knows where Bastien is." She let out a slow breath of air. "It's better this way. I'd only give into my emotions, which should have been kept locked away from the beginning. Alysies needs more than he has to offer."

Amerae touched her stomach, wincing with a huff. "Forgive me for disagreeing, but your emotions are what won us our kingdom back. I once lived a life of servitude under King Seber. All of Alysies has. Look how far we've come. We won't go back to what we were, no matter how high the cost. All the lords, my brother Marus included, will fight for Alysies. And if Bastien brings our queen the happiness and love she deserves—and has more than earned—he has *everything* to offer this kingdom."

Faelyn smiled wistfully behind stinging eyes. Her blurred gaze wandered to the windows, to the faraway treetops and steepled roofs.

Amerae doubled over and grabbed her belly with both hands. "Oh, that one was much stronger than the ones before."

Faelyn held onto her friend. "Fetch the midwife," she yelled back to her guards. "Come on, Amerae. Let's get to your rooms." She let Amerae finish breathing through her contraction, then wrapped an arm around her waist, half carrying her back the way they'd come. "You know there are easier ways of getting out of a council meeting than going into labor."

Amerae laughed between pants. "You think this is real labor? It's been false so many times now."

"I don't know, but we'll make sure you're okay at least."

Unfortunately, Amerae and Nolan's suite was far, far away. Amerae only made it halfway before she was in too much pain. The midwife met them, and the guards carried Amerae the rest of the way. Once Amerae was in bed, Faelyn held her hand until Amerae forced her to leave for the meeting.

As important and historical as this meeting was, Faelyn could only half focus as the hours ticked by. With Nolan's help, who was equally distracted, they recounted the battle. They put a plan in place for evacuations and where to station the troops, and issued orders for the lords to come with their armies. All plans they'd had in place for years in case of Daltieri attack.

"They won't make it to Pavora, my queen." Commander Rane said.

"Good." She glanced at the door. "We'll meet daily to discuss progress. More when necessary." She stood, all others standing. "Nolan. Let's go."

They hurried from the room. Side by side, they rushed back to Amerae. Servants and courtiers shot them worried looks, stepping out of their path. Yes, it probably wasn't the way to act in light of the news of war—the queen and the captain of her guard hurrying through the castle. She had a thousand things that needed her attention right now, a thousand people waiting to talk to her and awaiting her decisions, but she wouldn't be able to concentrate on any of it.

What if something had gone wrong? What if they couldn't stop the bleeding, as happened with Faelyn's mother? Fear-induced adrenaline lanced her heart. Still two corridors away, she ran. She didn't care who saw, who was watching, what they thought. Her friend wouldn't die this day.

Nolan hesitated only a moment, then he was running right with her. His eyes were intent, but worry leaked all around him.

"She'll be okay, Nolan. I won't let her die." If magic had been granted to her for no other purpose, it would be to save Amerae's life.

Her assurance eased some of the creases between his eyes.

An eternity passed before they skidded to a stop at the door. The yells and grunts of labor came from within. They hesitated. Panting, they exchanged a questioning glance.

Faelyn put a hand on the doorknob. "I'll go in. I'm a woman, after all."

Nolan flushed. "Right. You go in. I'll just go mad waiting out here for someone to tell me everything's all right."

"I'll hurry." She cracked open the door.

The high-pitched cry of a newborn echoed down the hall. She turned to Nolan and grinned, then burst through the door and hurried down the hall into the bedroom. The physician and midwife, along with several nurses, stood around an exhausted Amerae. They began to bow, but Faelyn held up her hand to stop them.

Glistening with sweat, her hair mussed, Amerae leaned back against her pillows, smiling. Clutched to her chest was her precious baby. The pink-cheeked infant nuzzled against her. Tufts of blonde hair stuck up from its head.

Amerae met Nolan's eyes. "It's a girl."

Faelyn looked behind her. Nolan stood, wide-eyed and pale, his eyes locked on the bloody afterbirth.

"Are you okay?" Faelyn stepped to block his view. "Why don't you wait in the—"

Nolan's knees gave out, and he fell forward. One of the nurses screamed. Faelyn darted and caught him, easing him to the ground. Huffing, she stood and locked eyes with Amerae. Both of them burst into laughter.

"He's used to blood and gore. I didn't think this would bother him." Faelyn circled to sit carefully by Amerae's side.

The midwife spoke up. "This is why we don't let the men in. They can't handle seeing their wives pained." She pushed down on Am's belly.

Amerae sucked in a breath. Faelyn's brow creased in concern, and she channeled her healing magic. With her hand above Amerae's abdomen, she eased the pain and some of the damage.

Amerae's features softened with relief. Her head fell back with a nod of thanks. She shushed her newborn, then at the nurse's urging, offered her breast.

Emotion threatened to overwhelm Faelyn. What must this be like, to be a mother? Would she ever get the chance to experience it herself? To be the mother she always wanted. "She's beautiful, Amerae. What are you going to name her?"

"Nolan and I talked about it, and we want to name her Mary, after—"

Faelyn gasped. "After her great-great-great grandmother." Fresh tears sprung to her eyes.

Mary had raised her from a baby—had been the mother she never had after her own mother died in childbirth. She'd been nothing but kind, protective in the way a mother should have been, loving when her father turned her away time and again. Nolan descended from Mary, and had remained loyal to Faelyn even under Daltieri rule. He'd been the key to their success in the battle to win back their kingdom.

Amerae could not have picked a better name.

Amerae's warm hand patted hers. "I know what Mary meant to you. Her memory will be honored through my daughter."

Faelyn clutched Am's hand. "Thank you," she whispered.

The baby, Mary, fussed. Faelyn crossed to where she'd left Nolan on the floor. He needed to be present for this moment.

With her palm glowing white, she placed it on Nolan's forehead. He awoke with a start and pushed to a sitting position, rubbing his face.

"You have a beautiful daughter, Nolan. Take care of her and my Amerae."

He grinned, and Faelyn helped him to his feet. She left the room, turning back only once to see the happy family encircled in each other's arms.

That's what she wanted in her life someday, a chance to be the mother she never had, with a man at her side to be the father she always wanted. Her thoughts turned to Bastien, but she pushed them away.

Now it was time for war.

CHAPTER

FORTY

Stomach rumbling, Bastien led his horse on foot through the outskirts of Pavora. The gelding had picked up a stone a few days back, and his hoof was still bruised. That was before a legion of Alysian soldiers had marched up the road behind him. He'd heard them coming and hid behind a distant hill. At least 2,000 of them on horseback and foot rumbled by with carts and banners stitched with their lord's coat of arms. That was not the last legion he'd crossed paths with. Faelyn must have been warned about the upcoming attack. How much did she know?

He'd run out of food and was forced to use nearly the last of the coin Cinda had snuck into his saddlebag to stable his horse. The poor thing would go no further.

The sun rose above the rooftops, chasing away the chill of autumn. He wished it would help the stench. Pavora wasn't an unclean city—cleaner than most actually—but even clean cities couldn't avoid the stink of human refuge and moldering trash. The tinge of fear and worry hanging over the people made it clear they'd seen the soldiers pass this way.

A cat darted across the paved street chasing a rat. A door banged up ahead as an old man stepped into the alley from his thatched-roof home, stretching and rubbing his stubbled chin. Bastien nodded a polite hello as he passed, but the man didn't return the greeting, simply eyed him warily.

The sights, sounds, and smells reminded him of Docimer, easing his tension. The homes and shops became more plentiful as he walked on, and more and more people filled the streets. Bakers set out trays of fresh goods in their windows. Women toted baskets of laundry to the public fountain. Men kissed their wives goodbye, heading wherever their daily jobs might take them. Many towns-people rode south in wagons packed with provisions. City guards patrolled the streets dressed in blue uniforms with swords, watching the people as they fled.

Bastien earned more than a few curious glances, but he wisely kept his head hooded with his black mage robe. His sandy hair had grown some, but still not long enough to hide his ears.

Hopefully no one would think twice that he wore mage robes but didn't carry a staff. If he was discovered before he reached the castle, finding Faelyn would be much more difficult. Already, he itched to lay eyes on her, finding himself walking faster than he should, attracting more attention.

Wherever the boundary began in which he could sense her, he hadn't reached it yet. What if she wasn't at the castle? What if she wasn't in the city at all?

He shuffled along the edge of a row of shops, the street now thick with people, horses, and the sounds of city life. Children laughed and screamed, ladies gossiped—mostly about the mysterious man in the hooded mage robe. A wood-chopping noise sounded from the street over, and across the street, a woman beat a rug, sending dust flying.

Scents of cooking pots wafted by every now and then, making his mouth water and stomach rumble. He patted the coins in his pocket, wincing at their pitiful jingle. Two guards rode up on horseback on the other side of a fountain across the square. They met a third, who spoke, then pointed to Bastien.

Damn it.

He should have entered the city under cover of night, but that would have meant waiting longer. He ducked into a shop boasting smells of a delicious breakfast. Inside was dark, with round, rickety tables and few patrons. They didn't spare him a glance but continued their conversations.

"Don't fret none," an older man said to his companion at one of the tables. "Our beloved queen will protect us, just as she did when she ran those bastards out of our town. You've been working on those buildings, you know she's been preparing for this." He took a sip from a mug.

The younger man hunched over his plate. "You can't possibly think this war won't touch us. We've seen our armies gathering to the east."

The older man nodded. "It'll touch us, no doubt, but we'll be fine."

Only a counter divided the kitchen from the rest of the room. A middle-aged man looked up from a pan of eggs he was frying and smiled.

"Eggs and potatoes for ya?" he asked. His tone was warm and inviting.

Bastien stepped to him and pulled out two copper coins. "What can I get for this?"

The man's smile faltered, and he eyed Bastien's robe. "Is that yours, son?"

"Yes, I'm a mage on an errand to the castle."

The door opened, letting in a flood of light. Bastien didn't need to turn around to know it was the guards. Swords clanked at their sides, boots stomping confidently into the room as if they owned it.

The cook greeted them before turning back to Bastien, stirring the eggs while he spoke. "I'll give you a full breakfast and payment as well if you can heal my son's leg."

The guards stepped closer. "No breakfast for us, Barden," one of them said.

Bastien's pulse accelerated. "Where's your son?"

The cook, Barden, one hand on a spatula, shrugged his shoulder toward a door. "My home is through there. If my son's broken leg isn't mended, he can't work, and winter is coming."

A heavy hand fell on Bastien's shoulder.

"You're stirring up a lot of interest," the guard said, his voice deep but not threatening. Yet.

Bastien turned, fighting the urge to flee from authority. If he could keep his smart mouth shut, maybe they'd let him be. "Can't a traveling mage get some breakfast?" His tone came out more irritated than he'd meant it to.

The guards frowned and shifted their stances. The lead guard, who had spoken to him, had a short beard, probably to hide his youth—he was not much older than Bastien. "So, you're a mage. What's your name, and where are you from?" His attitude went from curious to distrusting.

Bastien called a bit of magic forward, returning the guards' scowls. "I'm Bastien, and I hail from Thomats School of Magic. I've a message for the queen."

"Hmm. And where is your staff, mage from Thomats?"

Bastien hesitated. If he told them he didn't have one, they'd arrest him. If he attacked and knocked them out, he'd be pursued, then arrested. If he fled, they'd find him and arrest him. Nothing he chose would keep him from imprisonment. Again.

Barden spoke up from behind him. "Lord Bastien's staff is beside my son. My wife is safekeeping it until he's had some breakfast. Then he's going to heal him."

Bastien groaned inwardly. This old man didn't need to lie to the city guard on his behalf. What if they decided to check for the staff?

The guard eyed them both skeptically.

Bastien flashed a weak smile.

Barden stepped forward and shoved a plate of food in Bastien's hands. "Eat up, young mage. Sit anywhere you'd like." He nudged Bastien forward.

The guards locked dubious eyes as he shuffled past, head low. He sat at the nearest table, shoveling food in without tasting it, all senses tuned to the guards' every move and emotion. They were confused, curious, and uncertain. The smallest thing could sway them to either pursue their questioning or turn away.

"Since you're done eating, time to heal Barden's son." The head guard rested a hand on the pommel of his sword.

Bastien looked down. His plate was empty. He'd eaten the food in no time, too wrapped up in the danger of the situation, both his own and Barden's. He stood. Nothing left but to play the part.

"Thank you for the fine meal. I must have been hungrier than I thought." He inclined his head to Barden, who shot him a nervous smile.

The few patrons watched with intense curiosity.

"You guards have more important tasks than tending to my injured child," Barden said. "Don't let me keep you. I'll have my wife pack you a lunch." He cracked eggs into a bowl of flour. "She's made an apple pie."

The guard swallowed saliva and elbowed the other guard. "His wife makes great pie."

The senior guard's lip curled in admonition. "Get on with it, Barden." His tone turned dark and threatening.

Barden balked, wiping his hands on the apron tied at his waist. "This way." He opened the door leading to a dark staircase.

The senior guard unsheathed his sword, pointing for Bastien to go first. Bastien followed Barden up the squeaky staircase to the level above. There was only one large room with a couple of beds in the corner, a line of hanging laundry, a wardrobe and washbasin. Barden's wife—a thick woman whose wide eyes showed her clear surprise—stood by her teenage son in one of the beds. He winced, reaching toward his leg and rocking back and forth. Sweat soaked his nightshirt and pillow and poured off his head.

Bastien stepped ahead of the group and paused, horrified. The boy was near death, his skin like thin parchment. "I thought he broke his leg."

Barden pulled back the covers. The leg was swollen. Red and purple lines extended from a barely closed jagged wound.

"He broke it, aye, but he also cut it. We followed the healer's instructions to keep it clean, but we've not enough coin to have him come back." Barden bit his knuckle. "Please help my son."

Bastien gazed into the desperate man's eyes. The guards shuffled closer. Barden's wife fretted beside them. *How do I manage to get myself on this side of trouble over and over?* While he likely could heal the boy, he didn't have a staff. Would they recognize him if performed magic without one?

He glanced to the son and back. He couldn't refuse to heal the boy. His life was in Bastien's hands. An idea came to him.

"No need to retrieve my staff, misses. I was trained specially in healing at Thomats. I can project my own self-healing onto this boy." *Please believe me.* He did what he could to imbue his words with truthfulness.

The wife nodded, casting a look at her husband. The guards hovered, so Bastien knelt at the boy's side and took a deep breath. He brought his magic forward, focusing on healing until his palms glowed white. Gasps resounded around the room. The boy winced away from the light, eyes remaining closed.

Bastien placed his hands against the boy's leg. The skin was fire-hot, and the boy moaned. The mother cried out, but Bastien ignored all that. He pushed his magic, and it flowed easily into the leg, finding the source of infection and mending the bone, then the skin. It took much less time and energy than it had with Pinea, though he'd been exhausted then. It was almost as if it came easier this second time.

The wound closed, the boy's face relaxed, and he breathed the even rhythm of blissful sleep. Barden and his wife slumped into each other's arms, weeping and thanking Bastien.

The head guard sheathed his sword, and Bastien felt his awe.

"That was well done, Lord Bastien. I've never seen anything like it. You're welcome in Pavora anytime." He inclined his head. "Good day, Barden." The pair slipped out of the room and away.

Bastien breathed a long sigh of relief. Barden took his hand in a solid grip, pressing his forehead into it and weeping. "I didn't think you could do it, really, but we'd given up all hope. We thought he was gone to the Hereafter for sure." He grabbed for a pouch at his waist and shoved it into Bastien's hands. It clinked. "I'm sorry I doubted you. Thank you, thank you."

Bastien weighed the pouch in his hands. By the sound and feel, there were maybe a few coppers mixed with silvers inside. "What's your son's name?"

"Christopher, my lord," Barden's wife said from where she held her son tight in his bed.

"Take care of him." Bastien left them still hugging and celebrating. He dropped the coin pouch at the top of the stairs and exited the building with a smile on his lips.

Maybe he could be worthy of Faelyn's love after all.

CHAPTER
FORTY-ONE

Faelyn sat at a large wooden table surrounded by walls of polished rock, with beams of thick timber stretched overhead. Around her sat her generals and the lords of her kingdom who'd already come to her call for aid. They'd spent the last few hours on the ground floor of this newer building of the citadel, which was designed and built for the purpose of housing the council room closer to the soldiers and action during times of war.

Outside, the troops trained and drilled. Supplies were tallied, and more were being gathered. Missives had been sent, and part of her personal army would march tomorrow for the border where Daltieri and Kestrea intersected Alysies in the town of Crosston. More troops continued to arrive from around the kingdom, as well as mages.

Kian had sent word a couple weeks ago and was expected to arrive in a few days. Faelyn repeated that in her head each morning as she woke before dawn, her day already filled with more than any one person could accomplish, though she stayed up late trying. She needed him by her side. As amazing as she was, Niri would need help organizing the mage recruits.

The conversation in the room had broken off into several heated discussions. Some thought it best to wait for more information before sending troops, but Faelyn disagreed. If they didn't begin the march to protect their border—a several weeks journey for a force that size—Daltieri might take it without contest. The regular border militia couldn't hope to defend it alone. A large enough army would still be left for reserves until they had more information, and the troops who hadn't arrived would provide relief. Once Creadel sent reinforcements, it was simply a matter of strategically placing the troops and not being overrun with numbers.

The shouting became too much, the anger in the room beginning to raise her own anger. She raised her hand. "Enough."

The voices died down and, still grumbling, they turned toward her. Faelyn rose and smiled.

She paced, rounding the table, past those seated or standing along the walls of the room. "I know tensions are high. We are facing a very real threat, the most powerful this kingdom has ever encountered." She stopped at the head of the table. "But I look at us assembled here, and I know we will not fail." The leaders' frowns lessened slightly. "We all fight for a common purpose, that good will triumph over evil, that we can resume our lives of peace. Attacking a peaceful kingdom without provocation is evil. So we must work together for those looking to us for protection against the dark. We—"

Faelyn gasped and clutched her hands to herself. A connection snapped in place, reverberating with incredible force. *Bastien.* She hadn't noticed him drawing nearer, but now he was so close. How close?

"My queen!" Shouts of alarm rang out.

Nolan rushed to her side.

Tears of joy gathered at the corners of her eyes. She held up her hand as her heartbeat steadied. "I'm sorry. It was nothing. I—"

"Your Majesty." A runner entered the room, bowing quickly and charging toward her with a letter.

Door guards caught the young runner, throwing him back. He blushed deeply, eyes downcast as the letter was snatched from his hand. The scene bought her time to shove thoughts of Bastien from her mind. No matter why he was back, she couldn't see him. An aide brought the letter to her. She opened it, quickly scanning the contents.

She looked up, meeting the eager eyes of her leaders. "Daltieri and Kestrea forces are marching south. The report says they number twenty thousand strong." Double what they'd prepared to send tomorrow. "They'd been camped, waiting. They'll reach the border in a week."

Someone cursed. Faelyn was tempted. Their troops would never make it in time. And now they'd have to spend more time preparing more soldiers. Faelyn crumpled the letter. She should have foreseen this. She should have had an army ready at the border, waiting for this inevitability.

"How many do we number in Crosston?" she asked

"Roughly three thousand, my queen," one of her generals said.

The room hovered in ominous silence for a beat before the conversations roared up around her again. She sat, mind reeling, trying to ignore the pull to her heart. She threw a shield of air around herself—unnoticed by the others—but it did nothing to lessen the feel of him, or her desire for his arms around her. The memory of his warm lips on hers and her longing for more, more, more.

She rubbed her temple. *Focus.* "Send the troops, but we must decide where they will meet the enemy. Crosston will be taken."

Further down the table, General Rane spoke quickly to the commanders around him, arms moving in quick, jerky motions. He looked up. "I'll send scouts ahead of the force to choose the spot with a strategic advantage. We'll gather information and slow them down as they approach Pavora. It will buy us time to evacuate."

Faelyn nodded. "Prepare more troops to relieve those as soon as we can send them, tomorrow if possible."

"That will leave us nearly defenseless here." Lord Gilmore, who owned lands in the south, stared open-mouthed around the table.

"Only until the other lords arrive," Faelyn said. There were twenty-two lords of various holdings around Alysies, though only ten would travel to Pavora, adding their numbers to hers. The rest were needed to defend their lands along the Daltieri border and the coast.

Murmurs of agreement went around the room.

"Is that your final word, Your Majesty?" Lord Gilmore asked.

Faelyn glanced at Nolan, wishing more fiercely than ever Kian was here. She nodded ever so slightly. "It is."

Commander Rane grunted some commands, and aides and runners scattered out of the building.

Let the Fates guide me true. This kingdom will not fall.

"Until tomorrow then." She picked up her skirts, knowing it'd be much sooner than tomorrow. Events were happening quickly now, as they knew they would when this time came.

She left the council building, stepping out to the chaos of the training grounds, but she couldn't focus on the soldiers running to and fro, the whack of practice swords, or the thud as a fresh recruit dropped theirs in the dirt. Instead, she scanned the horizon. Her gaze jumped over buildings and over to the distant stone wall and trees beyond. Bastien wasn't there. She focused harder but couldn't tell how far away he was.

"Queen Faelyn?" Nolan said from beside her, a reminder she didn't have time to stand around.

She closed her eyes and allowed some of her emotions for Bastien to seep to the surface, remembering the way his pale blue eyes looked right into her. The pull became finite, and she pivoted to face where it felt strongest. She opened her eyes.

"Bastien has returned. He's somewhere west of us, perhaps at the castle." She pointed at the tall castle turrets bolstering banners of blue.

Nolan's eyes narrowed. "What would you have me do?"

Faelyn took note of his choice of words. If he'd asked her what she wanted, the answer would have been to let Bastien come to her and embrace like long-lost lovers. But he'd asked what he *had* to do. That answer was even simpler. Send him away.

Though, what if Kian traveled with Bastien, bringing him back? Maybe he saw Bastien's worth in their efforts after all. She stomped her foot in frustration.

"Find him for me, Nolan. See if Lord Kian accompanies him or if he's here on Kian's leave. If not…" Her heart ached at the words. "See to it he's denied entry into the castle until we hear word."

Her eyes drifted to the dirt beneath her. Guilt weighed down her shoulders. Kian had written about his findings, that Bastien's past was not a threat to the kingdom, but had stated he was to remain where he was—wherever that might have been. If Kian hadn't approved Bastien's return, he must still think of Bastien as a distraction. But Bastien had abilities that might one day rival hers.

"Yes, Queen Faelyn." Nolan bowed and retreated west.

Faelyn watched him go, and it took every ounce of effort not to call him back.

Now that she was unoccupied, no less than half a dozen pages, aides, and runners approached, bowing. She took a deep breath through her nose. She had a long afternoon of hard decisions, preparation, and convincing herself she'd made the right choice.

CHAPTER

FORTY-TWO

The lightness Bastien felt after helping Barden's son stayed with him, but it had been nothing compared to the moment the connection to Faelyn returned. It'd nearly brought him to his knees with joy, right there in the middle of a busy street. She was nearby, and he'd be able to warn her of his Fating. His steps quickened after that, then more so when the castle turrets came into view, white stone rising into a blue sky, dark blue banners etched in silver billowing in the breeze.

Now the outer wall, topped with crenellations perfectly spaced for archers, stood just beyond a short valley and down a wide stone road. Guard towers flanked the road where the town stopped before the castle. The guards eyed him but allowed him to pass. He wasn't the only one. Many townspeople headed toward the castle, on foot or with their ox-drawn carts of goods. He wasn't even the only mage, though he earned a stern look from the woman who passed him. He smiled and saluted her, but then the crowd carried her away.

Bastien reached the open castle gate flanked by another set of guard towers more heavily manned than the ones before. An Alysian soldier stepped into his path. The soldier's arms were stiff at his

326

sides, face stern beneath jaw-length dark hair and brown eyes. He raised his chin, and Bastien recognized him as Faelyn's head guard. Nelson. No, Newton. Something like that.

"Neal!" Bastien said. "Well met. I was wondering how I'd find her. I'm glad she sent you."

Neal's stern features came to rest in his mouth, weighing down the corners. "Captain Nolan at your service. Where is Lord Kian?"

"How would I know where his lordship is?" Bastien said. Why did that matter? "He didn't accompany me to Thomats."

Neal—no, Nolan—looked up to the watching guards and exaggeratedly shook his head from side to side.

"Um, I have an important message for Queen Faelyn." Dread crawled up Bastien's spine. Behind Nolan, guards exited a side door and positioned themselves across the road like a human wall. Wary townspeople were ushered past. *Damn it.* "You're going to arrest me, aren't you?"

"That wasn't part of my orders, but if you attempt to enter the castle, I will ensure it is done."

Bastien swallowed against the painful lump forming in his throat. "These are Faelyn's orders?" Nolan didn't react in any way.

Half of him couldn't believe it, the other half saw the reality of the situation. Who was he to her? He'd been so eager to assume she'd welcome him back with open arms. Despite the hurt, he still had to warn her.

Bastien took a step toward Nolan. The guards drew their swords.

He raised his empty hands. "I can accept she doesn't want to see me, that I'm not good enough for her kingdom." The words spat like venom, burning the air and burning his insides. "Just please pass on my message."

Nolan crossed his arms.

"I had a Fating of the future before I left Thomats. Daltieri and Kestrea will join forces to attack Alysies."

Nolan smirked, and the guards behind him chortled. "They delivered a declaration of war weeks ago. Their army marches south."

Bastien took a long step toward Nolan. The guards shouted, but Bastien raised his hands again, and Nolan called them off.

Bastien spoke quietly. "An entire fleet of their combined forces is poised to land on the shores of Caprina. The town will be overrun. I've seen their plans. Nothing you can do now will prevent them from coming, but if you act now, you might be able to save the town."

Nolan locked eyes with Bastien for a long time, weighing his truthfulness, one man to another. After an age, Nolan's stance relaxed. "I will tell my queen what you've seen, but don't expect her to take the word of one who hails from Kestrea."

Bastien kept his face neutral, but inside, he bled. Is that how Queen Faelyn truly saw him? "Let me join the army. Let me volunteer. I want to fight, and I know I can help."

Nolan reached to his belt and untied a leather pouch. "This will help you get far from Pavora, and far from causing Queen Faelyn more grief."

Bastien sneered at the coin pouch. "Tell her one more thing. I'll crawl on hands and knees to the Hereafter if that's what it takes to see her again." With a flick of his robe, he turned and left the castle gate.

He could have used the money, but he wasn't about to take charity. The guards at the city gate eyed him more menacingly this time. *Acantha above.* Could nothing go right in his life? Even when he tried, he failed. He'd be damned if he was going to duck and run. He'd find some other way to see her if he couldn't get into the castle.

There would be no giving up on her, nor would he fail her. Her name would not be added to the list of people he'd let down.

Faelyn was speaking to the master of arms in her meeting room at the citadel when Nolan entered.

"Thank you, Rupert. Please let me know when you have a final count on the uniforms."

Rupert bowed and left, muttering about not enough hands for the job of outfitting all the new recruits.

She paced the small, bare room. "Did you find him?"

Nolan shut the door behind him, filling her with foreboding. "I did. I intercepted him as he attempted to enter the castle grounds. He was wearing a mage robe but carried no staff. He hadn't seen Kian."

Faelyn twisted her hands around each other. "Did he say where he'd been?" Her mouth snapped closed. Kian hadn't told her for a reason. She wasn't supposed to know so she couldn't follow. Nolan waited for her to retract her question, but she couldn't.

She met his steady gaze, a challenge.

"Thomats School of Magic, Your Majesty."

Thomats! She smiled involuntarily. Kian had sent Bastien to Thomats. Was that because he trusted him and his Fating that he would one day help her? Or because Cinda was there, the best mind reader in the kingdom? Perhaps Kian only wanted her to read Bastien's memories to make sure he wasn't a spy. Then Bastien had escaped and stolen a mage robe.

Faelyn sighed.

Nolan continued. "He was warned to leave Pavora. I sent a pair of guards to follow him."

Well, he wasn't gone yet, that much was certain. The pull to him was as strong as ever.

"Did he say anything?" Her nerves were stretched so thin, she might snap at any moment.

"He had a message for you. Two, in fact, though I hesitate to say."

Faelyn tilted her head. "Why?"

"I'm not adept in gauging the truthfulness of a mage's word. He could be trying to purposefully mislead you."

Her lips thinned. "Tell me, Nolan."

"Of course."

As Nolan recounted Bastien's Fating, Faelyn's stomach dropped, horror washing over her. When he was done, she had to sit for fear her legs might fail. "A coastal attack. We are not prepared." She breathed, trying to calm herself. There simply hadn't been enough time to reverse a hundred years' worth of damage to her kingdom. "Creadel will help us defend our shores. We'll be fine. Though I am glad for the warning."

"Forgive me if I'm overstepping, but I advise caution if you're considering making decisions based on the words of a potential Kestrean spy."

Faelyn narrowed her eyes and stood to her full height. Irrational anger flooded through her. How dare he insult Bastien? "Kian claims Bastien is not a threat to our kingdom. If he was a spy, we'd know it."

Nolan bowed his head low. "Forgive me."

She breathed through her nose and shook her head. "What was the second message?"

"I don't recall it in full. Something about crawling on hands and knees."

"To the Hereafter." She brought her fingers to her lips. "Thank you, Nolan. That will be all." Nolan bowed. "And don't arrest him. Even if he doesn't leave Pavora right away. Let him be."

"As you wish." Nolan left, closing the door behind him.

Faelyn slumped into her chair. She couldn't shake the feeling Nolan was disappointed in her. Maybe she was just disappointed in herself, at her weakness. She barely knew Bastien. What angered her the most was that part of her hoped Bastien would find a way to reach her, despite her orders. She could almost admit that's why she hadn't ordered him arrested.

She needed Kian. Needed his guidance and steady assurance.

She stood, smoothed her dress, and straightened her circlet. "Guard," she called.

The door guard stepped into the room and bowed.

"Send runners to call the lords and generals to the council room immediately." They'd have to change strategies.

FORTY-THREE

Nolan, that bastard, sent guards to follow him. Bastien ran, darting in and out of streets and alleys until he was satisfied he lost them. The good mood at not having lost his touch from his reckless youthful days didn't last long—only until he remembered why he'd been forced to run in the first place.

Doing his best to keep the scowl off his face and not startle the townspeople, Bastien spent the rest of the afternoon circling the palace and citadel, trying to find a way in. The castle grounds were expansive. Walking westward through the alleys of Pavora, he kept the wall in his sight. Strong, protective magic radiated out from the stone as a warning the wall would not be breached. The city kept going on and on, and so did the wall. Where it curved around, the city curved with it.

He hadn't made any progress by the time the sun set and the townspeople headed home. Where the castle wall ended, the citadel wall began, just as high but made of a cruder stone without any floral or ivy adornments. Magic still permeated it just as heavily. Within the wall, the sounds of people giving their all in preparation for war continued. He wished to be inside more than anything.

Warm light from the street lamps bathed his surroundings, nearly masking the evening's chill. Candles glowed within nearby houses. He was in a richer part of the city, where the homes were mansions two stories high with fences surrounding small yards.

He couldn't stay here. He stepped on but then stopped. The draw to Faelyn was noticeably stronger beside the citadel than at the castle.

Faelyn was in the citadel. He could feel her not far beyond the other side of the wall. So close. If he could just talk to her, maybe she'd allow him back into the army. They wouldn't let him in the gates, so why not scale the wall?

The battlements were heavily guarded. He needed a diversion.

Bastien slid away from the streetlight and into the shadows beside a quiet house, keeping an eye on the guards at the top of the wall. A dog barked nearby. The soldiers training in the citadel yelled. Carts rolled through the streets, but even those sounds became less and less as he concentrated. He nestled down between a pair of bushes and slowly built up his magic.

When the meeting adjourned, Faelyn sent Nolan home to be with his wife and baby. She excused her guard and left the citadel council room. Outside, it was night, but the oil lamps burned bright so work could still be done. More lords had arrived with their armies during the afternoon, as well as a courier with a note from Cinda outlining Bastien's Fating. All of it meant more meetings, more supplies, more organizing. Now, when she should be resting for the coming day, she wanted a walk.

She pulled her cape tight against the chill in the air. Late autumn would set in soon and rain would be a fact of life. Her breath fogged before her as she looked up at the stars. Bastien hadn't left, though she didn't attempt to pinpoint his location. Not heeding the dirt path or caring where she went, she passed between the stone bunkers and training grounds, enjoying a moment to herself.

Soon, Amerae would be well enough to begin light duties. Kian would return, then she wouldn't be so alone in this. She'd been tempted many times to use the piece of his mage crystal and speak to him, but there were drawbacks. She wasn't sure if she wanted to subject herself to the baring of her soul that occurred when the crystal linked them. Kian knew of her feelings for Bastien, but experiencing them was something different. She didn't long to hurt him further or give him a reason to stay away. Selfishly, she also wasn't prepared to handle feeling his pain any more keenly than she already did when they were together.

Faelyn looked up to find she stood beside the south wall. Funny, there was no path here, and the lack of lamps meant it was darker, though not to her eyes. She had trod through an open grassy area to stand at this spot without really noticing. The stone towered high, with no opening anywhere nearby. The pull to Bastien was strong, though, now that she was paying attention. She placed her palm against the wall. The binding magic within the stone and mortar pinged and zapped beneath her touch.

Bastien was close. Very close.

A rumble in the distance diverted her gaze behind her, over the expanse of the compound. Dark clouds roiled on the outskirts of the citadel, lightning flashing within. An autumn storm was not ideal. Shouts rang out as soldiers ran to secure the weapons and take cover from the coming rain. Water was not good for their armor. She cringed, thinking of the armies camped to the east. Most were outside the shelter of the city. There simply wasn't enough space.

She took a few steps and stopped. The clouds advanced quickly, but there was no wind—hardly a breeze fluttered her hair. With air magic, she sent her awareness to the sky to explore the unusual phenomenon. It reeked of magic. She nearly recoiled, but there was a familiar flavor to it, like roses and springtime.

Blotting out the stars, the clouds rolled over the citadel, and with them, a powerful gust of wind slammed into the compound.

"What is that idiot doing?" Faelyn threw up a shield as the strong gust hit her.

Tents and lean-to's toppled. Weapon racks pitched over, crashing into fences. Thatch flew off some of the roofs. Soldiers piled out of the bunks, scrambling to secure what they could. Then the rain came. Those armored dove for cover. Faelyn gathered her magic to push back the storm, but then something thudded to the ground behind her.

Before she could turn, strong arms wrapped around her. In her surprise, her shield faltered. Rain poured over her.

Bastien twisted her around and placed his hands on the sides of her face. She met his cool blue eyes burning into hers and knew no one had ever seen her the way he did. His perfect lips parted in wonder, face glowing like she was air to his lungs.

The rain weighed down his short hair revealing long ears over a smooth jaw.

"You idiot," she said, her voice milder than intended. "You could have destroyed the citadel." She breathed in deep—taking in the musky scent of him—and found the action lighter and easier than it'd been since he'd gone. Had breathing always been such a struggle before they met?

His lips formed the most beautiful smile, and he chuckled. "I'm still learning." His voice was pitched low. One hand slid to cup the back of her bare neck.

A million thoughts whirled through her head, but she shut them all off save one and rose up on her toes. Their mouths collided, lips intertwining, slippery and sweet with the falling rain.

Bastien wrapped his arms around her, pulling her close, and somehow her hands became entangled in his mage robe. She wanted him closer, and closer still. She parted her lips, and their tongues slipped over each other—emotions given declaration with the dance of their mouths. Shivers ran from deep in her belly outward. The taste of him, his warm breath on her, filled a missing part of her, and she knew she'd never get enough.

His back slammed against the wall. When had they moved? She didn't care. For a moment, only a moment, she would give in to what her soul desired. Her heart thrummed, and her breathing turned ragged, but the sounds of him commanded her attention. He breathed through their rapid kisses, the turning of their heads and tangle of their lips. A low moan built in the back of his throat as if their kiss physically pained him.

But no, it wasn't this moment that caused him pain. She felt it too. It was the loss of all the moments they'd never had together. She owed herself this, for all the moments she'd deny herself later.

A shield of air burst out around them—Bastien's doing. The rain stopped mixing with their kisses. The leftover drips helped his hand slip over the curve of her back. She smiled against his lips at his efforts and added her own: a shield of water to mirror them from outside sight.

She broke free of his mouth, panting. "How did you get over the wall?"

Cheeks flushed, he held her arm and let his fingers slide down her cheek. "I formed handholds with earth magic." He leaned down for another kiss.

She moved her head back. "That wall is spelled against that kind of tampering. I spelled it myself."

Bastien stared at her mouth. "I didn't meet any resistance. More proof we are meant to be together." He leaned down again.

Faelyn stepped out of his embrace. Hurt flashed from his essence but did not show on his face. She glanced around at the bubble around them, listening as the rain splashed against it.

What was she doing? Had she totally lost her mind? She opened her mouth to object—but he cut her off.

"Wait. I know what you're going to say. I know why I was sent away. Not because I can't be trusted, but because of this." He gestured at the shield around them, then her. "There's something between us besides being the same. The Fates want us to be together, but they haven't made it easy. You were born a queen and I a street thief. Yet here we are." A shy smile formed on his lips.

"If you know what I'm going to say, then why are you here tormenting me?"

"I read about you at Thomats. My heart broke when I learned of what you've endured to come this far. You've done so much to overcome the destruction wrought by the Daltieri kingdom."

He stepped closer, and she didn't back away. His voice was warmth and honey to her raw heart. Here was someone acknowledging her pain and accomplishments, who understood her struggles.

"I know you, Faelyn. You're not harming your kingdom. You never could. But I will not cause you pain. I only want to be a part of your life. I've done nothing honorable, and I don't deserve to be by your side, but give me a place in your army so that I may fight. Let me be one more body to protect your light against those who wish to cover it in darkness."

"I don't need you to save me, Bastien. I can save myself. I won't let you distract me from being the ruler I was meant to be." She turned to go. "Goodbye."

He sucked in a breath and fell to his knees on the wet ground. "On hands and knees, Faelyn. We need each other."

Her eyes widened, then narrowed. "Stop saying that. Every time you do, it's like a jolt to my soul, wrenching me back to you." She bit her lip.

"We're meant for each other." He reached for her, desperation now plain on his face. For once, his essence mirrored his appearance. He was in turmoil.

She hesitated, then dropped to her knees and fell into his embrace. His arms pulled her close, and she wrapped her hands behind his neck, resting her cheek against his. Her heart had never been torn in such a way. More than torn—tortured, ripped, bled, and prodded over and over again.

"You're wrong, Bastien. You've done plenty in your life to prove yourself worthy to be by my side. You're here." She squeezed him. "Despite my best efforts to push you away and all the pain I must have caused you, you came back to me." She couldn't believe what she was saying, and yet there was nothing else to say. "I don't know what the future holds for my kingdom. I've run off every political match that could have aligned me with a kingdom of substance. Even with every lord at my disposal and Creadel's help, we're still outnumbered. There just hasn't been enough time to rebuild Alysies to what it once was." She shook herself. "I have to do what is best for my kingdom. But maybe I've been wrong about what that is." The words burned true inside her. "I'll find a place for you in my army."

He grinned and brought them to their feet, then scooped her up, twirling her through the air, warm and dry inside their shields. When he set her down, this time *she* kissed *him*.

"You'll have to leave the way you came and come back tomorrow through the gate after I make arrangements," she said. "I'll give you a place with Niri amongst the mages. I don't know what can become of you and me, but I can do this."

His smile brightened his face like a sunlit day, making her stomach do delightful flips.

Someone shouted her name from a distance. Nolan.

"I have to go. Up the wall, hurry!" She pushed him, and he grinned, pulling her back for one more lingering kiss that thrilled to her toes.

In unison, they dropped their shields. Rain no longer fell, and the stars were shining again. Faelyn stepped away but turned back before she reached the lamplight. Bastien was watching her, a smug smile on his lips. He turned to the wall. Handholds formed above him one at a time as he climbed up and over, arm muscles coiled beneath his taut skin where his robe slipped away. His magic was amazing, and he was barely trained.

Time would tell if she'd made the right decision, but her heart said it was. She couldn't bear to send him away once again. He didn't deserve the pain she'd already caused—it hurt her as much as it hurt him.

Nolan shouted her name again. She rushed into the light on the path, then calmly made her way back to the courtyard in front of the council room. Soldiers spotted her through the dark, and her name echoed throughout the citadel. Not good. Water puddled everywhere, and repairs were being made to roofs and downed fences. She spotted Nolan as he ran toward her.

Panting, he hastily bowed. "My queen, are you well?" His voice was close to panicked, which never happened to him. "The guards lost sight of you and alerted me of your disappearance."

"I am well, thank you, Nolan. I went for a walk and got caught in that unusual weather. I took shelter, but now I'm ready to go home."

Nolan eyed her for a long time. "The carriage is waiting, Your Majesty. This way."

Her guards returned, surrounding her just a bit more closely than usual. As a true servant to the crown, Nolan didn't ask any further questions. Faelyn rode home with the heat of Bastien's kiss flushing her cheeks and the promise of a new day.

FORTY-FOUR

That night, when Bastien knocked on the door of the bleary-eyed restaurant owner, he was welcomed in with open arms.

"Lord Bastien! You're back!" Barden tossed a heavy arm over Bastien's shoulders and led him inside, the lingering scent of roasted chicken making his mouth water. "You're a hero in these parts. Everyone's come to see my boy's miraculous recovery." He sat Bastien down at a table, then went to the kitchen and returned with dinner and a mug of cider. "What brings you here so late?"

Dawn was still a long way away, but Bastien didn't feel the least bit tired. In fact, this was the most awake he'd ever been. He had a long day ahead of him, trying to earn his spot back in the army. "I need a place to sleep, just for the night." He grinned. "I've been accepted into the army within the ranks of mages."

"Well, of course you have. And of course you can! You're welcome here anytime." He watched with a pleased smile as Bastien ate. "My wife and son are sleeping, so we'll have to be quiet, but you can sleep upstairs."

"Thank you, Barden. That's very kind." Bastien quickly finished the food, and Barden showed him upstairs. A blanket and pillow were offered, then Barden left with a chuckle of satisfaction. Bastien sensed the cook's joy in repaying the favor.

He settled down over the thin blanket, listening to their quiet breathing. The usual noises outside Thomats were absent in the big city. The chirps of crickets and coos of night owls were replaced by late-night travelers and wagons bumping over cobbled streets. Moonlight streamed into the small room, the white light reminding him of Faelyn. She couldn't deny the connection between them now. Even if her senses returned, reminding her she was so much more than him, she'd told him to come back. And even if she turned him away when this war was over, it'd be worth it. He'd be able to help her and protect her. His Fating would be fulfilled.

But, of course, his actions had become more than that—more than some vision. More than his desire to finally do something worth a scrap of value in his life. Because now that he'd met her, he knew the world would cease to exist without her light in it. There had never been anyone as fierce and strong, as powerful and beautiful as Faelyn. His Faelyn, he'd one day call her.

It all started tomorrow.

⚔

Bastien awoke better rested than he'd been in a long while. After ensuring his hood covered his ears, he tossed the cotton blanket off and stretched. Sun had replaced moonlight in the window, easing some of the chill that permeated the room. The family was not in their beds. From downstairs came the sound of clanging pots and muffled voices.

Breakfast!

Bastien shot for the door, then doubled back to roll his blanket. He examined his work. He'd rolled it like he was living on the road with Tave again. Did people roll their blankets in a normal home? At the House, he'd only ever kicked it into a corner and hoped it was there the next night. A servant took care of his bedding at Thomats.

He left the blanket as it was and plodded down the steps.

Barden, his wife, and his son, Christopher, looking none the worse for wear, smiled in greeting at he came through the door. They each continued their tasks, kneading big bowls of batter, frying eggs on the stove, and drizzling honey over delicious-looking biscuits. Bastien's stomach rumbled. He had time for just a quick bite before he needed to head to the castle.

"Good morning, Lord Bastien. You're just in time for us to open. Would you mind unlocking the door?" Barden, elbow-deep in dough, nodded toward the front of the shop.

"Of course." Bastien stepped from behind the counter and weaved his way through the few tables. He unlatched the door and opened it. The cool morning air washed over him as he poked his head out to survey the scene.

Rough hands grabbed him by the shoulders and hauled him into the street. "It *is* you!"

Bastien saw the grinning face of Tave before he was pulled into a bone-crushing hug.

Behind him, Micah glowered beside an indifferent Brock.

Bastien recovered his wits as Tave, still grinning, let go. "So you didn't get killed."

"Nah, of course we didn't," Tave said. "We thought you might have, though. We knew you got caught and thought there was no way they'd spare you. So, we're in town, taking care of a little business, and we heard of this Lord Bastien performing miracles on injured children." Tave eyed him up and down.

Bastien shifted in his fine mage robe.

Micah rolled his eyes.

"Looks like you've survived all right, *Lord* Bastien." Tave made a dramatic bow. "That is a robe of Thomats School of Magic, if I'm not mistaken—and it's not a fake." He pinched the fabric between his fingers.

Some of the delight in meeting his old comrade was quickly fading. "I've been training there."

"Indeed?" He glanced over his shoulder to Micah and winked. "Where's your staff?"

"The queen's army kept it, I suppose. I don't need it anymore." Bastien pulled the robe from Tave's grip.

Tave leaned toward him. "Finally figured that out, huh?"

Bastien's mouth formed a tight line. If Tave knew he didn't need a staff, then he knew about his fae heritage. "How long have you known?"

Tave hooked his thumbs into his belt—not much more than a length of rope. "A few days after we spent a small fortune on your staff, we were camped outside of the town of Caprina. You thrashed and called out in your sleep. A name, Ollie or some such. When I got up to check on you, you rolled over. I saw your ears. After I picked my jaw off the floor, a lot of things about you made a lot more sense."

"Why didn't you tell me you knew? Why make me train with a staff?"

"If people found out you didn't need a staff to access magic, they'd ask questions. If they found out you were fae like their beloved queen, I might have lost you and your abilities a lot sooner." Tave shrugged, and Bastien clenched his fists. "Now don't look like that. It was just a guess, anyway. That is, until Micah noticed you'd been healing yourself when your staff wasn't even lit up."

Bastien narrowed his eyes, and Tave threw up his hands. Townspeople eyed them as more and more traveled up the street, some entering Barden's restaurant.

"I guess I shouldn't have expected anything more from a band of thieves." Bastien had spent his youth with this lot, but he hadn't realized how despicable they were until he'd lived life on the other side. He had a sudden appreciation for his short time in the army and at Thomats.

"Don't think you're any better than us, *Lord* Bastien," Brock said.

Micah smirked.

"I don't know why people are calling me that. Because I'm a mage, I suppose. Anyway, I'm late. You all take care." Bastien stepped past Tave, watching Micah closely.

"Hold on there," Tave said. "Now that we found you, we can't just let you leave." The three of them shuffled forward.

Bastien turned, incredulous.

"You still owe me a debt." Tave smiled, though Bastien sensed his nervous energy. "For the staff. I'd ask for it back, but it seems that's not possible. You'll have to pay us what's due."

Bitter anger worked its way under Bastien's skin, but that's where he left it. He didn't let it show. "What about the coach robbery?" That was to be his last job before he was free of his debt, the one that got him caught.

"We had to run—actually, swim—away after you failed to hold up the wall. We barely made it out with our lives," Tave said.

Magic built around Micah until his staff glowed.

Bastien allowed a slow smile of warning on his face. "They had a master mage, and she has since trained me well. Whatever you think you can do to stop me won't work. I'm leaving."

He turned and hurried down the road. They'd attracted too many eyes, and negative attention was the last thing he needed. Tave cursed and barked something to Micah. They gave chase. Water in nearby troughs shifted, then lifted with Micah's magic. Bastien nearly laughed. Micah's water magic had always been weaker, especially now that Bastien had some formal training. What did he hope to accomplish?

Townspeople stumbled to a halt, gawking. Some screamed and ran as Micah's water rose higher, now chasing Bastien down the street. *Enough.* He stopped, turned, and threw a shield of air directly in front of the advancing thieves. With audible smacks, they hit it like a brick wall and collapsed to the ground. Micah's water dropped on either side of Bastien, splashing over the bottom of his robe.

He shook his head and turned north to the castle. Nothing would ruin his second chance to prove himself to Faelyn.

A whoosh of air was the only warning before a board slammed into his face. Pain exploded and was quickly gone with the release of consciousness.

CHAPTER

FORTY-FIVE

"Has he arrived yet, Nolan?" Faelyn paced the citadel council room.

She hadn't specified what time Bastien should return, but she assumed he wouldn't be much later than dawn. Now the sun rose high, nearly midday. The troops had departed at first light to head north to the Daltieri border. She'd made a grand, but quick speech as time was not on their side. More than anything, she longed to go with them, to fight on the front line and save as many as she could, but she was needed here. The pull to Bastien, though not as strong as before, was still present and was motivation enough to remain in Pavora.

"The citadel guards have not seen him, Your Majesty." Nolan stood dutifully beside the door, acting as both guard and confidant.

Her shoulders drooped. She'd made all the arrangements to have Bastien placed with the mages and to continue his studies under Niri. Faelyn's trust was not direly misplaced, she was sure of it, despite the doubt radiating from Nolan as he stood appearing indifferent. A war meeting was due to start any minute to continue discussing plans for the armada Bastien had seen in his Fating. She

345

wasn't overly concerned. Still, plans had to be adjusted and orders issued.

But where was Bastien?

Nolan shifted, drawing Faelyn's attention.

"Please speak your mind, Nolan." What he wanted to say was nearly audible anyway, and the silence in the room was enough to drive her mad.

"Would you like me to send guards to find him?"

Faelyn looked at him with surprise, and he offered one of his rare small smiles.

He went on. "I do worry about you. You've been melancholy ever since he was sent away. Niri trusts him, Lord Kian wanted him trained, and you clearly care for him. Since you've asked what I think, I think a mage who has the power to conjure the storm we saw last night, it's better he's on our side." Nolan took a breath and resumed his 'guard' stance, as if his speech had cost him emotional energy.

Faelyn couldn't help her smirk. "Yes, send a pair of guards. I can't think of why he wouldn't be here, but if they find him, tell them to observe and report back." Hopefully he had a good reason, like caught up healing another of the town's children, and not something horrible, like real trouble. She pushed that thought quickly away. Wherever he was, he couldn't be hurt or in distress. Bastien was one man who could take care of himself.

Bastien awoke, his head pounding. He blinked, looking over a dark, dank room. His ankles were tied securely to a chair, wrists bound behind him, and a rope around his chest and middle. The room was made of mildewed wood, swollen as if from heavy rain or flooding. A basement perhaps? No windows, only a single door. He had no idea how much time had passed. Dried blood flaked off his face as he turned his head.

Micah stood leaning in a corner. He lit his staff up just before Tave came through the door, followed by Brock and a woman he'd never seen before. Wearing a leather vest and tight trousers, hair unbound, she watched Tave possessively, and the three spread out in front of him, joined by Micah.

Bastien felt nothing but disappointment. He'd looked up to Tave for many years, Micah too. He'd strived to be a good member of the gang and do his best, always with his eye on the ultimate goal: earning his freedom. Tave called them brothers in arms. Bastien had been nothing but a tool to them after all.

Tave glared at the woman. New bruises under his eyes meant he'd somehow broken his nose, hopefully when he'd run into Bastien's wall of air.

"You're a fool to think you can keep me here." His mind picked over what elements would best help to free him and harm his captors. He'd read that Faelyn could steal the air from her enemies. Maybe he'd try that.

"I'm real sorry about this, kid," Tave said. "We didn't know how else to get you to listen. Vayla here wasn't supposed to smash your face in, just stop you if you tried to escape."

Bastien focused hard on the rope binding his wrists. The minute fibers were made from a plant. And what was a plant if not part of the earth? He could manipulate earth and plants.

Though it wasn't easy, he'd had a mentor pass him off under Cinda's guidance, so he knew what to do. He channeled the magic. Micah straightened in alarm. The fibers loosened, and his wrists dropped free. With a heavy frown, he crossed his arms.

Tave grinned and shook his head. "It's a shame you won't join back up with us. You've got real talent. I knew it from the moment you nearly burned us all alive."

The bindings dropped from his ankles and body. "How long was I out?"

The woman, Vayla, tightened her grip on a vicious-looking knife.

Tave patted her shoulder. "Only a few hours. Look, I should have known better than to ask for payment for the staff." He shrugged. "Can't blame a thief for trying. Consider your debt repaid. Instead, I'm here to offer my services to his lordship."

What? Bastien nearly laughed, might have if he wasn't so pissed. Tave had a mind that was always calculating, always two steps ahead of everyone else. Whatever his initial reason for cornering Bastien, it no longer existed. He'd moved on to grander plans, but what did that mean he knew?

Bastien stood, knocking his chair back with a clatter. Brock jumped, and Micah's staff grew brighter.

Tave raised his hands showing he was unarmed. "You're free to go, of course, just hear me out."

"And the moment I leave, your cruitie will knife me in the back?"

Tave glanced sideways at Vayla. "Put the damn knife away."

She glowered but complied.

"We've heard rumors, and while you were napping we asked around. Alysies's beloved queen has accepted you into her army. She fights a war she cannot win against not one, but two formidable enemies." Tave pointed his thumb at his cohorts and himself. "We know the ins and outs of the kingdom borders better than any spy, and you know it. We've been traveling these routes forever."

Bastien snorted. "You want to be the queen's spies now?"

"No, but we'll be traveling anyway. Let us bring you back news."

"For a price." Always a price.

"For a price, if it's worthy news," Tave said.

Bastien considered. By the time they returned, he may just have earned what money they'd require for their services, and if it helped Faelyn... "Alright. Just keep in mind I can sense when you're lying, so it will do no good to fabricate news."

Tave adopted a look of mock horror, mouth and eyes going wide. "You'd accuse us of fabrication?"

Brock chuckled, and Vayla grinned.

Bastien ignored them, crossing to the door and opening it. A dark staircase led up to a room lit by sunlight.

"I'm sorry I disappointed you, kid." Tave's words were genuine and gave Bastien pause. "You've seen goodness, and it's opened your eyes to the bad within us."

Behind Tave, Micah looked away, frowning.

Bastien sighed. "I know where you are and how you feel, but it doesn't have to be like that. We can all rise above. None of us have to be less than we desire. None of us are trapped like we think we are. The hardest step is the first."

And with that, he stepped up the stairs and away from his old gang.

"You're just going to let him leave?" Vayla argued from behind.

"None of us could ever hope to stop him," Micah said quietly. "He grew too powerful, like I always said he would."

Tave laughed. "You didn't say that. I did!"

Despite himself, Bastien left what appeared to be an abandoned riverside warehouse, smiling.

The war meeting ended, lords, generals, advisors, and messengers all hurrying to their tasks. It had been productive, and more ships would be dispatched from the southeastern ports to hopefully offer relief to Caprina in a few weeks' time. They didn't know how far in the future Bastien had seen the enemy coming. Faelyn had issued swift instructions, all while keeping her senses open. She still held on to hope that Bastien would come.

Nolan entered as the last of the group left. He bowed in greeting. "The guards spotted him, Your Majesty. They are just outside should you desire to speak to them."

"Yes, please. Send them in." Nerves prickled the back of her neck.

The way Nolan spoke without offering his own information didn't sit well with her.

Two guards entered wearing the standard thick leather guard armor over blue tunics. They bowed in unison. At Nolan's prompting, the senior guard gave his report.

"There was an altercation this morning north of the Pavora market. Upon questioning the witnesses, Lord Bastien fought with a group foreign to Pavora."

Lord Bastien?

"The fight ended when he was knocked unconscious by a member of the party. From there, we tracked him to an abandoned mill near the western shore of the river. We snuck in close and listened to what we could. We believe the group to be a band of thieves. Lord Bastien was once a member, and they hope for him to be again. When we were sure he wasn't being harmed, we left without interfering, as you requested."

A dark weight settled over her. She met Nolan's glance before he quickly adjusted his gaze. Had she let her heart and imagination run wild? This had to be the same gang he'd been with when Niri captured him. Bastien couldn't leave his past any more than she could.

"Thank you, soldiers." Her voice came out breathless, and she cleared her throat. "Captain Nolan, see that they receive my commendation for their work. I may call on them again."

Pride beamed out from the two young men as they bowed and followed Nolan out. If only she could absorb their joy to squash her irrational disappointment and anger.

She brushed the silver tray holding her goblet of water and considered smashing it against the wall. The only thing stopping her was logic. It wouldn't solve anything, only make her feel worse when the servants cleaned it up.

Bastien hadn't *chosen* to go with them. And at least he was safe. A band of his old thieving friends was hardly a threat, especially after what Cinda had said in her letters to Niri regarding the advancement in his abilities.

She looked up at a knock at the door. Amerae entered, dressed in full training gear, practice sword at her side. Her brow creased with concern.

"Oh, Amerae." Faelyn rushed to her dear friend's embrace. "I'm so glad you're back."

Amerae smoothed her hand down Faelyn's back. "You'll be okay, my queen. You'll make the right choice."

"Nolan talked to you, then." It was right that he had.

"He's concerned for you, as am I."

Faelyn pulled back. "I worry I'm using Nolan for my personal issues rather than the kingdom's, where he's better suited."

Amerae's kind face was reassuring. "He's happy to serve in any capacity. By serving you, he serves the kingdom."

Faelyn took Amerae's hands. "I'm sorry I haven't had much time to see you and baby Mary."

"I understand. But, I'm here now and ready to get back into shape."

"Good, we need you."

The two shared a warm smile. Something shifted with the pull to her soul, drawing Faelyn's gaze behind her friend, though she only saw the open doorway and the citadel buildings beyond. Bastien was close to the bordering wall.

Amerae was watching her, so Faelyn turned her attention back. "Don't overdo it on your first day. We have some time before we see action here. Use it to prepare wisely."

"Yes, Queen Faelyn." Amerae inclined her head. She left with only a single backward glance, though Faelyn sensed her concern long after.

It was the same concern she held for herself. Faelyn turned and glanced at the tray with the goblet she longed to throw. She huffed and grabbed her sword. A spar would do her good.

FORTY-SIX

Bastien jogged toward the citadel gate, cheeks burning with embarrassment at being so late, and anger at Tave for being the cause. A coolness snaked down the connection between him and Faelyn. He'd messed up. He'd hurt her trust. He had to get it back.

Slowing, he crossed the walkway to the outer guard station. Two of them stepped forward to intercept him.

"Stop right there, mage. No one enters without authorization. Remove your hood." The lean guard winked, drawing Bastien's notice.

Bastien smiled, finally recognizing his old friend beneath the helm. He pulled back his hood and shook his hair from his eyes.

Chrisso laughed, dropping his tough-guard act. "I knew it was you. They said you were due this morning, but you were just waiting for my rotation, huh?" He sheathed his sword, and the two shook hands in a firm grip.

"It's good to see you, Chrisso. Looks like you've done well for yourself." He'd been in training last Bastien knew.

"Not too bad, but a far cry from where you are." Chrisso clapped him on the back, and they made their way through the tunnel under the wall, leaving the other guard behind. "Word is, Lord Bastien, that you've earned the queen's favor. A mage as well as fae. And here I thought your only skills were putting no-good captains in their place."

Bastien covered his joy by studying the compound as they came out the tunnel and crossed the grounds. Soldiers and guards were everywhere, standing in line at the mess hall or marching in formation. Blue banners billowed in the cool breeze on every building. Those that were being built when he left were now completed. Young runners hurried up and down worn paths while captains shouted orders and practice swords clanked in the distance. The citadel had been a busy place before, but now it was full to the brim.

Chrisso must have seen his surprise. "We've done a lot of recruiting since you were last here, and more pile in as the high lords arrive and word of the war has gotten around the kingdom."

Bastien marveled at the enormous amount of money and resources this effort must have taken. Faelyn's foresight had prepared them well. He looked for her, scanning across fields of troops and between buildings, but of course she wasn't nearby. Still, he felt the draw to her toward the west, so he continued his search. He caught the eyes of the passing troops as he wound through the compound. They whispered or even pointed, saying his new name, Lord Bastien.

He considered putting his hood back up, but there was no point now. "Why do they call me Lord?"

Chrisso glanced sidelong at his pointed ears. "Far as I can tell, it started as a nickname when you beat Captain Flinn in that duel. No one's been brave—or stupid—enough to do that." Chrisso gave a shrug. "Or it could be the ears. It definitely spread that you had fae traits and were sent to train at Thomats. The townspeople, you know how they like to talk. Well, they picked it up from some of the soldiers flapping their mouths, and now it's stuck."

Bastien didn't know how he felt about the name. He had yet to do anything deserving of it, but he would. "Where are we going?"

"I've been given orders to take you to the north of the compound. The mages have their own housing and training facility there." Chrisso caught his eye. "Looks like I won't be seeing you around."

"I'll come visit when I can. You've always been kind to me."

Chrisso waved off the comment as they reached an entrance with its own guards. Two stories high of smooth stone and a heavy wood door flanked by blue columns. An aether shield surrounded the building, putting a metallic taste in his mouth and holding the flavor of Faelyn—a wild, untamable feel as crisp as a summer wind. Though spirited and free, he got the sense she'd be a leader no matter where the Fates had placed her.

"Good luck, man." Chrisso saluted and walked back the way they'd come.

Bastien turned to the entrance. The guards stared straight ahead.

"Good afternoon, fellas." Bastien waved as he walked toward the door. To his surprise, they didn't try and stop him.

With the faint feel of static, he passed through the thin shield and opened the heavy door. A stone staircase lined with wall sconces greeted him. He followed it down, down, down, winding around until the pressure in his ears changed and he finally reached the bottom. A double set of wooden doors revealed nothing of what lay beyond, but he felt much magic within, as if from multiple sources.

None of the magic spoke of Faelyn. In fact, the draw to her was fainter here, as if he'd left her behind beneath the layers of earth between them. The feeling was near to losing a limb, though not as agonizing as when they'd been separated before. He'd become used to having her companionship, even if they weren't physically together.

He pulled the door open and stopped in his tracks. This was a cave, tall and wide. His gaze shot upwards. *Acantha above!* Almost the whole ceiling was made of water. It was Pavora Lake. It was like looking through a giant window, but instead of sky, there was the lake. The light of the afternoon sun filtered through. Fish swam in the clear water.

Bastien's jaw dropped. He'd never seen such a feat of magic, even at the best school of magery in the continent. They'd built this entire complex under the lake. Like one big bubble arena.

Someone laughed beside him, making him jump.

Niri smiled, winded. "I rushed over here as fast as I could when they told me you were coming, just so I could see the look on your face. It was worth it, too." Pieces of red hair had sprung loose from her braided updo, sticking out in wispy curls. "We call it the Hollow. No enemy would suspect its presence."

Below the water dome was a vast open area. Mages sparred or worked on individual spells within their own personal spaces separated by invisible shields. None wore robes from their individual schools, though. They wore fighting gear in Alysian blue, similar to that of a standard soldier except for swirling silver lines adorning the front and back. Doors and walkways led off to corridors where more mages entered and left. There must have been hundreds of people within eyesight alone.

"How?" was the only word he managed.

"Queen Faelyn has worked very hard to create this space since she became queen. It's impenetrable, spelled by the finest, and kept entirely secret from the outside world." Niri beamed with pride.

"Thomats doesn't have anything like this." It had been difficult to find safe places to train with his more dangerous magic.

"Thomats is a school. This is a war compound. We don't work on basics here. We hone what we learned in school and apply it in ways that will thwart our enemies." She gestured to the open area with her staff. "They don't teach you how to fight at Thomats. Here we do, and doubly so now that we've entered the war we've always known was coming."

He watched the two mages closest to them spar behind their invisible shield. The woman fought with water, the man with fire, both with mage staffs brightly lit. He shot a fireball toward her, which she ducked, holding a shield of water to avoid the heat. The fireball slammed into the shield and dispersed.

Bastien bounced on his toes, anxious for his turn.

Niri chuckled again. "It's good to have you back, Bastien. I was against sending you away at first—I didn't know what Kian had in mind—but it has done you much good."

"It has. Your daughter taught me well."

"She had nothing but good reports. Come." Niri turned and walked along the outer edge, where the wall was dark rock.

Bastien followed a little behind. His eyes warred between the wondrous lake overhead and the amazing displays of magic from the sparring mages before him. One pair, two men, simply stood in front of each other, staring intently. Sweat poured off their brows, and their legs shook. He felt the magic streaming from them and saw it in their glowing staffs, but could not for the life of him figure out what they were doing.

Then one doubled over, eyes rolling into the back of his head before he collapsed. The other let out a gust of air and smiled tremulously. The shield instantly dissipated, and healing mages rushed in from one of the many stations dispersed throughout the dome.

Niri followed his gaze. "Their ability is mind control. We try to pair mages up based on their ability, at first, then expand from there to situations they may encounter against mages in battle."

Bastien nodded, realizing he'd stopped to stare again. "When do I get to do that?"

"Soon." She sounded pleased. They continued walking around the dome. "We're working on your pairings. No other mage, besides Queen Faelyn, can control all five elements, so we're still deciding. You could be a good trainer for the junior mages who will soon face enemy mages of various abilities simultaneously. But we're not there yet. Cinda told me of your hesitation when it comes to mind magic, so we'll get to that as well."

He cringed. The prospect of elemental sparring had him salivating, but facing a mage with any mental abilities almost made it not worth it. Almost.

Niri led him into a hallway lit by wall sconces in the absence of light from the lake. "Do not worry. It will be nothing like what Cinda did. Almost nothing. But you need to learn how to protect yourself from all kinds of magic."

She showed him into a large cavern carved out of rock where mages sat at long tables eating meat and potatoes off wooden plates. "This is the dining hall. Further down the hall behind us is where the junior mages sleep in bunks, not unlike those from your army days. The senior mages have their own rooms they share with a room-mate. You will have a room to yourself." She showed him to a line and handed him a plate.

Why a room to himself?

Younger boys filled his plate with food from large trays. They sat at a table away from the curious eyes of the other mages. Grateful, he ate while she talked.

"Every day you will receive a match list. You must adhere to this list and no trading with anyone. We pick your partners with a purpose. Eventually, you'll face more than one at a time. If you're uninjured, you'll have private training with me or one of the other master mages."

Bastien soaked up every word. He didn't want to mess up his second chance. "How long do we have?"

Niri nodded as if she was expecting the question. "Queen Faelyn advised this morning that we have a month at most." She lowered her voice. "I know you're no ordinary mage-in-training, Bastien, so I will tell you what I know when I know it, but you must not repeat what I say."

He swallowed his last bite of potato. "I promise."

"A screen, if you please."

It took him a moment to realize what she meant, then he conjured the necessary air magic to create a shield so they couldn't be overheard. A lot of the mages in this room likely had the ability, in one form or another, to listen in on their conversation. It would take a while for him to get used to living in this kind of environment.

"Good." She straightened. "Troops left for the Daltieri border to meet the enemy that is marching on Crosston. The town will be lost, but our troops will set up a defense to intercept and hopefully defeat those villains."

Bastien's jaw unhinged, but he caught it before his lips parted. "How prepared are we?"

Niri frowned. "As prepared as we can be. We've only begun to rebuild what was left in the wake of driving Daltieri out and recovering from the damage done during their hundred years of rule. Our army has grown swiftly, but the border runs long. Our queen has done the best she can. Aligning us with Kestrea was supposed to be the cornerstone of the plan. Without that stone, everything collapsed."

He broke away from her gaze, feeling a judgment that wasn't really there.

"Your Fating made us aware of their second phase of the plan, the armada, and we are doing what we can to make ready." She paused for a long time. "I was at Thomats during the battle for Pavora. I wasn't forced to witness the atrocities and the death toll, but I will this time. You will too. So we must be ready." She handed him a slip of paper. "Come."

She gestured around them, and he dissipated his shield, glancing at the paper.

Laneira – Ice mage

He grinned and followed Niri. After quickly changing into a training uniform, she led him back to the bubble arena. They crossed through blocks of sparring mages, lights flashing and muted booms from their spells.

"You'll have a longer list once we finalize your schedule. For now, Laneira should suit you," Niri said.

They reached an empty quadrant of the open arena floor. A pair of medic mages identified with M's on their armor sat at a table of medical supplies and water. A woman stood waiting, hands clasped as if she was the calmest person in the world. Blue hair flowed to her elbows. Even her skin was faintly blue in a blatant display of how she identified with her ice powers. Her gaze went right to Bastien's ears, and he got the odd sense she wanted to bow to him but didn't.

"Laneira is nearly a master already and will be a good start for you." Niri backed away, and the ice mage stepped closer, nodding.

Niri continued. "Nothing internal, no mortal wounds, and if someone indicates they concede, you must withdraw. The bout goes until someone gives up, becomes too injured to continue, or your time runs out. Shake hands."

One of the medics cast an air shield around them.

Bastien cocked a grin and extended his hand. Excited energy lifted his gait. He hadn't done much with ice, but he'd done plenty with fire and water.

Laneira's hand was cold in his, her staff already glowing. He compensated by warming his hand before he let go.

"Oh, and Bastien, do not harm her mage crystal by magical means," Niri said, voice muted behind the shield.

He raised an eyebrow. The thought had never crossed his mind.

Niri hid a smile. "Our great queen turned the tides of the battle with that trick."

Bastien blinked. Mage crystals were naturally shielded from such attacks. He'd have to ask her how she did it.

"Begin."

Magic gathered to Laneira, diverting Bastien from thoughts of Faelyn. In the breath it took him to decide on fire and pull the magic forward, Laneira showered him with a wave of ice. His feet locked in place. He began falling forward, but the rest of her ice caught him, locking him in a solid block. The stinging cold bit at the exposed skin on his cheeks and hands. He couldn't breathe, couldn't move a muscle. Through the clear blue ice, Laneira turned to Niri, ready to claim her victory.

Panicked anger coursed alongside the searing heat he threw against the ice. There was no way he would go down like this in his first match. He'd be the laughingstock of the mage community, shaming Niri and her daughter. Not to mention, word would get back to Faelyn.

The ice around him melted, then cracked. He switched elements and blasted air out from all directions. Chunks went flying. Laneira threw up an ice shield, but he struck it with a wave of molten flame.

The ground beneath him turned slick, and he slipped. His legs flew out from under him, and his shoulder slammed into the cold, hard ground. *Ice!*

He growled and pushed himself up, reforming the fire to melt through her shield. A solid sphere of ice the size of a kickball raced toward his head. He conjured his shield of air, like a second skin. The sphere hit harmlessly and smashed to the floor.

His fire broke through her shield. She darted out of the way, landing on her knees as the towering flames slammed into the wall where she'd stood.

Using her staff to regain her footing, face contorted into anger, she shot up a hand.

"No, Laneira!" Niri shouted. "No internal wounds."

Laneira's eyes widened in horror, and her hand dropped.

Bastien used her distraction to wrap a sphere of flame around her, panting from the volume of magic. He didn't burn her as he would a real enemy, but she couldn't escape. She tried to counteract the fire. Ice shards pierced into his flame, melting before making it through. His weariness grew, legs shaking the longer he held the spell. Even pride wouldn't keep him from admitting that she was a formidable foe.

Soon, a muffled shout that sounded like, "Concede," came from within the roaring flames.

Bastien dropped the magic, nearly sagging with exhaustion. He'd never last long in a real battle if he didn't build up his stamina.

Laneira stood from her crouch, sweat pouring off her. Blue hair now limp and sticking to her face around livid eyes.

"You fought very well." Bastien held out his hand. "I can see why we were paired."

She took his hand, and the cold burned his skin.

He held it when she tried to pull away, burning him further. "What were you about to do when Niri stopped you?"

"Freeze the water in your body." She jerked her hand from his, taking a layer of his skin with her, and stormed off. The arena shield disappeared just before she stomped through it.

He looked at his raw hand, already healing. "She wouldn't have been able to anyway. I had my shield up."

Niri stepped forward, tusking over his hand and looking to where Laneira had gone. "She's never lost a match. I thought it would do her some good to be humbled."

His eyes widened. "You knew I'd win?"

She raised an eyebrow. "I'd hoped. Given your progression with all the elements, you had quite the advantage."

"Well, in a real fight, things might have gone much differently." Bastien scratched the back of his bare neck, arm heavy with weariness. "It's difficult to train when we have to hold so much of ourselves back."

"That's Laneira's constant complaint and struggle, but it's a necessity." Niri frowned. "She can freeze water, even through a mage shield."

Bastien looked sharply to where Laneira drank from a cup at a medic table several arenas over. "I've never heard of such an ability."

Niri turned to him. "She'll want a rematch, and I might not be there to stop her next time. Just watch out for it."

He nodded, looking around the room with new appreciation at the multitude of mages, sparring or waiting their turn. He caught several eyes staring at his ears. Most looked away. Some gave him subtle nods.

"You'll want a rest after expending such energy," Niri said.

He was tired, after being knocked out, tied up, and escaping just to be immediately tried by ice. He'd used a lot of energy. Yet he couldn't deny the potential influence he wielded in this place, and not just magical. He and Faelyn were the same. The mages were already beginning to respect him; he could feel it in the air. Niri herself was attending to him. He could only gain more respect through his ability—proving to them just how alike he and Faelyn were.

"A little water, and I'll be fine. I'd like to go again," he said.

Niri nodded her approval, and he got to work.

CHAPTER

FORTY-SEVEN

Queen Faelyn watched from her oversized wooden chair at the long table as Nolan entered the citadel's council room. "That is all for right now," she said to the amassed lords and leaders. "We will adjourn."

Time was always against them, so her people no longer wasted time lingering to curry favor with their queen once they were dismissed. They each vacated the room, much to Faelyn's pleasure, until only she and Nolan remained. She pulled a shawl closer around her shoulders at the chill let into the door. They hadn't had the time or resources for her mages to heat the newest citadel buildings as they did the castle.

He approached and bowed. "I have your report, Your Majesty."

Faelyn ignored the flutter of her heart. It'd been three days since Bastien arrived. The pull to him practically shouted, but she'd not laid eyes on him. He didn't leave the Hollow, and she did not go in. Rumors had flown across the castle about his ability and connection to her. Nolan, without question or complaint, brought daily reports in between strategy meetings, war preparation, and plans to evacuate the town next week.

"Thank you, Nolan. Go ahead." She took a sip of water, feigning the disinterest they both knew was a lie.

"Master Niri has increased his opponents to two at a time, though they each only possess one ability. He's doing roughly ten matches a day and has yet to lose."

Ten was very impressive for someone who'd just begun. Her chest rose, filling with inexplicable pride, but she kept her face blank. "Has he gone up against any mind mages?"

"No, Your Majesty."

She waited. He'd given her the surface information, but they both knew she wanted more.

"He sustained injuries, some burns and cuts, but has shown a great capacity for healing himself, almost to rival you. His stamina continues to improve. Master Niri has him scheduled to spar twelve tomorrow. From my personal observations, he's working hard, shows eagerness to improve, and has made quite the impression with the junior mages. They swarm him at meal times."

She couldn't help a small smile. "And his title?" She didn't know where 'lord' had begun, but it'd spread, with many using it when referencing him. She'd even heard rumors of land he presided over somewhere in the Alysian north.

"Some of the seasoned mages have adopted it." Nolan hid it, but Faelyn sensed his disapproval.

"Thank you..." Her words trailed off with the touch of a familiar presence.

Her gaze snapped to the door. A moment later, Kian entered with dusty travel clothes and disheveled, peppery hair. Face impassive, he bowed. Did his skin have lines before? As if all his troubles were etched in new wrinkles. They didn't stop the grin on Faelyn's face. His presence made everything immediately right in her world, with a sense of peace and homecoming. She stood and rushed to embrace him as he rose from his bow, the scent of dirt and hard travel stirring old memories.

He returned her affection with a one-armed hug and a small

smile. The message couldn't have been clearer. She stepped back, hurt flashing over her skin. He felt a million miles away.

She cleared her throat. "How was your journey?"

"I have much to report." His hazel eyes glanced meaningfully at Nolan.

She nodded, and Nolan took his leave. Now it was only Kian. "Would you like something to drink?" She walked to the refreshment table and poured him a cup of water. With her back to him, she studied his emotions. He was sad, but what she sensed just before he shielded himself from her magical prodding scared her the most. She gasped and spun around.

He was afraid.

"What's wrong? What is it?"

Kian took the water in steady hands and set it down without drinking. "Creadel isn't coming. They refuse to send more aid."

She heard the words, and they made sense as words should in the right order, but she still didn't understand. The walls closed in on her. "They've always helped us," she breathed.

"Not this time, Faelyn." He raised his arms, as if readying to catch her.

He knew then, what this meant for Alysies, even without having heard her carefully laid plans in his absence. Creadel troops were integral to defending the coastal cities from the Daltieri armada already on its way. Without them, like the border to the north, the towns would be overridden.

She swallowed back the bile rising to her throat. "Did you beg, plead, offer them money? Better trade agreements?"

"All that and more, my queen." He watched her carefully.

Her mind raced. "Then I will go to King Wesli myself." This was the worst time to leave for Creadel. By the time she returned, Daltieri would already be in Pavora. Just the thought of Prince Rory's superior smirk upon finding her absent made her blood boil, but they *needed* those troops.

"Faelyn." Kian reached to touch her cheek, then withdrew. "The king could not be reasoned with, not even when I warned him they would be next, should Alysies lose this fight. Daltieri did not attack Creadel when they ruled before, and King Wesli has no reason to believe they would now." His frown deepened. "He's insulted you did not seek out an alliance of marriage with his eldest son and heir, choosing to align with Kestrea instead."

The words exploded out of her. "Then why didn't you promise my hand!" Bastien's blue eyes flashed before her mind. She winced, but quickly wiped it away. "I'll do anything, *anything* for my people, Kian."

His brow creased with sadness. "I did. I knew it's what you'd want, so I told King Wesli you'd gladly marry his son." He shook his head. "He said he knew about the fae mage, *Lord* Bastien, and heard you shared a great love with him. A commoner." His voice turned dark. "He didn't desire to subject his son to the same pain Prince Rory must have felt upon finding you two in such an embrace."

Her insides burned until she saw the room through a haze of anger. "His words, not yours?" she hissed.

"His words."

He didn't need to add that he agreed with the king completely. It was written all over his face and in everything he didn't say.

"He asked you to stay, didn't he?" Anger loosened her tongue. Kian had always been loyal to her, but he was, after all, from Creadel. If he'd ever wanted to leave, the conditions were ripe.

"He did."

"And you can't be bothered to say more than two words on the matter?" Even decades of existence couldn't temper her emotions. "Have you come to collect the rest of your belongings then? You needn't have bothered. We could have sent back what was left after Daltieri finished burning the kingdom to the ground." She picked up the cup of water and flung it across the room. It clanged over the long table, bouncing to the floor. "Go if you must. I watched my family die the last time the enemy marched on Pavora, and I ran away without looking back. I'll never run again."

She stared over the table, hands forming fists. Why? Why did the Fates make her life so difficult? Anger warred with self-pity and shame. She was a queen, above such behavior, but even she was allowed a moment of weakness, right?

She stepped away to retrieve the cup, but Kian caught her upper arm. "I'm loyal to you as always," he said, conviction in his tone. "We can win this war without Creadel. I'm sorry I left, but it wasn't a complete loss. I hired troops on the way here, and collected some loyal to my house. About five thousand have joined the ranks. Some mages too." He let go.

She took a shaky breath. "I'm sorry, Kian. Sometimes it's too much to bear. Your news is a shock, and you've been so cold lately."

His jaw clenched. "I had time to think on my journey. I realized I've never stopped trying to make you love me."

She turned away.

"Yes, it's the great topic we can never talk about, but there's something else." Anger tinged his voice. "You love him. Bastien. I see it in the way you look at him, in the way he looks at you."

"That doesn't mean I can ever have him, or deserve the happiness he might bring me. You know that." Choosing Bastien would be repeating her father's mistakes when he chose himself and grief for his wife over his kingdom, leading to disaster.

Kian scoffed. "That excuse may have worked for me, because you never loved me, so what was left to choose but political gain? But Bastien is here now. You can't deny the Fates created you for each other."

She was glad her back was still to him so he couldn't see the tears in her eyes.

He took a deep breath. "There is no great alliance waiting to come between you and your... love anymore. Embrace it fully, Faelyn, and be happy. That's all I've ever wanted." The words rang powerfully despite the softness of his voice.

Even under the crushing blow of the news of Creadel, a heavy ache eased from her chest. He was right. There were no kingdoms left big enough to make a difference. And he'd given his blessing, which mattered more than all the rest.

She turned, tears spilling over. He gave her a smile, both sad and hopeful. She couldn't help throwing herself into the embrace of her best friend.

This time, both of his comforting arms wrapped tightly around her. "We're okay, you and I. Just let me talk to him first."

She pulled back, and he smiled mischievously. "All right," she said slowly. "Why?"

"He has to pass my test first, of course." He reached for his mage staff.

"What kind of test? What if he doesn't pass?"

Kian raised an eyebrow. "You better call a meeting. We have a lot to cover."

"Right." She wiped her tears and stepped away. Their entire strategy had hinged on Creadel support. Now that had to change. "Nolan," she called, and he entered. "Send out the runners for an emergency meeting."

CHAPTER
FORTY-EIGHT

Bastien awoke and lit a mage light, the floating ball illuminating the cavern room. It had taken two days to remember his bed was carved into the wall and not bash his head sitting up. He rolled out of bed and dressed in his fighting gear. After that first match, he'd been issued his own clothes and armor. The freedom of movement without the robe had been refreshing. A knock came just as he finished lacing his boots, and someone pushed his daily sparring list beneath the door. He snatched it up. Some of the names were becoming familiar, though he hadn't sparred the same person twice. Mostly, he looked for their abilities and to see if he would fight more than one.

Scanning the paper, he nearly choked. There was only one match on his list today.

Lord Kian Foster, Head Advisor to the Queen
Master Mage of Water
Master Mage of Aether

Two abilities. Faelyn's head advisor and twice master mage. The

369

paper trembled in his grip. They'd only given him one match in case he was too injured to continue.

Numb, Bastien slipped from his room and made for the dining hall. Several mages greeted him as he passed, but his usual carefree attitude was absent behind his anxiety. He ate because he'd need every ounce of strength, but the food was tasteless.

On his way out, Niri had to step in front of him before he realized she'd been calling his name.

"No need to worry, Bastien." She patted his arm. "I was planning on testing you against mages of more than one ability anyway."

"A master mage?" he asked warily.

She gave a tight smile. "You're not far from testing at master level yourself, but there is one thing you should know."

"What?" Could it be any worse?

"He has a similar ability in reading emotions and magical intentions as our beloved queen. Best to disguise your nerves if you can." She bit her lip, eyes creasing, and hurried off toward the arena.

His heart hammered.

Even Niri wasn't confident in this match. He took a deep breath and strode after her. Why shouldn't he win? He was strong. He controlled three more elements than Kian, even if he didn't do them so well.

When he entered the bubble arena, the crowds were thick. He nudged his way through until the mages caught sight of him and parted, whispering as he passed. Coins shuffled from hand to hand as bets were placed over his fate.

Once through the crowd, Bastien stopped, blinking. A ring of what looked like every mage in the complex circled the perimeter of the entire arena. Kian stood in the middle, thick arms crossed over his chest, and looking every bit as strong as Bastien had boasted of being just a few moments before. His mage staff was tucked into the crook of his elbow, and his fighting leathers were crisp and polished. A sword hung at his side. Were they allowed to bring weapons? His graying hair and wise eyes were the only indications of his age.

Niri stepped beside Bastien and patted him on the shoulder, which became more of a shove toward the arena. "Do your best."

Choruses of 'good luck' rang from the nearest mages as Bastien made his way to the middle of the gigantic space. The staff of one of the mages at the edge of the circle lit up, and he created an air shield around them. The whispers and murmurs became muted, the shield thick enough to drown most of the sounds.

"Lord Kian." Bastien nodded and swallowed. "I never had a chance to thank you for what your goons did for me—locking me up and starving me and such." He knew he was covering nerves with sarcasm, but if he could trick himself, maybe he'd fool Kian, too. Besides, what Kian had done was pretty low.

Kian unfolded his arms, face stoic. "Don't hold back, because I won't."

"Begin," Niri's muffled shout came from behind, catching him off guard.

Bastien drew magic to him.

Kian's staff blazed. He smirked—and disappeared.

Bastien drew a breath and swiveled. Teleportation wasn't one of Kian's listed skills. He glanced back and forth, but Kian was nowhere to be seen. A blast of electricity threw him crashing to the floor, and Kian suddenly appeared in front of him.

"How?" Bastien pushed himself to his feet, ignoring his aches.

Kian's stern face didn't show any evidence of pride or superiority, just a confidence in his unwavering ability to win—which was worse than if he'd been showing off. "I taught Faelyn that trick, or rather, she taught herself. She's an amazing woman." He vanished again, but Bastien sensed his presence hadn't moved. He'd simply disappeared.

Unseen power surged from where Kian stood invisible. Bastien threw up a shield, but too late. Kian's magic hit him and trapped him in a continuous strike of lightning. His limbs locked up. A metallic taste filled his mouth and soured the air he struggled to breathe.

He'd experienced this before—during training at Thomats. With his own surge of power, he infused aether into an air shield, cutting off Kian's attack.

Kian hadn't moved—his concentrated magic gave his position away. Bastien threw a wave of fire, but Kian created streams of water around him that diverted the flames and turned to steam. The shimmering heat gave an invisible outline to Kian's form.

"You're very lucky." Kian's words came casually as he counteracted the flames with seemingly little effort. "For years, decades, I've tried to win her love. I thought I had once, long ago, but she gave me up for her kingdom." A great sadness weighed his essence.

Bastien threw everything in his arsenal—fire, water, air, lightning—but Kian found a way to avoid it all with streams of water and fancy shields, like a person outpacing a gnat. The watching crowd cheered at the show, though their shouts barely penetrated the shield. They clapped and pumped their arms as Bastien's magic filled the arena with an ineffectual display of light and flame. His hands shook, and he ended the fruitless assault.

Kian reappeared, pacing, using his staff as a walking stick. "I knew she loved you when she chose you over Alysies. That moment on the loading dock was a moment of unrestrained passion." He faced Bastien. "But I know Faelyn. She's lived several lifetimes. She wouldn't have let go of her self-control unless she wanted to."

"I never meant to make her choose." Bastien breathed with a desperate hope, even while he knew it must be a trick. He listened hard, waiting to see what Kian would say next.

The surge of magic was the only warning before a wave of water slammed into him from behind. The momentum carried him forward, shield and all. He flailed, water rushing and tumbling him end over end. His arms thrashed. Panic overwhelmed his training as memories of being carried down a river of his own making, arrow in his back, flashed in his mind.

His shield failed, and water flooded his open mouth. He struggled to right himself, but the water was so deep, there was no up from down.

Focus. He concentrated, trying to force the panic away. Amidst the roiling waves, he sensed an open line, a force tethering him to hope. The draw to Faelyn. He latched onto it with his whole might. She was thinking of him, rooting for him not to fail. His eyes shot open beneath the water. Kian stood in a dry circle while the water careened around him. He must have summoned the lake to fill up such a space.

Bastien gritted his teeth. Drawing magic, he threw a strong current toward Kian's legs. The water hit, knocking Kian down face-first into his own torrent. Bastien had to act fast. Still being tossed by the waves, he thrust out a hand. Mimicking his movements, a watery hand grabbed the top of Kian's staff and yanked. The staff tore free of Kian and shot through the watery arena—into Bastien's grip.

The swirling water came to a stop, leveling out. Bastien pushed upright out of the flood. The water came to his knees, held at bay by the shield of air surrounding the arena.

Kian struggled to his feet. The fuming anger on his face was nothing compared to what Bastien sensed from him. There was no rule saying you couldn't part a mage from his staff, but he hadn't seen anyone use that tactic. It was likely considered cheating. But there were only two people who didn't need a mage crystal to access their magic, and Bastien was one of them.

Kian drew his sword. This was a magic spar, and he'd just robbed Kian of his ability to do magic.

"You're resourceful," Kian said, hefting his weapon. "That's good. You're going to need it." He advanced, sword pointed forward and shoulders hunched like a charging bull. Water splashed aside as if eager to be out of the way of such fury.

Bastien couldn't believe Kian's perseverance. The fight was as good as over. He could destroy Kian a hundred ways now and Kian wouldn't be able to do anything about it. But, he didn't want to.

Bastien set Kian's staff down carefully into the water, then sent the current to carry it away to the shield's outer wall. He didn't have a sword, so he'd make one, as he'd read mages of old doing. He focused his magic, directing it toward his hands in the form of fire. A sword of red flame extended out, and he gripped the hilt, feeling no heat.

The watching mages roared their approval.

Kian hesitated. Some of the anger faded, his face relaxing. "Our queen needs someone strong, but just, at her side."

Why was he saying all this? Bastien held his sword up out of the water. "I know I'm not worthy to be by her side, if that's what you're hinting at, but I hope to be. I've sworn to protect her and all she loves with my life, including her kingdom."

Kian flashed a half-smile, then rushed and made the first swing. Bastien raised his sword and blocked. Sparks showered from the flames, sizzling the water, and the bout was on. Kian slammed powerful blows into his guard, and with no magic to back them up. Bastien defended, twisting and blocking, unable to find an opening and half-surprised he hadn't been sheered in two already. A large portion of his concentration was spent not utilizing magic to defend himself. His mind had become accustomed to using it naturally ever since Cinda had unlocked his past, but he would not give in and claim his unfair advantage.

Kian feinted left, but Bastien read his intent and charged for the opening, water splashing. Kian parried, but barely.

"Good," Kian grunted. He pivoted and swung overhand.

Bastien raised his sword to block, but Kian's momentum carried their swords down. The front half of Bastien's sword plunged into the water, which hissed and boiled. Hot steam rose, blinding them. Kian pulled free and struck. His sword cut through Bastien's leathers and went deep into his side. He cried out, his magic instinctively flaring. A deluge of water swept Kian off his feet, cracking his head against the floor. Water rushed back over him, submerging his still form.

Bastien gasped from the pain in his side. Blood poured from his wound, but his body already began healing. He pushed the water from Kian's body and held it at bay.

He glanced at Niri who was waving frantically, pointing up. Bastien looked toward the bubble dome and understood; the shield couldn't be dropped for the medics until the water was gone. Several water mages had their staffs lit up, but they couldn't get their magic through the shield.

Wounded, weak, and shaking, Bastien pooled his magic around him until he glowed white with it. He'd emptied a pond before, he could do this. Like lifting a boulder with his bare hands, he concentrated until the whole body of water rose from the floor. His limbs shook with the effort, the water rising higher and higher. As it came above Bastien's head, someone dissipated the shield. The water mages stepped in. Together they moved the water back into the lake above.

Bastien hadn't realized he'd collapsed to his knees until he released the water magic. His hands slapped against a pool of his own blood as he fell forward. He'd directed so much magic to moving the water, his wound hadn't healed. It burned with searing pain. Dark spots bloomed in his vision. He lay on the hard ground, only one more thing to do before he could rest.

By feel alone, he located Kian's mage staff, seeking out the dormant crystal. Feet pounded all around him as mages filled the arena, some rushing to Kian, some to him. Shouts for water and more medics rose above the crowd. Using air magic, he tugged the staff. A cry of surprise rang out from someone who must have already picked it up. The staff flew, bumping into legs, until it rested by Kian's side where it belonged.

The black spots bloomed larger. Medics rolled him to his back. Bastien pushed magic into his wound, as he'd done hundreds of times. The medics assisted him, and slowly the wound closed. Bastien smiled, he'd done it all without passing out, though he might never get up again. His throat was sandpaper dry. Even a swig of lake water sounded good.

"Well done, Bastien." Niri stood above him, holding a cup, her face stern. "That was the sloppiest, most reckless spar I've ever witnessed." She crouched down and lifted his head, tilting the cup to his lips.

He drank it dry. "Is Lord Kian all right?" Bastien couldn't see him for all the people milling around. He concentrated, trying to feel him out.

The gossip was already starting.

"Lord Bastien defeated Lord Kian!"

"He took his staff. It wasn't a fair fight."

"Of course it was fair. You have to use what you can against the enemy."

"Lord Kian is fine," Niri said. "He's waking up just now."

The draw to Faelyn suddenly intensified. She was in the Hollow!

A hush fell over the mages. Bastien sat up, head spinning and nausea roiling. He couldn't see her for all the people in the way.

The closest medic frowned. "You've lost a lot of blood, Lord Bastien. Allow us to transport you to your room to recover."

"Nonsense." Bastien stood, searched for Faelyn's face, then promptly vomited up the water Niri had given him, plus a gallon of lake water he hadn't realized he'd swallowed.

Niri tsked, and Bastien wiped his mouth, shooting her a look. She glanced at the medic and nodded. Before he realized what that meant, the medic's staff lit up and Bastien was dragged to unconsciousness.

CHAPTER

FORTY-NINE

Faelyn's strategy meeting had taken the rest of the day and began again the next morning. Kian's blessing remained at the back of her mind, even as her lords and advisors argued over their troop numbers again and again. They were short, and there was little time and money to finance more recruiting. Kian's additional troops—hired with money from his own lands—helped, but he'd been absent from the morning meeting.

Kian's talk of testing Bastien occupied the rest of her attention. What kind of test would Bastien have to pass to earn Kian's favor?

Faelyn was discussing fleet movement with the council when she stopped midsentence. Intense spikes of magic came from within the Hollow, stronger than ever before. A thread of panic shot out from Bastien, and she gasped aloud.

She excused herself and rushed across the citadel compound. The magic and desperation had only grown stronger. It became obvious that Kian had challenged Bastien. A sharp pressure ached in her side when Bastien had been wounded. She'd run the last of the way, holding her skirts and leaping down the stairs, and then all the magic abruptly ended.

In her heart, she knew everything was fine. Kian would never kill Bastien, and the mages running the arena were prepared for any foreseeable problem, but she couldn't help fearing the worst. The thought that Bastien might be in trouble scared her as nothing had in over a century of existence.

She burst into the arena. Everyone bowed at the waist, revealing Bastien. He stood in a pool of blood, vomiting a lake full of water, then collapsed to oblivion. Fear stabbed her through, and she cried out before logic caught up to her—the healers had used their magic to send him to sleep.

Curious eyes followed her as she weaved her way through the bowing mages attempting to look calm and serene. Niri watched her, head lowered.

Faelyn willed her cheeks not to burn. No matter what she did now, if there was anyone left who didn't know of her feelings for Bastien, this little scene would take care of it. She placed a glowing hand on Bastien's forehead, the warm nearness of him tingled through her skin. She sent a quick pulse of magic. It did nothing but heal some fading bruises not already taken care of by his own magic.

She spoke quietly. "Niri, you and the medics see Bastien to his room." Louder, she said, "All rise." The room straightened, watching her. Healers took Kian—dazed but whole—and Bastien away on stretchers. "I am pleased with the progress you all are making, and how well you've adapted under these dire circumstances. I regret I haven't been present much, but Master Niri gives good reports. You all will be vital to our success, so continue to follow her lead and the good examples laid out here today by Lord Kian and Lord Bastien."

She smiled at his name, and a murmur overtook the crowd. Without further ado, she turned and made for the edge of the arena. As soon as she passed out of the main room, conversation exploded behind her.

"The queen! She's truly a beauty."

"Her voice is like a song."

"I bet she's sleeping with Lord Bastien."

"Of course she is. Who wouldn't?"

"I wouldn't believe he could defeat Lord Kian if I hadn't seen it with my own eyes."

A laugh burst from Faelyn's lips. She wandered the hallways, giving Bastien time to be settled. There was so much she needed to be doing above, but she couldn't leave until they spoke. What had Kian said to him? Had he let Bastien win?

She passed a door and sensed Kian behind it. Without stopping to think, she slipped inside. A woman Faelyn didn't know knelt beside his bed. Long, straight, gray hair framed her face as she straightened and hastily bowed.

Faelyn stopped just inside the door. "I'm sorry. I should have knocked. Have you finished healing Lord Kian?"

The woman's cheeks turned crimson. "The healers left moments ago, Your Majesty. I am Auvie. A friend."

"Oh." Faelyn should leave, but Kian was her head advisor. Still, Auvie's essence dripped with embarrassment, as if she'd been caught. Caught at what? Faelyn dug a little deeper, not knowing if Auvie would notice the intrusion.

Faelyn sensed a deep affection and concern for Kian. "I don't believe we've had the pleasure of meeting, Auvie. What is your ability?"

Auvie's gray-blue eyes met hers, but it was Kian who spoke. "Auvie speaks to the animals." There was something off in his voice —a tenderness? —but she didn't sense it from him.

Impressive. Controlling animals was rare magic. Her mind flashed to what abilities she and Kian's offspring would have.

Both women looked as Kian sat up with barely a wince.

"It was nice to meet you, Auvie."

Auvie slowly bowed, recognizing her dismissal. She held Kian's stare before finally retreating.

Kian flashed a warm smile and patted the chair beside his bed. That warmness had been absent so long, Faelyn had almost forgotten how easy things used to be between them. She ignored the chair and sat on the edge of the bed instead. He chuckled and bumped her shoulder.

Faelyn broke into a smile, then shoved Kian's legs over and swung herself and her voluptuous dress on the bed, stretching out beside him. He grinned, and they lay back on the same pillow. Her maids would have a fit if they saw what she was doing to their careful job of her hair.

"Auvie seems nice." Her tone was pleasant, but she couldn't and didn't disguise her burning curiosity.

"She is." Kian crossed his hands behind his head, elbowing Faelyn on purpose.

She scoffed and moved over. "You know, if you won't tell me about her, I have certain connections, being queen and all."

He laughed. "Auvie's a good friend. She studied in Creadel where animal magery is more common, and traveled here after joining one of my recruitment groups a few years ago."

"And you never thought to tell me she loves you?"

Kian paused for a beat. "I don't know that she does, really."

She sat up. "Oh, she does, and now I know why you threw the fight with Bastien." She nudged him with her elbow, then grinned. "I'll leave quickly so she can come back to swooning at your side." Maybe Kian was oblivious, maybe intentionally, but she couldn't be happier that perhaps he'd have a chance at love after all.

He looked to the door as if he'd never realized why Auvie had been in his room.

Faelyn wanted to press the issue but now was not the time. She'd have to secretly hope Kian's blessing for her to be with Bastien would help Kian free his heart to love another.

"How's your head?" she asked instead.

He blinked as if coming up from under a spell. "I'm well. Simply tired." He looked back toward her. "And I didn't throw the fight. He legitimately won. In fact, he had the chance to end it sooner, and chose to fight like a man."

Faelyn beamed but kept it inside. The main reason for her visit couldn't wait a moment longer. She had to know if Bastien passed Kian's test. "Did you have a pleasant talk?"

Kian took her hand. "We did. He passed. I'd trust him with your life. He's a good man, Faelyn."

A weight lifted from her chest. "A high commendation indeed, from you." She teased, but he would know how much the words meant to her. "Well, I will leave in case your lady friend comes calling." She felt lighter than air. It'd been too long since she'd been able to tease and play with Kian. She stood and brushed her dress and smoothed her hair.

"Beautiful, as always. Give my regards to Bastien." He sank deeper into his pillow, missing the glare she shot him.

Faelyn laughed silently as she left his room and followed the pull to Bastien. He wasn't far, only a few halls closer to the dining area. The rooms were smaller there, the wooden doors set into the cavern walls closer together. This time, she knocked.

No one answered, so she let herself in. Niri and the healers were gone. Bastien lay sleeping on his bed, which was set within the wall, his essence filling more than just the small space his body occupied. A taper candle burned on a small table beside him. Faelyn pulled up a stool and studied him while he slept. His breaths rose smooth and even beneath his muscled chest, easily seen through a thin, cream-colored tunic. A blanket was pulled up to his waist while his hands, so masculine and strong, rested at his sides. His sandy hair was pushed back, fully revealing his ears. The sharp angles of his jaw and his prominent cheekbones completed the handsome picture. His full lips parted in sleep, and Faelyn imagined how they'd feel trailing kisses down her neck.

She shivered and leaned closer. With a light touch, she stroked the edge of his ear, but he didn't wake. Her fingers traced down his face to his chin. Tingles ran up her arm. He stirred, and she pulled back. His blue eyes blinked, then opened wide, taking her in with a gasp of surprise.

"Are you well, Bastien?" The words came out almost nervous,

and there was a burning in her cheeks, but she refused to look away from his captivating gaze. She didn't need to hold back anymore.

He found his voice. "Queen Faelyn." He propped himself up on his elbows, but that was as high as he could go in his small space. Caressing his jaw where she'd just touched him, he studied her.

She felt his magic probing her emotions, so she opened them up, hoping he'd sense her longing. "Kian tells me you fought well, that you won."

He blinked. "I did win, in a way. But that's not the most important thing I took from our spar." His lips curved into a shy smile. "Kian said you care for me, and didn't add 'But it can never be,' at the end. I'm scared to hope that your being here now means something."

She dropped her eyes. "What do you think it means?"

"That I may be worthy of your love." His words rang full of passion and hope, yet she sensed fear underneath. Fear of rejection. Fear of pain.

The pull to him had never been stronger. The desire to ease the pain of his past and the pain of her previous denial took her words away. Her gaze drifted to his mouth, set in a hopeful part. Further up, his eyes were pleading, though he tried to hide it with a quick smile.

She licked her lips and slowly reached for his hand. Her fingers found his, warm and sure, and as they twined together, his expression changed. The smile slid away with an intake of breath as she squeezed his hand, and his cloud-blue eyes filled with unspoken emotion: relief, love, and hunger.

Bastien swung his legs over, sitting up on the edge of the bed to fully face her. Every movement assaulted her senses. The shift of fabric, the air flowing in and out with his warm breath as he drew closer, the beat of her heart in her ears. With both hands, he reached out and took hold of her face, calluses brushing over her skin. He studied her mouth, then her eyes as he dipped closer.

Faster. Slower. Make this moment last forever. Kiss me, now.

Their lips met, breath intermingling as they both released whatever restraint they'd been holding onto.

There were no guilty thoughts left to flood her with doubt. No fear of repeating past mistakes. Only Bastien, his nearness, his strong presence, and his warm touch as their lips danced.

He cupped the back of her neck, and she grabbed his muscled arms as their kisses increased in intensity. She pressed into him, leaning over until he led her off the stool to lie next to him on the bed.

She didn't question, didn't doubt, didn't hesitate. She wanted this, more than anything, to share this moment and her love. He stopped their kisses long enough to take her by the hands and look deep into her eyes. His fingers moved over hers, then gripped them as if afraid she'd slip away.

They'd been here before, close enough to touch, fingertips away and yet unable to reach each other. Not this time.

The pull to him flared, stealing her breath away. "Do you feel—?"

"I feel it," Bastien whispered. "I've always felt it." He dropped her hands and wrapped his arms around her, pressing her even closer.

The pull made it hard to think, to do anything beyond touch, kiss, and caress her Bastien. His kisses intensified her need, and just as she'd hoped, his lips left hers and trailed down her neck. Each press of his mouth left a burning gateway leading straight to her core.

Of their own volition, her hands tugged at the hem of Bastien's shirt. He emitted a startled gasp that left her smiling as she pulled the fabric over his head. She bit her lip. Her hands roved over his chest, so muscled and strong, and down to his stomach.

With agonizing slowness, he helped her remove her dress and underclothes. Every fiber of her wanted him to wrap her up in his nearness, but he took his time, savoring each moment. His fingertips and kisses ran down each naked length of her, over each curve, until the world didn't exist anymore and there was only him and her, breathing and memorizing each other and knowing without doubt they were each created for the other. Hovering above her, he reached, caressing her cheek with the back of a hand, love in his adoring eyes.

When they came together, warmth and tenderness, the pull to him crescendoed, towering toward Acantha. But still, he gazed into her eyes between kisses, as if he knew this was right, that they could give themselves permission to love each other fully. She knew it too. No longer would she regret the circumstances that had given her the opportunity to open her heart to him.

She'd never felt so complete, so loved, so wanted. His was the kind of love she'd sought her entire existence: unconditional and pure.

CHAPTER

FIFTY

Bastien lay beside Faelyn's sleeping form. Happiness filled him, as if he'd been waiting for this moment longer than he'd been alive—the moment he could love someone freely with his whole heart, and she could love him in return.

He stroked the length of her arm, studying her; the mounds of her curves, the swoop of her waist before it rose into perfect hips, the roundness of her calves before they ended in her petite feet, so soft as he rubbed them with his own callused ones. When was the last time she'd had decent sleep?

Her cheeks were still flushed, hair mussed every which way. He pushed a strand behind her long ear. She'd never looked so beautiful. Kian was right. Bastien was the luckiest man in the world.

Her eyes opened, and she smiled a sleepy smile. "You're going to distract me constantly now, aren't you?"

"I certainly hope so." He pulled her closer and gave her a long, lingering kiss. He met her forest eyes. "Do you believe we knew each other before we were born?"

She snuggled into his neck. "Of course we did. I'm sure we laughed and spent time together every day." Her lips turned up in a sly grin. "You were probably in love with me, relentlessly trying to catch me as you are now."

He chuckled. "Undoubtedly. And you probably tried to remain friends, until you couldn't deny your heart anymore." He kissed her forehead. "I bet I was in agony when you left for Thera."

"Took you long enough to find me."

A knock pounded on the door. More than one voice sounded outside. Bastien frowned, not ready for their bubble of happiness to break.

Faelyn gasped, reaching for the blanket. "That's Kian."

Kian banged again. "A rider from the north has brought news, Your Majesty." His muffled voice paused. "It's not good."

Faelyn jumped out of bed. Bastien's mouth dropped as her beauty stunned him.

"A moment." Her voice was calm and steady, though she pulled on her garments, piece by piece, with fervor.

Bastien snatched up his clothes from around the room. Even the gravity of the situation couldn't take the smile off his face. Kian had known to find Faelyn here.

They hastily finished strapping and tying. Faelyn opened his door just as he spotted her crown on the small table. He lunged and placed it on her head, drawing Kian's gaze. It landed lopsided, but she straightened it absently, clearly not concerned with being found out, but with whatever news Kian had brought.

"Tell me, Kian, what is it?"

Kian glanced back meaningfully at Bastien.

"Go ahead," Faelyn said. "Whatever you would say to me, you can say to him. From this moment henceforth."

Kian blinked a few times, but that was the most surprise he let show. Bastien, on the other hand, felt he might have to hunt for his jaw after they left.

"The Daltieri army moved ahead of what our sentries reported. They doubled our number with fresh mounted troops. Daltieri obliterated the garrison at Crosston a week ago, starting with poisoning the water supply, then advanced. The reinforcements we sent north did not have time to set up a defense perimeter. They were decimated. Stragglers began arriving an hour ago. The enemy will be here within three days."

Faelyn's breathing became audible though she stood stock-still. Bastien couldn't see her face, but her essence screamed of horror, anger, and betrayal. Between the rumors, his fating, and Niri, he'd pieced together their plight; Daltieri wanted to reclaim Alysies—a kingdom they believed belong to them. Their king used Prince Rory's embarrassment to turn Kestrea to their side. Two kingdoms against one, and no one was coming to help.

"What else, Kian?" she breathed.

"Their armada attacked Caprina. They've taken over and have received shiploads of troops for the past several days. They will regroup and act as relief for the northern army."

Faelyn reached back her hand, and Bastien took it. Her icy fingers clung to him in a crushing grip. "How were we caught so off guard? How did this happen?"

Bastien thought hard. His vision had told him the enemy would attack the coast, but not when. They'd been counting on more time, and now they had none.

"Daltieri planned this," Kian said. "They suborned our spies, armed their armada, and readied their troops. I believe they planned for this even before the opportunity arose to share costs with Kestrea. Probably since the day we tossed them out of our kingdom." He let out a slow breath. "We've found some of theirs disguised as our own. They were placed along the border and main roads to intercept those who might carry word of the invasion."

Bastien stepped next to Faelyn. "But Alysies has prepared for this." He'd seen the evidence of the massive might himself. "Pavora will not fall."

Both looked at him.

"No, Pavora will not fall," Faelyn said softly. She turned to Kian.

"Call a meeting. Our scout reports are no longer safe. We evacuate the town at first light."

Kian turned to the people down the hall. "Go," he said tersely. Several guards, runners, and aides took off running. "I'll see you up there." He met Bastien's gaze before turning and hurrying away.

A flicker of fear crossed Faelyn's face before she fixed her features.

"You don't have to pretend when it's you and I." He placed a hand over her heart. "I know what lies behind the mask. Let me be your safe haven."

"The mask keeps the tears from falling and the walls from crashing down around me." She wrapped her arms around him. "You are my safe haven, and I'll take comfort in the knowledge that you know what I hide from the world. That will have to be enough, for now."

He nodded and pulled her closer, feeling nearly whole again. "Go win this war, my Faelyn."

She took a shuddering breath. "I want you at my side, but that would be a waste of your talents. Find Niri, she'll know where you're needed most." She backed away, their hands slipping over each other's arms until they clung together by fingertips alone, then she was gone.

Bastien laced his boots, strapped on his sword for the first time in weeks, and headed to find Niri. The news hadn't reached the majority of the mages as he made his way to her office. Only the occasional master mage passed by at a hurried pace. The rest stopped Bastien to clap him on the back and congratulate him on a fine victory and such a quick recovery. He smiled good-naturedly, ignoring the mischievous gleam in their eyes when the junior mages mentioned how concerned Queen Faelyn seemed about him.

Niri's office was set on the opposite side of the bubble arena, just inside the inner hallway that ran along the length of the open space. The buzz of voices preceded him as he approached. Master mages already congregated outside. Niri's clerk stood in front of her door, holding a sheet of parchment and reading off orders.

"The company assignments for the evacuation will be posted within the hour. Your mages will report to their assigned units before first light. Within the units, you will assist as needed relative to your ability. Barricades will be necessary to keep the citizens on the right path, healers for the injured, mages to assist with emotional states, ensuring a calm evacuation... you get the idea. A special team will assist Master Niri and the queen personally. Anyone with questions, see me in front of the master list. You've been trained what to do, now go."

Most of the mages hurried off. It was all so efficient and military, but he shouldn't have been surprised based on the way the matches had been conducted. He turned to go, but the scribe called his name.

"Bastien." He held up his quill to get his attention. Several remaining mages glanced at Bastien. "Master Niri hoped you'd be here. She wants to see you in her office." He waved toward the door.

Not knowing what to expect, Bastien stepped inside. Niri sat in a room of scattered papers and half-melted candles, but it was bright with mage light.

The person at her desk stood, taking a sheet of parchment with him. "I will compile them immediately."

Niri motioned Bastien to a seat. "Thank you, Caler." The mage left, closing the door behind him. "Thank you for coming, Bastien. I want to discuss your responsibilities in the evacuation. Kian said you have Queen Faelyn's highest approval."

He nodded, and the ghost of a smile formed on her face.

For all the urgency, Niri appeared collected, her red hair up high as usual, though her hands trembled. "In an hour, the assignments will be posted and you'll find your name on the special team assigned to me. While most of the army's mages will assist with evacuations, my team will strengthen fortifications and double-check contingency plans." She scribbled something down with her quill. "But that's not what you'll be doing. Word has gotten around town about your ears, your abilities, and rumors abound that you have a love affair with our beloved queen, and might even be the next king." Her eyes became stern and bore into him.

Bastien stared right back, unblinking and unashamed. He did love Faelyn, and if they survived this war, he'd do whatever it took to remain by her side. The thought of him, a street thief, becoming king was laughable. Faelyn wanted him nearby now, and there was no time to consider the rest. "What would you have me do?"

She straightened, some of the sternness dissipating. "Word has also circulated that a certain Lord Bastien saved the life of one of Pavora's citizens and is being hailed a hero of the people, a true mage with a kind and generous heart."

He felt his cheeks go red. He'd never meant for his actions to fulfill selfish desires.

"Oh, don't be so self-conscious. You did a good deed. Take credit where it's due. But, fortunately for me, that puts you in a prime position to fit my needs. I want you to head into town tomorrow and go where you are needed. Motivate the people to leave calmly, coax those who are resistant into compliance. Short of the queen herself, you may be the only one suited for this task." She paused. "Queen Faelyn always planned to abandon the town and make a stand. We need you to help ensure Pavora is emptied."

Bastien sat back, shocked. He'd never thought he'd be suited for anything of the sort. His life before Faelyn had been a series of bad decisions and an ill-reputable existence.

Niri's voice softened. "People change, Bastien. You aren't the street thief anymore. The people need you. Queen Faelyn needs you. I know the Fates had greatness in mind when they sent you from Acantha."

Her words reached deep into the recesses of his black soul, scraping some of the stains away. "My goal since I was a child has always been to do whatever it took to survive another day." He and Olin lived by it.

"This is still a game of survival, to be sure," Niri said.

"But now I live for so much more than that."

Niri nodded and gave a small smile. "Good luck tomorrow."

Bastien rose. "Thank you, Master Niri." He bowed and left Niri scribbling at her desk.

He'd take on this task. Even if the people chose not to listen, he would try his best. This was his chance to be more, for himself and for Faelyn.

CHAPTER

FIFTY-ONE

Bastien awoke alone to the slide of parchment shoved under his door. He rushed over and scooped it up.

Evacuations to begin immediately. Report directly to Commander Rane at the Citadel Command Post

The letter dropped from his hands, and he threw on his spare fighting leathers, free of the bloodstains his other clothes still bore from his match with Kian. Heeding Niri's words, he pulled his hair, now long enough for a tail, back to fully expose his ears. His whole life, he'd hidden them out of fear. Now he would display them with pride.

He grabbed a giant chocolate chip scone on his way out of the Hollow, stuffing the sweetness in his mouth huge hunks at a time. Mages rushed everywhere, hardly sparing him more than a glance. Kian and Niri were nowhere to be seen, and Faelyn's draw told him she wasn't in the Hollow.

Quick steps took him to the citadel command post. The early sun was just turning everything blue, and a fine layer of frost covered the roofs and trampled grass. Groups of soldiers poured out the open citadel gates. Mages were scattered amongst them, traveling in pairs. Bastien was the only one solo. Heads turned his way, eyes flicking from his blue mage attire to his ears. He lifted his chin and let thoughts of his evening with Faelyn distract him from the task ahead. He'd never met Commander Rane but heard he wasn't much better than Captain Flinn, bullying his way to the top.

Clumps of people stood outside the command post, not far from where Faelyn's presence felt strongest, where she must have been conducting her meetings and making plans for war. More people were coming and going, carrying out orders and bringing in new ones. The mages gave him respectful nods as he entered the building.

Commander Rane, identified by the horde surrounding him and the braids at his shoulders, didn't look up from barking orders at some poor young runner. A captain Bastien didn't recognize stepped in his path.

"Lord Bastien." He nodded. "Here are your orders to be carried out immediately."

Bastien accepted the paper, and the captain retreated.

Under the command of Master Niri, and in accordance with the evacuation plan as approved by Queen Faelyn of Alysies, Lord Bastien will assist the Alysian army in the evacuation of Pavora. A squad awaits Lord Bastien's orders at the South Gate.

Bastien glanced up, but no one met his eyes. Could this be right? They'd given him command of a squad? To do what? He folded the paper and tucked it away in his pocket. Heavy steps took him to the south gate. How many people made up a squad? He hadn't got that far in his training before Kian sent him away.

When he arrived, Captain Flinn stood in front of a group of around twenty, watching him with scorn, disgust twitching his long mustache. Chrisso grinned from among the ranks. The memory of Flinn forcing him to cut his hair and revealing him to Faelyn churned his stomach.

Fantastic.

"Are you my squad?" Bastien asked, then immediately wished he hadn't. This group was the only one not mobilizing, and the intensity of Flinn's hate could only mean one thing.

Captain Flinn rolled his eyes. "Awaiting orders from the amazing *Lord* Bastien."

Chrisso made a swiping motion across his mouth with the back of his hand and then pointed. Bastien arched an eyebrow and raised his own hand to his mouth. Melted chocolate was stuck to the side of his lips. He quickly wiped it away.

As if taking on this role wasn't hard enough, he had to be stuck with Flinn. At least Bear wasn't here. But what to have them do? Niri's words came back to him.

He stepped past Flinn, ignoring him to address the soldiers. "You all are part of a special team. We are to move around as needed, assisting those unwilling to evacuate." As he spoke and they took in his ears, their internal attitudes turned away from skepticism. Soon, it wasn't only Chrisso who emitted respect. It was everyone except Captain Flinn. "Let's go."

The soldiers and a reluctant Flinn followed him from the citadel. They started with the nearest houses not already marked as cleared by the squads ahead of them. Most of the townspeople were ready to go as soon as the soldiers knocked, though they had to be convinced to leave behind a lot of unnecessary items.

As Niri predicted, the townspeople did look up to him. As soon as they heard who he was, they responded to his guidance. His squad evacuated several families needing assistance that had been passed over by the previous squads because of their resistance. He fell into the role as if he was born for it.

As the day wore on, they drew closer to Barden's restaurant in the center of town. The air was thick with alarm. Bastien quickened their pace in his eagerness to make sure Barden and his family had evacuated. Through the crowds clogging the streets with their belongings, troops surrounded the restaurant, swords drawn.

"What the..." Bastien ran. "Soldiers to me!"

Their pounding steps followed as he darted between townspeople and others who'd stopped to gawk. A captain stood at the door to the restaurant shouting for someone to open up.

Bastien threw himself between the captain and the door. "What is going on here?"

The captain glared. "Step aside, mage, or my troops will..." His words trailed off as he noticed Bastien's ears. "Lord Bastien. My apologies. This family refuses to evacuate, and I'm under orders to remove them from the premises by force if necessary."

"I know this man. I'll handle it." Bastien turned to the door. His troops lined up beside him, forcing the other squad to make way. Captain Flinn approached, a scowl on his face that Bastien had ignored all day. "Barden, it's me, Lord Bastien.

"Lord Bastien?" came Barden's muffled reply. The scrape of a wooden beam being removed preceded the opening door. Barden peeked out, his normally-smiling face set in a fearful frown as he took in the soldiers surrounding his home.

"Let me in," Bastien said quietly, sending feelings of comfort. "Let's talk."

Barden opened the door a little more.

Captain Flinn drew his sword and knocked Bastien aside as he barreled into the restaurant. The door smacked into Barden, sending him sprawling backward. Barden's son and wife cowered in the back of the room.

"You've been ordered to evacuate," Flinn said. "Your delay is costing lives."

Midstride, sword raised, Flinn's limbs locked and he stopped, nearly toppling forward. Bastien blinked. He hadn't thought, he'd just acted, binding Flinn in place. He'd never done that before.

He strode into the room until his gaze bore into Flinn's wide eyes. He ripped the sword from his grip. "You are under *my* command, Captain, and I've not given you the liberty of deciding your own orders. These people are my friends and loyal citizens of Pavora. They will not be removed by force." He took Barden by the hand and helped him up. His wife and son rushed to him.

"Thank you, Lord Bastien. Thank you," Barden said. "We don't mean to cause trouble, but there's looters, you see. Our restaurant would be stripped bare if we left it now."

Bastien's troops gawked from the door.

"Gather your things. I will cast a shield to protect your home." Bastien gave Barden a warm smile.

With a glint in his eye, Barden smiled back and nodded. Then he and his family grabbed the bags already packed by the door. With a last look, they retreated, leaving a seething, immobile Flinn and the troops at the door behind.

Bastien looked Flinn in the eyes and spoke loud enough for all to hear. "You've heard my past and think you know who I am. But you have no idea what I've become and what I'm capable of. You see a street thief, while all I see is a lifetime of skills built up to serve our queen and rise above people who would see me brought down." He drew closer, and Flinn's mouth parted in anger brought on by fear. "We're on the same side. We serve the same queen. Regardless of what you think you know, I will command your respect."

He released Flinn from the magic binding him in place.

Flinn gasped and stumbled almost to his knees. He hesitated, then spoke with anger but a new respect. "I'm sorry, my lord." He bowed his head.

Bastien hid his surprise and glanced at his troops. Chrisso was grinning while the rest had bowed their heads as well.

Outside the restaurant, Bastien pulled the magic from within him, his skin emitting a soft white glow. With a push, he sent out a combination of air and aether to create a strong shield to protect their home from looters and vandals. The army would keep crime to a minimum, but he'd promised Barden, and it wasn't a difficult spell to cast.

Bastien returned Flinn's sword. "Let's finish what we've started and protect the people of Pavora."

FIFTY-TWO

Two days of evacuations left Bastien exhausted. A runner opened his door, awakening him from a hard sleep.

"The Hollow has been summoned to the citadel courtyard," the young man said before darting to the next door.

Bastien threw on his gear and hurried out. Was the castle under attack? Mages piled up the stairs in a steady climb of bodies. Panic filled the air, but everyone was oddly silent, as if they feared giving voice to their assumptions.

The sun was just rising, bringing colors back into the world and a bit of warmth to the chilly air. Most of the Alysian army was already lined up, facing a tall platform upon which stood Faelyn, Nolan, and Amerae holding her tiny baby. The mages followed directions to form lines as well, calming as they realized danger was not immediate. Bastien ended up in the front rank with Niri by his side.

"Do you know what this is about?" he asked.

"Yes, and you'll find out soon enough."

He looked up to find Faelyn gazing right at him. Her forest eyes shone, radiant from her golden gown reflecting the sun's morning rays and looking every bit the regal queen. He grinned, and she gave him a small smile, a promise for the evening to come, before turning to address the people.

"Alysies," Faelyn called. Her wind magic effortlessly carried her voice across the large group. "I know we all have tasks to do, and I commend you on how well you've done. I have an announcement, a happy one to combat our troubled times." She turned to Amerae who handed over her baby without hesitation. "I have chosen an heir." She held up the baby, dressed in a white gown and blanket against the cold. "I, Queen Faelyn Eva Rylandor of Alysies, under the authority given to me by the people and my inherited title, bestow upon Lady Mary Kinlyn Maddux the role of heir to the throne of Alysies, unless and until I give birth to any natural born children." She kissed the baby on her cheek and then handed her back to Amerae.

A smile formed on Bastien's lips at the lingering image of Faelyn cradling the tiny infant.

"This is a big moment for her, Bastien," Niri said. "Her father failed to name an heir before his murder, and Queen Faelyn vowed to never repeat his mistakes."

He stared up at Faelyn, appalled. "But she was the heir, right?"

Niri frowned. "No. The king denied her the throne."

His eyes widened, and he opened his mouth to ask more questions.

Niri cut him off. "She'll tell you in time."

The crowd cheered, hailing Mary and Queen Faelyn as she smiled over them, but Bastien's despair hung heavy. They didn't see this the same way he did. Faelyn was preparing the way in case she didn't survive this war.

After the announcement, when everyone was dismissed to continue their preparations, he didn't get the chance to see Faelyn. Niri assigned him to oversee Mary's evacuation. Special care had to be taken to see her safely away. He didn't have to do much, other than stand guard in case there were enemy assassins who would try to get to Mary before she left.

Nolan must have said his goodbyes earlier because only Amerae was present to see their daughter off. She placed the baby in the arms of a nursemaid sitting in a covered wagon surrounded by soldiers. They would watch over her at the home of Amerae's brother, Lord Marus, on the western shores of Alysies.

Bastien was closest to Amerae when she let go of the baby. She turned to him, tears streaming down her face, and threw herself into his arms, sobbing. Stunned, it took a breath before he awkwardly held her. Then his hold tightened, and it felt right, like he was comforting his own sister.

"It will be okay, Lady Amerae. Your daughter will be well taken care of, and it won't be long before you see her again."

She nodded against him, her sobs slowing. "I know. I just love her so much." She pulled back, shaking her head. "I'm sorry. I shouldn't have—" She stepped back further.

He took her hands. "It's okay. Really."

She gave him a tentative smile through her tears but remained by his side as the wagon bearing her daughter rolled out of sight. When her tears began anew, he placed his arm over her shoulders while she leaned into him for support.

"I'm sorry I've been so hard on you," she said when she'd recovered.

Surprise colored his tone. "I understand, Am. I would have been hard on me, too. Anything to protect Faelyn."

Her eyes warmed. "I'm glad she has you."

"And I'm glad she has you." Faelyn needed people to protect and assist her, but nothing was more valuable than good friends. It meant a lot that her friends were finally accepting him.

Afterwards, he reported back to the Hollow. Niri relayed that the wards on the outskirts of Pavora Woods had been tripped, and the trustworthy scouts had reported the main body of the enemy would reach the city at dawn. Faelyn ordered everyone to feast and celebrate the coming victory. As a reward for his hard work, Niri insisted he stay for dinner in the bubble dome, and said she'd save him a seat next to her.

"I will, Niri. I promise." He'd eat as fast as he could and then head for the castle. There was no way he'd stay away from Faelyn on the eve of battle.

Niri had already briefed him on his role: never leave Faelyn's side. He didn't intend to.

When he arrived for the feast, tables had been pulled from the dining hall and into the bubble arena. Everyone found a seat under the dome, stars shining through the water. Platters of savory meats steamed on the tables along with roasted vegetables and long loaves of crunchy bread. In the center, a mage with a beautiful singing voice amplified by the element of air sang a merry tune accompanied by lute and piccolo players. The mages dug in, talking, laughing, and enjoying the evening.

Bastien could almost forget what loomed ahead.

Beside Niri, at the table with the other master mages and army leaders, Bastien felt less out of place than he thought he would as he piled his plate high. He wolfed down the delicious food, barely caring he was eating as if someone might take it away at any moment—a long habit that he'd have to break eventually. He'd need his strength. Besides, no sense wasting a good meal.

The others chatted around him, everyone avoiding speaking of the upcoming battle.

"So, Bastien," Niri said. Her voice raised, drawing several mages' attention. "When do you plan on taking the tests to become a master mage?"

Bastien swallowed a large mouthful of biscuit, then dabbed his mouth with a napkin—he'd learned several points about manners during his time at Thomats. Niri asked about a future that might not come to pass. He was meant to save Faelyn, that much he was sure of, but would he? Would he survive this war against a formidable enemy? Would Niri, or any of the mages around him?

He smiled. "As soon as your magnificence deems me ready, Master Niri."

She returned his smile, shoulders relaxing. "That's Most Magnanimous Magnificent Master Niri, to you." She winked.

Chuckles erupted down the table and from tables nearby. Bastien along with them.

He finished scraping the last of his peas into his mouth. He pushed back from the table and flashed a grin at Niri who gave him a knowing look.

He paused.

Unease furrowed his brow.

The alarm sounded, shrill and loud, bells charmed to ring when the citadels' did. Dread punched him in the gut. They were early.

Niri stood. "We're under attack." Her voice came out winded, full of disbelief.

A powerful blast of invisible, silent magic struck from above. Bastien raised his face to the bubble a breath before the other masters did. The magic was the work of hundreds, maybe thousands of enemy mages spelling in tandem.

"Shield yourselves!" he screamed.

Mage staffs lit up around the room—but not everyone had the ability to create a shield.

Another strong blast of magic hit the bubble. Bastien threw his own shield around him, just as the unthinkable happened. The impenetrable bubble popped.

Bastien grabbed Niri, pulling her to him, as the entirety of the lake fell upon them. The weight of the water slammed into his shield. He gritted his teeth to keep it strong and big enough to protect both him and Niri. Her horror splintered into him like shards of glass, and he opened his eyes. Currents swept through the room as the water rose extremely fast, rising above his shield. Tables floated away, slamming into walls and unconscious bodies. Mages floundered, flipping end over end while trying to keep hold of their staffs.

Only the water and air mages remained grounded, protected by their shields while the rest of the cavern filled with water. Those he could see had one or two mages within their circles, sometimes more. Bastien's mind reeled. He had to get their leader to safety. He and Niri could float to the top, but he'd have to leave everyone else to die. Faelyn's army would be decimated without her mages.

Niri fell to her knees, shaking uncontrollably. The water had already climbed halfway up the enormous arena. More pounded down from overhead, crashing into the space in a constant waterfall.

"Niri!" he yelled over the roar of the water and the roaring in his ears. A mage, leg bent at an odd angle bounced up and over his shield with the current. He jumped and punched his hand through the shield. Grabbing the mage by the ankle, he pulled him and several gallons of water into the bubble.

The mage fell to the floor, coughing up water.

Bastien turned to Niri. "Get a message to the others. We have to re-form the dome."

Niri stood, gripping his arm and her staff. Bastien sensed the magic as it pulsed away from her. The mind mages within sight touched their foreheads when they heard her. The message was being relayed.

He took a deep breath, gathering his strength. With all his might and more, he pushed against the water, and the weight crushed him. He fell to his knees. Niri cried out, crouching with him as his shield shrank.

Beside them, Laneira, the ice mage he'd first sparred against, was crushed entirely. Blue eyes framed by long blue hair widened as her ice shield shattered. Water flowed over her and the other mages within her shield, sending them swirling with the push and pull of the currents. She grabbed as many hands as she could and formed a new shield.

Bastien screamed and pushed. His bubble expanded. Looking up, the fall of water into the cave seemed to slow, but it might have been merely hope. Water still roared down on top of them. The cave was three-fourths full, and surely all the underground halls and bedrooms were underwater. A staff swirled by without an owner, and Bastien's heart wrenched.

Like individual threads, Bastien felt to where the mage's magic originated, and to where they cast it into the body of water above. Individual air and water elements mixed with his. With an unspoken agreement, they collectively pushed against the falling water. Bastien's heart leaped. Though the water in the cavern remained, the water flowing in slowed almost to a stop.

"Keep going, Bastien," Niri said, fists clenched around her staff. "Almost there."

Bastien sensed the enemy mages a breath before the cavern walls began to rumble.

Niri reached for him. "They're trying to bring down the cave!"

FIFTY-THREE

As soon as the silent attack began, Faelyn spun around, eyes locking on Kian's through the soldiers she'd been inspecting. "Sound the alarm!"

The pair of them, followed by a company of troops and every mage within earshot, hurried across the darkened citadel. She sensed them, the enemy mages. They'd evaded the magical wards and now stood on the opposite side of the lake, attacking in perfect synchronization.

Without question and in perfect order, her army's drills and practices fell into place. The bells gonged and troops mobilized. Before the first of them had even begun to pour out of the barracks, though, Faelyn clutched her heart as the agony of hundreds dying ripped through her.

She ran.

"Faster, Kian!" Faelyn flew through the ranks. The distress and volume of magic screaming from the Hollow nearly brought her to her knees with each step.

She put on another burst of speed. They reached the Hollow doors, but all appeared to be normal. She stopped and listened.

Troops advanced inside and down the stairs. There wasn't a hint of fighting or war to be seen, just the pounding of silent magic, and a roaring that sounded like a nearby waterfall.

Cold horror slammed into her. *The dome!*

The troops returned upstairs, roiling water at their heels. Each supported a mage, wet from head to toe.

"There's no getting in, my queen," one soldier said, wide-eyed with panic. "The water's above the door."

All her people. Bastien. Bile rose in her mouth, which she swallowed forcibly. She felt him inside the arena, magic raging. Not dead yet.

"Up top, with me," she shouted, running toward a set of stairs that led up the outside of the citadel wall.

"Bring the mages," Kian shouted to the troops.

There was no looking back to see who followed as she leaped the steps two at a time, building her magic like a billowing storm cloud inside her. The enemy was out there. They'd destroyed her impenetrable dome. Her mages were drowning.

A rumbling rolled from deep in the ground and through the wall. The stone shook like an earthquake, but the spells in the citadel walls held. Faelyn sprung up the last few steps and rushed through gathered guards, pushing to the edge of the battlement. The wall was a flat drop to the ground below, with the lake stretching beyond. A violent, glowing whirlpool churned in the water, directly where the dome had been. The horizon was dark, no hint of the mage light that should be seen like stars in the distance. They had shielded themselves from sight.

She sensed a spike in Bastien's magic, and it snapped her back. Her troops knew what to do. This was her task. She hurled her magic at the horizon. Like an invisible wave, it slammed into the enemy shield near the water's edge. Her magic connected with a crack as loud as thunder. Their shield splintered along the line of contact and then broke into a million pieces of black that faded into nothing. The night sky lit up like day with the blaze of a thousand Daltieri mage staffs.

The guards beside her cried out, then moved as orders were shouted for archers. Runners flew down the stairs to carry the news. At her elbow, Kian sucked a breath through his teeth. He was straining, focusing his efforts on the whirlpool. But the enemy mages hadn't relented. The ground rumbled again beneath their feet, jostling her from side to side. She couldn't restore the dome while it was still being attacked.

An orange glow of torches flanked the lake, advancing toward the enemy. Her troops had mobilized to stop the threat, but they wouldn't arrive in time to save the Hollow. She gritted her teeth. Time to put some of their careful planning in place.

"Fire the disrupters," she commanded.

A guard sprinted off to the center wall station.

Faelyn itched to pull the lever for their trap herself, but she had to focus on the water below. Five breaths later, a rumble built into a great crash across the lake. She watched intently, the area well-let by the enemy staffs. The mages startled, breaking off their attack to stare at the ground. The earth beneath their feet vanished, dragging many into the hidden caverns her people had dug years ago. Those that could ran for stable ground.

Faelyn threw the full force of her magic into the waters below. The whirlpool was gone. Too few mage staffs glowed from under the surface. Were they too late? She sensed Bastien and many others still working their magic, driving the water up.

Agony and desperation, and her frustration at the slowness of restoring the dome steeled her resolve. She grabbed the top of the battlement and pulled herself up.

"Faelyn, get down!" Kian shouted.

She was an easy target for mage-driven spells or weapons, but she didn't fear them. She sprinted two steps and leaped as far as she could off the edge. Air magic propelled her over the lake as she dove for the dome. Hands outstretched, she hit the cold water with a painful jar. The weight of her armor and sword aided her hard kicks to the Hollow below.

Individual pockets of mage light shone through the water. Those that could control those elements were doing what they could, but it wasn't enough. What about the rest? She kicked harder.

Bastien's surprise and concern washed over her, but she could not pick his bubble out from the rest of the mere dozen below her. She dropped through a small air gap where the room should have opened, gasping a deep breath, then hit water again.

There was so much horror to behold, but no time. With her own shield around her, she sank until her feet reached the floor. Her hands thrust up, giving focus to her magic. She concentrated on the dome shield as Bastien and the others slowly lifted the water out of the cave. The shield thickened, then thickened more, as she added layers of protection. Those who survived would be safe in the Hollow.

When water no longer covered her shield, she dissipated it, winded. Only a couple feet of water remained in the cavern. The wails of the survivors assaulted her. Exhausted and grief-stricken mages fell to their knees or leaned against each other for support. Troops and her personal guards poured into the arena and assisted with evacuations.

"We must find the wounded," Bastien shouted, his voice strong and alive. "Hurry!"

Faelyn sought him through the carnage. His gaze bore into hers, and she wanted nothing more than to run into his arms and feel him whole, but she couldn't. Still, relief washed through her. He was safe, if wet. He gave her a look of longing, then ran toward the nearest group of screaming mages.

Soaked through, Niri held an injured mage who struggled to keep his face out of the remaining water. Faelyn concentrated, sending the last of the lake up above.

"Niri, are you all right?" She stooped next to her long-time friend.

Niri glanced up with a blank look, as if she were lost. "So much death, so much destruction."

Faelyn's brow creased with concern, and she placed a hand against Niri's forehead. "We must press on. Our people need us." She sent feelings of restorative peace into Niri, quick as a flash, then removed her hand.

Niri grabbed her arm. "Don't go outside the wall, my queen. Bastien's Fating. Peril awaits you outside the wall."

Faelyn patted Niri's hand and spoke slowly. "I'm to remain in the command room, to coordinate our efforts, remember?"

Niri nodded, so Faelyn stood, catching her breath before finally allowing herself to survey the damage. Tables, chairs, and empty platters littered the room, along with piles of debris washed from rooms and offices. Except for the torches the troops brought with them, only mage light lit the dark space, and too few at that. The steady drip and splash of water wasn't enough to overpower the screaming, or the horror and grief that permeated the air.

Faelyn's eyes lit upon a discarded staff, then another, then a pair of legs peeking from underneath an overturned table. She gasped and rushed to the fallen mage. With a thought, the table sailed away. The woman's long, dark hair covered half her face, eyes closed, no mage staff in sight. Faelyn knew without checking that she was dead. The life essence had left her.

She knelt and picked the hair off the woman's face before placing a palm on her forehead. "Hereafter, accept my sister's soul to have and to keep."

An essence, weak but there, had her rushing to the hall nearest her. Down the long tunnel, she opened a door and found a mage bent over on the floor of a disarranged bedroom, vomiting lake water. Faelyn rushed to him, glad to have found someone alive.

The second-tier alarm rang out; the enemy troops had been spotted.

Faelyn rushed the mage out of the room and passed him to the nearest healer. She quickly located an officer in charge. "Get everyone out of here. Comb for wounded. Check every room. Those that have survived need to regain their strength quickly. I need a final count as soon as possible."

"Yes, Your Majesty."

Guilt heated her skin at turning their loss into a problem of numbers, but she had no time to give in to sentimentality. She couldn't rule as an efficient leader if the weight of their tragedy crushed her to the ground. There was no choice but to carry on.

Faelyn reached the stairs leading up from the Hollow. She'd see for herself just how bad their odds were. Bastien drew closer, and then his hands were on her. He spun her around and crushed her to him. Her magic multiplied, easing her weariness. She breathed him in, panting with the effort of not being able to draw him in deep enough.

"I have to stay near you. To protect you," he said with a squeeze, as if he'd never let her go.

She peeked over his shoulder, seeing more bodies than mages, and barely held the horror at bay. "And you will, but first you need to help here." He started to protest. "Do this for me, Bastien. We need our mages, and I am needed elsewhere. You'll find me when you're done."

His lips formed a frown, but he kissed her forehead. "On hands and knees."

Reluctantly, she let go and raced up the stairs. Her personal guards followed, but she stopped them. "Stay here. Help evacuate the mages." They bowed and immediately left to help.

The Hollow doors crashed open to the sounds of war. Soldiers rushed over the hard-packed ground in the dark of night, obeying as their captains and generals shouted orders. Arrows twanged, being released from the tops of the wall on all sides. Another enemy force must have arrived from the south. Disguised under more undetected magic? Explosions and fire lit up the eastern sky.

A company of guards led by Kian approached her.

"Kian, I need you to take over leadership of the mages. Niri is too shaken up. Bastien is leading the recovery in her stead but has orders to find me as soon as it's done. I need all who survived to be revived and ready."

Kian watched her intently as she spoke, bowing when she finished. "Yes, Queen Faelyn."

The overwhelming urge to hug him came over her. They'd been here before, she and Kian. He'd fought side-by-side with her to save Alysies once already. She'd thought she'd watched him die that night, but the Fates had spared him. Was this the last time they'd see each other before the Hereafter?

His ability meant he sensed what she felt. His eyes softened, turning almost sad, but his lips formed a smile. She hugged him fiercely, but briefly, then let go, rushing off to the command room without looking back.

Nolan spotted her along the way, palpable relief rolling off his steadfast shoulders. He hurried to her from a side path and fell into step beside her. They'd long ago worked out that there was no need for him to bow during battle.

"Tell me, Nolan."

He took a shaky breath that caused Faelyn's gut to roil. Nolan was never anything but calm and sure.

"Their mages have regrouped, healing those injured but not killed in our attack. We estimate there's sixteen-hundred left of the two thousand they brought."

"Two thousand!" Faelyn had just over 2,000 herself, before the collapse of the dome, but she'd recruited relentlessly for years—decades—to reach those numbers. How had Daltieri acquired so many?

"The army arrived while we were busy fighting off the mages. They went around the lake, flanking us on the north and east, while a second force we only learned about before they'd arrived came from the south. They were the ones who decimated Caprina. Ten-thousand troops from the north. Roughly the same from the south. They are burning the city to the ground."

Faelyn's mouth worked, but no sound came out. They approached the command room, ignoring the dozen runners outside trying to shout their reports over each other. With great effort, she shoved away the emotions that would numb her from being able to lead. "They could take shelter in the town. Why would they burn it down and put themselves at risk without cover?" She glanced to the south above the wall. Pillars of smoke lit up the night sky, reflecting the orange glow of fire. Thank Acantha they got everyone out, that Bastien was there to help.

"It's a controlled burn, Your Majesty, by their mages. I believe they are doing it to provoke you, to distract us and the soldiers who will be devastated by losing their homes."

"And the lords?"

"Lord Trey and three others of the western territory have met the army to the east. Lord Williams is fighting bravely with the others on the east."

She perched in a chair at the nearly empty table in the council room. "And the south?"

"The enemy is at the gate, ramming it as we speak. They are Kestrea forces, and not equipped with as many mages, only about a hundred, but they are working hard at undoing the shield protecting the gates. Their troops are well defended by the homes of our people while they wait. Our archers have killed but a few."

She pushed up from her chair. "Show me."

Nolan glanced at her chair, hesitating, but then led the way to the south gate, one of the only entrances to the citadel. The yard was eerily empty. Where normally people trained or hurried from one activity to another, now everyone had their posts, whether it was to fight outside the wall, attempt a futile sleep to be ready for the next rotation, run weapons and supplies to the front line, or arrows to the archers, or cook the food that would be in constant demand to fuel their energy-gobbling adrenaline.

They passed between a pair of storage buildings and finally beheld her troops. The soldiers stood in lines behind the wall, resting, waiting until their time came. With more luck than they'd had so far, maybe it wouldn't come to that and they'd see no action.

Fear hovered over the troops as they gazed at the burning orange sky. The ashes of their homes rained over them.

"Announce me, Nolan."

He glanced her way and then nodded. In a practiced voice, spurred through the ranks by a little of her wind magic, Nolan said, "Make way for our fair and beloved Queen Faelyn Rylandor of Alysies, the conqueror of Daltieri!"

Faces swiveled, breaking into grins, then erupting into cheers. A wider path was made between the troops. Chin high, glowing with magic, Faelyn passed through the soldiers, touching some on the shoulder as she went. The effect on their essence was instant. Confidence and resolve chased away their fear.

She reached the stairs to the left of the gate and climbed up to the top. Archers lined the wall in both directions as far as she could see. A rhythmic pounding issued from the gate as the enemy struck with the battering ram.

The commander of the south gate, General Holmes, bowed. "We're able to drive them back, keeping them from attempting to scale the wall, but we can't do much damage since they take cover behind the houses. The gate is holding."

Another crash below emphasized his point. "I'll send air mages to work on the battering ram crew, sweeping them off their feet and knocking the battering ram off course. That will buy us time until they figure out how to counteract us." If they had any air mages left.

She moved passed General Holmes to the edge of the wall. Two archers flanked her, crouching behind the cover of the battlement. She shielded herself and cautiously peeked around. In the distance, the town blazed. Fire roared skyward, and where flames ended, billowing smoke began. The smoke poured in rolling waves, blotting out the stars. She'd expected this, that her city might become a casualty of war. During the battle of Pavora, the town had been spared, but each side had a much smaller army. That war had been a fraction of the scale of this one.

Directly in front of the castle, enemy archers lined the roofs of her people's homes. They fired arrows, then crouched below the roof line. The rest of the army stood between and behind the homes and shops in a seemingly never-ending line. Rank after rank of enemy soldiers scaled back and back beyond even where her night vision could detect.

"Aye, they've an effective strategy, firing and taking cover," General Holmes said. "From their vantage point, they've taken out some of our archers, but we can barely reach them."

Faelyn cringed at what she had to do next. The solution was so painfully obvious, she was surprised Kestrea hadn't prepared for it, but she sensed no magic.

With a quiet cry of fierce regret, she raised her arms and summoned fire.

The enemy soldiers had their target. Arrows clanked off the wall in front of Faelyn in a frenzy now that she glowed with magic. She poured herself into shaping the fire. Flames roared to life at the enemy front line. Great clouds of fire expanded out and back. The inferno didn't have to reach far to catch the first of the houses ablaze—the large mansions of Pavora's elite were framed in wood, if not entirely comprised of it.

The enemy rushed to escape the blaze, archers jumping off flaming houses and soldiers running from the burning frontline. They ignored the shouts of their leaders, trampling each other in their hurry. She sent wind to further the flames into their retreating lines. At the same time, she diverted some effort into directing the enemy mage fire raging on the outskirts of the city. Like a dam released, fire rolled like water through streets and narrow alleys, trapping soldiers in between. The enemy screamed as the flames licked at their skin, boiling them in their armor. The ranks vanished beneath the roiling blaze.

The screams were drowned out by the cheers of her soldiers. The battering ram crew, left without leaders, broke formation and scrambled to get back to their army, but the flames were thick and impenetrable. Alysian arrows sailed through the air, picking them off. The heat roared up the side of the wall, chasing away the cold and blowing Faelyn's pinned-up hair.

A few feeble attempts to control her fire came from the mages on the outer edge, but the blaze was already too large, too out of control. Soon, those in charge of the burn on the southern edge would divert their efforts, but the damage would be done.

Faelyn let the magic go, allowing the fire to rage unassisted. A tear rolled down her cheek. Her entire city would be forfeited. There'd be no Pavora for the people to come back to. If they won.

She brushed the tear from her face. The enemy's force was weakened, but Pavora's real prize was in the inferno's aftermath. No longer could the enemy shelter behind the buildings. It would have happened anyway, better to have happened on her terms than the enemy's. They could rebuild.

A runner came flying up the stairs, stopping to bow and catch his breath. "Your Majesty, we have a count of the surviving mages." He panted. "Eight-hundred and seventy-six. Also, I bring word that Lord Graymer and his contingent have fallen to the east, as have two more on the northern side, and one on the southern."

Her breath caught. "Has the north side been ordered to fall back?"

"Yes, Your Majesty, but their progress is slow. The enemy mages have regrouped, and ours are only just joining the fight."

"Hold the south gate, General Holmes," she shouted as she headed back down the stairs. There was no time for emotion. No time for thinking. Only surviving.

"Queen Faelyn." Nolan's tone as he followed her was one of urgency and warning.

Yes, she should be in the council room, the central location so she could coordinate the efforts, but their mages had been dealt a terrible blow. Less than half of them remained. Half! And she could not sit in a fortified structure while her army perished without key points of a plan long in place. They needed her.

"Find Amerae," she said as they whipped by cheering soldiers—they had no idea what was coming. "Tell her to report to the council room and act in my stead. She's trained for this." Faelyn had scarcely had a moment to think of her friend. The part of her not focused on the here and now, not strategizing their every move against the enemy, was wrapped up in Bastien. The pull to him told her that he remained in the Hollow, likely still healing those who could be saved.

Nolan hesitated while he jogged behind her, heading toward the eastern wall. "My lady battles on the northern front. Lord Gilmore refused to fight, to lead his people. She jumped in to take command."

Faelyn took the blow to her gut and used it to motivate her to run faster. Amerae's life was too important to throw away like this. She should be protected to the last.

They passed the mess hall, the barracks, stables, the citadel family homes, and the market, eventually reaching the wall. There was no gate here, but a sally port wide and tall enough for one rider at a time. Ranks of soldiers stood in lines, waiting for the inevitable siege to begin.

"Bring me a horse," she commanded.

"Me as well," Nolan said to the runner.

"No, Nolan. Not this time. You stay here." *Where it's safe.* "Lead the army in my stead. Until Amerae returns," she added.

"If it's so dangerous, let me go. You stay here."

Faelyn faced him full-on. Nolan rarely spoke up, and never to give her an order.

His mouth fell open, looking as surprised as she. "The kingdom will be lost without you. I'm no one, just another soul destined to depart someday anyway. My ancestor Mary didn't die to watch you throw your life away so carelessly."

Faelyn placed a hand on his arm. "Mary didn't die to watch me back down now, or to let her progeny go unprotected." Someone brought her horse. She took the reins and mounted. "This isn't my last, Nolan. I'll find her."

With a squeeze to the sides, her horse took off. The door cranked open just as she barreled through. Dense, scraggly trees protected this side of the citadel, but she followed the path cut through to the other side, heading north where the enemy hadn't reached the citadel walls. The sounds of battle grew more defined. Horses and people screaming. Thousands of swords clanging together in fierce fighting. Thunder reverberated off the wall behind her. An enemy mage somewhere must have been using lightning. She didn't want to think that it was explosions hitting her walls.

Her horse was strong and ready beneath her. Its powerful legs ate up the path through the trees in no time, and she found herself at the back of the battle, where triage had been set up. The surviving mages tended to wounded soldiers by the hundreds. Twenty soldiers to every one mage—impossible numbers.

The rest would be on the front, shielding and fighting with what abilities they had. Even with the raging fires, bursts of lightning, and blaze of mage staffs, the dark of night blanketed the battlefield. The numbers were too high for her to spot any Alysian lords or generals, nor Amerae. Had she already fallen? The fires to the south of the castle reflected off the smoke in the sky and cast the battlefield in an orange glow. From her higher vantage point at the top of the slope down to the lake and valley beyond, it was clear how enormously outnumbered they were. Her blue and silver soldiers were drowning in a sea of black and gold.

The Alysians were trying to withdraw, but they couldn't go two steps before Daltieri soldiers cut them down. A horrifying number of soldiers in blue littered the ground. The wounded were hobbling her way, those that could. The rest lay dying on their backs in the field.

Drawing her sword, she charged past the retreating wounded, past her healers, and into the battle.

She made herself glow, wrapping a shield around herself. A great cheer rose up from her soldiers—and the enemy. They piled over each other to get to her. She cut down any who stood in her way. How dare they destroy a peaceful kingdom? How dare they try to take what wasn't theirs?

"Retreat!" she shouted to her soldiers as she battled to defend them.

"My queen!" Amerae shouted. She fought on horseback, sweat dripping off her, but unscathed.

Faelyn rode to Amerae's side, spurred by the relief cushioning her heart. Rage further bolstered her as some enemy peeled off to pursue her retreating people.

Time passed slowly. Every time she thought it was safe to retreat, more enemy rose up against them, but she had done what she came to do. The rest of her people who hadn't been felled had fled. The last of the troops who'd remained to defend her were barely holding on. Amerae, Faelyn, and the enemy surrounding them were nearly all that remained. It was time to return to the citadel.

In the distance, the sun broke the horizon. A buzz of activity drew her attention from the air magic she'd been using to suck the breath of those nearest her. A chariot had arrived some distance away. Two figures exited wearing golden crowns.

King Seber of Daltieri and Prince Rory of Kestrea.

"Amerae," Faelyn shouted. "Our enemy draws near. We can finish this." She swung her sword, felling another soldier. The years spent training with Swordmaster Donoven gave her muscles flight, anticipating her enemy's every move with barely a thought.

"I'm with you." Amerae fought strong beside her, the shield Faelyn placed holding strong.

So long as her magic held out and the enemy mages remained at bay, they'd make it. Faelyn had shattered a number of mage crystals of those who attacked from afar, rendering them useless. Adrenaline fueled her as she did so many things at once. But she wasn't done yet; she could last a little longer, just long enough for their leaders to draw closer.

Only then could things be made right.

FIFTY-FIVE

Bastien finished a rather difficult healing on a mage whose leg had been nearly severed by debris. The wound was healed, but she remained unconscious on a righted dining table in the bubble arena. He leaned over the table, eyes closed and panting. She was one of the last deemed too injured to move to the safety of the citadel.

Kian oversaw the evacuation of the rest of the mages and assigned them their subsequent companies and roles. A woman with long gray hair kissed Kian full on the mouth before leaving to take care of the horses at the stables.

The enemy mages hadn't attempted another attack. They'd done their job and done it well.

Kian strode to him. "Take a rest, Bastien. You've done all you can here." He handed Bastien a cup of water.

Bastien spotted Laneira across the dome, supporting an unconscious mage. Her eyes met his, and she nodded. There was a kinship with what they'd endured. Too many had not survived.

Most of the bodies had been cleared away by the soldiers, but it wasn't quick work. Many remained piled against the wall where the currents had held them fast. He'd never seen death of this magnitude. Faelyn and Kian had. He'd never compare his own difficult life to hers again.

Bastien took a slug of water, then found himself gulping it. So much for pretending he wasn't affected. He wiped drips from his mouth.

The thread between him and Faelyn spiked with determination. He focused. The cup slipped from his fingers and clanked over the cave floor. She was making for the northern front, outside of the Citadel, the place Kian said was the worst. His head swiveled to the north as if he might see her, riding toward the fight of her life, through walls of impenetrable earth.

"You sensed her. She needs you." Kian's words were clipped, as if he'd rehearsed them, knowing he would utter them some day, and knowing he didn't want to for fear of what they might mean.

"She's outside the wall." Bastien turned to him, his weariness suddenly vanished. The time of his Fating was nigh.

"Go to her, brother. Save her. Save us." They clasped forearms, then Bastien was racing through the room. "Take my horse, just outside the Hollow," Kian called after him.

Bastien flew up the endless staircase. No one questioned him when he grabbed a sword and left with the horse.

An explosion resounded to his right. His horse reared, but he regained control just in time to see the south gate fall. It crashed inward in a boom of flames and flying rock. The enemy poured in, roaring above the noise. Some caught arrows and went down in a clatter of armor. Others yelled, charging into the ranks of Alysian soldiers.

The citadel had been breached.

Bastien raced to the east wall. Shouts of, "Clear the gate!" were called before him. They knew their queen was out there, and like Bastien, they knew he'd follow her.

He arrived at the wall and a scene of nightmares. Wounded soldiers and mages lay dead or bleeding everywhere. Wide-eyed troops poured in through the narrow opening, frenzied in their quest for self-preservation despite people shouting orders to make way for Lord Bastien. Arrows twanged repeatedly from the battlements. The enemy was within firing range. Bastien's brave horse nudged into the fray of people charging through the door, but the flood pouring into the citadel didn't ebb.

Fear stabbed through to him from Faelyn.

"Make way! Move!" he shouted, edging his horse forward, like a rock parting the crashing waves. Acantha help him, he had to get through. Their queen mattered above all.

"Bastien!" A familiar voice called to him. "Lord Bastien, over here!"

His gaze swept right, over the stream of people and ranks of awaiting soldiers. Someone waved him over. Bastien's mouth dropped open. *Tave!* He spurred his mount to where Tave stood beside the wall in a less crowded spot.

"You're trying to get out. I know a way." Without explanation, Tave took off on foot, traveling along a path that ran close to the wall, flanked by the abandoned citadel market stalls and shops.

"What are you doing here?" Bastien couldn't believe his luck, if indeed Tave knew of another way out.

"We tried to flee after we parted ways with you, but we met up with the enemy. We had no choice but to seek refuge here. There's a whole slew of people who followed us, doing just that."

They came around as the wall curved southward. Bastien was now going the wrong way. "Where is this exit? And how do you know about it?"

"It's a tunnel I use to smuggle goods into the market. A drain pipe. You can't take your horse, but mine may still be outside. We're almost there."

Bastien's hopes were renewed. "For once, I'm glad for your illicit ways, Tave."

Tave turned and grinned. "It's Netavion, but don't tell that bastard mage, Micah. There's some secrets that should go with me to the Hereafter."

Despite himself, Bastien laughed. Within a few minutes, the sound of trickling water reached his ears, and then they spotted Micah, Brock, and their new partner, Vayla, beside a drain pipe.

Bastien dismounted and handed the reins to Tave. "Thank you."

"You're welcome. It's what brothers are for." They shook hands, and Bastien rushed to the pipe.

Micah and Brock lifted a grate from over the top. "Good luck." Micah's features slanted with irritation, but it was probably the nicest thing he'd ever said to him.

Bastien accepted Brock's heavy clap on the shoulder, then hopped down into the drain. Micah's staff lit up, and the water stopped flowing, giving Bastien easier passage. The way under the citadel wall was narrow, forcing Bastien to stoop, but eventually he came out the other side. The flow of water resumed, where it would eventually meet the river. To the south, only blackened, smoking husks remained of what once was the greatest city in Alysies.

Directly east of him was the outskirts of the eastern woods, and tied up on a long tether were none other than two horses. He dashed along the short clearing, hoping not to be seen by any of the enemy. The furthest horse whinnied in greeting.

Tarten! Tave must have recovered Bastien's horse after their failed heist and kept him this whole time. Bastien rubbed his old companion's nose as Tarten stamped the ground. He saddled him using skills long drilled into him by Tave, and they were off, racing north. The smooth gait brought a familiar comfort.

He found the path used by the fleeing to navigate the woods. Few trickled by now, mostly wounded soldiers, staggering under their injuries and supported by a healer. Soon he broke free into a sea of dead. The bodies lay end-to-end, blues, greens, and back and gold, crisscrossing in a grotesque mosaic—his Fating come to fruition and given color to magnify the horror.

His nightmare was coming true.

In his Fating, he'd raced and raced, and never arrived where Faelyn was. He had no choice but to try. Tarten exposed the whites of his eyes, but didn't shy from the coppery-scented blood which covered the dead and ran in rivulets over the stained earth. He pushed courage into his steed, and they flew, jumping and skirting around bodies, trampling them when there was no other choice.

On and on Bastien rode. The enemy soldiers had pursued the broken, retreating army, but many had stayed, their eyes on a single prize marked by a blazing white light in the distance. They fought down the valley, scrambling after the queen. She stood horseless on a small hill, nearly back to back with Lady Amerae. Her sword swung in an elegant dance of death and destruction.

An endless circle of foes surrounded them, held only partly at bay by a small handful of tiring Alysian soldiers. Two figures approached beyond, well-dressed in capes that fluttered in the cold morning breeze, with crowns of gold glinting on their brows. They walked without hurry, waiting for Faelyn's inevitable defeat, the conquering victors.

Not while Bastien had breath in his body.

He sped on, going faster now that they were sloping down. Tarten stumbled, then crumpled beneath him, flinging Bastien through the air. He landed hard on a pair of corpses and their weapons. Tarten struggled to his feet, whole, but limping. He couldn't be ridden without risk of further injury. Bastien ignored his jarred bones, pushed to his feet, and ran. Shouts rang out at his approach, but they were too late. He drew his sword, reaching the back of the ranks surrounding his Faelyn. He no longer saw her, but felt her with all his being.

Bastien stabbed through armor. Soldiers cried and turned, engaging him. He was surrounded, though only a few were spared from the circle clamoring for the queen. He thrust and pivoted. They struck from all directions, unable to find purchase through his shield. The enemy mages made feeble attempts to thwart him, but it was from a distance and had little effect.

He blocked a heavy hit, then turned and stabbed another soldier through the neck. A cry of agony erupted from Amerae. His shield faltered. Pain exploded in his shoulder. He cursed and swung around to defend himself. He couldn't do anything for them but keep going. His shoulder healed itself freely since he was using little magic to fight, conserving it for Faelyn.

He was beginning to draw more attention, with more people joining the fray, but he also slowly drew closer to Faelyn, close enough now to see them. Their small hill gave them the advantage of height. He just had to reach her.

A shout rang out. "Seize her!"

The enemy converged like a deadly blanket. A sick feeling hit his stomach. He'd seen this before, somewhere. In a dream? He knew what was to happen.

The deadly soldiers charged. Amerae fell, crushed under the weight of bodies. Though he hardly knew her, her death shuddered through him. He barely blocked the next blow.

Only Faelyn remained, a glowing spectacle, a lone queen against an army. Her light shone through the morning fog like a beam to Acantha. In the distance, the king of Daltieri stood beside the heir of Kestrea.

Bastien hated those smug faces, those faces that aimed to destroy everything he'd come to cherish, everything he'd learned was good in this world and worth fighting for. Freedom. Friendship. Love.

He caught Faelyn's weary, determined eyes, and found himself drifting from her, feet carrying him toward those hated faces.

Maybe he never reached her in his Fating because he wasn't meant to. Cut the heads off the two-headed snake, and the body will writhe without direction. It might be the only way to get Faelyn out of here. He just had to get close enough.

He pivoted around her small hill, fighting with as much ferocity as he had started, with no idea where his strength came from. His breaths flowed in and out, fast, but in an even rhythm. His feet moved in time with his sword, which thrust and blocked in time with his pounding heart. Sounds faded to the background. His magic flared as needed, knocking his enemies back in quick bursts, or shielding from an attack he couldn't quite turn fast enough to block.

He was almost close enough.

"He's fae," someone shouted.

Bastien ended up in the middle of a pack of enemies and sent a ring of air hurling them away.

"His ears! He's like the traitorous fae queen!"

The fighting halted for the barest of heartbeats. That was all Bastien needed. He focused on the king and prince, still a great distance away, their smug smiles dropping. With a smug smile of his own, Bastien cut off their air. Their mouths gaped like fish, eyes bulging in fear. Their mages surrounded them, fighting in vain against Bastien's magic. Shouted orders and cries of renewed vigor flew from the enemy troops.

He held out his sword, ready for the attack, but to his horror, they ran from him—straight toward Faelyn. She was the one glowing on the hilltop. She was the one with the powers. Faelyn drew them away from attacking *him*.

A deadly, unstoppable wave of enemy soldiers rushed her, ignoring her sword, barely swayed by the flames she threw at them. Bastien couldn't think, couldn't act fast enough. He dropped the magic directed toward the king and prince and hurled it toward Faelyn. Flame, boulders, and crushing wind went flying, but he wasn't fast enough.

Just as he'd seen with Lady Amerae, the sheer volume of enemy soldiers overwhelmed her. He watched helplessly as she was buried beneath the onslaught.

Her light went dark.

Faelyn crawled over corpses and through the throng as they desperately searched for her. She ignored the agonizing pain from multiple stab wounds. The invisibility she'd placed around herself held, and she prayed it held around Amerae. She'd shouted for her friend to remain motionless no matter what. An order. A command from her queen. She'd cast the magic over Amerae the instant she was overrun, just as she'd done for herself. But if Amerae moved, the spell wouldn't move with her.

She pushed her way through legs, arms, and swords while the soldiers shoved in, each trying to get to the last place they saw her and seize her crown for themselves.

"Get him! Kill the fae!" It was the unmistakable, infantile voice of Prince Rory. They were after Bastien.

The pull to where Bastien fought told her where to find the prince and king, who must surely think they'd won. She'd felt the moment he'd gone after them instead of coming to aid her, and was glad. He'd chosen her people over her, knowing it was what she would have wanted. He was right.

Faelyn reached a clearing away from the scrambling enemy and stood. Blazing heat rushed by her cheeks and teared her eyes. Bastien had whipped up a cyclone, and it spun around him, infused with fire. His magic was tremendous, fueled by the fear and rage she felt in their connection. Soldiers surrounded him, the bravest trying to break through. They were thrown back into their lines, uniforms aflame.

He fought for their lives, but wouldn't last. This had to end now.

Faelyn charged, keeping her invisibility and shield firmly in place. The smoke and ash that blocked out the sun helped cover her movement. She wound through the ranks, dodging armored soldiers and horses, until only an empty field separated her from the king and prince. They stood apart from the fighting where they thought they were safe with their mages and soldiers. Exhaustion crept into her lungs, making it hard to draw deep breaths, but she gritted her teeth and sprinted across the short field.

"Protect the king!" Enemy mages surrounded King Seber as they sensed her magic. Their staffs lit up, and the earth quaked beneath her. Guards began ushering the king and prince away.

"What? She's as good as dead." King Seber protested, struggling to keep his horse from being led away or spooked by the earthquake.

"It's her. She's coming!" one of the mages shouted.

Prince Rory turned his horse and sped away, his guards hurrying to keep up.

Come back, you coward.

Faelyn increased her speed. A shallow pit opened directly in her path. She cried out, stumbling. Her arms flailed to keep her upright, but her knee twisted, and she fell, her concentration breaking.

"Light!" someone cried.

An enemy mage in front of the king raised her staff high in the air. Faelyn tensed for an attack. The mage conjured a great beam of light, shining it directly on Faelyn like a beacon. The balance holding her invisibility together shattered. She was exposed.

"Archers!"

A line of archers stretching out from the king released their arrows, filling the sky with the deadly shafts. Faelyn clamored to her feet and sent a blast of air to knock them off course. She looked down in time to see an arrow flying directly toward her at ground level carried by mage wind. She pivoted, but it slammed against her armored shoulder, nearly spinning her around. It did not penetrate the strong metal.

"Faelyn!" Bastien yelled. Profound relief poured off him.

She turned to him as he broke free of the enemy ranks. His face and silver armor were splattered with blood. Exhaustion lined his eyes. The two of them were trapped, the army separating them from her castle. Another volley of arrows sailed toward her. Bastien sent a wave of fire hurling toward them, burning the ones that would have hit their mark.

Faelyn panted. She was worn out. What had she planned to do against such numbers? Her wounds were barely healing. They had to retreat. Where was Amerae? Bastien took her hand, and the ache making it hard to breathe eased. The weariness in her magic lifted as if she'd had a full night's rest.

Bastien and Faelyn locked eyes. He'd come, just as he said he would, forsaking his life and his former kingdom for her. He was her equal, not just someone she loved. He was meant to be here with her.

The ranks behind them reformed and charged. The clang of swords made them turn. Amerae was up and fighting. She couldn't hope to last, but fought anyway, to buy more time.

Behind the rows of archers and mages, the guards had finally convinced King Seber to retreat—a true coward to the end. From this distance, the range for any magical spell should have been impossible, except the power in her magic told her otherwise, as if it'd been magnified. Hand-in-hand with Bastien, nothing seemed impossible.

She returned his desperate grip. Magic burst from them, bathing them both in white light. They charged across the field. Without even speaking, together they cast a net of magic. Undirected and feral, it burst out as a blue glow swimming through the air. The dome grew and expanded. The enemy lines ducked and scattered in fear.

The king had gone far, but the magic reached farther. Like pinpricks, Faelyn felt the moment their enemies passed under the net. King Seber's horse reared, tossing him to the ground. He shouted for help, almost too faint to hear beneath the fleeing troops. The power flowing between them was like nothing she'd ever felt.

The net completed its dome shape, trapping the troops outside the space. Only the mages remained, a dozen of them, standing in front of their downed king. They hadn't cowered from the magic. Seber clambered to his feet under the weight of his armor, wide eyes swiveling to his retreating soldiers.

"Ride back to your army," Faelyn said, words carried to him on the wind. "Ride back and order the surrender."

Being under their dome, she sensed the king's instant rejection of the plan. His forces still outnumbered hers.

Bastien shocked him with a flashing bolt of electricity.

"Do as Queen Faelyn says. Your breaths are numbered." Bastien's strong, sure voice followed hers on the wind.

She squeezed his hand appreciatively.

King Seber writhed on the ground. A few of his mages rushed to him. The rest raised a shield around him. Faelyn and Bastien called their magic again, and through it, she showed him how to follow their lines of power and shatter their crystals. The enemy mages cried out and enough were distracted that the shield dissipated. Some of them fled to the boundaries of the dome.

King Seber drew his sword. "I'd rather die than surrender to a false fae queen." Before Faelyn could react, he sunk the hilt into the ground and tipped forward onto it. The tip pierced his ceremonial armor and flesh. He dropped to his side, blood dripping from his mouth.

"The king is felled! Retreat!" The mages grabbed what horses they could and galloped off.

Bastien cursed, the very thing she wanted to do. "How do we get his army to surrender?"

A clamor of activity had them spinning toward the castle. Their hands dropped from each other, and the magic dome disappeared. Instantly, Faelyn's legs grew heavy and unsteady. Exhaustion weighed her down.

"Look at that," she breathed.

There was no foe formidable enough to attack them, yet the Daltieri army was fleeing. Regrouping around Prince Rory, perhaps? The ranks scattered, revealing Amerae. Bleeding from a wound in her side, she stumbled and fell.

Bastien rushed to her. The remaining enemy ran south toward the citadel, forsaking their dead and wounded. The sun peeked through the ash cloud high overhead. Had they been fighting that long? She took a long pull from the waterskin within the satchel at her side and stumbled across the clearing, away from Bastien.

"Where are you going?" Bastien asked beside a subdued Amerae.

"To retrieve King Seber's crown. We've no hope of returning with his body, at least until we find aid. We'll need the crown to prove his defeat." But it wouldn't be enough. The Kestrea army still fought.

At the castle, smoke filled the sky and screams burned into her ears. No relief squadron rushed to meet them. No soldiers had come to their aid. And that was a bad sign. Things had gone very wrong at the citadel.

King Seber lay prone, blood soaking into the grass and pooling beneath his wound. The crown had fallen off his head and lay point-down in the dirt. His was a legacy of war and rampage begun long before the days of Prince Samual and his ruthless mother, Queen Vatrice. They'd conquered her weakened kingdom in a mere day when she was but eighteen years old, taking from her everyone she'd loved and everything she'd held dear. Every possible future she'd ever imagined for herself had been dashed. There had been many, many mistakes on her path to redemption. Maybe one of them wasn't going after King Seber the very moment she reclaimed Alysies at the battle of Pavora, instead allowing him to build his army back up again.

She picked up King Seber's crown. He had sons and grandsons, brutal heirs already in place to take the throne. Fighting still raged behind her. They were still horribly outnumbered. But for the barest of moments, she allowed herself to feel the weight of a partial victory. The Daltieri king was felled in the name of a free Alysies, as her father should have done long ago, and as she should have done before today.

The sound of Amerae's whimper as Bastien helped her to her feet broke Faelyn of the moment. She rushed back and embraced her friend. "Let's go find your husband."

Worn and weary, the three of them made their way. Every time Faelyn felt she couldn't take another step, she grabbed Bastien's hand, drawing strength. Finally, they came close enough to the castle to catch the attention of a battlement guard.

"Open the east gate," he shouted.

One. One guard stood on the eastern wall. One of hundreds that should have been posted there. The sounds of a desperate, bloody battle grew as they reached the gate. The noise was inside the citadel. The wall had been breached. Faelyn drew her sword, which rested heavy in her hand.

"We can't fight, my queen," Amerae said from behind. "We are none of us in a position to hold our own."

Faelyn exchanged a glance with Bastien and hefted the Daltieri crown. "I need to get inside the citadel."

"We'll get you there," Amerae said.

Faelyn nodded.

The gate opened slowly, barely wide enough for one of them. Bastien let her lean on him. Hand in hand, they slipped through the gate and into chaos.

The sight stopped Faelyn cold. Dead bodies were piled everywhere. They lay over each other in every direction. She cried out, backing up into Bastien. Blood bubbled over the ground. Faelyn looked skyward, unable to handle seeing another fallen soldier in blue, another of her people whom she treasured, so casually discarded. Flame and smoke stained the air.

A pair of gate guards were engaged in combat, trying to hold a couple dozen enemy soldiers back from their queen. Bastien didn't hesitate.

He dropped her hand and drew his sword, jumping into the fray. "Protect the queen!" He beat back a pair of Daltieri soldiers in black, then pivoted, sending a pulse of air to the gate guard's attacker, sending him sprawling.

Amerae led her away, toward the stairs along the wall. Faelyn tore her gaze from Bastien and set the pace. He'd be okay, and she needed his distraction to get away. They'd find each other in the end.

Houses and shops burned as they passed along the citadel market. Faelyn put out what she could while trying to conserve her magic and allow it to build back up. Bodies of women and children who hadn't escaped to the castle—their last stand—littered the streets. Most of the fighting was taking place elsewhere, so they met little resistance, cutting down the random enemy runner. She feared what she might find as they traveled further.

A familiar presence slithered down her spine as they continued. Prince Rory was nearby. He hadn't fled after all. The sludge and hate wrapping around his heart permeated the air, even stronger than the tang of blood and acidic bile. Would he bow down now that his ally was dead? No. She'd have no choice but to end him, and she'd be glad to do it.

The remnants of a blast of air magic caressed her face, sending the tendrils of hair that had torn loose from her braid billowing. The magic felt of Kian. She stopped, her gaze shifting to where his power originated. The south gate, unseen through the buildings and flame. The center of the fighting where the noise was loudest and magic was thickest.

Amerae stood before her, sword up and scanning for any wandering enemy.

Faelyn pulled Kian's mage ring out of her pocket and slipped it on. He'd insisted she'd keep in on her ever since his return. The first time she'd experienced the sharing of his mage crystal, it had been forced upon her as he'd hastily shoved it on her finger. The feeling of him, his raw desperation that day, had coated her, panicked her. They'd used it few times since, when desperate times called for it, and it'd been easier to handle. She'd realized they were just friends, though their friendship ran deep. The ring and feeling of Kian became more a tool to communicate with him, and less a symbol of a romance that never was.

She knew just who to give it to should they survive the war.

Faelyn, thank Acantha. Are you hurt? Even Kian's thoughts were winded as he fought in the thick of things.

I'm fine. King Seber is dead. I sensed Prince Rory. Do you know where he is?

Kian's essence grew dark and grim with an underlying fury that worried her. *He's in the castle. Nolan followed with a company. I have to remain here or the citadel will fall.*

The castle! Where the defenseless sought protection.

Kian continued, knowing she'd need all the details. *The enemy has breached the citadel. Mostly Kestrea, but Daltieri soldiers are forming ranks on the horizon. More are filing in. We won't last long.*

She felt Kian tense, thoughts streaming through his mind, analyzing the magnitude of fresh enemy troops who'd just come crashing into the citadel. Faelyn moved to help.

No, his mind yelled. *You're needed in the castle. Keep going.*

Her steps rocked with indecision, but she tore her eyes away from the south gate. She removed the ring and slid it into her pocket. There was no helping him now, not with the castle in danger. Amerae was on her heels as they raced ahead.

Then the screaming began.

FIFTY-SEVEN

Taking in gulps of air, Bastien gawked at the seemingly never-ending enemy lines that bled back from the eastern gate and into the town's burning houses and shops. The crackling of flames and crash of collapsing buildings was nothing compared to the roar of the enemy and agony of the dying.

The citadel, with all its magical protections, had been breached.

The smoldering rubble forced the Kestrea soldiers into a bottleneck as they attempted to take the gate, held off by only a handful of Alysian soldiers. Word must have gotten to them that their queen would need safe passage, or they might not have been there at all to open the gate. Faelyn had the Daltieri crown. There was no choice but to stay and fend off the enemy to give her a chance to slip away.

Gripping his weapon, Bastien shuffled toward the melee. The screams and clashes of swords vibrated in his chest. His steps fell heavier without Faelyn's touch, and the funnel of free-flowing magic narrowed dangerously. An entire enemy legion had been sent to this side, and for what? Was the citadel so overrun they had troops to spare on an abandoned and defenseless section? Or had the enemy discovered Faelyn would come through the east gate?

Sweat poured down Bastien's face as he reached the enemy and slashed into their lines. His sword raked over metal and flesh, again and again as he pivoted and thrust. Smoke burned his eyes. Ash coated the ground beneath him. Where were the rest of the Alysian troops? Chrisso, Bear. Even Captain Flinn would be a welcome sight.

The Alysian guard beside him stumbled and was run through. Bastien moved to take his place, raising his sword to parry an attack. The blade landed heavily on his, jarring his arm.

"It's the thief," his attacker said with a note of surprise. "The murderer."

Bastien swung and studied the enemy's face. He gasped, nearly forgetting to block the next hit. Stern face. Two green medallions set in each shoulder to show rank.

He fought Captain Cerick.

Breath burst in and out of him at the sight of the captain's smug grin. This was the man he'd been raised to fear, who'd almost killed him once. Street kids knew to avoid Captain Cerick at all costs. Cerick's blows came more rapidly, each stronger than the one before.

"Did you think justice wouldn't come for you, thief?" Cerick struck. His sword slipped passed Bastien's defense, hitting his side and digging into the metal.

Not deep enough to bleed.

"I didn't kill your guards." Bastien's heart thrummed in his ears. Cerick represented everything that was wrong in the world; corruption, deceit, injustice. He *would not* let that poison infect Alysies. "But I will kill you. No one will take this kingdom from its queen."

Bastien met every heavy strike with a parry, studying Cerick's slash, parry, step, strike pattern.

"My nephew, my prince, will end her, and this kingdom will be his." Cerick panted as he slammed his sword into Bastien's. "And I'll end you, as I should have in Docimer."

Bastien took the hits on his blade, legs shaking as he searched for a way in and found none.

But he wasn't the same person he was back in Docimer, that

scared boy putting up a strong front, but with no hope and no future. He'd trained at the sword. He'd trained at magic. He had Faelyn's love.

When you've got everything to lose, you fight for it.

Cerick yelled as he swung a vicious strike. Bastien jumped back, missing the swipe to his throat by mere inches. Enough. He'd bought himself enough time. Looking Cerick straight in the eye, he let loose his built-up magic.

The earth rumbled beneath the captain, jarring him and his surrounding soldiers. Bastien struck, forcing Cerick back a few steps. Mouth gaping, Cerick leaped, but it was too late. With a great crack, the ash-covered ground opened beneath him. His terrified eyes were the last Bastien saw of him before he fell. The earth caved in around him, trapping Captain Cerick and several enemy soldiers underneath.

"Fall back," Bastien shouted to the remaining Alysians. He couldn't hold the enemy off any longer. What magic he had left needed to be conserved.

The few Alysians remaining turned and ran, right in the direction Faelyn and Amerae had retreated. The enemy surged after them.

Wide-eyed, Bastien shouted, "To me!" He raised his sword and took off down the path toward the middle of the citadel, avoiding the direction Faelyn had gone.

Pounding and shouting told him he was being followed. He ducked around buildings, the sounds of battle increasing as he went. The magic of the Alysian mages roared strong, and he followed it.

He rounded a flaming storage building and into the sight of Alysian soldiers. Their dwindled ranks lined up against the Kestrea army, who grossly outnumbered them, yet more still poured through the burning south gate.

Bastien threw himself to the side of the building, wood scratching against his armor, just as the enemy troops who'd followed him rushed past without seeing him, maybe fifty in all.

Orders were shouted. The troops at the back of the Alysian formation turned and raised their swords, meeting the enemy.

The soldiers' fury and fear coated the air as they cut down the enemy. The smoke couldn't cover the smells of blood and death. The shrieks of the dying and desperate rose above the sharp clang of swords and constant twang of bows along the battlement.

A blast of air blew cool against the heat of the flames. Mage air. Toward the front of the Alysian formation, Lord Kian fought alone against a trio of mages armored in green. The soldiers, friend and foe alike, gave them and their magical blasts a wide birth. The enemy mage crystals glowed brightly against the backlight of flames rapidly spreading to the rest of the citadel.

Kian bled from an unhealing cut on his forehead, helmet long gone. His shoulders bowed with exhaustion, but still he fought on, sword in one hand, staff in the other. The three Kestrea mages pressed forward, faces fixed with stern concentration. They meant to break through Kian's shield, and they were close.

Bastien swore. He couldn't leave Kian to fight on his own. Faelyn would be all right for a little longer. He tightened the grip on his sword and rushed through the skirmish at the rear of the Alysian formation. Swinging, he slashed and felled a Kestrea soldier, then passed into the ranks of Alysians awaiting their turn to fight. The fear was as thick as the stink of their sweat. They barely noticed him shouldering his way through as they breathed hot breaths, blood dripping from under the armor of most, having already had many rotations on the front lines. But they were holding, for now. Likely due to Kian's efforts against the mages. If he fell, and the lines fell, what kind of chance would Faelyn have even with the Daltieri king dead?

Bastien angled his approach so he'd come up behind Kian. No troops fought there as they were all keeping back out of harm's way of whatever spell the mages might let loose. The magic increased in intensity the closer he got, like electricity raking over his skin, stirring up his own meager reserves. The Alysians on the front radiated relief as he pushed past them. He stopped just behind Kian who sent a volley of aether at the mages. Two women and one man in green armor stood stock still, concentrating. Sweat beaded their upper lips as they attempted to break Kian's aether shield.

Bastien pulled his magic to the forefront, shaping it to become flame.

A squad of Kestrea troops broke from the front line, rushing toward Kian with raised swords. The pack was led by a tall, muscled soldier whose dark eyes looked surprisingly familiar beneath his helm.

Bastien's heart slammed into his chest.

Olin.

Olin had survived Kolb's gang. Olin was here.

Fighting for the enemy.

FIFTY-EIGHT

Olin had grown nearly as tall as Bastien, filling out with muscle—likely from being well-fed for once in the Kestrea army.

The weak, quiet boy whom Bastien had protected all those years charged at Kian.

"Kian." Bastien's warning came out a croak. His feet carried him forward, heavy, as if fastened to the ground.

His friend, his brother, had become his enemy.

Kian turned slowly, finally noticing the threat almost upon him. Bastien had barely made it halfway. Kian's magic increased, but Olin reached him first, his once-innocent face snarling in fury. Their swords met, clanging viciously even over the den of fighting all around them. Olin's squad took position around Kian while the enemy mages pressed in, eyes eager.

Bastien had stopped moving. Indecision and guilt rooted him to the spot. Kian and Olin struck at each other, Olin moving and parrying with long-practiced skill. Bastien shook himself. Of course he had to help Kian. He searched for the magical thread of the toughest-looking mage, the woman in the middle standing just a bit ahead of the rest. She hammered Kian's weakening shield with some unseen force. Not air.

Bastien surged forward, striking at the troops flanking Kian. The one on the left twisted to block Bastien's feint and was cut down. Bastien jumped back as the other swung at his middle and then lunged with a strike. While his body was engaged in combat, his mind and magic grabbed the thread of the lead mage. He sensed her surprise and swore he heard her startled gasp, just before he shattered her mage crystal. She screamed and drew a sword, charging Kian's back.

"Kian, turn around!" This time Bastien's words came loud and clear just as he downed his opponent.

Kian didn't hesitate, as if his instincts had warned him when to turn and engage—leaving Olin facing his exposed back.

Bastien charged and leaped between them as Olin swung. His blade met Olin's in a jarring clang, crisscrossing in front of their faces. Bastien held there, staring full-on with pleading eyes at the face he'd never forget. He was met with pure anger.

"Olin, don't do this."

Olin's brows furrowed in confusion, but he pressed on, grinding his sword into Bastien's. Bastien sent magic through Olin's blood frenzy, coaxing peace and understanding from him. Olin's eyes widened in surprise, then recognition. He stumbled back.

"Bastien?" His voice, confused and horrified, rang familiar, but deeper.

He couldn't know all Bastien had been through, only that Bastien had abandoned him and now fought for the enemy. Still, Olin was the one Kestrea soldier Bastien would never dare strike down.

"Olin." Bastien smiled with relief.

Olin's sword drooped. "Your ears..."

An Alysian soldier broke from the line. He flew toward Olin, sword before him like a battering ram. Bastien threw out his magic. Air blasted the soldier, knocking him back. He lost his sword as he rolled end over end until he came to rest at his captain's feet.

Acantha above, what have I done? Bastien stood paralyzed.

The captain looked to the unmoving soldier, then up at Bastien. His surprised eyes narrowed.

"Bastien." Olin's voice cut through the noise of battle as he lowered his sword. His tone was one of acceptance. He'd finally come to terms that he wasn't imagining things, but pain and anger swarmed his essence. Worse, betrayal.

The words spilled over. "I'm sorry I never came back. More than you'll ever know. But I was wanted for crimes I didn't commit. I couldn't return to Kestrea. I couldn't be near you without endangering you."

"Captain Olin, what are you doing?" The two remaining Kestrea troops in the mage circle stared at Olin, eyes shifting between him and Bastien. Beyond them, Kian battled sword-to-sword with the staffless mage. The other two continued the unseen magical attacks on his shield.

He'd made captain? There was so much Bastien wanted to tell Olin, so much he needed to explain and help him understand.

Magic hit Bastien in the gut, and he doubled over. He frantically tried to throw a shield of air around him, but the enemy mage blocked him, holding the air away from him. Adrenaline rolled coldly through him as he sensed a surge of magic.

A sharp tug grabbed his middle, and his body lifted. What kind of magic was this? His arms whirled, trying to grab onto something as his feet left the ground. He cried out, startled, still grappling. His hands met nothing but open air. The levitation magic covered him, filling his pores like an invading host of winged bugs. He floated above the melee, heart hammering in his chest, mind working furiously to think of how to counteract such powerful magic.

Kian felled the lead mage and engaged one of the two remaining. The other smirked up at him, the light of his staff casting an eerie glow over half his face, blending with the orange glow of fire.

Bastien thrashed, panicking, still rising. His magic did nothing to break through the mage's efforts. Much higher, and all the mage would have to do was release the spell, and Bastien would break his body. Bows twanged as a volley of arrows was released from behind enemy lines. Floating uselessly, Bastien braced for impact.

Someone grabbed his armored foot and yanked. The arrows whooshed by, just overhead. He looked down. Olin met his eyes with a nod. Pride and warmth flooded Bastien, clearing his head of panic.

Kian cried out. The mage had him on his knees, as if unable to control his own body. Was she a mind-control mage? Still tugging Bastien down against the force of the magic trying to lift him, Olin tensed. Bastien swiveled his gaze to see a band of Alysian soldiers, led by the captain, charging straight toward Olin and his two remaining companions.

"Let go, Olin. Fight!" Bastien shouted.

Olin raised his sword but didn't let go of Bastien's foot. "I don't know what made you join the enemy, Bast, but you saved me that day so long ago, and all those times before. You wounded Kolb, scared him so bad that he took your money that bought my freedom. Miss Bannings said you made her promise to help me. Now I'm going to save you."

Olin's companions jumped in front of him, but they were outnumbered.

Kian sagged to the ground.

Desperate fury erupted within Bastien. He shoved past the mage's magic with colossal effort and latched onto the thread of the two remaining enemy mages. Like lightning streaming down a tethered line, his magic shot straight into their mage crystals. They didn't shatter. They exploded. Pieces of crystal and wood shot out and embedded themselves in the mages as they screamed.

Bastien fell the last several feet, taking Olin with him as they slammed into the ground. The Alysian soldiers slashed and met nothing but air, losing their footing and toppling over. The captain remained standing, furious eyes locked with Bastien.

Bastien shot to his feet, hauling Olin up, which was much harder than he remembered. "He's on our side, Captain. He's one of Lady Amerae's spies."

The captain hesitated.

Olin glared, but with a firm shake of Bastien's head, the protest died on his lips. He nodded instead, hostility and betrayal rolling off him in waves.

A battle roar interrupted whatever the captain was planning to say. Bastien whipped around to see the army charging, trying to gain the ground the mage fight had occupied. Kian lay sprawled in the dirt.

There was only a heartbeat to decide what to do. He couldn't rescue both Olin and Kian. Like ripping his own heart out, he shoved Olin toward the safety of the Kestrea lines.

"Survive another day, Olin. I'll find you again." There wasn't time to say anything else. Olin's loyalties lay with his kingdom. Bastien could only hope his friend might live through this, but even as he thought that, he knew it'd be at the expense of Faelyn's people. His people.

Olin nodded and backed away, eyes conveying a last goodbye as he was swallowed into the ranks, lost in the bodies pressing in. Bastien sent a silent prayer for Olin to be okay. He launched across the clearing, reaching Kian and crouching over him just as the soldiers came upon them from both sides. He threw up a hand, and his shield flared, a bubble of air and light around them. His other hand draped over Kian. Healing magic poured out of him, clamoring to fix what had been broken. But it found nothing. It was Kian's mind that had been tampered with.

"Wake up, Kian. We must move!" He shook Kian hard, but his eyelids merely fluttered.

The Kestreans and Alysians collided in waves of green and blue. They threw each other against Bastien's shield, some using it to protect their backs or shoving off of it for leverage. Kian couldn't stay here. More mages would come. Bastien debated for all of a heartbeat before unbuckling and removing Kian's plate armor. It was a great risk, but he'd never be able to carry Kian and his staff with the extra weight.

He stood, his shield adjusting to his height, and hauled Kian over his shoulder with a grunt. They'd both lost their swords, but he grabbed Kian's staff, feeling the familiar power of the mage crystal thrum through his hands. Kian's crystal was fine indeed, not cracked like his old one.

Kian?

A wave of spring sunshine, breezy meadows, and wildflowers warmed his mind. He knew this person.

Faelyn. Bastien sensed her surprise, then her intense relief and a love he never thought he'd deserve. But, she had a piece of Kian's mage crystal. That meant... Were they engaged? Doubt flooded him as he expanded his shield ahead of them, forcing a way through the thick fighting while hauling Kian toward the castle. Like pushing boulders with each heavy step forward.

Bastien, where are you? What's happened to Kian? Worry lanced through her words, though he couldn't tell on whose behalf.

He huffed forward, nearing the back of the Alysian ranks. *Kian's with me. He's unconscious, attacked by enemy mages. We're beside the south gate, heading toward the castle.* Toward her, he realized. That was where the draw felt strongest.

He glanced over his shoulder once, fruitlessly trying to find Olin in the fray. The glow of mage staffs rose in the background. He cursed and moved faster, Kian a dead weight on his weary shoulder. He was an easy target with his glowing beacon of a shield, though they'd have to pass through the armies to reach him.

Faelyn's brief relief turned into excited shock. *It's the prince. I sense him. He's here in the castle.*

The pull told him she moved through the castle halls. He could almost see her grinning in anticipation of finally ending this.

Horrified anger, intensified by the crystal, preceded her words. *His soldiers are attacking the women and children who sought refuge here.*

Bastien snarled a fury that matched her own. Through the crystal's bond, he felt her guilt. For a brief moment, he glimpsed the weight of the crown she wore, the burden she placed upon herself to protect every last living soul in this kingdom and the way it tore at her. His thoughts turned guiltily to the Alysian he'd knocked unconscious to save Olin.

Bastien pivoted around a burning building and cut across the citadel yard. He scanned for a safe place to deposit Kian. If the prince and his soldiers were in the castle, Kian wouldn't be safe there. The small gateway between the citadel and the castle grounds was teeming with Daltieri troops in black and gold. They surrounded it, protecting it like it was their own, and even manned the battlements above.

Faelyn's nervousness and anticipation grew. She was getting closer to the prince. Bastien had to be there.

Fire. He needed fire.

Bastien paused long enough to drink the last of his waterskin. His first thought was to send a flaming wall to incinerate the enemy in a solid strike, but he was too depleted. He turned his shield of light and air into one of fire, shooting out from all sides, and ran. He couldn't see the way ahead, only the ground beneath his feet, and used his sense of the men in front of him to navigate his way to the gate. Men and women soldiers screamed, dodging or catching fire. Arrows twanged from above, incinerating harmlessly by the flames.

Everything darkened as they crossed through the tunnel beneath the wall. He put forth a burst of magic as he exited, sending fire to clear the way. He didn't stop running until the arrows and cries of the enemy died away—their job was to defend the gate, apparently. Only then did he switch his fire out for air, which took much less magic.

His legs shook, and sweat poured off him. Kian was dead weight on his shoulders. But he'd made it halfway to the castle entrance.

I've found him, Bastien. He's in the throne room. I'm almost there.

Hang on, I'm coming.

There were surprisingly few troops out front. Alive, anyway.

Plenty of bodies in blue lay dead and bleeding, crows picking at them. He grabbed a couple of the less-bloody swords on his way through. Not many troops had been stationed here, as the stronghold was the citadel. Or, perhaps they had been, but were called away to defend the gates.

He shook his head, trying to clear his weariness. The castle grounds went on forever, and Kian grew heavier and heavier. Bastien charged up a sloping drive to the castle keep, then ducked around a skyward turret to a side door. It was unguarded, but locked.

With a strong kick to the heavy wood, the lock lurched. He sensed Faelyn's anticipation, the breath before she made the final turn. *I'm almost in. Wait for me.* It was too much to ask, he knew. Still, he concentrated, listening for her response as the door finally burst inward.

Fear and blinding horror shot through the crystal. *No, no, no.* Faelyn's thoughts were paralyzed, convalesced around that single word.

"Faelyn!" he screamed out loud and through the crystal. *Talk to me, what's happening?*

He stumbled into the dark hall, eyes instantly adjusting. Screams and fighting sounded out from all directions, but there was only one direction he needed. He opened the nearest door—a closet of some kind—and set Kian down beside brooms and buckets. He glanced at Kian's staff and hesitated. Without it, he couldn't communicate with Faelyn.

But he wouldn't leave Kian defenseless. He tucked the staff in the crook of Kian's limp arm. *I'm coming, Faelyn.* Her resounding horror was all he sensed before he let go. The connection cut off, and then he was running.

FIFTY-NINE

If there was one nightmare come true that would be worse than all the nightmares that had plagued Faelyn over her long years, it was the scene unfolding before her now.

She stood at the entrance to her throne room, afraid to move, afraid to breathe. The enemy troops she'd evaded lined up at her back, held off by a wave of the hand of the man lounging on her throne.

Prince Rory.

Two mages flanked his stolen throne, staffs aglow with the shields they produced to protect him. Rory looked rested, barely upset by the war that had raged around him for what felt like weeks now. Resplendent in crisp green silk, he smiled, victor-triumphant, reveling in his moment of sure glory. His cape was the only sign of violence, flecked with blood. Not his.

Beside the throne, unmoving and bloody, lay the body of her most trusted advisor, Nolan.

Halfway down the aisle between Faelyn and the prince, held from behind by a guard with a sword to her throat, Amerae wept. For in the arms of the prince was the helpless baby, Mary.

Faelyn shook with uncontrollable fear. Her friends. Her family. Her future.

Even the cruelty and hate shown during their brief and regrettable engagement never led her to believe him capable of such atrocities. Such horror he'd brought into her peaceful kingdom.

"You should have kept her close, Faelyn," Rory said.

Words wouldn't come. Thoughts wouldn't form. History was repeating itself. Mary, her Mary from her youth. The woman who'd held her when the palace boys had been too cruel. The woman who'd bought her fighting leathers when no one else thought girls should learn to fight. Faelyn had sent Mary away to protect her when the invasion started, only to watch her die at the hands of the enemy. Just like she'd sent away baby Mary.

He cradled the sleeping babe closer. "Daltieri spies—my spies now—were beside themselves to share what they learned. This child, the named heir, being evacuated to a safe location?" He smiled and shifted on the throne, sword clanking against the wood. "You seem shocked. Surely you realized King Seber and I arranged this whole thing, right after my father forced me to sign my life away to rule beneath a fae freak." He tilted his head back and chuckled. "My father never caught on. And I have a real bride waiting at home for me. You've no doubt heard of the beautiful daughter of Daltieri, Princess Cassia."

She'd done everything right. Their army was stronger than ever, she'd named an heir, her people were well-fed and taken care of. How had it come to this? Indecision rooted her to the spot as deep as the horror and the sounds of her friend weeping. Nothing she could think of would work. Every power within her control would only put Mary in harm's way. Amerae, her dearest friend, a steadfast and loyal Alysian, locked tear-filled eyes with her, silently pleading for her to save her baby.

Faelyn lifted her chin.

"Hand over King Seber's crown, and I'll spare one of your friends," Rory said.

He knew how much these people meant to her. He'd been in this castle for months, learning their connections and secrets. And he'd use her friends to get what he wanted.

Hope bloomed in Amerae's eyes as she gazed at her daughter, and Faelyn's heart broke. Rory wouldn't spare Mary. He wouldn't repeat what had happened when Daltieri conquered Alysies and an heir to the crown had escaped.

Rory scowled, his vile hands clutching Mary closer. The baby whimpered.

Faelyn willed her voice not to shake. "I give you the crown, and you let Lady Amerae go."

Rory nodded, eyes eager as Faelyn reached into her satchel and pulled out the gaudy golden crown. He snapped his fingers. The guard holding Amerae lowered the sword from her neck and released her.

Amerae fell to her hands and knees, chestnut hair cascading around her face as she cried and crawled toward her baby.

"Am, be still," Faelyn hissed, heart ripping open inside of her.

The guard took measured steps, approaching Faelyn warily, then snatched the crown from her upraised hand.

Rory's grin widened. "How I wish I could simply imprison you. I'd like to study you, to learn of the history you've seen. Perhaps see how long a fae really lives. What they can endure." He sighed as if deeply regretful. "We both know I can't. You'd find a way out, another way of coming out the hero, which seems to be your tale. Not this time."

She stifled a gasp as the welcomed pull to her middle preceded a loud commotion behind her. Soldiers yelled over the clang of swords. She didn't turn. She knew who had come, as he'd always promised he would.

Her Bastien.

Warmth chased away fear and anxiety, steadying her, easing her up from the ground beneath her. She locked narrowed eyes onto Prince Rory. The mages to either side of him tensed, thickening their shields against any elemental attack. They had no idea what she was capable of. She breathed deeply, then slammed Rory with emotional magic.

Terror. Worry. Nervousness. Doubt. All the things Bastien chased away when he'd decided to take on an entire company to save her— she channeled them into the prince.

Rory raised his hand—to signal his guard? —but it hung, uncertain, as the emotions crowded his feeble mind. "Should we retreat?" He looked to the mages, and their shields momentarily faltered.

Faelyn latched onto their crystals, and they cried out. Rory glanced side to side, then down at the infant on his lap. He shook his head, squeezing his eyes tight.

"Stop it, stop it!" His emotions increased, pushing against her efforts, fighting to hold onto his victor state of mind.

The guards around the room lifted their weapons.

The mage crystals shattered. The shield around Rory disintegrated. The mages backed away, fear in the whites of their eyes.

Hand shaking, Rory pulled a dagger from his side. "You get out of my head right now, or she dies." He raised the dagger.

"No!" Amerae cried.

Faelyn stopped the volley of emotions and lunged, barely grabbing a handful of Amerae's sleeve before she ran to the dais. The fighting in the hall intensified. Flame whipped down the hall behind her, screaming of Bastien's magic. He was using everything he had left to reach her.

Rory's grip tightened on the dagger. Faelyn raised her hands, placating a desperate madman. She sent more emotional magic, but subtle, oh so subtle this time. Desperation. Doubt.

There was only one thing left to offer. One final sacrifice for her kingdom.

"You want me, Rory. You don't need the baby. You're not a murderer of infants. Your father wouldn't want this. Let her mother have her. I'll... take her place." She looked into Amerae's desperate, bleak eyes.

As Faelyn offered to trade one life for another, she sensed indecision war inside her friend, but Amerae didn't argue. No protest formed on her lips. Her queen for her child.

Rory tapped the tip of the dagger against the armrest, thinking. Even over the screams of the dying, the dagger plunked against the gold filigree in a twisted cadence.

He stood, shifting to keep Mary in one arm with the threatening dagger in the other. Her sleepy head lolled forward, startling her awake. She began to cry. Amerae's sobs renewed, and Faelyn took an involuntary step forward.

"Please," Faelyn said, tone desperate. "You're right. If you let me live, I will never stop trying to reclaim my throne. I'll give you my life to spare hers." And she meant every word, driving home that undeniable truthfulness into Rory's black heart. Mary's ancestor had died for her, so many people had suffered for her cowardice and long absence.

Prince Rory stifled his smirk. He'd kill the infant as soon as Faelyn no longer stood in his way, but Bastien and Amerae wouldn't let that happen. They were strong enough. They'd get Mary out, and her kingdom could rebuild upon the hope that infant gave them.

"Guard, train your arrow on this babe, and if soon-to-be-former Queen Faelyn tries anything, kill it." Rory's tone carried, still full of confidence and lacking the doubt Faelyn had hoped she'd planted.

A guard's bowstring went taut and pointed straight at Mary who still wailed, held awkwardly in Rory's arm. Amerae struggled not to cry.

"That's the mother, I presume?" He sneered in disgust toward Amerae. "She will take the infant, and you, Faelyn, will take her place."

Amerae gripped her hand. "My queen." Worry laced her voice.

Faelyn forced a smile born of need, and also a sense of peace. She was going to right some of her many mistakes. "Let's go get your daughter."

Under the threat of upraised swords and the glares of several

Kestrea guards, they slowly made their way to the front. The sunset in the windows ahead cast the room in a luscious orange, but she focused on the man fighting behind her, sending her love to him. The only goodbye they'd get.

"No!" he shouted over the den. The noise became more ferocious.

Rory craned to peer behind them, but he could not be allowed to know what was coming. Faelyn rushed ahead, pulling Amerae with her and startling the guards. Rory's gaze locked back onto her.

Faelyn glanced at Nolan once as they passed him, his life essence there, but faint. He lay face down, his injuries hidden. Could Bastien heal Nolan and save Amerae at the same time? Would he have anything left after battling the soldiers in the hall? She prayed to Acantha for a miracle.

They stopped at the top of the dais. Rory leered, eyes roving over Faelyn, then Amerae, who reached ever so slowly for her daughter, face crumpled in pain. Mary's tiny form was red with her cries, small fists and feet jerking, twisting her pale pink dress around. Rory glanced at the guard with the arrow nocked, and the guard nodded.

Rory shoved the baby toward Amerae, who pulled Mary to her breast, backing right into a pair of waiting guards. Rory grabbed Faelyn by the arm and tugged her to him, dagger at her neck.

She finally had a view of the scene that she hadn't dared turn her back to view before. Bodies in green lay piled outside the throne room doors, spilling through. Blood was everywhere, and the walls and some of the soldiers were blackened by fire. The fighting continued, but it was further away now. She sensed Bastien down the hall, his magic still going.

"They say you can heal yourself, my Faelyn," Rory said. His breath snaked over her bare neck, hot and sticky. "That no superficial wound will kill you. And make no mistake. You are mine."

Revulsion racked through her at the touch of his body pressed against hers. Her teeth ground together. There were a hundred ways she could end him if the threat to Mary was gone.

Amerae cried out, and Faelyn jerked her head earning a fine cut that dripped blood but instantly healed. The guard with the arrow stood but a few feet away from Mary, arm shaking from holding the bow taut so long. The guards flanking Amerae kept her from turning to shield her daughter.

"You have me," Faelyn spat. "Call them off." She directed fear into the bowman's heart.

Rory gripped her tighter around her hips. "You'd like that," he breathed. "No. It's time to take what's mine." He turned to the guard with the arrow pointed at Mary's heart. "Release."

The bowman released the arrow, the twang deafening. With her last dregs of magic, Faelyn threw a shield around Amerae and Mary. The arrow slammed into it and ricocheted to the ceiling just as Faelyn twisted away from Rory.

Cradling Mary in one arm, Amerae whirled and grabbed a dagger from the sheath of the nearest guard and rammed it into his throat.

Bastien appeared, breathless and bloody in the doorway.

The whoosh of Rory's arm came before an explosion of blinding pain erupted from her back.

CHAPTER

SIXTY

Faelyn's cry of pain pierced the room, down the tether connecting them and right into Bastien's soul, stealing the breath from him. Prince Rory stood above where she'd half-fallen to her knees, raising his knife for another strike. Faelyn's magic shielded Lady Amerae who held her baby girl. Mary. Faelyn's pained eyes met Bastien's.

Fear and fury overrode all senses, dousing his vision in a haze with only Faelyn clear in the middle. There was no plan. His sword clanged to the ground as he threw his arms up, along with every ounce of magic he had left. Power, hot and desperate, pulled to his hands from his core. Bastien released as Rory swiped down. A flash of lightning shot over Faelyn's head. The beam hit the prince in the chest, throwing Rory backward into the throne.

The knife didn't fall from Prince Rory's hands—it melted. His clothes flamed into ash, and his mouth opened in horror as he looked down. Blisters erupted over his exposed skin, bursting then blackening. Rory slumped into death, eyes sunken, features and limbs twisted with the misery of his demise.

Faelyn cried out and fell to her side, blood seeping from her back.

455

Bastien charged up the aisle, barely registering the slap of his bloody boots against the floor. Blood from his own wounds. Blood from those he'd killed. Amerae slew the guards around her. More guards advanced from around the room. Despite the dead prince, they drew their swords and charged Bastien.

Now halfway to Faelyn, Bastien reached for his sword. Gone. He'd dropped it. Three guards approached, and Bastien raised his fists. The guards stopped, eyes going wide. They grabbed at their throats, mouths gaping like fish as water bubbled between their lips. Bastien turned.

Kian. Kian rushed into the room, single-handedly taking out the rest of the threats. They exchanged a weary nod as Bastien stumbled down the last of the aisle. Amerae charged past him and landed beside a fallen Alysian guard who lay in a pool of his own blood. It was Nolan, Amerae's husband.

"Kian, heal him!" Amerae shouted.

Bastien barely heard her, barely registered Kian or the other mage he sensed had joined them, or his own exhaustion, or even his own name. He leaped to the top of the dais and sat, scooping Faelyn into his lap. Tears trailed down her face, running red with blood.

He had nothing. He had nothing left to save her, to heal her. "Kian!" he shouted. Faelyn's wet breaths were the only reply. "You can't die," he cried. "We've only just found each other. You're supposed to live a long life in my arms." Tears burned his eyes.

The thread between them thinned as the essence drained out of her.

"I've protected those I love, and I love you." Faelyn smiled faintly. "I didn't become my father after all." She pressed a cold hand to his cheek, turquoise eyes cloudy and far away.

With a jolt, magic crescendoed at their contact, as if whatever the two of them had left was magnified by being together.

"It's okay, Bastien." She barely stroked his face, and her eyes drifted closed.

"No, it's not," he whispered. "I won't lose you, too." He placed his hand over hers and twined their fingers together. His magic jolted again like a push to his gut, a demand. "I'm not ready to follow you to the Hereafter just yet. I've done nothing right in my life, but I can do this."

He placed their joined hands on her forehead and closed his eyes. Then he let go and gave his magic free rein. White light erupted from their hands, expanding to surround them. Bastien bore down, leaning over her until his forehead touched the back of his hand bound with hers. The magic shaped itself around her wound, but it wanted more. Needed more. He poured everything he had into healing his love—the pain of his past, his hope for the future, whatever his life was before he left Acantha to be born on Thera. The magic could take it all, if that was the price.

He was worthy of her love. She made it so. And he would spend the rest of his life making sure it stayed that way.

Her magic awakened and fought in tandem, bursting from the dredges of whatever was left. He bared his teeth against the strength of it. The light blinded him through his closed eyes.

Just as strong as it had come on, her magic abruptly stopped. He opened his eyes as she pulled her hand from his and threw her arms around his neck. His magic stopped, instant weariness threatening to take him under.

Then Faelyn's lips were on his. He pulled her to him, planting kisses in desperation through tears and sweat. She was okay. She would live.

Her hair was a snarled mess. Ash and blood streaked her face. She'd never looked so beautiful. Cheek to cheek, they held each other while the world existed outside of them.

Faelyn pulled away, ocean eyes looking up at him. "Marry me, Bastien. This crown, my people, my past, it's nothing without you in my life."

Warmth flowed into him, and he chuckled, wanting nothing more than to never let her go. He brushed a tear from her cheek with his thumb. "Perhaps it's best to not make such important decisions when you've barely escaped death."

She shook her head, but then someone groaned beside them, drawing her attention. "Nolan!" she exclaimed.

Bastien looked up, reluctantly drawing his gaze away from his reason for living who still lay across his lap. Kian and Niri—when had she arrived? —battered and bruised, knelt beside Nolan, their mage staffs just dimming. Nolan's front was sticky with blood, but he groaned again as he tried to sit up.

Amerae, still holding the baby, cried great sobs and clutched Nolan to her. All the enemy soldiers were dead.

"I heard you were having some trouble at the castle," Niri said matter-of-factly. Blood caked one of her ears, and her staff had a new gash in it, but she was whole.

The tension left Faelyn's body, and she sagged against Bastien.

Kian met his gaze, looked down at Faelyn in his arms, then grinned. After a moment, his smile retreated, and he cocked his head. "Bastien, how did I end up in the broom cupboard?"

Bastien laughed in earnest, a release from the stress of the moment. His movement startled Faelyn, who had drifted asleep.

Niri stood, using her staff for support. "Everyone drink some water. This is not over yet, and we're none of us in a state to fend off another wave of enemies."

Bastien's good mood vanished as he stretched his senses, scanning the area for enemies. He sensed none, nor any allies. He pulled Faelyn's waterskin from her satchel and tilted it to her lips. When the water hit, she woke just enough to drink it dry.

Kian shoved his toward Bastien. "You need this more than I do."

Bastien considered him for a moment before finally accepting it, though he left it half full. Kian scowled but drank the rest.

"Is Queen Faelyn okay?" Nolan's tone was weak. He lay flat on the ground, clutching Amerae's hand.

"She's fine, my love, merely sleeping." Amerae peered over at them with gratitude in her eyes, baby Mary asleep once again in her arms. "She saved us. They both did."

Pride seeped into Bastien's bones, warming his cheeks.

The sound of boots pounded in the hallway. He shifted, placing Faelyn behind him while searching out the newcomers. "They're allies." He felt no ill intent from them.

The newcomers rounded the corner, young and wide-eyed, bearing swords. There were only three, wearing Alysian palace livery.

Kian stepped toward them. "Four horses for her majesty at the main entrance."

They gawked at each other.

"At once!"

They took off. Kian grabbed the crown off Rory's head, then the Daltieri crown from the dead guard and held them toward Bastien. "The armies won't stop until they know their leaders are dead. Queen Faelyn won't be safe until this is over."

Bastien forced his eyes to remain open. "You expect her to ride through a raging battle right now? She can't even stay awake."

"No. I expect you to ride with her."

Bastien blinked at the crowns Kian held before him. The conviction in Kian's words brooked no argument, as if there was no doubt Bastien would accomplish this task and keep Faelyn safe.

Bastien took the crowns in one hand, his other still holding Faelyn against him. The weight of the gold sagged his arm. "Let's hurry."

Kian nodded his approval and then reached down, lifting Faelyn into his arms. Her body left a cold absence as contact broke between them. Bastien narrowed his eyes and nearly demanded her back, but then logic returned. There was no way he'd be able to carry Faelyn. He'd be lucky to even stand. He pushed himself up, and his limbs shook, but he didn't fall face-first down the dais. Niri took his elbow, and they made a slow procession down the aisle.

"Go, Amerae. Our queen needs you," Nolan said from behind him, still too weak to get up. "I can protect Mary."

"I'll send the guards back to you, Nolan," Kian said.

Amerae must have been convinced, because Bastien heard her kiss her daughter, then follow. They worked their way passed countless bodies toward the main entrance of the castle. The scale of destruction he'd wrought to reach Faelyn was enormous. Neither soldier nor décor had been spared. Hallways blackened. Furniture shattered. More than once, Kian looked back at him with wide eyes.

The horses with the three guards awaited out front. No enemy was found, but the awful sounds of fighting still came from the east. Thick walls of black smoke had overtaken the sky as the sun set. Kian sent the guards back to the throne room as the rest of them mounted. It took Bastien an embarrassing number of tries before he swung his leg high enough, grumbling about his heavy armor. Once settled, Kian handed Faelyn up to him. She muttered in her sleep, then sighed in contentment as Bastien positioned her in front of him, one arm holding her close, one hand on the reins. The crowns he'd secured to his belt.

Amerae, Niri, and Kian each mounted a horse, then turned to him. He blinked with startled surprise. They were waiting for him to lead. He sat taller in the saddle, scrambling for something to say. His days on the streets with Olin came back to him.

"We've fought an impossible fight here, outnumbered, outmaged, and yet we hold the crowns of their leaders while our beloved queen still breathes. Let's ride, and live to survive another day."

The group flashed eager grins. He urged his horse into a gallop, and they were right on his heels.

"Faelyn, love," he said into her ear. "Time to wake up." He sent a strong tug down the line connecting them.

She took a quick intake of breath and then pressed into him. "What are we doing on horseback?"

"Take the crowns, my queen. It's time to show them who's won."

A sense of eager urgency spiked through Faelyn. She twisted to remove them from his belt. One by one, their group barreled through the small citadel gate, now abandoned by the enemy. The reek of charred flesh and burning buildings slammed into him.

An involuntary gasp escaped him, echoed by Faelyn. The citadel was no more. Where once stood great buildings, some several levels high, were now piles of burning rubble. The fighting raged on, a mixture of green and black soldiers with only a small smattering of Alysian blue. Gone were their formal lines.

The trained warhorse sped toward the thickest of the melee. Faelyn grabbed his hand and held up the crowns. She bathed them in white light as he charged through the masses of soldiers still fighting. The crowns glistened in her light, contrasted by the darkening sky.

The enemy's attention flickered toward the crowns of their royalty. The Alysians roared their victory. They fought with renewed strength, yelling their defiance and barreling into the enemy horde.

Slowly, the order to retreat trickled down the Kestrea and Daltieri lines. The enemy soldiers balked and stumbled. Then ran. There weren't enough Alysians left to do anything but get out of the way as the enemy retreated. They poured through the shattered remains of the southern gate and the many holes in the stone walls. Those that stayed to fight were quickly downed or captured and added to the enclosure holding the prisoners of war.

An Alysian lord rode up, marked by his bloodied and torn cape and crests at his shoulders. Blood leaked from a gash in his helmetless head as he bowed.

"Marus," Amerae cried, riding up to him. "But you were fighting on the eastern side."

Marus nodded to her but addressed the queen. "We fell back to the keep when we received word King Seber had been felled. The fighting is over on that front."

A resounding cry sounded south of the citadel, drawing their gazes. A great clash of swords and magic had Bastien and Faelyn charging the gate, flowing with the enemy.

They rounded the rubble and beheld banners of red and tan, held by thousands of fresh troops clad in red.

"Creadel has come, Your Majesty," Kian shouted.

Faelyn gripped Bastien's hand harder. "They've come too late."

Their ally met the remnants of the enemy host, ripping through them. Faelyn hopped down from the horse, teetering. She stared dazedly at the ruins. Bastien followed her gaze. The citadel, the town, her army. All gone.

Except, in the far-off distance, one lone structure still stood amongst the rubble. Bastien squinted. Barden's restaurant! Bastien had cast a shield of protection from looters and vandals. Now the entire landscape had changed around it.

The army in red still fought, and Bastien itched to scoop Faelyn up and ride far away. The Creadel army could easily turn on Alysies once the enemy was out of their way. And meet no resistance.

Faelyn glanced southward sharply, as if she'd had the same thought.

A party broke away and rode toward them, resplendent in pristine armor, clean of blood and unmarred by the horrors of war. In the center, flanked by riders carrying Creadel banners fluttering in the evening wind, rode their leader. His shiny helmet was shut, sword sheathed, reins held loose in his gauntleted hands. The party slowed as they reached the end of their ranks, picking their way through the carnage, always on a direct path to Faelyn.

Bastien dismounted and stepped in front of her, planting an expression on his face he knew would hide his weariness and warn a would-be attacker away. Footsteps and shouted orders told him without looking that what was left of the Alysian army reformed their lines.

The party halted a good distance away, beside a cascade of rock that had once been part of the south gate. The man dismounted, then removed his helmet, passing it off to another soldier. His dark hair hung by his face, and his beard hid his age. Faelyn stepped to Bastien's side with Kian on her other side. Besides the crows and the screams of the injured and dying, the battleground was almost quiet, waiting for what this man would do.

"Lord Deminal," Kian said in surprise. To Faelyn, he said, "Lord Deminal rules the northern territory of Creadel, to the east."

Lord Deminal bowed low at the waist, then so did his accompanying party. He took in the battlefield. "Queen Faelyn, I apologize we've arrived so late. It wasn't our intention to miss the fight. I received word you weren't expecting Daltieri to arrive for a few more days, and we had some difficulty crossing the border."

Bastien felt the deep regret behind the formal words and instantly respected Lord Deminal.

Faelyn remained wary, face cold. "I was told King Wesli would send no aid."

Lord Deminal frowned. "Is there somewhere we can speak in private, Your Majesty? With your leave, my army will assist in tending to the wounded."

Bastien sensed Faelyn's burning curiosity and desire to hear Lord Deminal out. But if this lord of the north thought Bastien was leaving Faelyn's side, he was in for a rude surprise.

"Kian," Faelyn said, "Would you mind?" She gestured with a weak arm, indicating she wanted a sound veil.

Bastien thread his fingers through hers, squeezing as her magic zinged feebly between them. It was a testament to Faelyn's state that she didn't make the veil herself.

Lord Deminal glanced at their twined hands, then took a few steps closer as Kian's staff lit, casting over the three of them in the air.

Faelyn nodded toward the battlefield, riddled with bodies and burning buildings. "This is as private as we can get."

Lord Deminal nodded, eyes creased, and reached into a small satchel at his side. Bastien tensed, tugging Faelyn back.

Lord Deminal looked up, but slowly pulled out a cloth pouch and turned it out over his hand. A ring tumbled out. Faelyn stepped ahead of Bastien, watching Lord Deminal carefully.

"Your sources were correct, Your Majesty. King Wesli denied aid to our northern ally. Pride has become the undoing of many a kingdom, but in this case, my king and I do not see eye to eye. Our kingdom has prospered since you've become queen. Maybe more so for my lands, sharing a border with Alysies, but I was not going to let you fight alone. You're allowed to marry whom you choose." He glanced again at Bastien's hand in hers.

"Then I thank you, Lord Deminal, for having the courage to do what you believe is right," Faelyn said, all coldness vanishing.

"What is that?" Bastien asked, pointing. If Faelyn was too polite to ask, then he'd have to.

Lord Deminal looked at his hand as if he'd forgotten about the ring. "This is for you, Queen Faelyn." He held it out.

Faelyn moved to accept it, but Bastien intercepted her and swiped the ring from Lord Deminal's hand—he didn't trust anyone when it came to her safety. He held it up to his face. A sparkling blue stone sat between tarnished silver leaves. The metal had worn smooth on the inside as if it'd seen much wear. No magical properties. It was harmless. He passed it to Faelyn, almost sensing the eye-roll beneath her glare.

She gasped. "This... I know this." She looked up, as did Bastien, into Lord Deminal's smiling face.

"This is the other reason I've come, Your Majesty," Lord Deminal said, amusement in his voice. "I'm curious, what do you know about this ring?"

Faelyn slipped it on her finger. A perfect fit. "It belonged to me. I was wearing it when I fled the castle during the battle of Pavora. I gave it to someone as a wedding gift." She smiled. "Ellowen. Her family took me in when I had nowhere else to go. She became a sister to me."

Lord Deminal crossed his hands in front of him. "Aye. Ellowen married and become Ellowen Hertsel, as you know. She bore many children, though some didn't survive to adulthood. One was my wife's thrice great-grandmother." He reached into his satchel again and pulled out a plate of brass the size of a sheet of parchment. "Ellowen knew you, Your Highness, and knew of your long life. She knew of your greatness and believed in your destiny. She passed down the ring, and these words hoping someday they'd cross your path. My wife all but forced me to come to your aid."

Faelyn took the brass with shaking hands and pressed it to her breast. Tears spilled down her face. "Thank you, Lord Deminal. Thank you."

CHAPTER

SIXTY-ONE

The hours since the battle ended were almost as hard to bear as the battle itself. Magically and physically, Faelyn's body was at its limit, yet she still found the strength to cry. Her council sat on piles of rubble to take stock of what they'd lost, even while Creadel soldiers worked tirelessly to sort through bodies and wounded. They also served an instrumental part in putting out the remaining fires in what was left of her once-vast city.

Of the lords who'd joined them, only four endured—Lord Marus, Amerae's brother, among them. Less than half of their forces remained, and even some of them wouldn't make it through the night. Only a third of the mages survived.

When she could hear no more, she stood, and Bastien supported her as they trailed through the rows of wounded. She forced a brave face as they reached for her, gripping her hands and begging her to save them. They reached for Bastien, too. While he remained stoic, Faelyn felt him drain every drop of magic that had built back up out into the wounded.

The damage was of her nightmares. The citadel wall had been breached at six different points, including the south gate. Once the

466

magical barrier had been broken, it wasn't difficult for the enemy mages to come through. The majority of the city of Pavora was in ruin, and a decent portion of that was at her own hands.

She could call the townspeople back, but most had no homes to return to. And less timber to build from. The fire had spread into the surrounding woods, but she didn't know how badly. The dark of night settled too quickly, hampering any surveying efforts.

The fires set within the citadel had burned unchecked too long to save any of the buildings. The market, soldier housing, dining halls, armories, command center, storage buildings—very little of it remained.

Kian, more restored than the rest of them after his nap in the broom cupboard, took charge of those left among the mages along with Niri, who'd sent word to Thomats for aid. Nolan, Amerae, and baby Mary were resting in their untouched rooms, safe and happy together, under heavy guard.

Bastien and Faelyn made it to her rooms near midnight, Bastien carrying her. The sight of the castle had zapped the last of her strength. Only the main gate had been breached, but the damage done within had been heartbreaking. Treasures and heirlooms had been looted from all over, but that wasn't the worst—they'd get some of it back once they sorted through the enemy dead. No, what made her unable to bear the walk to her own room was worse than that. Rory and his host of soldiers had laid waste to the guards, servants, and families who'd taken shelter at the castle. They hadn't gone far when Bastien had waylaid them, but far enough.

The smoke of the funeral pyres would clog the gates of the Hereafter. She was the Queen of Ruin.

Bastien made it through her suite, which was surprisingly untouched, and laid her into bed. Only a small part of her cared she was still filthy with blood and ash. He collapsed beside her, as tired as she. Then he held something up, pinched between his thumb and forefinger. A red rose.

"It's more than a tragedy, Faelyn, but not everything is lost," he said as she took it, inhaling the sweet scent and admiring the perfect, unmarred bloom. "And you'll always have me."

Her eyes stung and her heart lurched. She caressed his smooth face, staring into his clear blue eyes where he rested on the pillow beside her. "And you'll always have me."

He'd saved her life, saved her kingdom, and saved her heart.

That day she'd kissed him and Prince Rory saw, he'd saved her from a life she never wanted, a life she would have resented. She would have sacrificed the core of who she was, and it only would have hurt her and therefore hurt her people.

Her eyes drifted closed, but she pried them open. There was one thing she had to do before sleep took her. She pulled out the brass letter that she hadn't allowed herself to read earlier. The memory of Ellowen hadn't crossed her mind in many years, though she'd been like a sister to her as she hid away on the farm in northern Creadel. The way she'd treated Ellowen on the day of their parting, that bitterness and resentment inside her, was just one more mistake on her list of many in her past. But, Ellowen forcing her to leave had been the best thing she could have done for Faelyn.

Faelyn,

I etch this in metal, hoping it will survive until it finds you again. We did not part on the best of terms, but I hope time has helped you forgive me for forcing you off the land which was rightfully yours. I've deeded it to you in my will under the name Queen Faelyn Rylandor of Alysies. That's how much I believe in you. You'll claim your title one day and become the greatest queen who ever existed. Remember, especially when times are tough, there is love, and love can take us through even the most impossible obstacles. I love you.

Your sister,

Ell

Faelyn didn't realize she was crying until Bastien wiped the tears from her face. She blinked up at him, and he pulled her to him in a desperate embrace.

"We will rebuild, my love. We have time." He caressed her hair.

She nodded against him. They did have time, and more importantly, they had each other. She tilted her head back and kissed him, salty lips sinking into each other until sweet oblivion overtook her.

Faelyn drifted to sleep in Bastien's arms, warming his heart where the horrors of battle tried to only allow fear and bitter cold.

After the meeting with Lord Deminal, he and Kian had overseen the mages while Faelyn conferred with the scant remainder of her leaders. Nearly drained of magic, the mages still helped the wounded. Nighttime had settled when Bastien broke away from them to comb through the bodies, using his ability to sense emotions to help him pick the dead from the living. He searched and searched, but never found Olin, dead or alive. His friend had disappeared, hopefully to flee home. To survive another day. Once the heat settled between the kingdoms, he would visit his old home and find him.

Just when regret nearly overwhelmed him, he heard a familiar whinny.

"Tarten." Bastien grinned as his loyal horse tugged away from the Creadel soldier leading him. He had a slight limp but was otherwise unharmed. Bastien instructed the soldier to take Tarten to Auvie at the stables since she communicated with animals and would know what to do.

Finding Tarten alive was a bright spot in all the darkness.

At the tail end of Bastien's search, a pounding from one of the smoldering ruins had caught his attention. Completely drained, he'd drawn his sword and edged closer. The building was located near what was once the citadel market, but now all that remained was a pile of blackened, smoking wood and a charred frame.

The pounding sounded again, rattling some of the boards. Bastien stepped through the threshold and into the small space, sensing someone beneath the floor—many people—and one had magic. He hacked and kicked at a pile of rubble until he found a blackened trap door. He reached to lift it, but it shot open, making him jump back, sword raised. A man poked his head out, looking around until he noticed Bastien.

"Tave." Bastien blew out a relieved breath and sheathed his sword.

"Bast, my boy. What's the state of things?" He looked around, brown eyes widening, though this part of the market was too dark to see much past the glowing remnants of fire. "So you survived!" Tave said it like he was happily surprised, then climbed the rest of the way up the ladder.

The woman, Vayla, followed, reaching for Tave's hand.

"Where's Micah and Brock?" Bastien asked.

Tave gestured down with a smile, and Bastien peered into the hole where mage light—not his—lit the space. Micah and Brock stood surrounded by women and children.

Bastien's gaze shot to Tave, blinking.

Tave dusted ash from his jacket, smearing it. "The soldier we paid to store our wares here was gone. The Daltieri were slaughtering everyone." He trailed off, and Bastien could almost picture the horror he was recalling.

He clapped Tave on the shoulder. "You saved them. You're a hero."

Tave waved away the compliment.

"Don't shortchange yourself, Tave. You don't have to be who you once were. Your past mistakes don't have to dictate your future. You can rise above them."

Tave quirked his head. "You mean like you?"

Bastien shook his head. "No, I—"

"But you have risen above, Bastien. You're not the street thief anymore."

Bastien swallowed hard, then smiled at Faelyn as his mind focused back on the present. Maybe she would agree to give Tave and his crew jobs. Acantha knew they could use every able person.

He smoothed the golden hair from her face, feeling the softness of her skin. Leaning over, he kissed her lightly on the lips. Taking the rose from her loose grip, he held her hand. He'd seen that rose amongst the smoking rubble, and something told him she'd love it and maybe even needed it. She smiled in her sleep, fingers gripping back.

The coming days, weeks, months, would be hard, but they could do it. Together. She'd asked him to marry her. The thought lent him a few more precious moments of wakefulness, just enough to settle next to her and pull her close. His love, his family.

His fate.

EPILOGUE

Bastien walked down the sidewalk beside the busy street, hardly glancing as cars rushed by. He focused on the lithe creature before him, leading the way as she always did. Faelyn's form-fitting leggings stopped just above her ankles, her feet clad in low heels. A sleek coat hung to her knees, and her pale golden hair plunged to the middle of her back in waves. She turned her face to the side, revealing her smile—red lips graced by a perfect nose and long, defined eyelashes which batted a few times in amusement before she looked ahead again.

Movement earned a flick of his gaze—his reflection in the glass of a building. His steps slowed, then he stopped. Framed by long, sandy hair, his light blue eyes looked back at him. He glanced once at his jeans and dark jacket, then blinked at his surroundings. Tall buildings, the usual big-city traffic of cars and people, sidewalk shops hawking cheap knock-offs at the edge of a shady alley. This moment, this place seemed... familiar. As if from a dream.

"Bastien, what's wrong?" Faelyn's musical voice flowed through him, breaking into his trance. She smiled from where she'd stopped a few feet away, tucking a curl behind her ear.

After all this time, she still knew how to completely disarm him.

His lips turned up in a warm, answering smile. "I think I've fated this moment."

She stepped toward him. "Can you tell me what happens next?" She extended her youthful hand.

He took it, wedding band glinting in the high sun. "This." He pulled her to him, their bodies pressing against each other as if time had molded them to fit that way.

He placed a hand against her cheek, the other around her waist. She wrapped her arms around his neck, and their lips met in the sweetest kiss, a kiss he never seemed to get enough of, a kiss she was always willing to give.

Snow fell around them, a light flurry that drifted from a cloudless sky. The flakes melted before they hit the ground. He glanced up toward Acantha, then met Faelyn's wry smile. With a grin and a peck on the lips, she took his hand, and together they continued on, just like they always would.

The End

ACKNOWLEDGMENTS

I'd like to start out by thanking my beautiful ARC readers/street team/loyal readers. Some have been with me, Ardenis/Bastien, and Laida/Faelyn from the beginning, and some jumped on in the middle, but I am so, so thankful for them. For the reviews, posts, shares, support, amazing videos, word of mouth, and incredible opportunities. I appreciate all of you! You know how hard it is to be seen in this world, but this story deserves to be told! Kellye Filer, Angie Marie, Pia Murillo, Hayley Hamblin, my amazing Watchers (newsletter subscribers), and everyone who gave Fated Born a chance, loved it, and left a review or told a friend.

Can you believe this series is complete? It is such a bittersweet moment for me. I never thought I'd get the chance to become a published author, and now I have a completed trilogy! Remember, your dreams are worth your time.

Thank you to my mom and dad, whom this book is dedicated to. You are hard-working, loving parents, and the best grandparents—always spoiling my daughters.

To my husband, Jonathan, for *everything*. For your enthusiasm, support, encouragement, and bringing home charcuterie to fuel my writing and celebrate the wins.

To my daughters for your excitement, helpful suggestions, and keeping me up to date on young-people slang.

To Rachel, my first reader, my sister, who will drop everything and analyze character art with me, or get excited over new story ideas, and never fails to give me her (brutally) honest opinions, because she knows that's what I need and want.

To Christina, for reading Fated Sworn and loving it even when it was a steaming dumpster fire, for your unwavering support, and for letting me talk about author stuff all the time.

To my family and friends from all walks of life who've shown up for me and my writing journey in more ways than I could have imagined.

To my editor, Kelley, my cover designer, Franziska, and my character portrait artist, Alrun. You all brought this series to life through your skills and artistry, and I'll be forever grateful.

And certainly not least, thank YOU reader! Thank you for loving these characters like I do. Even if you just found this series, you're here now, and hopefully here to stay.

BOOKS BY KRISTIN L. HAMBLIN

Fated Born Series

An Upper Young Adult Epic Fantasy Low-Spice Love Story

Sorcery and Sacrifice Series

A Young Adult Clean Romantic Portal Fantasy

ABOUT THE AUTHOR

Kristin L Hamblin was born and raised in Tulsa, Oklahoma. She loves to read and write stories where fantastical things are possible, especially if they contain magic, adventure, and romance. Kristin lives in Oklahoma with her husband, raising their four daughters and a menagerie of pets, including two wiener dogs, Ruby and Sunny.

If you have any questions or comments about her books, or just want to say hello, she would love to hear from you on social media or at kristinlhamblin.com